Until We All Find Home

By Heather Wood

Finding Home by Heather Wood

Until We All Find Home
Until We All Run Free
Until the Light Breaks Through

Until We All Share Joy
(standalone novella concurrent with Until We All Run Free)

ISBN: 9781686379635

Cover art by Jenna Phillips

To David

You've always been the coolest person I know.

Thank you for appreciating the things I love:

God, family, Chicago, and the Civil War

-1-

July 15, 1861

"Does this bring back memories?"

Luke Dinsmore leaned towards his best friend standing at attention next to him on the railroad platform of Great Central Station.

Justin Young glanced over and nodded, sweat causing his black curls to stick to his forehead underneath his smart kepi.

It was beginning to get warm in the midday July sun in his brand new navy blue wool uniform, especially after the grand march the regiment had just completed down Wabash Street. In a few minutes, the 23rd Illinois Regiment would be boarding the train and heading south, to their new station at a garrison somewhere in southern Illinois, to the best of his knowledge. But first they had to wait through mayoral speeches and military band performances, and Justin could feel Luke growing impatient next to him.

Luke had been fascinated by railroads since he was a child and had been working at the ticket counter at the same station when Justin first arrived in the city five years prior, the occasion that prompted his question now. He had never had the opportunity to take a trip himself, and the only thing now standing in his way of boarding the giant iron beast was Mayor Wentworth's rhetoric.

Unfortunately, the mayor was waxing eloquent, which was ironic, considering that he typically paid little attention to the Irish population on the lower west side of Chicago; but now that the Irish Brigade was preparing to ship out, he apparently felt that a photograph in the paper of him honoring their bravery would appear patriotic and perhaps give him the needed boost in the looming election.

Through the crowd, Luke could make out his family members gathered to see him and Justin off. Only his mother wasn't there, because watching her beloved son leave for war was not something she was capable of stomaching, and if there was anything that Mrs. Dinsmore hated above all else, it was emotional outbursts. This explained why Luke was her favorite child, a fact that she never bothered to hide. He was one of the most easygoing individuals most people would ever meet, and his even personality was just the thing Mrs. Dinsmore appreciated when she had three daughters surrounding Luke in age.

His older sister Christina hadn't come today either, but he'd stopped including her in the numbers when she got married two years prior and moved to a farm way out west of the city. His younger sisters were there at the station though, Rebecca and Elisan, and his ten-year-old brother Titan.

What the rest of the siblings lacked in tender loving care from their mother was more than made up for in their father. Reverend Dinsmore had always been his children's close confidante and wise advisor, and he was there today pulling his daughters close on either side of him as they tried to regain their composure.

Luke wasn't completely sure if Rebecca's tears were more for him or for Justin, but the fact was that two of her favorite people were leaving today, and for all their pride in their new uniforms, the sight of them made her feel ill. There was no doubt that Luke was her very best friend in the world, but lately her relationship with Justin had been heightened. There wasn't an official courtship yet, but there was something growing there, with the escorts home and filled dance cards and the unspoken understanding in the way they looked and spoke to each other.

Luke had never actually asked Justin about her himself, or he would have known that Justin had already talked to the reverend about his intentions. The war had interrupted his plans, for once states began seceding from the union, Justin had held back from taking the next steps with Rebecca. He was completely free, with no ties yet holding him back and therefore the most eligible recruit for the army once the first shots were fired. He knew this, and knew that he would sign up as soon as they asked for volunteers, so it seemed the right thing to do to leave Rebecca completely free should something happen to him and he didn't come home.

After five years, Chicago was home to him now, and it was all because of the Dinsmores. Standing in the Chicago summer heat next to Luke as the mayor droned on, Justin's thoughts wandered to the day he had first arrived at that station. He was just fifteen and alone, but he had childlike faith and youthful excitement at what the world was capable of holding for him. He had disembarked the train and was sitting on a bench in the station when Luke first noticed him.

It was his ritual at each station he came to; he would get off and spend some time praying, asking for a sign or some kind of direction whether this was the place he should stay or if he should get back on and keep going. The train had made its way from Paducah to St. Louis and up the length of Illinois, and so far nothing had kept him from reboarding and continuing on his way. He was thus lost in thought when he was approached by Luke.

"That was the last passenger train for the evening; the next one will be in the morning," Luke told the boy, and Justin looked up at his voice.

"Okay, thank you," he said without moving.

Luke almost moved on, but hesitated. "I noticed you've been here for a couple hours. Are you waiting for someone, or are you staying here overnight?"

"Am I allowed to?"

Luke shrugged. "I'm leaving for the night myself, but I'll be here in the morning and I won't tell anyone. The janitor won't bother you; he's a pretty understanding fellow."

Justin bit his lip and thought for a minute. Before he replied, Luke cocked his head.

"Where are you headed?" he asked, surmising that Justin did not, in fact, have anyone coming for him.

"Wherever I have a reason to stay," Justin admitted. "I was actually just praying about that."

Luke looked tempted to find out more, but instead he stopped himself.

"Are you hungry? I was about to go have dinner with my family, and we would love to have you join us."

"Are you sure?" Justin's eyes widened, but in his heart something was stirring. Of all the prayers he had prayed, this was the first time anyone had spoken to him at any of the stations. He was curious to find out what God was doing that possibly involved the lanky boy in front of him.

"Sure." Luke held out his hand, his blue eyes smiling from under neatly combed dark brown hair. "I'm Luke Dinsmore."

"Justin Young." Justin stood up and shook Luke's hand. He was on the short side of average height, and a full four inches shorter than Luke, although he figured Luke was about the same age.

"I'd been watching you, and I felt like I should come over and meet you," Luke said as they left the station together.

Justin glanced over as they headed south through Chicago's dusty streets, and he felt goosebumps.

"Where are you from?" Luke continued.

"I just came from Louisville. I'm originally from Grayson County, Kentucky, but I was in the orphanage in Louisville until my birthday this year, when I aged out."

Luke stopped walking and turned to him in surprise. "You're on your own? I'm so sorry. I take having my family for granted."

Justin shrugged. "It's been eight years since I lost mine. In some ways I've gotten used to it, but I miss them."

"Do you mind telling me what happened to them?"

Justin didn't mind. Luke had an honest face that most people found attractive, but they failed to realize that it was due less to genetics and more to the fact that he was a pleasant person, and that reflected in his face. He had a personality that made people feel comfortable talking to him because he made a conscious effort to be a good listener. From his father he had learned wisdom greater than his years, but mostly he just listened well, and he often found others' inhibitions were dropped around him and he had a knack at getting them to open up.

"My parents passed away, and I don't know where my siblings are. The best I can gather, they were divided up among the relatives, but I don't know where they are or if they are still alive." He paused. "Tell me about your family, since I'm going to meet them. What does your father do?"

"He's a minister," Luke said. "You'll like him; everyone does. He's a decent preacher, but mostly he's one of the nicest people you'll ever meet. I have three sisters: Christina, Rebecca, and Elisan, and my baby brother Titan. Well, he's six now, but he'll always be the baby."

"Do you usually bring people home from the station for dinner?" Justin asked curiously.

"So far it's only been beautiful women," Luke answered with a laugh, and Justin realized that Luke was already comfortable enough to joke with him, and it felt good.

Justin remembered arriving at the parsonage and meeting the family for the first time, and how they had all welcomed him as part of the family from the start. No one acted inconvenienced or like it was odd to have an unexpected guest, and the next thing he knew, they had persuaded him to spend the night with them. By that point, he knew beyond a shadow of a doubt that his prayer had been answered and that he would indeed not be on the train the following morning. He had insisted on not taking advantage of their hospitality, and the next night at dinner, voiced his intention of finding his own lodgings as soon as possible, since he was to stay.

"I know just the place," Reverend Dinsmore announced immediately. "One of our church members, Mrs. Katz, has an apartment above her bakery about ten blocks from here in the seventh ward. Until recently, a Negro family lived there, but they moved when the husband took a job north of the city. She's a decent woman, and I know she'll take good care of you."

Justin had lived in that apartment ever since, and in that time he had grown fond of his German landlady. The Chicago River formed the southern boundary of the neighborhood, and it was there that Justin found a job as a stevedore at one of the many lumber warehouses. He found that being of Irish descent, he blended in well to his neighborhood, which was largely populated by German and Irish immigrants. Nevertheless, he stayed quiet so as not to cause a disturbance with the revelation that he was actually a Protestant and was in the minority among working class Irish Americans by supporting abolition.

The first Sunday that he went to Reverend Dinsmore's church, he walked in the door to the strains of the pipe organ playing hymns for the prelude. He quietly took a seat near the back, and was taken aback to realize that the organist was none other than Luke's thirteen-year-old sister Rebecca, and she played simply but mistake-free. He was further surprised to realize that where he was seated in the rear, he was surrounded by black parishioners, and realized that unlike his church in Kentucky, they worshipped on the same level as white believers. If he had liked Reverend Dinsmore before, that fact alone made him respect the leader of this church all the more.

He fell in to his new life easily, and Luke and he had become fast friends. Justin worked hard during the week, and although Friday night dinners at the Dinsmores' became their standing tradition, he often spent more time than that with his new family each week, between parties, church events, walks to the lake, and games of chess with Luke in his father's library. Perhaps some church members had gossiped about "the orphan boy" and his proximity to the Dinsmores, and later about Rebecca Dinsmore's apparent interest in him, but the family held it on principle to never heed what the gossips were saying. They often reminded each other of this conviction, which was important since, as the minister's family, they were perhaps gossiped about to a greater degree than anyone else in the church.

As a whole, Justin was happy and grateful for his life. He loved Chicago, his neighborhood, and his friends; and he loved the excitement of the huge barges and railroads daily bringing lumber from the north woods and crops from Illinois farms on their journeys to the far reaches of the country. Chicago felt like it was in the center of everything, until the war started and turned everyone's attention south, and there the ache deep inside him was inescapable.

In all the years he had been on his own, in the orphanage and in Chicago, a day hadn't gone by in which he didn't think of his sister Kellie and his younger brothers. He didn't even have any idea if his siblings were still in the south, but it was where he had last seen them as a seven-year-old, so it was where he associated them with in his mind. Kellie was the next one in order after him, so she had always been his little playmate. Justin had lost much of his mental image of what she looked like, but he remembered her thick black curls bouncing down her back as they ran through the meadow behind their house together, and that was the picture he always carried in his mind.

His brothers were a toddler and a baby when he last saw them, and his other little sister Katie had died before his parents, so Kellie was the one he had the strongest memory of and the greatest desire to see. The day she was taken from him was etched in his memory. He remembered they were both crying as his five-year-old sister was driven away in someone's wagon, to go to he didn't know where, to live with . . . was it an aunt? He wished he could remember, but either way it was someone he didn't know, in some far off city. He had stayed behind because his grandparents wanted him. He was big and strong and could be a big help to them, and besides, they always doted on him. But they had lived only a year after his parents, and with no other family in the county, he had gone to live in the orphanage when they died.

The changing seasons always made the ache intensify, and he would try to picture what Kellie would be doing. She'd be ten now, he would think. Is she at school? Carrying water and scrubbing laundry, or sitting in a fancy parlor learning how to embroider? Does she go to church? Then, she's thirteen—is she at finishing school? Picking out ribbons for her dresses? Tending a hearth? At sixteen, was she taking suitors and attending fabulous balls?

Standing at attention on the railroad platform, Justin thought of Kellie again. She'd be eighteen now; was she still alive? Was she married? Or perhaps she had married young and had a baby now. Justin's eyes widened at the thought that he could be an uncle. But as always, there were no answers to go with his questions. Just questions. Why didn't anyone know his relatives or where they were from? Why didn't his grandparents think to offer to let him write to his sister? Wouldn't they have known this aunt, or was she an aunt on his other side? Was it even an aunt? Why were they his only other relatives in Grayson County, and where had they come from?

If there was anything he would have done differently, it would have been to try to find more answers before leaving Kentucky as a fifteen-year-old. He had left straight from Louisville without going back to Grayson County, but now he wondered if there was anyone left there who knew his parents and grandparents, or if their death certificates at the county courthouse held any further clues. Making such a big trip again armed just with questions had never really been feasible, though, and he had never seriously considered it.

Next to him, Luke wiped at the perspiration on his face and shifted his weight. He looked over at Justin, and the look on his friend's face stopped him. He knew that look of melancholy all too well, and knew what Justin was thinking about. Luke literally made a game of learning to be perceptive and understand people. He and Rebecca had started it one day years ago when they were bored waiting for their father in a meeting. They had played it often together ever since, becoming actually really good at it in the process. In the game, they would take a situation of someone they knew, and try to guess what they thought that person would do, based on what they knew about that individual's situation, personality, and motivations.

For example, when they found out, as pastor's children were wont to do, that Mrs. McKinley's husband had been caught swindling customers at his insurance business, they tried to guess whether she would leave him or not. Rebecca thought she would, because Mrs. McKinley was a pious woman who had little patience with others' shortcomings, but Luke thought that she would not, since she was financially dependent on him and had no other family in the area. In the end, Luke was right, as usual. He had a natural bent for reading people, but Rebecca had spent so much time as his protégé, that she had improved with time and effort.

Justin they knew better than anyone, and within the past year, they had the opportunity to make him the subject of their game. He had come to Friday dinner bringing a lemon meringue pie, as he always did. Cooking was a skill Justin had mastered at the orphanage, and he enjoyed it to boot.

That particular day, Elisan was in the front yard deadheading flower beds when he arrived and she came over, wiping her hands on her apron, to greet him and take the pie into the kitchen. In their brief interaction, he had teased her like older brothers did to their adopted younger sisters, and before she even had time to think, she had flung the pie at his face. It really was quite funny to think about later, for everyone except Elisan, who still got red at the memory of it. At the time, however, no one was laughing. Justin stood on the front walk, wordlessly wiping from his face the pie over which he had labored so hard. He had turned around and stalked home without staying for dinner, and Elisan had cried all evening.

She came to his apartment the next day bearing a lemon meringue pie that she'd made him as a peace offering. He sat at the table and ate the entire thing in front of her while she apologized endlessly.

Rebecca won this round of the game. Luke thought that would be the end of it, and that Justin's eating the pie in front of Elisan gave him the last laugh and all would be forgiven and forgotten. Rebecca saw Justin as a little more likely to hold a grudge and have fun making Elisan suffer, although he wouldn't be unkind about it. She was right, even nailing Justin's passive-aggressiveness, for ever after, he'd refused to make another lemon meringue pie. In fact, every single Friday dinner since, he had brought shortbread, which would be far less disastrous should they be thrown at someone's face. Rebecca felt great personal triumph at beating Luke at the Justin round.

Nevertheless, Luke knew Justin through and through, and he knew that as much as Justin loved his adoptive family, more than anything in the world he longed for his own, and it was a longing that marrying Rebecca and producing children of his own would not allay. Luke wasn't sure how much of that Justin himself was even aware of, since it was something he hadn't exactly voiced, but he knew by the look on his face that Justin was thinking about his family now.

If Rebecca was brokenhearted over Justin and Luke leaving, Luke knew Elisan wasn't crying for the same reason. Knowing Elisan, she was probably mad that she couldn't enlist too, and that she had to be stuck at home doing far less exciting things during the war. The Dinsmores all said that Elisan was the family spitfire, and she was often a topic of concern when church members met with Reverend Dinsmore. In fact, probably the only person in the church who was unconcerned about Elisan was her father. He knew, however, that for her strong will, hare brained ideas, and tendency to speak her mind, she had a truly good heart and that improving the lives of others was usually her motivating factor. He was known to say that God made Elisan to reflect His image in a way that no one else on earth could, and the meetings usually ended with the parishioner questioning the reverend's theology and informing him that they were praying for his youngest daughter. As such, she was the most prayed about person in the church, although her father never let her know that.

Even Rebecca didn't quite understand her younger sister, but she loved her dearly and often was bolstered in her own courage and faith by Elisan. Not that Rebecca was a mousy type—she was known to be fairly headstrong herself—but she usually did a better job of assimilating into society and finding ways to occupy herself within the boundaries determined by their culture. Elisan saw no boundaries, and tended to be surprised whenever she ran into one. It wasn't that she regretted being a woman; on the contrary, she was every bit as feminine as Rebecca. Elisan just held the unpopular belief that a woman could have fun and still be a lady. Rebecca had spent most of their childhood covering for Elisan, rescuing her from tangles, making excuses for the chaos left in her wake, and smoothing out any scuffles before anyone else found out. As a result, Elisan bore the consequences for her spunkiness far less than anyone might think, and she was keen enough to realize that Rebecca was the one to whom she was indebted.

Rebecca was sensible and practical, but she leaned towards making doing the right thing look easy and never came across as uptight about things. In fact, if anyone had a vice against Rebecca, it was that she made everything look easy. Rebecca enjoyed the types of skills that young ladies were expected to learn, and she mastered them effortlessly. She was known for her cooking and the way that ingredients came alive in her hands, and she was born with a natural talent for music and the piano. She was the type of person that all the other girls wanted to be friends with, but they also rather secretly hated her for being so much better at everything. Since her family was all the friends she ever needed, it was likely that she was never really aware of what her schoolmates thought of her.

Justin had come into the picture when she was just thirteen, long before she was being considered as a possible match for people's sons, so he was first in line, so to speak, when she came of age. Thankfully, he was cognizant of his position and realized that he would be an idiot to pass up a catch like Rebecca Dinsmore. He liked her; he had always liked her as a sister, but he was almost twenty-one now and beginning to consider his future. It was natural to picture her in it, and she seemed to be just as pleased with the idea.

The odd thing was that he was leaving for the war without sealing the deal, a fact not unnoticed by the people who cared, and it seemed to be a rather large risk he was taking. It wouldn't have been as big of a deal had he at least talked to Rebecca about it and let her know where things stood with them, but he hadn't. Communication was notoriously not Justin's strong suit, and he was occasionally clueless to social cues, though he made up for it by being amiable and having a great sense of humor whenever he was made aware of it.

The Dinsmores chalked these faults up to the fact that he hadn't had parents since he was seven. In reality, his being from a different part of the country, and a farming community rather than the city, also came into play, not to mention that he still lived alone, and that didn't do anything to help his ability to communicate effectively. They were as forgiving as if he were one of the family, but it still sometimes wreaked a bit of havoc, as in the situation with Rebecca.

The mayor finally finished his speech, and Luke audibly sighed with relief, but unfortunately, the marching band began to play. All told, the event amounted to two hours in length before the 23rd Illinois was finally allowed to board the train and take their seats. Justin gave Luke the window seat and he leaned out the window waving his cap as the train sped away from the platform and out of the city, the rails moving them towards cornfields and clean blue skies, and closer to the war.

-2-

September 18, 1861

Justin's pulse raced and he licked his dry lips as he peered across the open square from his position behind the Union fortifications. A week had passed since the Irish Brigade had arrived in Lexington, Missouri, and until now, they had been occupied building the fortifications that now surrounded the Masonic College in town. Over the last couple of days, however, it had turned into a siege by the Missouri militia, who had just received reinforcements, and the Irish Brigade's provisions and water were running dangerously low.

Finally, that morning, the rebels had attacked and taken the Anderson house across the way. The Yankees had been using it for their hospital, and now Colonel Mulligan wanted them to take it back. Justin's bayonet was fixed as he stood nervously with the other men in his company, waiting for the order to counterattack.

In that moment, he deeply regretted the impatience that he had displayed waiting around the garrison in Quincy over the last few months, and wished that he could get back to safety and drinking water. The insignificance of this obscure post that they were defending from state militia—were they even real Confederate soldiers?—hundreds of miles from the rest of the war didn't do much to boost his morale. Regardless, the Irishmen surrounding him seemed pretty eager to show off their manhood. Everyone except for Luke, who was serene and quiet beside him.

Oh, dear God, Luke. College Hill hardly seemed like a hill that Justin was willing to die on, and definitely not worth losing his best friend for. *But Missouri is a border state,* Justin told himself, trying to convince himself of the importance of this battle. *We can't let the Confederates control the border states. And if we can push them back, we can get some water again.* That was one good thing about the battle finally beginning; at least they would be able to get water again. Despite his personal feelings about the location of the battle, Justin was resolute that he would be no coward. He believed in the cause for which he was fighting, and he had Luke that he needed to look out for—Luke who had a family that he needed to get back home to when the war was over. Nothing was going to happen to Luke on his watch.

The order came to march, and the company took off in double time around the square in the direction of the house. Justin burst into the house through the front door that the sergeant and corporal in front of him had battered down, and the gruesome hand to hand struggle for the house began.

"Are you doing okay?"

Justin must have asked Luke that question a hundred times over the course of the past three days, but never in his life had he felt so personally responsible for another human being.

"I'm fine. It's just a cut," Luke insisted, touching the bandage on his upper arm. "Promise me you won't tell Rebecca about it. It will be all healed by the time we get home anyway."

Justin nodded, but he was sure that he would never recover from the memory of watching that knife come at Luke in the Anderson house the other day. That was one nasty fight that he hoped he would never have to relive, and thankfully, they hadn't had any more hand to hand combat since that episode. They had taken the house at the time, but then the rebels had come and taken it back just a few hours later, so it was all for naught anyway. The battle had continued in the days since as the Irish Brigade held on to College Hill and what provisions they'd had ran out completely.

Things had been quiet for about an hour now, and everyone waited, exhausted, to see what was happening. Word was that there had been a white flag, so firing ceased, but there was still confusion over who had raised it. Justin had seen Colonel Mulligan striding past at the time of the flag sighting, demanding information from his staff and ordering a message to be sent to General Fremont, so he apparently had not been responsible for the ceasefire. Justin figured that it had to have been a Union officer though, based on the fact that he'd run out of ammunition three hours ago and out of food two days ago, and he didn't think that the rebel militia could have fared worse than that.

"So much for those reinforcements they said were coming for us," Luke commented.

The regiment sat glancing around at each other, speculating amongst themselves about what was happening, while some dozed. Hearing a small ruckus, Justin looked up and saw Colonel Mulligan returning, so he poked Luke. Mulligan's officers approached him from around the square for a brief rendezvous, then the colonel turned to the enlisted men waiting on all sides.

"Gentleman, we are surrendered," he announced. "We will lay down arms and exit this post, then sort out your parole with General Price and bring provisions immediately. You have fought bravely, befitting to the name and reputation of the Irish Brigade, but the numbers were not in our favor this time. It was an honor to serve with you, and we will get you all taken care of as soon as possible."

The men cheered for their admired leader, but Justin turned to Luke.

"What does that mean? Are we prisoners, or going home, or what?"

Luke yawned and stood up slowly. "He used the word 'parole,' so that sounds promising."

"I just heard the word 'provisions.' I'm ready," Justin replied as Colonel Mulligan left and the captain under him began directing the relinquishment of their weapons.

The Irish Brigade marched out of the trenches with only their personal effects in their possession, down the hill towards the town where the rebel commander, General Price, waited outside the courthouse. Parched and ravenous, the men were overjoyed to find baked potatoes, bread, and water waiting for them, and threw themselves on the ground to inhale their rations.

They had no sooner finished eating when General Price stood up on the steps of the courthouse, and Justin got his first real look at their opponent. Sterling Price was in his fifties, with gray hair, fluffy sideburns that drew attention from his receding hairline, and a dignified presence in his double-breasted gray coat.

"Men of the 23rd Illinois, Governor Jackson is here, and he has some words to share with you. You will rest here tonight and march out in the morning for the railroad, where you will board and be returned to General Fremont in Quincy."

Justin and Luke looked at each other, wide-eyed at the news, as the governor mounted the steps. Justin pulled a sheet of paper out of his knapsack and, ignoring the governor's speech, began scratching out a letter to Rebecca.

October 5, 1861

The paroled 23rd Illinois sat around the garrison in Quincy for another week waiting for orders when news finally came through that they could expect to be mustered out within the week. Justin overheard some of the men grumbling about the quick end to the war for them, trying to figure out a way to muster up again and keep fighting now that things had finally started to get interesting. Others were anxious to head home to their wives immediately.

He sat alone by the fire making another pot of coffee since there really wasn't anything else to do; even drill had been suspended since the parole, because they technically had been set free to not fight anymore, and Colonel Mulligan wasn't with them, having turned down parole from General Price for himself.

Justin thought they were lucky; they had been so close to getting sent to a prison camp, but instead they were free men, and it was sounding more and more like they would be going home soon.

Luke smelled the coffee and sauntered over to find him.

"I knew it must be you," he said, taking a seat on a stump and pulling his mug out. "I could smell that coffee across camp. Are you sharing?"

"Happy to," Justin replied. He waited a minute to ensure the coffee was as hot as he wanted it, then carefully lifted it off the fire and filled their mugs.

"What do you think you'll do once we're mustered out?" Justin asked.

"Oh, I have to go straight home," Luke said without hesitation, holding his mug up to his nose as the steam curled across his forehead. "The girls told me that if I reenlisted, it would be the death of Mother. She hasn't been holding up very well since I left." Luke took a careful sip. "What about you?"

Justin toyed with the handle on his mug and took a deep breath.

"Maybe I'm a coward, but I don't really want to reenlist. I think this battle was enough for me, and if they're going to let us go, I think I'm going to take the chance," he admitted. "It would give me an opportunity to go to Kentucky before I head home."

Luke did not look at all surprised. Since they left home, Justin's memories had been eating away at him more than usual, and he was free from commitments. It made sense to go now.

"What do you think you'll do there?"

Justin swallowed his coffee. "Visit the cemetery, for starters. I haven't visited my parents since before I went in the orphanage. I'd like to go to the courthouse for their death certificates to find out where they're from, then maybe I'll have clues to where my aunts and uncles would be. I'll probably go to church and ask around if anyone knew them. And before I come home, it would be nice to swing by the orphanage and see Mr. and Mrs. West, since I lived with them for six years."

"Seems like you'll be gone a while," Luke said. "Do you want me to come with you?"

Justin shook his head. "It's okay. Mother needs you, and I shouldn't delay you. I'd enjoy your company, but I'll be fine."

Luke looked dissatisfied, but knew Justin was right. "Yeah. I wish I could see where you grew up, though. What if you find them? What if you find Kellie, and she's married or something? Do you think you'd come back to Chicago?"

It was the hot question, the type that didn't have an answer and no one really was prepared to face.

"I guess there's no way to know." Justin let out all his breath. "Could be that I find her and she's happy with her life and not interested in reconnecting. Could be that I never find her, or that she's not still alive. I won't really know until I try." He took a drink. "I have every intention of coming back to Chicago though, and Mrs. Katz is holding the apartment for me. We'll just have to see where this trip leads."

Luke fell silent and sipped his coffee, clearly not happy about the thought of Justin possibly not returning.

"Do you need money?" There was the expense of travel and lodging to think about, and Justin wouldn't be working.

"No, but thanks for checking. I've saved some up and I have my army wages, so I should be fine. By the way, I wrote to Rebecca today," Justin said. "Do you have anything you'd like to send?"

Luke shook his head. "I just wrote to the girls yesterday, and nothing has happened since then."

"Okay, I'll go ahead and send it. I hope we get mustered out soon. It's getting terribly dull around here." Justin set down his mug and stretched. "Since the war's over for us, hopefully the boys out east can get this thing wrapped up by themselves."

"Oh, I don't know about that. General Scott seems to be taking the long road to getting things done, and it didn't go very well for them at Bull Run. They need to get a general out there who will march straight down to Richmond and burn the place. This war is going to last forever if Lincoln leaves Scott in charge." Luke reached into his pocket. "Game of cards?"

Justin glanced at him side-eyed. "I think I've played more cards this week than I have in my entire life," he said drolly, then sighed and poured himself more coffee. "All right, deal me in."

October 8, 1861

Justin held his parole papers three days later as the sergeant at the garrison reviewed the return of his army issued supplies. He had stopped at the mercantile for new clothes as soon as the Irish Brigade mustered out, since he was heading into a border state and figured that identifying with one side of the war may not be the wisest idea. He wasn't sure where the residents of Grayson County stood in their loyalties and did not want anything to turn people off from speaking to him.

"Most of the men are sticking around to see if the general will let them muster up again," the sergeant said suggestively, looking Justin in the eye.

"Thank you for the information, Sir. Unfortunately, I have some things I need to take care of, but thankfully others are available to continue fighting the good fight." He knew that he had no obligation to stay, and the sergeant couldn't prevent him. The parole said they were supposed to muster out. For that reason, he was surprised that only a third of the men were leaving.

Luke and Justin walked together towards town, where Justin would board a stagecoach southeast, and Luke a train north. For the first time in five years, they were going different directions without knowing when their paths would unite again, and it wasn't a good feeling. Neither felt that it was necessary to talk about it, so they waited at the Quincy station silently after purchasing their respective tickets. Luke's train arrived first, and they stood up together.

"I wish you the best, brother," Luke said, turning to Justin. "They're out there somewhere, and I'm praying your search is successful."

Justin nodded around the lump in his throat. "Thank you. I'll be back soon. Give the girls a hug and a kiss from me."

They stood for another minute in the silence, then embraced, patting each other on the back firmly. Luke let go and started for the train.

"Safe travels," Justin called after him. Luke raised his hand in farewell, and disappeared from view.

Justin stood on the platform, feeling emotional. It was strange having Luke leave him, but at the same time, he was filled with anticipation for what Kentucky held for him. As he stepped up into the stagecoach an hour later, his future felt uncertain and exciting.

Justin leaned against the window and watched the miles go by through southern Illinois, too caught up in his thoughts to engage with the other passengers. Would he be heading back to Chicago by the end of the year to marry Rebecca like he had always planned? Or would he find Kellie somewhere and end up settling down near her? What if he got to the point where he actually had to choose between them? That was an unpleasant thought, and since it was a bridge he could not cross in advance, he put the thought from his mind. Then he began to wonder if he was prepared to find out that Kellie was no longer living, and if it would be better to not try to find her than to discover such a painful truth. For the past thirteen years, she had left a hole in his heart, so what would be different if she had died? He would still have the hole, but without the questions, and she would be at peace. On the other hand, it was possible that he might find her in a desperate situation, in which case he would be able to be of some help. His mind was made up; the risk seemed insignificant in light of even the tiniest chance that she needed him more than he needed her.

He had always wondered if she would have ever tried to find him. Of the four siblings, Justin felt that he would have been the easiest to track down, since church members in Grayson County were the ones who had gotten him into the Louisville orphanage, and that was a trail that shouldn't be difficult to follow. From there, he had kept in touch with the orphanage head, Mr. West, so his Chicago address was known and would be to anyone looking for it. No letter had ever come.

After stopping in Paducah, the stagecoach route took Justin directly through Grayson County on its way to Louisville, and he disembarked at the county seat, the unincorporated town of Leitchfield. Stepping off the stagecoach with just his knapsack, as he had left so many years ago, he felt the surreal juxtaposition of being in a place he had known in a past life, but which had evolved with the years just as he had. He paused in the town square, attempting to reconcile his vague memories with what was now there and piece his thoughts together.

It was dusk, and breathing the fresh evening air felt as good as standing and stretching his legs after two days of travel. The courthouse loomed before him, perhaps a bit smaller than he had perceived it as a child, but it was a beautiful building and was lined with maple trees turned the fiery shades of autumn. His family only ever came all the way in to town every couple of months, but he remembered it well. It was always exciting as a youngster, and he especially remembered exploring the general store while his mother shopped, surveying the shiny new tools and guns on the wall.

Justin took a deep breath and turned in the direction of the hotel. As anxious as he was to jump in and begin interrogating every person he passed, for the moment he wanted to be alone in the quiet, so he took dinner in his room. There was no rush, and he wanted to pay respects to his parents before doing anything else in town. His racing thoughts fought his tired body, and it was late before he succumbed to sleep.

-3-

The sun was just waking up the next morning when Justin began making his way down the quiet road to the church just outside of town. The crisp autumn morning felt delicious, and Justin's heart swelled with contentment. For the moment, just being back felt enough, and he was grateful.

He was surprised when he arrived at the little white building sooner than he expected, and realized that the town had grown out around it. The cemetery behind the church had spread out as well, and it took him a minute to get his bearings and locate his parents' graves. Then he saw their names, and stopped. The three dark gray slabs stood next to each other, simple and solemn.

Henry Donovan Young. 1817-1848.

Sinead Kellie Young. 1818-1848.

Kathleen Young. 1844-1847.

In an instant, Justin felt his eyes fill with tears and emotion washed over him. For the first time in a long time, he didn't push away the grief but allowed himself to feel it, and accept the tears, and remember. He tried to remember their faces, and tried to translate his memories of them as an adult and not as a child, so that he could know who they really were as people beyond pa and ma. But his memory was shaky and cloudy, and he failed to see them as well as he wanted to.

He thought of the day his mother died. She hadn't been well since the baby was born, and it was obvious by the pallor in the faces of the adults that it had become grave. The doctor was there, and his grandparents, and the preacher. He remembered his grandmother gathering him and his siblings close; they were all sobbing, and she simply held them for hours, probably to keep them out of the way. They wanted to see their mother, and they didn't understand why the door was closed and they were on the outside. They didn't understand when the doctor left, and their father only came out late that evening when men came to take the body. His face was ashen, but he was concerned for them and asked about their dinner. Then he hugged them one by one, and the baby was crying, and he'd taken the baby and rocked him and hushed him gently. So his father had loved them well, despite his own grief, but never in the years since had Justin's heart stopped aching from not getting to say goodbye to his mother.

The next few months were challenging as the whole family managed without her. Justin's grandparents moved in to help with everything, and they all did their best to take care especially of the motherless baby. And then, in the midst of all of that, one day his father was thrown from his horse in a freak accident. That day's memories were significantly less clear for Justin. The weeks after his father's death were completely blurred from his memory, not at all like the crystal clear precision he had of his mother's death. The next clear memory he had was Kellie crying and being driven away from him.

Justin pressed his handkerchief against his face as his shoulders shook, and he cried until all of his tears were gone. As the hours passed, he sat on the grass by his parents, and his grandparents next to them. He talked to them, and he prayed, and he took out some sheets of paper and wrote a couple of pages to Rebecca.

The morning was gone, and it was past lunchtime before Justin realized he was hungry and began to think about heading back to the town square for food. He was just about to get up when he saw a clergyman walking across the cemetery towards him. Justin stood as the older man approached.

"Mr. Phillips," he greeted with recognition the minister he had known for the first nine years of his life.

The man straightened up and looked Justin in the face. "You're one of the Young boys," he exclaimed.

"Justin," Justin replied and shook his hand.

Mr. Phillips nodded. "I was going to guess you were Justin, but didn't want to presume. You look very much like your father. How are you?"

"I'm well." He turned back to the graves. "I wish I could remember what he looked like."

"You were all so young when they died. I've always wondered if any of you would make your way back here," Mr. Phillips told him with a sad smile.

Justin looked at him expectantly. "Can you tell me about them? That's why I'm here. I don't know much about them, and I would like to try to find my other relatives."

Mr. Phillips opened his mouth and then paused. "I was just going back to the manse for lunch. Will you join me?"

Justin's eyes widened. "Yes, thank you. That would be an honor."

He picked up his knapsack and followed the minister back across the cemetery and up the road to the first house neighboring the church. Justin remembered Mr. and Mrs. Phillips as kind and helpful friends, but they had several young children when he lived in the county, and were limited in their ability to help the Young family.

Mrs. Phillips greeted him warmly and quickly set another place at the table. "Our youngest, Lucy, just got married this summer, so we're alone now. It's nice to have a young face here and remember your family," she said as she poured him a glass of lemonade. "Where have you all ended up?"

"That's just the thing," Justin began. "I only know where I ended up. I've not had communication with any of my family since I went to the orphanage."

Mr. and Mrs. Phillips looked at him in surprise, taking their seats at the table.

"What about your aunts and uncles?" Mrs. Phillips asked.

"What aunts and uncles? Do you know anything about them?"

Mr. and Mrs. Phillips looked at each other and shook their heads.

"No, I'm afraid we don't. All I know is that they were out east somewhere. Your grandparents sent the children to them, so none of them ever came here," the minister said. He took a breath and held his hands out. "Let's say grace and then we can continue while we eat."

He blessed the food, and Mrs. Phillips filled their plates, a thoughtful look on her face. "When your mother's family immigrated, they came through New York, but I don't know where they lived and met your father before coming here. Henry and Sinead were newlyweds when they came to the county with your mother's parents. Sinead was never very strong and used to frequent the hot springs, so that is probably what drew them here, and your father started a farm."

Mr. Phillips nodded. "I think Sinead had siblings that came from Ireland with them, but they must have settled somewhere else. It's hard to believe that no one kept you connected to them and your siblings."

"It was such a tragedy when your mother died," Mrs. Phillips added softly. "We were absolutely broken-hearted for you all. Four sweet little children. We were thankful your grandparents were here, and they took the responsibility of finding homes for each of you themselves, so we didn't really know where everyone went. The best I knew was that relatives were taking care of everyone, and it didn't seem our place to interfere even though we hated to see the children split up."

"I don't remember anything after Pa died," Justin confessed. "I only remember Kellie getting taken away from me, and I didn't understand why."

"She was such a sweet little thing, with her big blue eyes and black curls." Mrs. Phillips smiled. "She was a doll. And the way she used to try to take care of the baby by herself. She had an unusual name, Kellie. But it was your mother's family name, and it just fit her."

"I miss her." Justin took a deep breath and let it out. "Was anyone else friends with them? Who did they spend time with?"

"Well, Ira Campbell, your old neighbor. He was Irish too, although his family has been in Kentucky for generations. Your father and he used to get on well together and help each other out," Mr. Phillips said after thinking it through.

"I remember him. Do they still live by our old place?"

Mr. Phillips nodded. "Ira's alone now, since his wife died a couple of years ago. I think he would be happy to see you, and I'm sure he knew your parents better than anyone in town would have."

"Then I think I'll go there next. Thank you," Justin said, and took a bite.

"What have you been up to since you left the orphanage?" Mrs. Phillips asked curiously.

"I moved to Chicago when I turned fifteen. I work at the docks on the river, and I have a little apartment and some good friends. I joined up when the war started, but we were just paroled in Missouri, so I came here before going back home."

Mr. Phillips looked surprised. "That was fast."

"Yes," Justin said. "I found that I didn't care for war anyway."

"We have members at church who are joining up on both sides. It's such a volatile situation here. Even families are going to separate sides," Mr. Phillips said sadly.

"Can you imagine, raising a gun at your own family? What a terrible thing this war is. I'm glad that I got out when I did." Justin tapped his finger softly on the table, then straightened up. "I wanted to thank you for what you did to help me get into the orphanage. It was a good place, and I was happy there. I'm planning to stop by there to see Mr. and Mrs. West before I head back to Chicago."

"The Wests are good friends of ours from our seminary days," the minister said. "I'm glad to hear of your experience there. Our son Robert went up to help them out for a year, but he just left to take a teaching job at a boys' school there in Louisville."

They finished the meal, and Justin thanked them for lunch and their time before preparing to take his leave.

"How long do you plan to stick around?" Mr. Phillips asked as they stood and made their way to the door.

"Maybe just a day or two," Justin replied. "I am going to see what records the courthouse has of my family as well as speak to whoever I can find."

"Why don't you stay here?" Mrs. Phillips suggested. "We have the room, and it's quiet here. We'd be happy to have you."

Justin looked back and forth between the minister and his wife, and Mr. Phillips nodded in agreement. "Well then, I'm much obliged. Thank you."

Justin stopped again before going out the door. "I'm not sure I can remember the way back to our old place," he admitted, and Mr. Phillips gave him directions before he headed out.

It took Justin over an hour to walk to Ira Campbell's farm, but the day was nice and the countryside was lovely in its fall splendor. Justin found Ira stacking firewood by his house, whistling as he worked. When the farmer saw him, he stopped, took off his hat, and wiped his brow.

"You're—" he began.

"Justin Young. How are you, Mr. Campbell?"

"Justin! You have really grown up. Welcome home." Ira Campbell's eyes twinkled under his bushy red eyebrows and his matching red whiskers smiled broadly.

"Thank you. Can I give you a hand?"

Justin grabbed some logs and helped Mr. Campbell finish his project. Once the logs were all stacked, Mr. Campbell headed toward the porch and Justin trailed behind.

"What brings you back to Grayson County?" he called behind him.

"I'm looking for information on my parents."

Mr. Campbell reached into a bucket of water for the dipper and offered Justin a drink first, then he poured the cool water into his own mouth and wiped his face.

"Ah." He leaned against the railing. "They died so young. Henry was a good friend. What do you want to know?"

Justin shrugged and sat on a step. "Anything. Everything, I guess. I'm starting with nothing, I only know their names. Mrs. Phillips said that my mother's family emigrated from Ireland. Do you know if my father did too, or if he was born in America?"

"Yes," Mr. Campbell replied. "His parents immigrated before he was born, and he didn't have the Irish accent like your mother did."

"Do you know where he was born?"

"Well, now." Mr. Campbell looked into the distance, "Seems it was out east somewhere, maybe Philadelphia or Baltimore. He came here to get out of the city and find a piece of quiet. He never was one for crowds. We were neighbors for about a decade, and he was a good man. Hard-working and generous. I could always count on him if I needed a hand. And they always went to church." He took a deep breath and stroked his big red whiskers. "It was such a shame when your mother died. Henry was trying to keep everything going and care for all the children, but he was heartsick. And when he died, we all lost a good man."

Justin dropped his eyes and silently kicked at the dirt for a minute. "Did he have any siblings, do you know? Or where his relatives were?"

Mr. Campbell thought before replying. "I believe he had a sister. His mother died a few years after they moved here, but he couldn't go back for the funeral. Maybe about when you were born. I think his father had already passed. I wish I knew where the sister lived, but it's been so long, I can't say for sure."

"As far as I know, my siblings were all sent to live with different relatives," Justin said. "I have no idea where they are or who took them."

"My wife Betsy helped your grandparents write letters to all of them after your father died. I remember they were trying to look for relatives to take them. Betsy would have known their names and where they lived since she did all the writing, but I wasn't directly involved and she died a few years ago. Of course, the letters were all sent, so I don't have a record of them."

Mr. Campbell looked regretful, but Justin was confused.

"Why did she help them?"

"Well, they didn't know how to write," Mr. Campbell explained patiently.

"My grandparents were illiterate?"

"I suppose so."

In his bewilderment, Justin tried to piece together memories of his grandparents. He'd never realized that they didn't know how to read or write, but now he couldn't picture them doing either. His grandmother always told them Bible stories, but he didn't have memories of her actually reading the Bible to them. For the first time, he understood why they had not helped him keep in touch with his siblings, since writing wasn't something that they did themselves.

"Huh," was all he said.

"Do you want to go over and see the old place? There's a family there now, but maybe they wouldn't mind you poking around a bit."

Justin shook his head. "I don't need to bother them. I doubt there is anything left to see. Do you know if my parents were friends with anyone else?"

"I reckon they were friends with all the neighbors in the area. Your pa would help people out, and everyone liked him. But they were more acquaintances. I don't think anyone knew them as well as we did. We were the only ones they had over to play cards on Friday nights."

Justin spent the rest of the afternoon chatting with Mr. Campbell, and even though he didn't have any more real information to share, Justin enjoyed his company. When he realized he had an hour walk back to town before dinner, he stood up to take his leave. He shook Mr. Campbell's hand and thanked him.

"I'm staying with the Phillipses tonight and will be around another day or two if you think of anything else. I appreciate it so much, sir."

Mr. Campbell slapped his back jovially. "I should be thanking you for your help, and for a good afternoon of memories. It was nice to see your face and remember old friends. Good luck with your search, boy." He smiled and gave a friendly wave as Justin made his way back down the dirt road towards town.

Justin stopped at a crest in the path and peered over at his old home across the way, but it was too far to see much, so he continued back to the manse for dinner.

Mr. Phillips greeted him at the door. "Dinner's almost ready, but I want to show you what I found," he said, ushering Justin to the settee.

He pulled out a large ledger book and set it across his lap. "I looked in the church records and found the baptism entries for you and your siblings. Your parents' and grandparents' burial information is in here too. It's just a record, but I thought you'd like to see your names."

Justin touched the page with wonder. "I would, thank you. It was so thoughtful of you to pull it out for me." He ran his finger down the page of baptisms, beginning in 1840, and came to his own name.

Justin Henry Young, parents Henry and Sinead Young, date of birth July 22, 1840, date of baptism August 28, 1840.

Next he found Kellie, and read *Kellie Arlene Young*. He stopped and reached over to his knapsack on the floor. Pulling out a paper and pencil, he jotted down the full names and birth dates of his siblings, with the exception of Katie.

Kellie Arlene Young. December 5, 1842
Jedidiah Finley Young. January 27, 1845
John Donovan Young. April 6, 1847

Kellie, Jed, and Jack. Justin sat staring at their names. Would he ever see them again? How could he possibly find them? Where could they be? It wasn't until Mrs. Phillips announced dinner that Justin broke out of his reverie and stood up to join his hosts.

By the time Justin made it out of the courthouse late the next morning, most of the town seemed to be aware of who he was and why he was there. Even though he had records of his siblings' births already, he went ahead and requested copies of their birth certificates and his parents' and grandparents' death certificates, since he wasn't sure that he would ever be back. He took the documents to a nearby bench outside of the courthouse and sat down to peruse them, anxious to see his parents' birthplaces most of all.

He read them and reread them. New York, New York, his father's death certificate read. New York? Finding his Young relatives in New York would be like finding a needle in a haystack. It may as well have said that he was born in the United States of America, especially if he only had a sister using a married surname still alive. Sinead's and her parents' certificates all recorded Cork, Ireland as their birthplaces. No further clues or new information were on the rest of the documents, but at least he had them now if he ever needed them.

Justin sat in the midday sun, lost in thought. Although he processed his disappointment in the dead end, he was grateful to be back at his childhood home and speak to people who knew his parents. It made them feel real again, to someone who had carried them as a distant memory for two-thirds of his life.

He spent the remainder of the day strolling around town, perusing the general store and making conversation with the proprietor and townspeople who stopped him to chat. Some of them he vaguely remembered, and most of them he didn't, and even though none of them had been close with his parents, it was special to hear from so many who remembered their family.

At the manse that evening, he informed the Phillipses of his intention to take the stagecoach up to Louisville the following day. He gave them his Chicago address, should any other Youngs ever show up in town searching for him.

"If you need anything while you're in Louisville, be sure to look up our son Robert," Mrs. Phillips said. "He teaches at the St. Andrews School for Boys, and I'm sure he would be glad to see you."

Justin thanked her and offered to take anything up to him that she'd want to send. Robert was a couple of years older than him, but they'd been in Sunday School together as boys, and he was grateful for the Phillipses' kindness to him. He passed a relaxing evening visiting with the minister while Mrs. Phillips prepared gifts for Robert, and retired early to rest for the next leg of his journey.

The next morning, Justin headed out on foot with a parcel of treats for Robert and another with more baked goods for the orphanage and letters to the Wests. He wanted to stop by Ira Campbell's again on his way to Louisville, and figured that he would catch the stagecoach further up the road. The doctor was just beginning his morning rounds when he overtook Justin on the road and gave him a lift, so it was still early when he arrived at the farm. Justin showed Ira the documents, but the farmer scratched his head.

"New York? That just don't sound right. Henry must have been born there and then moved, 'cause I don't think your pa grew up in New York. I would have remembered that, and I'm pretty sure your ma came through New York but didn't stay there. I seem to remember they met and got married somewhere in the Maryland or New Jersey area." He looked regretful. "I wish I could remember more for you, boy, but it's been a long time since we talked about these things."

"Don't apologize; I enjoyed hearing everything you did share about them," Justin insisted. "I can't tell you how much your time has meant to me, and how I appreciate the opportunity to get to know them a little more."

Leaving Grayson County, he felt like he was leaving newfound friends, and the reception he had received was more than he had hoped for. The new information, coupled with being physically present where his parents had lived and died, helped him to know them better than he ever had before, and he realized that he knew himself better as a result.

The rest of the day's trip to Louisville was uneventful, and he reached the orphanage after dinner time. A middle-aged woman in a ticking apron covering her brown calico dress answered his knock, and when she saw who it was, she opened her arms wide.

"Justin!" Mrs. West exclaimed, wrapping him in a motherly hug. "Horace, come and see who it is!"

Her husband, a medium-built man with graying hair, rounded the corner with two elementary-age boys at his side and broke into a grin. "Come in, come in!"

Justin handed the house mother the parcel from Mrs. Phillips and was ushered in to a large sitting room, where two older boys were lighting fires in the fireplaces. Justin remembered when that had been his job, and he introduced himself to them.

"I remember you!" The shorter one straightened up, and Justin realized that this had been one of the smaller boys he'd helped learn his letters as a little chap. "I'm Roy, and this is Abe," he said, indicating his dark haired companion.

"I remember you, too," Justin said with a friendly smile. "Are you the biggest boys here now?"

"No, there are a few more; eight of us are in the upper class now, including the girls."

"Well, I hope to get to know you more before I leave. I was going to catch up with Mr. and Mrs. West now, but perhaps tomorrow we can play a game of chess," Justin suggested amiably.

"Certainly!" The boys finished their job and left for the next room as Justin took a seat on the couch across from Mr. West's armchair.

"I was just down in Grayson County and wanted to stop by and see you while I was in the area before heading back home."

"We're glad you did," Mr. West replied. "Did your time in the army run out?"

"No," Justin said, and told him about the battle of Lexington and the paroled Irish Brigade.

"I'm thankful you're out safely. War is a terrible thing, but the cause is important." Mr. West sighed. "We need to rid this country of slavery once and for all." Most of Justin's abolitionist views had been nurtured in the orphanage, where every life was seen as valuable, and he knew that Mr. West would have expected nothing short of him doing his part in the war.

"How are things here?"

Mrs. West entered carrying a toddler in time to hear Justin's question. She took a seat and cheerily began to bounce the baby on her knee.

"We have thirty-one children now, more than we have ever had before," Mr. West said. "They're a good group. It's challenging, but each one is such a unique blessing to us. And God provides all that we need, sometimes before we ask."

"Do you have other staff?" Justin asked.

"Right now we just have Abigail, the teacher, and Daisy, who handles the little ones." Justin remembered the free black woman who had come on staff when he lived there, and her children who spent their days playing at the orphanage.

"Robert Phillips was here last year. He tutored with the upper grades and helped with a lot of the maintenance. He took a job at St. Andrews this year, and we are so pleased for him. It's a great fit for his skills."

Justin waved his finger. "I was going to ask you if you had anything you needed help with while I'm here. I'd be happy to tackle a project or two before I leave."

The Wests looked at each other. "I'm sure we can find something for you to do, but you don't have to," Mr. West said. "You're welcome to stay as a guest."

"Nonsense. It's the least I can do."

"Well then, maybe we can patch some holes in the roof and paint a couple of shutters tomorrow," he conceded. "I have to say, our biggest need right now is probably the tutor. Some years we can get by with just Abigail. She's excellent at handling so many children in varying levels at the same time, but upper math isn't her strong suit. And you know I'm far better with words than numbers myself. We have a couple of boys who seem to be gifted in mathematics, and I'm afraid we aren't able to cultivate their gifts as well as I would like. We have been praying for a math teacher this year."

Mrs. West looked at Justin. "You were always good at mathematics," she mentioned, quite pointedly.

Justin immediately started to shake his head. "I don't know," he began. His first instinct was to keep with his plan to head back to Chicago within a week or two, but he stopped himself.

"Why don't you pray about it? We could use you, and it's just for the school year. It would be such an answer to prayer."

Justin's mind raced, but he nodded. Stay for the school year? He loved the Wests deeply, and they had done so much for him, but he had been looking forward to getting home to Luke, Rebecca, and Chicago, in that order. Eight months was a long time to delay his return, but on the other hand, it wasn't forever. Since the Wests didn't seem to expect an answer immediately, he changed the subject.

"I forgot; I have a package to deliver to Robert myself. I should do so in the morning while his mother's treats are still fresh."

"You can take the carriage," Mr. West said. "We can paint shutters another time. I'll give you the directions to the school in the morning."

Justin was surprised when he was offered a private room for the night, as he had expected to bed down with the boys like he always had. The orphanage had a tiny bedroom in the carriage house that had been used by Robert and various maintenance men throughout the years, and the Wests had left it vacant in faith that their math teacher prayers would be answered soon.

Despite the late hour and his long day, he jotted another page in his letter to Rebecca before heading to bed. He had an uncomfortable feeling about the job offer, the kind of feeling that told him that he would probably not be going back to Chicago anytime soon. He decided to leave the subject for the next time, and prepared his letter to be posted.

-4-

The next morning, Justin left his letter on the console in the orphanage foyer on his way out to St. Andrews. It was Saturday, so Robert didn't have class when Justin arrived at the faculty building. Robert opened the door, broom in hand, and Justin held up the parcel.

"I'm Justin Young. I've just been down in Leitchfield, and your mother sent this for you."

Robert's eyes lit up and he held the door open as his bearded face turned into a smile.

"Come in! It's been a long time." He set his broom against the wall and offered Justin a seat. "Thank you for bringing the package. What brings you to Louisville?"

"Oh, I stopped by to see the Wests," Justin said. "I heard you helped out there last year."

Robert untied the parcel on his small table and began unpacking it. "I did. I remember you lived there. They mentioned from time to time when they got letters from you. You live in Chicago now?"

"I'm supposed to. It's looking a little like I'll be living here this year, though. The Wests asked me to stay on and teach upper math."

Robert stopped, a jar of homemade pickles in his hand. "I was sorry to leave them, but I was offered this job, and it was the position I had been hoping for. So you think you will?"

Justin hesitated. "They've done a lot for me, and I don't have a real reason not to. I'm trying to wrap my mind around not heading back home for several more months, though."

"What do you do in Chicago?" Robert asked.

"I work in a lumberyard on the river. I love it, but there's not much going on in the winter, so it's a good chance to not head back right away."

"I've never heard anyone say they love working in a lumberyard before," Robert said, his eyebrows arched. "You have a girl back home?"

"Yes, I do."

"Do you think she'll wait for you?"

"I think so."

Robert just nodded understandingly and finished putting things in his cupboard. "You'll really like the boys at the orphanage. It was a pleasure to teach them; they're so eager to learn. If you need anything, just let me know."

Justin grinned. "So it's settled? You've decided I'm staying?"

"If the boys are going to be aging out of the orphanage soon, and your lady is willing to wait, it sounds like it's settled to me." Robert took a seat. "Especially if they will have the opportunity to be mentored by someone who has been in their shoes and has headed into adulthood successfully after leaving the orphanage. I'm sorry." He seemed to realize he had overstepped. "It's not my business. I've fallen in love with those boys, and I'm thrilled to think of how valuable your time would be to them."

Justin sat considering the argument carefully. "You're probably right. Anyway, I should get going since I told Mr. West I could help with some projects today."

"Well, if you're staying, let's get together sometimes. I'm free on Saturdays, and I'm sure I'll see you at church," Robert said, standing up to shake Justin's hand.

"I'll be there tomorrow," Justin replied, as Robert opened the door.

"Thanks again for the package from Mother."

Justin paused in the hall. "I was glad to, and it was good seeing you again. Tomorrow, then."

That evening after dinner, Justin was surrounded by boys in the sitting room as he played Roy in chess, explaining each move he made as the game progressed. He found it enjoyable, especially the look in Roy's eyes when he executed a well thought-out move and took one of Justin's pieces. After Justin won the game, he promised more games with other boys the following afternoon before Mrs. West came to usher them off to bed.

Justin waited until the children were down for the night before he spoke to the Wests again about teaching. Mrs. West settled in by the fire with her never-ending pile of mending, and her husband had his newspaper, which he usually read aloud to her in the evenings. He didn't open it, and the three sat chatting comfortably together. Eventually, Justin mentioned the job offer.

"I'm not much of a teacher. I've never taught before, so I might not be that good at it. But I can stay until summer and help how I can," he announced mildly.

Mrs. West let out a happy sigh, lowering her mending into her lap, and Mr. West looked at him with satisfaction.

"That sounds perfect, since that will keep you humble. Rely on God to guide you, and He has already given you talent in mathematics. He brought you as an answer to our prayers."

"God bless you, dear," Mrs. West said with an affectionate smile.

Mr. West folded his hands soberly. "The salary isn't much, you understand," he began, but Justin shook his head.

"Please don't give me any salary at all. All I need is room and board, and enough money for my train ticket home in the summer."

"Justin!"

Justin was resolute. "Please, use the money for other things you need. I don't need it, if I have food to eat and a place to stay. Besides, I can't imagine the children will spend all day on math. I'm sure if I need anything, I can pick up odd jobs in the afternoons or Saturdays when I'm not tutoring."

The Wests were hesitant but grateful, realizing that as an orphan himself, Justin was used to not needing very much to get by.

"It will be so good to have you home again. What do you need to get settled?" Mrs. West asked.

"I think the room has everything I need. I do need to go to the tailor's on Monday since I only came with what I'm wearing."

"Take as much time as you need to get everything in order before you start. And we can cover the expense of the clothes you'll need," she told him, but still Justin refused.

"I have a bit of money saved up. I promise, I'll be fine. Thank you, but I know you need it more than I do."

Mrs. West reluctantly conceded, but she was inwardly proud of the integrity of the young man she and her husband had mentored and launched into the world.

It felt good to be back with his old friends in a place where he had many happy memories, and for the ability to meet a need that they had. Still, Justin's heart twisted when he thought of the many months that would pass before he would see the Dinsmores again, and he hoped that what he had told Robert about Rebecca was true.

When he retired for the night, he sat propped up in bed, closed his eyes, and pictured the way she always looked at him, with her mouth turned up contentedly and adoration in her eyes. Nothing else in the world compared to the feeling he got when she looked at him like that. There wasn't much doubt in his mind that if he proposed, she would accept, nor was there a question if he was sure that she was the one for him. In fact, now that he had hit dead ends looking for his family and was out of the war, there wasn't anything left to stand in his way from making an offer as soon as he returned home. With such a pleasant thought on his mind, he blew out his candle, burrowed down under his quilt, and dreamed the sweetest kind of dreams.

December 14, 1861

Justin was glad to be in Robert's warm apartment after his chilly commute on a Saturday afternoon in December. He'd made a habit of spending most Saturdays with Robert and attending social events together, since the two bachelor teachers had similar interests and found each other's company invigorating. He had brought some leftover cake that he'd made with Mrs. West the day before for some of the children's birthdays, and Robert made a pot of coffee to go with it and get them through the evening's festivities, a Christmas party hosted by a couple from church.

"I wanted to ask you about Christmas break," Robert said, handing Justin a mug of coffee and taking a seat with his own. "I'm heading down to Leitchfield next week and wanted to invite you to come along. My whole family will be together and the food is good. We would love to have you join us."

Justin blew out all of his air and raised his eyebrows. "Goodness. That's a tempting offer, and I appreciate it. I'd love to join you, but I think I'll stay and have Christmas at the orphanage."

Robert didn't press. "I knew you'd come to like those boys," he said contentedly, and Justin chuckled.

"Yes, but that isn't all there is to it. Christmas with the Wests was always special. It wasn't the presents, though people at the church were always generous. It's . . . every year they are so excited about Jesus coming to earth. It's infectious, and a bit addicting." He smiled at the memory of those formative Christmases he had spent with them.

"How do you feel about missing Christmas in Chicago though?" Robert asked.

Justin combed his fingers through his black curls.

"I just have to avoid thinking about that. Honestly, when I was there, I fondly remembered Christmases here, and this is probably the last Christmas I'll ever have here. I have to remind myself of that."

He perked up and added, "It's fun being on the other side of things this time, though. Now I'm coming back as an adult, and I get to add to the magic of Christmas for the children. I'm starting to form ideas of how I can make it fun for them."

"You almost make me wish I was staying too." Robert was clearly impressed. "I haven't seen my little nephews and nieces in a while though, and as their only single uncle, I need to go spoil them and be the one to get them outside for snowball fights when they're cooped up."

He groaned and stretched out. "I'll be interrogated about ladies when I get home. My mother and sisters can't wait to see me get married, and they're never satisfied with my excuses. If you came, they might be more polite about it, at least."

"In that case, I'll definitely stay here," Justin said teasingly. "But you can practice your excuses on me. What are they, anyway?"

Robert rolled his eyes. "Well, this year, it doesn't seem like most women are interested in a man that's not in uniform."

"Sorry, I haven't been looking myself, so I didn't notice that they weren't. It's too bad. If everyone went to war, no one would be educating the children."

"Last year when I taught at the orphanage, I was too busy to be social," Robert continued. "And being from a small town, there weren't many options for me before I moved to Louisville." He set down his coffee mug. "I'm not worried about it. It will happen when the time is right, and I've been so invested in the students that finding a wife hasn't been a priority."

"You can always head outside to the snowballs if your interrogation gets too intense," Justin encouraged him. "Then your family can talk about you freely without you around."

Robert laughed, and Justin thought of his adopted family and how he missed this kind of banter. "If I come back with frostbite, you'll know it was especially rough. And I'll blame you," Robert assured him.

"I really do appreciate the offer to join you. I hope you all have a happy Christmas together."

Justin leaned over to look out Robert's window at the barren landscape, brick buildings, and gray skies. Christmas break was almost here already, and that meant that the school year was halfway over. Robert saw the far off look in Justin's eyes and quietly took the coffee mugs to the dishpan, giving his friend space to be alone in his thoughts.

Justin was pulling a large evergreen tree through the front door of the orphanage with some of the boys on Christmas Eve when he glanced over and saw a letter on the console with his name on it. He heaved the tree upright and directed the group as they managed the tree into the sitting room, where Mrs. West was waiting with several children and boxes of decorations. It would have been easier had he handled getting the tree into the bucket of water himself, but everyone's spirits were so high, he allowed the boys the satisfaction of setting it up, even though it made it a significantly more precarious ordeal. Eventually they made it through, and the tree stood securely.

Once finished, he turned to see where he could jump in and make himself useful. Older girls were placing candles in candle holders and tying bows for the boughs, and several small children were threading popcorn onto strings. Justin took a seat on the floor by some of the littlest ones and leaned over to untangle their threads as they poked the popcorn with their needles. He could smell gingerbread baking, and it reminded him of all the Christmases he had been a child decorating in this room.

He was so engaged in the festivities that it was several hours before he retired to his room with the letter, quickly lighting the fireplace and jumping under his quilt fully dressed to open the envelope. Inside were letters from Elisan and Rebecca. He opened Elisan's first, cheered to read of the family's Christmas preparations.

Elisan wrote of their Aunt Em who was visiting from the east for Christmas with her husband, Uncle Phil. Justin recalled these relatives visiting for Christmas only once before several years back, and how engaging and gracious they were. Reverend Dinsmore's sister had married a respected doctor in Baltimore and as he was doing well for himself, they circulated with the gentility of that city. It was a treat for the Dinsmores to have a visit from their adored aunt and uncle, and Christmas was setting up to be a delightful soiree for the family.

To Elisan, however, the Christmas tidings she related to him were diminished by the report of greater news that preoccupied her mind and most of her letter. Aunt Em had invited her to a spring tour of Europe with herself and Uncle Phil, and Elisan was to return to Baltimore with them after Christmas to stay the couple of months until the ship set sail. Needless to say, the prospect of such an adventure had set her over the moon, and she gushed on for the length of a couple of pages about her pending trip. Justin smiled affectionately as he read of all of her hopes and dreams and what a fabulous time she was having with her beloved aunt, and he looked forward to reading Rebecca's placid and more practical opinions of the news.

As expected, Rebecca's letter had far fewer adjectives, and although she was thrilled for her sister, she was reticent to be apart from her for such a long time. They had never been separated before, but Rebecca took consolation in the fact that Justin would be returning home in the space that Elisan would be away. She asked individually about the boys at the orphanage that Justin had mentioned, and how his Christmas surprises for them had developed.

He read her letter in her voice, as he always did, and he closed his eyes and saw her face. She was a calming presence in his life, even from a couple of hundred miles away. Justin reread both of the letters before setting them aside and picking up his Bible, ending his Christmas Eve with the greatest letter of all, reading until he fell asleep.

February 21, 1862

It was a frigid day in February, the type of day that was so cold, Justin was actually grateful to not be spending the winter in Chicago. The ground was covered in days-old snow, but the roads were cleared and the city had begun moving about again.

Mathematics had been tough; they were at a challenging point which some of the boys were having difficulty grasping, and Justin was running out of patience and ways to explain the same thing. It had been weeks since anyone had been outdoors for long, and everyone needed some sort of reprieve from the monotony of winter before they all went stir crazy. Never had Saturdays with Robert been so necessary for preserving Justin's sanity, as that and church were his only outlets away from the house. Everyone poked along, doing their best to keep their spirits up and looking forward to seeing the sun again.

Justin was surprised to find an envelope with Rebecca's handwriting on the console, since a letter had just arrived from her three days beforehand. Math was over for the day at least, and everything else could wait, so in an uncommon move, he took the letter and headed to his room in the middle of the day to read it. He needed something to help break up the funk in his mind, and the unusual timing of the letter set his mind racing. Seated on his bed, he curled his knees up and gently pulled the paper out of the envelope. Inside was a second envelope alongside a thin letter from her. On the top page, she had scrawled an obviously hurried explanation.

Dear Justin,

This letter arrived at the bakery for you, and Mrs. Katz gave it to me to send you. I did not want to delay it in any way, so I'm sending it immediately with my half-finished letter. Please write soon. We are all anxious to know about it.

Yours,
Rebecca

Justin picked up the envelope she referred to, his hands trembling. It was addressed in a handwriting he didn't recognize, to his name in the 23rd Illinois Regiment. The army information was crossed off, and next to it was written his Chicago address in a different script. The original postmark was from Baltimore, Maryland, and the return address read *K. Burns, 83 Cary St.* Justin took a shaky breath as he eased the envelope open to find a single slip of paper.

My dear sir, it began. *If this letter has found the right Mr. Justin Young, then you are my long lost brother.*

If not, please forgive the error, and be so kind as to respond and let me know to direct my search elsewhere.

If so, however, your younger sister Kellie is anxious to hear from you after all these years and to be reunited with my dear childhood companion.

Justin stopped reading. He held the paper between his fingers as a lump formed in his throat. For the space of several minutes he sat unmoving, staring at the fire, trying to gather his thoughts together while offering heartfelt albeit scattered thanks to God through the bedlam in his emotions.

In an instant, his world had changed. In an instant, what was lost for what was now nearly fourteen years had been found. In this benchmark moment, alone in his bedroom, the trajectory of his life changed forever.

Justin's hands were still shaking several minutes later when he reached for a paper and pencil, but then he stopped and instead leaned over and picked up his wallet off of the bedside table. He leafed through it, then resolutely tugged his boots on, and grabbing his heavy overcoat and hat, headed quickly out the door for the telegraph office.

On the freezing mile-long walk crunching through the snow, he figured and refigured his wording, so when he arrived, his message was prepared.

To: Miss Elisan Dinsmore, Care of Dr. P. Estes, 327 3rd St, Baltimore
FOUND KELLIE IN BALTIMORE 83 CARY ST. TELL HER LETTER COMING. JUSTIN

It was more expensive to send a telegram than a letter, and Justin knew that a more practical person would have saved the money in the name of patience. After all, after fourteen years, what was one more week of waiting for a letter to reach her? But to him, it was fourteen years too long, and giving Kellie a personal connection in the form of Elisan would certainly accelerate things.

His spirits were high as he walked back to the orphanage, and he didn't feel the cold. The message would reach Elisan by the next day, and she would know what to do; and if anyone was quicker to action than Justin, Elisan Dinsmore surely was. Of all the chances, of all the cities she could have been in, of all the years her aunt had invited her to visit. Now, after fourteen years of silence,

Kellie reached out and found him at the exact time that Elisan was there. Justin had a little less than an hour until dinner, so he went directly back to his room, sat by his fire, and reread Kellie's letter before picking up his pencil and drafting a proper reply.

My dear sister,

I trust you know by now that you have located the brother whose heart has longed for you for the past fourteen years. I cannot express the relief and joy that your letter has brought, and I am anxious to see you with my own eyes as soon as I am able. The earliest I can come is in June, if you would like to see me. I must know how you are, and all that your life has held since we were separated. Must I wait to hear in person, or shall we catch up through pen and paper? I am well, but never have I been so well as I am now that I know you are alive. Your last name has changed; are you married? Do you have contact with our other brothers? Please don't delay in replying.

I am most affectionately your brother,

Justin H. Young

On his way in to dinner, Justin left the letter by the front door of the main house to be sent in the morning. He considered waiting to share his news until he could do it privately with the Wests after the children were in bed, but as it really had no need to be private, he made an announcement at dinner. To a group of orphans and their caregivers, there was no better news than Justin's, and they shared his joy in a way that no one else could. His heart swelled to see children dancing around the room as Mrs. West pulled him into one of her excellent hugs. It was touching to see others express so much happiness on his account, and the air felt light for the first time since Christmas.

He answered their questions as well as he could, and assured them that he had no intention of leaving before the end of the school year. The children were all grateful, but Mrs. West questioned his decision that evening in the quiet sitting room.

"You really are free to go now, Justin," she insisted. "We aren't even paying you anything, and you've been waiting your whole life for this."

Justin leaned back, relaxing into the warm armchair. "I'm not going, Mrs. West," he stated bluntly. "I've made a commitment and I won't be convinced to break it." So that was that.

Justin retired early, propping himself up in bed to read Kellie's letter again and study every curl of her penmanship. It wasn't until he had read it through twice more that he remembered that he had never read Rebecca's half letter, and he pulled it out now. He had far too much adrenaline to sleep anytime soon, so he honored her request of a quick reply and wrote her a couple of pages about Kellie's letter, his telegraph to Elisan, and his hope to head to Baltimore the moment that school let out in the summer.

Even with the completion of Rebecca's letter, his mind raced for most of the night and allowed him little sleep. Regardless of what the response from Kellie would be, he resolved to begin picking up as many extra jobs in town that he could on evenings and Saturdays for the remainder of the semester, and tried to calculate how much money he could save by the summer. It was a futile exercise, as such things are incapable of being known with so few details in hand, but it kept his brain active for several hours.

The next day he was exhausted but chipper and completely distracted during his own class. Elisan should have received his telegram by then, and his letters went out before lunchtime as the day dragged on and he marked time. The funk his brain had been in the previous day had disappeared, but the commotion that replaced it was equally unhelpful for mathematics instruction. He gave the boys lists of exercises to solve to pass the class time and free him from having to focus enough to teach anything, perfectly aware that it would be a couple of weeks before he would have a response from either Elisan or Kellie.

To his complete astonishment, he received a telegram from Elisan the next evening.

CALLED ON YOUR LOVELY SISTER WITH AUNT TODAY. DYING FOR YOU TO MEET HER. SENDING YOU EVERY DETAIL. ELISAN

Elisan had apparently not changed one bit in the past nine months. Justin smiled at the thought of Elisan showing up at Kellie's in the Estes carriage, although he could not picture what kind of home Kellie received them in, but it sounded as if the visit had gone well. The telegram sat out on his bedside table with his letter from Kellie and he read them both in the morning when he got up and in the evening before bed every day as he impatiently waited for more correspondence. Elisan's letter arrived a few days before Kellie's, almost two weeks later.

4 March 1862

Dear Justin,

I can hardly believe I've met your blood sister and seen her with my very own eyes! She is adorable. She looks like you, but her eyes are blue and she's far prettier. She's a slight little thing, but then you're not very big either. I don't know if you heard that she was married and is a widow now, so she's in full mourning and not going out much. It doesn't seem like she has many friends anyway, but we invited her over and hope to see lots of her before we leave in June. Yes, June—our trip was pushed back because of some kind of war stuff, so it looks like I may even be seeing you if you come after school lets out. It's too bad to be delayed, but I'm having a fabulous time here anyway, since auntie goes to the best kinds of parties and I have so many new clothes. Chicago seems to be kind of slow getting new fashions, and I love what is coming out of London this year. It will be terribly exciting to go there myself! Back to Kellie, I tried not to tell her too much about you because you know we Dinsmores are biased towards you in every way, but I told her that she's lucky to have a brother like you and I'm glad that we've been able to borrow you from her all these years. She reminds me more of Luke than you—steady, serious, and a good listener, but she's engaging and not dull like Rebecca. Oh I didn't mean that you're not a good listener, just cross that part out. It's that Luke is particularly talented at it and Kellie's not as flighty as you. Dear me, I didn't mean that, either. I think I'll end this letter before I end up cutting out the entire bottom part since nothing is coming out right. Get yourself here as soon as possible.

May I still consider myself your younger sister? If so, I remain

Yours,

Ellie D.

7 March 1862

Dear brother of mine,

What a pleasure it was to receive guests who are intimate acquaintances of yours, and your letter the following week. Thank you for sending them both. I was quite surprised when Miss Dinsmore showed up on my doorstep informing me that she knows you and that you sent her to me. It was the first I have heard from any of my siblings since I came to Baltimore as a child. She told me about your personality and how she and her siblings consider you to be their brother, and she said that she has first-hand experience that you are an excellent brother to have. I can't wait to see you for myself, although hearing you described by a friend made you more real to me than anything else could have. I have been searching army rosters of both sides for our brothers as they have come available to me, and you were the first to respond. It is quite likely that my letters are not making it through the lines to the Confederacy, as my search there has been less fruitful. I have some leads, and believe I may have located one if not both of our younger brothers in North Carolina regiments. It remains to be seen if they are interested in reconnecting with their birth relatives.

Your assumption is correct, I have been married. However, I lost my husband, Nathan Burns, in the Battle of Bull Run and am on my own now. He provided for me and I have a little cottage, but my greatest hope now is to find my family. I know now that you are no longer in the army and that my letter must have taken the long road to find you, and it must have been my prayers that brought it to your door. To think, you were in an orphanage then and now. I wonder how it was for you. I'm grateful that our aunt raised me, although we were never close and I never see her now. Ah, how much to tell you now, and how much to wait until I see you? June, you say? That's in three months, but after fourteen years, it is but a short wait more.

I send you my love.

Your sister,

Kellie Burns

-5-

2 April 1862
Justin dear,

I must write you with haste before something terrible happens. I have only known Elisan Dinsmore a short time, but as you have known her so much longer, you must intervene and prevent a catastrophe. She won't listen to me, and her guardians seem unconcerned. What to do? It may already be too late. Apparently, she was at a party with her uncle and happened to meet the brother-in-law of the surgeon general of the Confederate States. Before I knew what was what, she had determined to accompany this man and his wife to Virginia as guests of the wife's sister, with the intention of locating the two North Carolina privates I believe are our brothers. They are leaving next week, so my letter may be too late reaching you. Has she always been this spontaneous and stubborn?

"Yes, she has," Justin said out loud to his empty room.

I'm afraid she fails to realize that Virginia is a war zone and that nothing about her can pass as a southerner behind Confederate lines. I have lived in two border states in my life, and I assure you that I have nary met anyone who is as thoroughly a northerner as Miss Elisan Dinsmore.

Justin laughed out loud and pictured Elisan giving an impassioned speech about the evils of slavery in the middle of the Confederate army before he read on.

Perhaps that will protect her from being taken as a spy, though? If she were more subtle, she might be seen as more suspicious. Dear me, I will pray to that end. Her uncle is entrusting her to the care of his good friend and assures me that this man will let no harm come to her, but I have not slept since she called on me yesterday. What sort of parents does she have? Would they condone such behavior, and will they ever forgive me if something happens to her? She has asked me to provide letters to the boys and a photograph to take with her, but I'm afraid that if I do, it will only be encouraging this suicidal errand. I seem to be the only one here who does not think this is normal behavior. Is it normal? Please advise immediately; I am sure I shall not sleep until you do.

Your sister,
Kellie

8 April 1862
My dearest Kellie,

I'm afraid there really is nothing to be done about Elisan. What is abnormal for every other creature on earth has always seemed to be the kind of actions she gravitates towards, and in case you haven't been made aware, she is a force to be reckoned with. Furthermore, I doubt that her parents would do much to prevent her; her mother is unaffected by her daughters, and her father trusts her God-given instincts perhaps a bit too much. This may be more than they are willing to accept, but there is nothing to be done. When I met Dr. Estes, he seemed to be an intelligent man, and he trusts his friend that she's accompanying. So, let her go, and perhaps she will be successful and bring back good news? I will be waiting for updates from you. In the meantime, don't lose sleep over the girl, when her own parents are sleeping soundly.

Fondly I remain,
Your brother, Justin.

April 16, 1862

Elisan tapped her foot as she sat in the front room of a brick row house in Richmond, Virginia and looked out the window. Dr. Preston was expected to return at any minute, and he should finally have all the papers they needed to head into the Confederate camps. The Prestons had taken almost as much interest in reuniting the Young family as she had, although they had never met any of them, and were doing all that they could to use their connection with Dr. Moore to make Elisan's errand successful. Dr. Preston and his wife came to Richmond at least yearly to visit her sister, Mary Moore, and were familiar with the place and its people. They had been helpful guides to Elisan the past five days as she adjusted to the city while waiting for Dr. Preston to make the necessary arrangements for her meetings.

She had gone walking with Mrs. Preston and Mrs. Moore through the city and up past the beautiful white capitol building, which had been designed by Thomas Jefferson. Richmond was teeming with people who had been flooding there for work and refuge since the war began, and the streets were chaotic and full. Virginia had never been high on her list of places she wanted to visit, but she was surprised by the beauty and hospitality of the state and was now glad that she'd had the opportunity to come.

It felt strange to be in enemy territory, and stranger still to be welcomed so warmly by people she was so philosophically opposed to. She found herself unable to reconcile the friendliness she saw in southerners with their willingness to enslave other human beings, and filled journal pages with her many thoughts on the matter while she waited. The most difficult part of the trip for her by far was seeing slavery for the first time in her life, even in the Moores' own home, and she had to work hard to keep her mouth shut. The thought of slavery had always made her sick, but to actually experience it in person was rattling to the core.

Elisan saw the Moores' carriage arrive with Dr. Preston inside, and he soon entered the room where she sat with his wife and sister-in-law. Dr. Preston was tall and thin, with prematurely gray whiskers, spectacles, and a ready smile for everyone he encountered. He had been a colleague of Philip Estes' for many decades, although he didn't practice medicine as actively anymore. He was now involved in medicinal research and lectured at universities regularly, and looked the part of an academic.

Elisan straightened up as he entered the room, hoping that things were finally in order so they could begin the day long journey to Yorktown, where General McClellan currently held the Confederate bunkers in a siege.

Dr. Preston looked to her as soon as he entered, and held up the papers.

"I have our letters," he said. "You may want to wait before leaving, however. I just learned that Jed Young is actually here in Richmond."

"He is?" Elisan said in bewilderment, and the doctor nodded.

"It appears that he arrived the day that we did. He's being held under house arrest while waiting for his court martial."

Mrs. Preston and Mrs. Moore were as shocked at the news as Elisan was.

"Why, what did he do?" Mrs. Preston asked.

"They didn't tell me."

Elisan came to her feet. "May we visit him?"

"Yes, he's able to receive visitors. If you like, we can go after lunch, as there isn't anything else we need to be doing," Dr. Preston said. "I have confirmed that he is indeed the one you are looking for. I spoke to the captain in charge of transporting prisoners to the military courts, and he described him like the photograph you have: Irish descent with curly black hair."

Elisan's heart raced with excitement and she felt goosebumps to know that she would be meeting Justin's younger brother herself that very afternoon. Meeting Kellie had been a great honor, and she did not take lightly the weight of her mission to inform Jed Young that his siblings were alive and were anxious to know him.

It seemed that many things about Richmond were altered due to the war as the new nation made the city into its capitol and made do using current buildings for things other than their original purposes, such as hospitals, prisons, and offices. The men waiting for their military court proceedings were being kept in half of a residential house near other government buildings, the other half of the house being the headquarters of the signal corps.

Cholera had had its impact on the military court, and now the powers that be were scrambling to get the necessary people in order so that they could continue with their business in a timely manner. The city as a whole bore a sense of making-do as the infant nation struggled to find its footing, but Virginians were resilient people and rolled amiably with the chaos that their capital had become. The military court issues were just one more setback in a long line of them, so no one seemed particularly bothered by it at this point.

Elisan arrived at the holding house with Dr. Preston later that same day, wearing her neatly tailored emerald green calico day dress with a plain white cotton collar and cuffs, black and white bonnet, and a gold leaf pin at her throat. She carried a small satchel with the documents and photograph from Kellie, pulling a light brown cape around her to protect her dress from the mud.

At the door of the house, Dr. Preston spoke to the guard, and the two visitors were ushered into a small, vacant drawing room to wait while he was retrieved.

Dr. Preston's information was correct; as soon as Jed walked into the room, Elisan knew he was Justin's brother. She was most surprised by his height; Justin and Kellie were so short, she didn't expect Jed to be six feet tall. His curly hair was much longer than Justin's was, and he obviously hadn't shaved for at least a week. He wore Confederate gray wool pants with a yellow stripe down the side, a red and blue plaid collared shirt, and suspenders peeking from under an unbuttoned gray vest. He looked casual but not dirty, and he was clearly unsure of why he had visitors.

Dr. Preston came only as Elisan's chaperone, and sat back as an observer. Elisan stood up as Jed entered, and the moment that she saw his smoky gray eyes that crinkled in the corners, so similar to Justin's, she almost became emotional. She paused, swallowed, and stuck out her hand.

"Jed. I'm Elisan Dinsmore. It's nice to meet you."

Jed shook her hand silently as his eyes slowly scanned her face. Elisan took a seat, and he followed suit.

"I'm here on behalf of your family," she began. "Your older siblings, Justin and Kellie. They have been searching for each other, and for you, and are anxious to know if you are alive and well."

Jed sat and stared at Elisan. She didn't know what to do with his silence and lack of emotion, and wasn't sure if she should continue or wait. Since it was a major piece of information, and she didn't know yet if Jed had even been aware that he had siblings at all, she decided to give him some time to let the news sink in.

Finally, after about the space of a minute, he spoke for the first time.

"Where are they?"

"Justin is in Kentucky teaching for another month, but he usually lives in Chicago. Kellie is in Baltimore. They have not seen each other yet, but made contact and have been corresponding this year."

Jed nodded and was silent again as his eyes dropped to his hands, and Elisan waited. After a few more minutes, he looked up.

"Who are you?"

"I'm friends with Justin." Elisan smiled. "He's been like a big brother to me for the past several years in Chicago, and he and my brother are best friends. I'm here because . . . well, it's a long story." She couldn't think of a quick way to condense it into a sentence or two.

"I have time."

Of course he did. It just seemed awkward to ramble on explaining everything to someone who was staring at her emotionlessly and whom she knew nothing about.

"Did you know you had siblings?" Elisan asked instead.

"No. Well, I don't know. Maybe. Not now."

"Do you know where you're from? Or anything about your family?"

Jed shook his head. "I think I was born in Kentucky," he said, but he looked at Elisan with obvious distrust and didn't offer anything more.

Elisan reached into her satchel and handed Kellie's photograph to him.

"This is your older sister Kellie and her late husband on their wedding day," she said. "I was able to meet her about a month ago in Baltimore. She's the sweetest girl, and is the one who has been gathering information and trying to find everyone. To the best of my knowledge, your younger brother Jack is in the 5th North Carolina, and I was going to find him next. He was a baby when your parents died."

Jed held the picture and gazed at it, and it seemed as though he believed Elisan for the first time. He wiped his nose and sat with his fingers pressed to his lips, looking at the photograph of the woman who unmistakably resembled himself.

"You look like Justin, too," Elisan finally said softly. "Kellie has blue eyes, but you have gray eyes like Justin's."

She handed him Kellie's letter. He took it and looked at it, but didn't read it, his eyes going back to the photograph.

"What does it say?" he asked without looking up.

"You can't read?"

"No."

Elisan reached out and Jed returned the letter to her, and she read it out loud. In it, Kellie explained how much she had always loved and missed her brothers and how she came to begin searching for them the previous year. She told him how much it would mean to her if she could see him again, or better yet, if all of the siblings could get together, and that she would do whatever possible to make it happen.

Elisan finished reading, then folded the letter back up and Jed took it back. He still didn't say anything, so Elisan went ahead and told him about her family's relationship with Justin, her visit to Baltimore, the telegrams, and all that brought her to now be in Richmond.

As she talked, Jed seemed to warm up more and more, and he began asking questions and nodding to her story. Eventually, she believed he was comfortable enough that she ventured asking him about himself.

"Who raised you?" she asked. "Justin and Kellie never knew who took the children or where everyone else ended up."

"Nobody raised me," Jed replied in a surly tone. "I grew up in North Carolina."

"Kellie had records that you were in the 1st North Carolina Cavalry. What brings you here?"

Jed looked her dead in the eye. "Insubordination."

"Oh, really?" Elisan's eyebrows arched and she returned his gaze challengingly.

"Yup. To the 43rd North Carolina officers."

"But that wasn't your regiment, was it?"

"Not till my horse died and they stuck me in the infantry."

Elisan didn't know that was how things worked, but she realized Jed had just said three entire sentences to her, and she felt ecstatic. "I'm sorry about your horse."

Jed nodded acceptance at her sympathy.

"What are they going to do with you?"

"Hard labor, probably. But I'm not going back to the infantry. Didn't sign up for that bull."

"Can you get another horse?"

Jed snorted. "Not likely. I'd have to buy my own."

Elisan sat quietly for a minute thinking, and then she said, "Do you think they'd let you out?"

"I dunno."

"Do you want out? You could come back to Baltimore and meet Kellie."

Jed looked back at the photograph he still held. "She wouldn't mind having a brother who was court martialed?"

"Not Kellie," Elisan answered decisively. "What did you do, anyway?"

"I told you."

Elisan decided to play his game, and she sat silently and just looked at him until he decided to talk some more.

"I wouldn't kill a boy." He shook his head. "They put me on a firing squad the week after I got out in the 43rd. The officers did it on purpose cause they didn't like me anyway, but I wasn't gonna shoot the kid. He just wanted to get back to his ma 'cause he was too young to be there, but because he asked his buddies to desert too, they said he was incitin' and put him on the firing squad. I didn't even pretend to take the shot. It didn't save his life, but it put me here."

Elisan knew that Jed was her age, but he clearly thought of himself as older than the seventeen that he was. She noticed, and wondered if he even knew how old he was. "So do you want to get out, or not?"

"Of course I do. That's not how this stuff works, though."

Elisan looked at him dubiously. "How many men in the Confederate army have been court martialed for refusing to be on a firing squad? Who were also just found by their families? I can't imagine there's a lot of precedent you're dealing with here."

"You're one of those women who thinks she can always get what she wants, aren't you?"

"I am not," Elisan retorted, a little offended. "I just think that if you didn't sign up with the 43rd, you shouldn't have to serve with them."

"Yankee woman," Jed muttered under his breath, then to her, "You don't know nothin' about these things."

"Fine. It's your life. I think you should ask, though, and it wouldn't hurt anything. When is your hearing?"

"S'posed to be tomorrow, I guess."

"Where is it?"

Jed gave her a half smile. "They don't let Yankee women into these things, Miss."

"My name is Elisan. I'll wait outside then."

"Are you leaving now?" he asked.

"Do you want me to?"

Jed shrugged. "Seems like you do what you like anyway."

"I don't know why you've made your mind up about me like that. I'm just trying to help you," Elisan said, put out.

"Nobody asked you to help me."

Elisan didn't move. "You're the first rude Young sibling I've met," she told him quietly, and the two of them sat looking each other over in the silence.

Jed took a breath. "I didn't mean to offend you. I appreciate the information about my family."

"You're welcome."

Silence. Elisan had finally become comfortable with it, and realized that it was the only way to get anywhere with the introvert in front of her.

"Do you want to send a message back to Kellie or Justin?"

Jed shifted in his seat. "Guess we'll see what happens tomorrow. I'll see you then."

Elisan stood up and held out her hand. "I need Kellie's picture back."

"I'll give it to you tomorrow." Jed stood up, towering over her. He stuck his letter in his pocket and shook her hand. "Nice to meet you, Miss."

He turned and left the room, and Elisan stood in the middle of the room staring at the door as Dr. Preston joined her. He offered her his elbow and escorted her from the building, waiting to talk until they were outside.

"He wasn't at all what I expected," Elisan admitted as Dr. Preston helped her into the carriage.

"What did you expect?" Dr. Preston climbed in next to her and took the reins.

"I don't know. But Justin and Kellie are so warm and lovable. I don't know what to make of Jed."

Dr. Preston glanced over at his young charge as the carriage bounced along back toward the house. "He said he raised himself, and you are a stranger. I think it's natural that he would be distrustful and need more time to process everything you told him. It's quite a lot, especially if he didn't know he even had siblings at all before today."

Elisan sighed. "Yes, sir." She watched the buildings go by and sighed again. "He was exhausting. I'm tired now."

"I thought it was interesting that he would rather be court martialed than be on a firing squad," her companion said. "And that he told you that about himself when he wouldn't open up about anything else."

"Yes, it was interesting."

As they pulled up to the Moores', Elisan turned to him. "I guess I'm planning to go tomorrow. It seems that he's expecting me now."

"That's fine," Dr. Preston assured her. "We can try to head toward Yorktown the next day."

"Are you sure you have time for all of this?" she asked, worried about becoming an inconvenience, but Dr. Preston smiled warmly as he helped her alight.

"We have all the time in the world. We just have to get you back to Baltimore before your ship sails."

"Oh, that's still two months away! I promise I won't take up that much of your time," Elisan declared.

At supper that evening, Dr. Preston raised the topic of the proposed trip to Yorktown two days hence.

"I believe I can actually plan to go with you, since we have an extra day to prepare," Dr. Moore replied. "I can take the opportunity to check on the military medical corps myself. I'll send a message ahead so that they can have our accommodations arranged and get a headquarters set up."

Elisan was ready to leave for Jed's hearing the next morning when Dr. Preston came downstairs.

"I'm afraid Mrs. Preston isn't well this morning," he said as he picked up his hat and coat.

Elisan's eyes darted to his face in alarm. "Oh no! I hope it's not anything serious," she cried.

Dr. Preston shook his head reassuringly as he opened the door for her.

"It doesn't seem to be, but she needs to rest."

Elisan wondered if their trek to Yorktown would be delayed or affected in any way, but she didn't say anything more as they drove to the military court building. They did not have information on the time of Jed's hearing, and discovered upon their arrival that they were a couple of hours early and confirmed that they would have to wait outside for the duration of the proceedings. Elisan was nervous for Jed's sake and as they waited on a bench on the porch, she fidgeted and prayed for his hearing, passing the time as the minutes dragged on.

"What did you think of yesterday?" she asked the doctor after a while. "I didn't know what to say. Do you think I should present things differently when I meet Jack?"

Dr. Preston smiled graciously. "You did just fine, Miss Dinsmore. Perhaps only don't tell him if he's being rude. The culture is different down here, and we don't know what these boys have been through in their lives."

"Okay," Elisan said, and fell silent again.

They waited for another hour, until eventually the door opened and Jed came out, escorted by two Confederate guards. He was free to move about and was dressed in his full uniform, wearing his jacket and black slouch hat today.

"Jed," Elisan said, coming to her feet.

The three men stopped, and she turned to the guards. "May I have a minute?" she asked, and when they nodded, Elisan and Jed stepped to the other end of the portico together.

"How did it go?" Elisan looked up at him. Jed handed her a paper with the orders written on it, which she took and didn't look at.

"I got two months hard labor." Jed paused. "But I told them I wanted out, so they said I could get out if they made it four months."

He waited for a reaction from her, and she tried to hide her smile.

"So did you take it?"

"I did."

"I'm so happy for you!"

Jed grunted and looked into the distance. "It's four months of hard labor. They had better be worth it."

"They're worth it," Elisan softly assured him, and then asked, "Where are you going to be? How can they reach you?"

Jed blinked at her. "How? I can't read, Elisan," he reminded her.

"Don't you have anyone who can read to you?" she persisted, realizing that he'd used her Christian name for the first time.

"I wouldn't count on it," he replied indifferently. "I believe I'll be at the government works outside of Richmond with General Winder. If they can find him, they should be able to find me."

Elisan allowed him to be silent for a few minutes, then he asked, "What are you going to do?"

"I'm going to Yorktown tomorrow to look for Jack."

"Are you comin' back?"

Elisan blinked, shocked that he'd care what she did. "To see you? Won't you be working?"

Jed shrugged nonchalantly. "It's only ten hours a day."

"Do you want me to come back?"

"I want to know if you find Jack."

"Oh." Elisan was incredulous, and elated that he had interest in his family. "Okay. Yes, I'll come back then."

"Okay, then." Jed reached into his pocket and handed her Kellie's picture. "I guess you'll just show up whenever you want, as usual."

"Since I can't send you a telegram, I don't have any other choice," Elisan bantered back.

Jed glanced over at the guards, and they waved at him to indicate his time was up. He took a deep breath and let it out, then looked her in the eye and squinted. "Thank you, Miss Elisan. For taking the effort to come and do all this for my family. I'll be seein' you."

Elisan blinked back sudden tears. "It's my pleasure, Jed," she whispered and spontaneously gave him a hug. Jed did not hug her back, and when she pulled back, she saw the startled look on his face.

The guards came for him, and he wordlessly turned and walked away. After a few steps, he stopped and turned back to her.

"Tell Justin and Kellie." He paused, then added, "and Jack, that I added two months of hard labor for them."

Elisan could only nod around the lump in her throat. In his own way, Jed was telling her that he loved his siblings too, and that he wanted to see them as much as they did, and she knew how much that would mean to Justin and Kellie.

She stood watching him go, and her thoughts turned to Jack. He was the baby of the family, and would be just fifteen years old. Elisan had no idea what a fifteen-year-old was doing in the Confederate army, but of all the Young siblings, he would be the least likely to be aware of the others' existence, unless for some reason he was raised by someone who cared. The chances of a fifteen-year-old boy in the army being raised by someone who cared seemed to be pretty slim, and Elisan wondered what she would find in him. She swallowed her tears and turned back to the bench where Dr. Preston patiently waited.

-6-

Elisan was disappointed when Dr. Preston informed her after dinner that night that he would not be going to the army lines the following day. Mrs. Preston was not improved and he needed to stay with her, but he seemed confident that Elisan should go ahead on her mission with the Moores. He gave her the permission letters he had obtained on her behalf should she need them, but with the surgeon general of the Confederate States accompanying her, she likely would be fine without them. Elisan felt anxious about going without him, since she felt safe in Dr. Preston's presence and he had become a good friend, but she didn't want to delay the trip any further.

The carriage ride with Dr. and Mrs. Moore was uneventful, and the following afternoon, she arrived at a farmhouse between Williamsburg and Yorktown. She bedded down in a private dressing room adjacent to the bedroom prepared for the Moores. The arrangement suited her, since she had never been around so many men before, and she was grateful that no one could enter her room without going through theirs first. Her bed was comfortable, and she slept well despite her concerns for the homeowners that had been displaced for them.

In the morning, she washed and dressed and came downstairs to a breakfast of eggs and toast prepared by an army cook. Dr. Moore had already eaten and was on the porch speaking to some soldiers, but he came in when he noticed she was up. He had friendly eyes and big whiskers on his cheeks that looked almost comical, but he was quite good at what he did and was respected in the medical field as well the military, as far as Elisan could tell.

"Miss Dinsmore, I've gotten a sergeant to take you down to the 5th North Carolina. I hope you don't mind. I'll be here and there throughout the day, but these men should be able to find me if you need anything."

Elisan was alarmed to hear that she would be alone in the Confederate army, accompanied only by strangers. She tried to hide her fear, and thanked Dr. Moore for the trouble he went through to obtain an escort for her. She made sure that she had her papers on her later that morning when she prepared to leave with the sergeant, but she was nervous nonetheless.

The sergeant came with horses for them, and then there was several minutes' consternation over the need for a lady's saddle. When one was found in the barn on the property, they set off in the direction of the Confederate lines. By the time they finally neared their destination an hour and a half later, Elisan had begun to wonder about lunch, if she should have brought her own or if there was any way to obtain some in the camp.

When they reached the headquarters tent for the colonel of the 5th North Carolina, Elisan's escort left her to speak to the colonel. She waited by her horse, looking around to see if she could identify the last Young brother. Jack was the one that Kellie hadn't positively identified. There was a John Young in a South Carolina regiment, but Kellie seemed to think that Jack more likely grew up in North Carolina, like Jed. And there was always the high probability that the fifteen-year-old actually had not signed up at all.

Elisan watched her escort speak to Colonel Garrett, gesturing her direction, as other officers and aides listened in. She had not gone unnoticed by the men milling about, and was horrified by the stares and whistles she was receiving. Never had she been exposed to such inappropriate behavior whilst completely unchaperoned, and she began to wonder if it perhaps had not been such a good idea to just hop down to Virginia so impulsively. She glared at anyone who whistled at her, so within a few minutes, most of the camp was talking about the Yankee female and speculating about her, having made up their minds that she did not have a pleasant disposition.

One of the sergeants who had been standing with the colonel approached her, gesturing to the gawking men to go away as he did. When he reached her, she saw that he was tall, blonde, quite good looking, and carried himself with poise. Due to the lack of consistency among the Confederate uniforms, she was able to tell quickly that his was sharper and neater than the others'; he was dressed precisely and had a black necktie around his crisp shirt collar. His black boots were muddy, but the buckles on them gleamed as brightly as the gold buttons on his coat. Everything about him told her that he was an aristocrat, and he seemed out of place among tents and mud.

"Sergeant Thomas Blake," he said, bowing slightly to her. "I apologize for the behavior of the men."

"Thank you." Elisan offered her gloved hand, and he raised it to his lips. "Elisan Dinsmore."

"I understand you're here for Private Young," he said, straightening. "And you came all the way from Chicago."

"Yes. I've more recently come from Baltimore, though."

"You have a lovely name. It's unusual."

Elisan smiled. "It came from my grandmother, who moved to Cincinnati from Dublin and then married a Scotsman of all things. I like having it, but I usually have to remind people that the 'i' is long, unlike *Elizabeth*."

The sergeant opened his mouth to respond as the colonel waved them over, so instead he gestured to her and they approached the tent together. Colonel Garrett spoke directly to her when she reached him.

"Corporal Dietz will get Private Young," he said, indicating the man to his left. "You can use my tent; I'm going out now. Sergeant Blake, look after her," the colonel added, and turned to walk away.

Taken aback by his abruptness, Elisan called "Thank you," after him. Her own escort tipped his hat and went back to where their horses stood. Corporal Dietz left, and the other officers scattered, leaving Elisan alone with Sergeant Blake again. He swept his hand toward the open tent and entered behind her. She took a seat on one of the two chairs inside and the sergeant took the other.

"Where are you from?" Elisan asked, striking up a conversation while they waited.

The sergeant took off his kepi and sat erect, facing her. "My family owns property in Johnston County. It's near Raleigh."

"Do you own a plantation?"

"Tobacco," the sergeant replied proudly. "It's been in my family for a hundred and fifty years."

This was the first southern plantation owner that Elisan had ever met, and he was everything she hated about the Confederacy. But he was so polite, not to mention handsome, that she had trouble accepting that he was the enemy. The way he had rescued her from the rudeness of the men outside affected her opinion of him as well.

"I understand you're acquainted with Jack's family," he said.

"You call him Jack?" Elisan asked, and the sergeant laughed.

"I guess we do. He's just a kid, and he's friends with my little brother. I suppose since I'm a sergeant now, I should call him Private Young."

Elisan's interest was piqued. "What can you tell me about him?"

"Well, like I said, he's just a kid. We all like him, though. He doesn't really talk about himself or where he's from, but I know he's an orphan. He has a great sense of humor." Sergeant Blake grinned. "You'll see for yourself. He's a good kid. Scrappy, though."

"You said he's friends with your brother?"

"Yes, ma'am. Both of my younger brothers are with me. Charlie's a private, but Andy's just a drummer boy. He's the one I referred to, but we all kind of hang out together, us, and Jack, and the Grants, and Pick. Well, we did before I became a sergeant."

Elisan thought the man's obvious pride in his rank was funny, but she tried not to smile at him. "I've not talked to very many Yankees before," he said politely. "What's Chicago like?"

"Muddy," Elisan said with a laugh. "I like it though, because my family's there and they're a truly great family. My pa's a preacher."

She wasn't sure why she added the last part, but it just came out, as was apt to happen with her. Sergeant Blake took interest in this statement, however.

"I'm a Christian too," he said brightly.

Elisan's mouth came unhinged and she squinted at him. "Then tell me this," she challenged boldly. "How you can be a Christian and not have a problem with owning other people."

Sergeant Blake was clearly surprised by her question, but he didn't get defensive. Before he could open his mouth, there was a movement outside the tent, so he was saved from replying immediately.

"How about I explain to you later," he suggested. "It looks like Jack is here. And then you explain to me how northerners think they can impose their way of life on others who aren't like them."

They turned towards the opening as Jack Young ducked into the tent.

"Oh!" he exclaimed when he saw them, and then seemed embarrassed by his reaction. "Sorry, I thought the corporal was joshin' me that there was a lady here to see me."

Elisan and the sergeant laughed, and Elisan knew in an instant that she had found Justin's baby brother. The boy had the signature black hair, but of the four, his was more wavy than curly. He was very skinny and between Justin and Jed in height, and his baby face had not yet grown whiskers. Of the three brothers, Jack was easily the most handsome, a fact that Elisan tucked away to inform Justin of when she wrote to him, and had Kellie's bright blue eyes.

For a moment Elisan couldn't speak, as she surveyed him with an awareness that she was the first person in fourteen years to have laid eyes on all four Young siblings. She collected her thoughts and straightened up.

"Have a seat," she said, but there were no empty seats. Elisan had intended for the slave owner to give up his and leave them, but he didn't, instead pointing to a trunk for Jack to sit on.

"Good morning," Elisan said to Jack as he sat. "I am Elisan Dinsmore, and you are exactly the person I'm looking for. I was wondering what you can tell me about your family."

Jack hesitated, glancing from Sergeant Blake to Elisan. "You don't mean Richard, do you?" he said cautiously. "Cause he kicked me out."

"Who is Richard?"

Jack relaxed. "So you don't mean him then. I think he's my uncle, but I haven't seen him in a long time."

"Oh. No, I mean your parents and brothers and sister."

"I don't have those," Jack said, looking suspicious again.

Elisan grinned, giddy to impart her news. "Yes, you do. I've met all of your siblings myself, and they have been looking for you."

Jack fell silent, just as Jed had when she'd told him the same news.

"How do you know you have the right person?" he finally asked. "If I have a family, why did I live with Richard?"

Elisan looked at him compassionately, realizing that she needed to slow down, like she'd had to with Jed. "You're the youngest, and I know it's you because you look like them. Your parents died when you were a baby, and the children were all separated and sent to live with different people. The older ones remembered everything, and they have been looking for everyone." Elisan told him about Justin first, and then Kellie.

Jack's eyes filled with tears as he heard about his family for the first time and how anxious his siblings were to find him. Elisan showed him Kellie's picture, and he looked at it as the tears ran down his face.

"She's so pretty," he said. "My sister."

Jack showed the picture to the sergeant, who admired it as well.

"She does look like you," Sergeant Blake noted.

"Her husband died at the Battle of Bull Run," Elisan said. "He was in the Union army."

Jack wiped at his face with his sleeve. "I'm sorry her husband died. She looks like a nice lady. We weren't engaged at Manassas, so I didn't shoot him, at least."

"I just met Jed this week," Elisan continued. "He's in Richmond, and was just court martialed so he'll be up there a while. He was in the North Carolina cavalry, but ended up getting stuck in the infantry and wasn't very happy about that."

Jack looked at her side-eyed and humphed. "Cavalrymen think they're better than everyone else, but they just ride around for show anyway."

"Oh, that's not the worst of it! Justin was in the Yankee army last year, but he's out now," Elisan said, laughing.

Jack looked up at Sergeant Blake and grinned. "Half of us are Yankees, and half of us are rebels. Can you believe that?"

"Jack's not much of a rebel anyway," Sergeant Blake teasingly said to Elisan. "He only joined up for the food."

"It's true." Jack shook his head sadly. "I'm afraid everyone knows that about me. I wish I'd known how bad the food really is."

"Kellie sent a letter for you," Elisan told him, pulling it out, but then she stopped. "Can you read?"

Jack shook his head, and Elisan read it aloud, and he started to cry again. Elisan handed him the letter and a handkerchief, and he dried his eyes.

"I wonder how I can meet them," he said. "I guess we'll have to wait until the war is over."

Having finished sharing most of her information with him, Elisan leaned back. "Couldn't you at least make it up to see Jed? He really seemed interested to know if I found you."

Jack looked at his sergeant, who shrugged and nodded. "You can request leave for a few days," he suggested. "You haven't taken any yet, so they'll probably give it to you."

"How long does it take to get permission? I'll be around for a couple of days, since I'm here with the surgeon general down from Richmond. Maybe you could even catch a ride back with us," Elisan said.

"It's worth a try," Sergeant Blake replied. "Colonel Garrett would be the one who would approve it, and I have a feeling he would."

Jack was getting visibly excited. "That would be incredible. Can you help me with the paper?"

Sergeant Blake agreed, and Elisan smiled at the boy's joy. "I'm curious to know how the Confederate Army is allowing fourteen-year-olds in their ranks anyway," she said with a shake of her head, causing Sergeant Blake and Jack to both stop and stare at her.

"I'm fourteen?"

"No, you're fifteen now, but your birthday was in April, and you joined up last year, didn't you?"

The two men still looked at her incredulously, and Elisan saw that neither of them had realized how young Jack really was.

"Well, I just had them put sixteen on the paper, since I didn't know," Jack admitted. "I didn't know I have a birthday, either."

"Everyone has a birthday," Elisan said mindlessly.

Sergeant Blake turned to her now. "What are you going to be doing for the rest of your time until you go back to Richmond?"

"I'm staying with the Moores out on the road to Williamsburg. I think it's about an hour ride from here, but the officer that brought me this morning seemed to have trouble finding this regiment so it took longer. I really just came down here to find Jack, so I'm not sure what I'll do until they're ready to go back."

Jack stood up. "It's about lunch time now. Have you eaten?"

Elisan shook her head and the sergeant turned to his private. "I'll find her something from the officers' rations, Jack."

"Oh you don't have to do that, I'll be fine," Elisan insisted, but Sergeant Blake stood up as well.

"Come on, we'll get some food."

Elisan stepped out into the spring sunshine and took a seat by the fire as Jack and the sergeant prepared lunch with the rest of the men, some of whom were already eating. By this time, Corporal Dietz had gossiped about Elisan's errand to a few men, so everyone knew what she was doing there. Elisan enjoyed the novelty of observing a military camp, and sat watching the interactions among the men with interest. She easily identified Sergeant Blake's brother Charlie, since he was the spitting image of his brother, and she wondered if they were twins. Jack came back with his friend and introduced Andy Blake to her, and the two sat with her as they munched on cold beans and hoecakes.

A minute later, Sergeant Blake came and handed her a cup with beans and bacon. "It's not much," he said by way of apology. "That's how things are around here."

"Oh, don't apologize. Thank you for sharing."

Sergeant Blake turned to his youngest brother seated on a stump next to the lady. "Miss Dinsmore promised me a conversation, so scat," he said good humoredly.

Andy stood up wordlessly and moved to the next stump over, and Sergeant Blake took the seat next to her. For the next hour, she bantered with him over the causes of the war and their views on the conflict. Elisan truly enjoyed hearing from a real southerner for the first time, even though she remained staunchly opposed to his views.

They were thus engaged when another private she hadn't seen yet sauntered into camp. He wore his kepi jauntily, had an impressive set of whiskers for his age, and actually carried a gold cane, to Elisan's complete amusement. He saw the woman immediately, and let out a loud whistle.

"Well, lookee here, what did Sergeant Blake dig up?" he called as he approached the campfire.

"She's here for Jack," Sergeant Blake stated, and the soldier whistled again.

"I mean, I knew Jack was a real man, but this one is something else," he declared. "Good going, private!"

Elisan felt her entire face and neck heat up, and she stood up.

"Elisan Dinsmore. I'm here on behalf of Jack's brother," she said tightly. "I was delivering a message to him."

The private's mouth hung open at the sound of her distinctly Chicagoan accent. "A Yankee woman? Better be careful, Sarge. You know what those Yankee women want. Rebel babies. Keep your pants on," he warned.

Sergeant Blake came to his feet next to Elisan. "You will shut your mouth, private," he said authoritatively, his hands in fists. "Miss Dinsmore is a guest of the surgeon general, and she's here as a favor to Jack. You will not speak to her like this."

He turned to Elisan standing next to him. "I'm sorry. He doesn't usually treat ladies like this."

"I never treat ladies like this," the private corrected, taking a seat. "It's different with Yankee whores."

"Shut up, Pick!" Sergeant Blake shouted.

Elisan's eyes widened. "Pick? He's a friend of yours?" she asked, recognizing the name from his list of friends.

Sergeant Blake lowered himself back into his seat, looking genuinely embarrassed, and Elisan followed suit. "I really am sorry. I've never seen him with a Yankee woman before. I know he hates Yankees, but this is unacceptable."

Elisan looked across the fire at Pick. "I always had the impression that southern men were gentleman. You were inappropriate before you even found out I was a Yankee."

"I could smell it," Pick said dismissively.

"Well, I don't know what southern women teach their sons, but you've made me glad I'm from the north, where children are taught manners," Elisan said hotly.

Pick laughed. "Naw, I knew who you were before I came up. The boys were all talking about you and how stuck up you were, like all Yankee women. Now I know you're brazen too. Southern women have dignity. They know when a man's just joking and to hold their tongues."

"It's probably because they're too humiliated all the time to speak," Elisan retorted under her breath, and she suddenly became aware that everyone in camp had stopped to watch the exchange.

"I really should go," she said, standing back up and looked around for her escort. The horse she came on was alone, however, and the man was nowhere in sight. "Where's the sergeant that came with me?" she demanded.

Sergeant Blake cleared his throat and pulled on her skirt to get her to sit back down.

"I sent him away," he admitted quietly, leaning over. "I told him that I'd bring you back myself."

Elisan looked at him in horror. "Why on earth would you do that?"

Pick was across the fire laughing, and Sergeant Blake was red-faced.

"I just didn't want to keep him waiting when I didn't know how long you were going to stay. I'll take you back now, if you like."

Elisan looked around the fire and didn't know what to do. She had been having such a nice time before Pick came, and now she glared at him angrily for ruining her visit, not escaping the notice of her new friend.

"Pick, apologize to the lady or leave," Sergeant Blake ordered, but Pick only shrugged casually.

"I'll stop now," he conceded. "I'm just saying, I'm not making it up. I've heard stories and Yankee women actually come in as spies and you know how they get their information." Although everyone knew what he meant, he took it upon himself to spell it out anyway. "They flirt and manipulate and next thing you know, they've got the Johnny Reb in bed . . . "

"Pick, stop!"

"I'm just saying, be careful. Sarge is a ladies' man, and he isn't always careful," he added to his listeners.

"I'm not a spy," Elisan said tartly. "And I don't want . . . anything."

Pick shrugged again and leaned back, lighting his pipe.

Sergeant Blake turned to Elisan. "I am sorry I didn't ask you before I sent your escort away. I really only didn't want to inconvenience anyone when I could take you back. That's all there was to it, I promise."

Elisan nodded but her lips were pursed, and she still felt annoyed. Charlie came back just then with a banjo he had borrowed from someone, lightly picking at the strings. He had missed the whole ruckus, and now he stood by Pick and started talking to him.

"Are you two twins?" Elisan asked the sergeant, and he shook his head.

"We're eighteen months apart. The funny thing is, he actually is twins with our sister, and they don't look anything alike. People mistake us all the time. But Charlie doesn't talk much, so that's how you can tell us apart. His girl works down at the hospital; she came up from Carolina with us because she couldn't be away from him." He paused. "I feel bad for him, he would have married her if the war hadn't started last year, and he only came up here because of me. He's a patriot, but he doesn't care much for war."

Elisan enjoyed hearing about his family, and she relaxed again. A bugle sounded shortly, and the men all stood up.

"We have to go drill now, Miss Elisan," Jack told her. "Will you wait? I'd love to hear more about my family later, if you have time."

Elisan realized that he had been patient during her entire conversation with the sergeant, hoping to get more time with her.

"I have time. How long does drill take? I should get back before dark."

"Just an hour or two. We'll get you back in time."

Elisan agreed, and the men went off, leaving her alone in the camp with a couple of men on guard duty who didn't speak to her. She didn't want to appear suspicious, so she didn't move from her seat for the length of the drill.

Elisan visited with Jack and his friends for the remainder of the day, and didn't have any further trouble with Pick. Although she saw him a few times, he didn't come near to where she was, and she was glad. Sergeant Blake helped Jack with his leave request and submitted to the colonel before suppertime. Once this task was completed, he saddled their horses and escorted her back to the farmhouse, as he promised. They chatted comfortably on the way, and she took mental notes to include in letters to her family of what southern gentlemen were like in real life. She asked what sort of character Pick was, and if he really was normally well-mannered, as he claimed.

"The thing about Pick, is that he's richer than everyone else in the company put together," Sergeant Blake explained. "And that's really saying something. His father owns half of Raleigh, and he funded this company. I think sometimes Pick thinks that because he's rich, he can get away with whatever he wants. I've never seen him that rude before, but he definitely is a character. He isn't a Christian either, so we've included him in our circle and are trying to be a good influence on him. I'm terribly sorry for what happened today, Miss Dinsmore."

"It's Elisan," she said distractedly.

"Then you'll have to call me Tom. I've only been Sergeant Blake for about a week, and as exciting as it is, it is pretentious." He gave her a friendly smile, and she smiled back.

"Congratulations on your recent promotion then," she said.

When they were almost to the farmhouse, he asked her what her plans were for the next day, adding, "We have drill first thing in the morning and again in the afternoon like today, but other than that, we're pretty free to visit if you want to come back."

"Tomorrow's Sunday," Elisan reminded him.

"It is? Then we don't have drill, but we will have chapel. You're welcome to come to that too."

Elisan didn't want to commit until she knew what the Moores' plans were, but she assured him that either way, she would be back before leaving for Richmond, to see if Jack was going to be joining them.

Elisan accompanied the Moores to a service at a nearby church the next morning. After lunch, Dr. Moore took the carriage down to the lines to visit a friend and gave Elisan a lift to the 5th North Carolina, promising to pick her up on his return that evening. She brought her new friends some fruit from the house and spent the afternoon visiting with Jack, Tom, and their friends. She was disappointed that she couldn't send a telegram to Justin on Sunday, but the relaxed pace at the camp was enjoyable. Strains of hymns wafted throughout the camp at different times of the day as soldiers picked up their instruments, and a couple of times everyone joined in singing when they weren't playing cards or writing letters home.

Jack dictated letters to Elisan for Kellie and Justin, and he was ecstatic.

"It's the first letters I've ever sent, Miss Elisan," he said. "I've never had anyone to send them to before."

Tom was around, looking even more dashing than the day before, and he attended to her every need. He asked if she needed another escort that evening, and was visibly disappointed when she said that she didn't. No leave requests were looked at on Sundays, but since the Moores decided not to head back to Richmond until Tuesday, it gave Jack another day to wait for his approval.

He and Tom arrived at the farmhouse the next evening with the approved request in hand. Elisan sat out on the porch with them chatting for over an hour and basking in the beautiful evening. Jack was concerned about how he would get transportation back to the company when his time was up, and he raised the topic with Elisan. His leave was only for three days, two of those days needed for travel to Richmond and back, and the return trip hadn't been arranged yet.

"Don't worry about it, Jack. We'll pay for it," Elisan said reassuringly, but Jack looked dissatisfied.

"I don't want to take your money, Miss Elisan," he said. "I hate for you to do that for me."

"It's not just for you, it's for Justin and Kellie. And Jed. They all want to see your family getting together, too," she reminded him. Besides, her aunt had given her enough of an allowance to cover her needs for the trip, and she still had most of it left.

Tom stood up. "I should be getting back," he said, holding his hat in his hands. "I'll expect you in a few days, Jack."

Elisan joined him on her feet as he and Jack saluted each other, before following him down to where the horses were tied up.

"Thank you for all of your kindness this week," she said sincerely. "You showed me what a true southern gentleman is, and I'll always remember it."

Tom grinned. "It was my pleasure. And I enjoyed getting to know a smart Yankee lady. May the best cause win."

He untied his horse, but didn't mount right away, apparently reticent to leave. "It was nice to meet you, Elisan. I guess I'll never see you again."

"I guess not."

Tom stood and looked at her, and then he leaned down and kissed her on the lips, and she let him. He straightened up, smiled affectionately at her, and then kissed her again, longer.

"To remember me by," he said, and swung up on his horse. Tipping his hat at her, he rode off into the darkness.

-7-

It wasn't until Wednesday morning that Elisan was finally able to get a telegram sent to Justin from Richmond.

JED AND JACK ARE HAPPY TO BE FOUND. LOVE ELLIE

Jed would be working all day until six o'clock, so the only chance for Jack to meet him was going to be that evening, since Jack would need to catch his ride back to the company the next morning. He was well taken care of in the Moores' home and passed the day happily; Mrs. Preston had recovered, and the atmosphere in the home was upbeat. Mrs. Moore filled the boy's belly until he was beyond stuffed and packed sacks of food for him to take back to camp with him. He was offered a bath and a real bed, and was doted on in every possible way.

After an early supper, Elisan and Jack headed to the government works on the outskirts of Richmond to meet Jed. Jed was in his barracks, lying on a cot and staring at the ceiling when the lieutenant brought Elisan and Jack to his room. Jed looked up when he heard them approach, and when he saw Elisan, he sat up, swinging his feet down off the cot. He was about to say something when his eyes landed on Jack and he froze.

"This is Jed," Elisan said to Jack.

Jed stood, blinking silently, but Jack hurried up to his brother and wrapped his arms around him.

Elisan backed out of the room when she realized that they were both sobbing, and anyway, so was she. She sat on the floor of the hall and leaned her head back against the wall, wondering what it felt like to be the brothers meeting the first immediate family member they ever remembered, grateful that she had been allowed to have a part in their reunion. She thought of Justin, and wished for nothing more than for him to have this moment with his siblings as well. Maybe that day would come. At least he was coming to see Kellie as soon as possible, and that was just a month and a half away.

Although she couldn't make out what the boys were saying to each other in the next room, just hearing Jed's voice made her smile, knowing that he was talking to Jack much more than he had with her, and it was satisfying. They belonged together. They were family.

Before Jack headed back to Yorktown late morning, Elisan took him to the photographer to get his daguerreotype taken. She had gotten the inspiration the night before while she was waiting for the brothers, and was excited to have his likeness to take back to Kellie. It was unfortunate that Jed couldn't get his done too, as neither had been photographed in their lifetime, but there was no way Elisan could think of to make that happen.

Jack was proud and wore his full uniform, making sure that his knife and rifle were clearly visible in the shot. With his black wave of hair falling across his forehead, he was incredibly good looking, and Elisan couldn't wait to get the finished product. She was sad to see him go, beginning to think that Europe would be a letdown after the excitement of the past month's adventures.

She went back to see Jed that evening at his request, bringing along a sack of food for him. After meeting Jack, he had decided to dictate letters for his older siblings after all, and Elisan was happy to comply. He was noticeably warmer toward her than he had been before she brought him his brother; still taciturn and serious, but polite, and she made a conscious effort to give him the silence he seemed to require. She was unsuccessful in getting him to open up much further, and after he answered five of her questions with "I don't know," she quit trying and began to wonder if he really didn't know anything about his childhood.

Not wanting to take from Justin the honor of sharing his own life with his siblings, she was careful not to overshare as well. Communicating with Jed was exhausting, but it felt meaningful and she actually had begun to like him and hang on every word he said. He came across as honest and straightforward, meaning what he said and exaggerating or punctuating nothing. She got the feeling that although he didn't say much, what he did say she could take to the bank.

An hour had passed when the lieutenant came to let Elisan know that she had to leave. As she rode back to the house, she thought about Jed and the trust she had been building with him. Something about him seemed old, to the extent that she felt like she too had aged just by being with him. He carried a sadness that permeated his being, there was no light in his eyes, and his presence made her feel like crying. She thought of the natural joy that Justin and Kellie both had, and hoped that the spirit of life in them would one day be able to shine a light into Jed's darkness and bring healing. And she hoped that maybe, one day, she would see him smile.

The month of May passed slowly for everyone as letters flowed back and forth across the country. Letter delivery between Virginia and Maryland was unreliable, but Justin had better success with the delivery of his letters from Kentucky to Virginia. He buckled down at the orphanage and taught his heart out while picking up as many odd jobs as he could in his spare time, making preparations to leave the moment class ended the first week of June.

Sometimes a couple of weeks would pass before he would realize that he had not written to Luke or Rebecca lately, and feeling guilty, he would quickly scratch a note out to them. His family took all of his attention, and as impatient as he was to meet them while still trying to do his best for his students, not much mental room was left for anything else.

Elisan saw Kellie as often as she was able up until the last week of May, when she was tied up with shopping and preparing to finally set sail. When it came down to it, Justin would be arriving in Baltimore only a couple of days before she would be leaving, and although she wished they could have more time, she was grateful that she would get to see him at all. After all, Rebecca hadn't seen him since he left for war either, and there was no guarantee when he would be making his way back to Chicago.

Jed continued to mark days off of his work requirement, and after being engaged in the Battle of Williamsburg, Jack and the 5th North Carolina made their way up the peninsula towards Richmond.

The day finally came when Justin bid the Wests, Robert, and his students farewell for what he expected to be the last time and boarded a train for Baltimore. On the train, he read in the newspaper of a large battle that had taken place outside of Richmond a few days prior, and he knew that it was likely that Jack had been in it. It wasn't until Pittsburgh that he was able to obtain a copy of the casualty lists, but even then only the Union army's were to be found. Justin determined to get his baby brother out of the war as quickly as he could.

It was pouring rain the night of June 5, 1862, when Justin arrived at the Estes' mansion in Baltimore, physically exhausted and full of adrenaline. The butler ushered him in out of the rain, and his carpetbag was taken to a bedroom where he could make himself presentable before joining his hosts in the drawing room. Elisan and her aunt and uncle had already had dinner, but when they heard that Justin had arrived, Aunt Em sent for a plate of food to be prepared for him.

When he entered the room several minutes later, Elisan's emotions exploded. All propriety and the presence of her relatives were forgotten as she flung herself across the room and threw her arms around Justin's neck. The two laughed and cried together as they hugged, reunited after what had been an extraordinary year. Justin leaned his cheek on her hair and held his adopted little sister in a long hug. He had missed the Dinsmores terribly, and the debt of gratitude he owed Elisan in particular flooded his heart. Letting go, he held her at arm's length and looked her in the eyes.

"I don't have words, Ellie. I can't thank you enough for all you did, for finding my family, even putting yourself in danger." He shook his head and would have carried on in his attempt to express his gratitude, but they were both crying, and she squeezed his hand.

"They're so special, Justin," she told him earnestly. Elisan tried to wipe at her tears, but they continued. "I honestly didn't do very much. Kellie found them, and Dr. Preston and Dr. Moore made the connections for me. I had the easy and fun part; I just showed up and hugged everyone. Each of them is so, so special. You are really lucky to have the family that you have."

She could see how much it meant to Justin to hear that, and he hugged her again.

He suddenly remembered himself, and realizing that her aunt and uncle were in the room, came over to greet his hosts and take a seat by the fire, where his dinner was handed to him. He was too excited to eat much, and Elisan sat next to him chatting merrily away, taking the opportunity to take a good look at him for the first time. He looked older in just a year, a fact that was no doubt colored by her having been with his younger siblings more recently, and he had grown a neatly trimmed beard which suited him nicely.

Having been away from her own family for several months and engaging in the mentally exhausting work of acclimating to the personalities of so many new people, Elisan thoroughly enjoyed being with someone who knew her well and could offer understanding and familiar teasing. She was able to relax and really be herself without worrying about talking too much or speaking too brashly. If she did, Justin would just make a joke about it, unlike with strangers, when such a misstep would keep her up half the night with anxiety. She promised him that she would take him to see Kellie first thing in the morning, and it was late before the conversation died down enough for them to retire to their rooms.

Despite his exhaustion, Justin didn't sleep much that night, and he sat up to reread all the letters he had received from Kellie, from Elisan about his siblings, and the ones his brothers had dictated to him. When he awoke in the morning, letters were scattered around him on the bed, and he took the time to carefully put them all back in order again. He ate an excellent breakfast, and took a walk around the Estes' gardens to clear his head until Elisan and the carriage were ready to go.

The carriage bore them through Baltimore to the other side of the city, where small cottages lined up in neat rows with small, manicured lawns and flower beds between them. It stopped in front of a small stone cottage, and the footman dismounted and opened the carriage door.

Justin sat looking at the house, and cocked his head towards it.

"My sister lives here?" he asked Elisan, who nodded and waited.

To her astonishment, instead of disembarking, Justin leaned forward and covered his face with his hands. Elisan sat in the silence compassionately as the years of unknown, years of waiting and fears and doubts and hopes melted away. She gave him a couple of minutes, then leaned forward and touched his knee.

"Go on," she said softly. "She's waiting for you."

Justin dried his eyes a couple of times, and looked at her.

"Are you coming in?"

"No."

His face clouded and he almost pressed her, but she stopped him.

"Go see Kellie. I'll send the carriage back tonight and you two can come have dinner with us."

Justin squeezed her hand, stepped down from the carriage, and walked towards the door. He stood on the doorstep, knocked on the door, and took a deep, shaky breath as he waited for Kellie to open it. A minute later, he stood face to face with his sister, and Elisan tapped on the window for the carriage to drive away.

-8-

As the door opened, brother and sister took in each other for the first time in what had now been almost a decade and a half. They had been small children before, and now they were grown adults, having lived separate circumstances and developed into who they were meant to be on their own. Strangers as they were to each other now, the ties of the same blood had always fiercely held them together across the years and miles that separated them.

"Justin," Kellie whispered, recognizing him immediately. The curly-haired boy who had been her playmate and protector was a twenty-one-year-old man now. He stood five foot five inches and was trim and fit, with plain but neatly tailored clothes, a clean black topper in his hand. His honest gray eyes had not changed, but despite having a beard covering half of his face now, he looked exactly the same as she remembered him.

Before Justin stood his sister, whom Elisan was correct in describing as slight; Kellie was only five foot two, and a black lace day cap covered the back of her jet black hair. She was dressed from head to foot in simple black crepe and wore no jewelry. Only her face was white and her sapphire blue eyes and pink lips stood out even more as her only accessories in a sea of mourning. At just nineteen, she was already a widow and alone in the world, and for all the heartache that her short life had borne, she carried a serenity the likes of which is rarely found.

"Kellie."

Justin stepped inside the open door and wrapped his sister in his arms, as if all fourteen years needed to be made up in a single hug. He held her tightly, never intending to let her go again, pressing his face against her hair. Kellie clung to him, resting in his arms as over and over the word "home" came to her mind. She was home. And God was so, so good.

Many minutes and many tears later, Kellie took Justin's hand and pulled him into the sitting room adjacent to her small dining room.

"Come have a seat, and tell me everything," she begged. "Even if you already wrote it in a letter, begin at the beginning and tell me all about where you've been and who you've become."

As he took a seat on her couch, Justin glanced at the lamp table and saw two daguerreotypes on display: Kellie and her husband on her wedding day, and a handsome Confederate soldier boy.

"Is that Jack?" He reached over to pick it up without waiting for an invitation and studied the likeness of his youngest brother. "I say. He's really grown up."

Kellie leaned over his shoulder. "Elisan said he was terribly proud to get it taken."

This reminded Justin that he still had not found out about the recent battle, and still looking at the picture, he asked, "Have you seen the casualty lists for the battle at Fair Oaks? I was unable to secure the Confederate ones, and I wanted to make sure he's okay."

"He is," Kellie assured him. "We get both of the lists here. It sounds like it was a pretty large engagement though, and they're all moving up in Jed's direction now."

"I'd like to get them out of there," Justin stated quietly, and Kellie turned quickly toward him.

"Do you have a plan? Do you think they want to? I mean, Jed will be out in a few months, but what about Jack?"

Justin's eyes were still on Jack. "He's just fifteen. He's underage, and I have his birth certificate to prove it. I don't think they can make him stay, if he wants to leave." He glanced up at Kellie. "Do you want to go down there?"

Kellie looked astonished. "Us? Go down to the war? It's perilous down there right now, and you were a Yankee soldier."

"I'm a civilian now, and don't have to have any military identification on me. We have both been living in border states, and I can even pull up a Kentucky accent if I need to," Justin replied steadily. "Do you want to?"

"Of course I do."

"Now that we have found them, I don't want to lose them. I'm worried for them down there, and I want to bring them to safety."

"We could wait until Jed's time is up in August and go get them both," Kellie suggested. "The war may be over by then."

"Or we could go now and at least meet them while we can," Justin countered. "I don't think it will be over by then with McClellan in charge. And if it was, Jack could be taken prisoner or something."

Kellie looked at him suspiciously. "Are you always as impulsive as Elisan Dinsmore?"

"I'm not being impulsive. They're soldiers in war, and I have no guarantee that either of them will survive until August. Elisan said that she hardly felt like she was in a precarious situation the whole time she was there, and Dr. Moore could offer us the same protections."

Kellie searched his face intently, then slowly nodded. "Okay," she said softly, and Justin gently placed the picture back on the table.

"Elisan said not to take the railroad, because that's too unpredictable and dangerous down there," Justin said, but Kellie waved her hand.

"It's okay, I have a horse and little wagon."

"You do?"

"Yes, Nathan was a salesman and they were his. I keep them at the livery down the street."

Justin had never owned a horse in his life, and this seemed like an exciting luxury. "It will be a long trip, but if we expect to be flexible, we should manage fine together."

Kellie patted his hand. "I don't have anywhere else to be but with you anyway."

Justin's eyes wandered around the small room, sparsely furnished but well-lit and cozy. "How did you remember all of our names? You were just five when you left," he wondered aloud, and Kellie grinned broadly at him.

"I would have remembered anyway, but they're all in the family Bible I have."

"The WHAT?" Justin stared at her, flabbergasted. "What family Bible?"

"It's the only thing I took with me," Kellie replied, standing up and retrieving it from a shelf. "That morning, Grandmama told me I was leaving and said to pack my things, so I took the Bible and a few clothes. I was kind of afraid—kind of hoping, actually—that they would come after me when they realized it was missing."

Justin gently touched the worn leather cover. "Grandmama couldn't read. She didn't miss it," he murmured, opening it and examining the beginning pages. "I had no idea this existed. If you hadn't taken it, it would have been lost with everything else. I have nothing."

He held it on his lap as if it were a long lost treasure, because it was, and took a deep breath, remembering his sister's original question.

"So you want me to begin at the beginning?"

"Yes," Kellie said with certainty. "I want to know everything. I want to know what you had for dinner on September second when you were ten years old, so don't leave anything out."

Justin laughed and held her hand. "From the day you left until now, every single day was the same, sweet sister. I thought about you and missed you without exception."

"I missed you too."

"I'll tell you my story, but before I forget, we're invited to the Estes' for dinner tonight, so we have until then."

"And then you'll stay here with me tonight?"

Justin grinned at Kellie, his real, flesh and blood sister. "If you want me to."

"Of course I want you to. It's been so lonely lately."

Justin pulled her close. "I'm here now. I'm here. And I promise I'll take care of you as long as you want me to."

A week and a half later, Justin and Kellie checked into a boardinghouse in Richmond. It had taken them three days to make the trip, and finding an available boardinghouse had turned out to be a difficult feat. The effects of the war were everywhere, the streets crowded with wounded soldiers, refugees, medical and military personnel, and salesmen hoping to see a boost in their businesses. Eventually they found a room, and Kellie lay down for a nap to recover before supper, feeling faint after the trip in the June heat.

Justin took the opportunity to head out immediately to see what he could find out about the locations of his brothers. The air in the city was tense as the armies were close now, and although they hadn't been fully engaged since the first of the month, they were moving closer and shots could be heard now and again. Many of the wounded from the Battle of Fair Oaks had filled the hospitals in Richmond, adding to the frightening reality of the war for the citizens of the Confederate capital.

It was more difficult than Justin expected to get the information that he needed, but after a couple of hours he found an army sutler willing to take him to the 5th North Carolina the following morning. They were stationed up near Mechanicsville, only about ten miles from the city and conveniently closer to them than most of the other brigades.

Justin had letters from Dr. Moore should he have trouble getting through the lines, but he had no desire to presume further on the busy man who had already done so much for them. The siblings' tentative plan was for Justin to head out to the lines in the morning and touch base with Jack. Depending on how that went and how much time it took, they might or might not make it over to meet Jed the same evening. Since they couldn't see him until the evening anyway, it seemed feasible, but too many variables went into the execution of the plan to know ahead of time.

They hadn't informed the boys that they were coming, the unpredictability of their travel being the biggest reason, and Justin still hadn't exactly figured out what he would say when he met them. He lay awake that night on a cot at the foot of Kellie's bed thinking about how different meeting his brothers felt from meeting Kellie again. She had remembered him and wanted him all along; no one really knew what Jed remembered or wanted, and Jack was a complete stranger who hadn't even known his family existed. Although Elisan had sent positive reports from her visits with them, a great deal more uncertainty was wrapped up in these meetings for Justin. Not knowing what else to do, he prayed about it and choosing peace, soon fell asleep.

Justin was grateful to discover the next morning that the sutler did still mean to bring him along in his foray to the lines. He half expected to never see the man again, not knowing who to trust in a place where swindlers were clearly having their heyday, but they were on the road to Mechanicsville before the sun was high. Kellie's horse loped along, tied to the back of the sutler's wagon so that Justin would have a way back when he finished with Jack.

The sutler warned him that General Longstreet's men would be at drill for most of the morning before he dropped Justin off, and he was correct. The camp was quiet and mostly empty, so Justin announced himself at Colonel Garrett's headquarters tent and showed the aides his paperwork while waiting for Jack to be available. To his surprise, the aide left and spoke to the lieutenant who was running drill, and the lieutenant ordered Private Young to fall out.

Jack was equally shocked when he followed the aide and discovered a guest was waiting for him. He had never seen the man standing between the tents before, but having already met Jed, it was natural to presume that this was his oldest brother.

Justin greeted him with a big smile and handshake, and he quickly saw that Elisan had not been wrong in her description of the boy's youthfulness and vitality. Jack was drenched in sweat in his wool uniform from drilling in the heat, and after leaning his rifle against the tent, he took off his beat up felt hat and wiped his forehead.

"It looks like things are heating up for a big battle soon," Justin said. "How did you make out at Fair Oaks?"

Jack gave Justin a side eye. "I wouldn't call it that here if I were you. Rebs are callin' that battle Seven Pines and I don't want you to get shot here."

"Ah. Thanks for the heads up. Were you engaged there?"

Jack nodded. "It got pretty hot, but we did okay. I'm not sure what is happening now, it's like everyone is sizin' each other up and gettin' into position. It could be tomorrow or it could be next week, but we'll be the last ones to find out when the battle's comin'." He squinted at Justin. "I didn't know you were comin'. Have you seen Jed yet?"

Justin shook his head. "We just got here yesterday afternoon. I'm not sure if we'll make it to see Jed tonight or tomorrow. Do you know where he is?"

"We? You don't mean Kellie came, too?" Jack exclaimed.

Justin grinned. "I do. We got a room in Richmond."

Jack's eyes grew big and he swore under his breath. "You had better take care of her. It's dangerous in these parts. Please don't let anything happen to her," he begged.

"I'm trying, that's why she didn't come with me today. Do you think you could make it over sometime? Maybe we could all visit Jed together?"

"I don't know if they're givin' out much leave these days. And it's been a coupla months since I went over there, so I dunno if they've moved him. I can ask the sarge what he thinks."

Justin glanced around the camp. Drill had ended, and soldiers were starting to make their way back to their tents to scrape up lunch.

"I'll try to get some time off tomorrow," Jack finally said after thinking it through. "I'll prolly have to spend the night in the city, since it takes so long to get down anywhere. So come back tomorrow afternoon after drill ends, and I'll try an' be free to come see Kellie and Jed with you and you can bring me back the next mornin' before drill. I think the colonel'll be more likely to approve that."

"Do you want me to talk to him myself?" Justin suggested, but Jack replied in the negative.

"The sarge likes me, and the captain likes the sarge, and the colonel likes the captain, so we can prolly get somethin' worked out," he explained, and Justin knew exactly what he meant from his own days in the army. There didn't seem to be anything else to say, so Justin took his leave and let Jack get back to his company.

He returned the following afternoon with the wagon and Kellie, who had a long black veil covering her face as she did whenever she was in public. Justin had spent the morning determining Jed's exact location in the trenches, although he had yet to speak to Jed himself. Their anticipation was high with the thought that they could possibly have all four of them together that very day, but with so many unknowns in their way, they avoided talking about it. Justin pulled the wagon off the road near where the sutler had left him the day before, and went on foot through the tents to retrieve Jack. His brother was waiting for him, waving his leave slip with a big grin on his face when Justin approached.

"Is Kellie here?"

"She sure is; come on!"

Jack didn't need to be asked twice, and Justin had to double time to keep up with him back to the wagon. Kellie pulled her veil back and carefully disembarked from her perch, ready to embrace him when he came up.

"Kellie! You're even prettier in real life!"

Jack picked her up and swung her around, even though she was four years his senior, and she laughed and kissed his cheek.

"Look at you!" she cried, pulling back and taking a good look at him. "You're a sight for sore eyes," she said, hugging him again.

"Does Jed know we're coming?"

"No," Justin replied, helping Kellie back up in to the wagon. He swung up next to her and picked up the reins as Jack climbed up on the other side, sandwiching their sister between them. Kellie hung on to Jack's arm and the two of them chatted merrily all the way to Jed's camp as Justin drove, listening in. Jack kept grinning down at Kellie and squeezing her arm, asking her questions in his southern drawl and chatting away.

It was still light at six o'clock sharp when they arrived at the base camp for the work crews, the warehouse used for the men's quarters and some outbuildings claimed by the officers for offices and supplies. Justin pulled the wagon up to the low stone wall surrounding the property just as the crew was returning for dinner, each laboriously pulling his ball and chain along.

"There's Jed," Jack piped up, jumping to the ground.

He hurried off alone toward the group while Justin gave Kellie a hand down, waiting by the wagon to see what would happen. They identified Jed across the yard when he straightened and stopped at the sound of Jack's call, stepping out of line to meet him. Jack gestured towards them, and Jed looked over, then back at Jack, wiping sweat off of his face. He began moving towards them as the rest of the crew headed into the building. Kellie and Justin started across the yard to meet them halfway.

"You came," Jed stated in amazement, looking around at his three siblings. "I'm sorry I have to greet you like this," he added, gesturing toward his ankle. "They'll take it off when I go inside. And I haven't cleaned up."

"Don't be sorry at all," Kellie said, giving him a hug despite the dirt and sweat covering him. "You're here because you did what you believed was the right thing to do, and I'm proud of you." With her arms still around him, she patted his back. "It's so good to see you," she added. "The last I remember of you is you running around the cabin in your diaper and spilling beans on the floor."

"I'm a lot more careful to not spill beans anymore," Jed assured her. He held her with one arm and reached across to shake Justin's hand. "It's good to meet you again. You all are stayin' where it's safe and not runnin' into any trouble?"

Justin nodded. "So far it hasn't been too bad, but it's dicey out in Henrico, and the citizens in Richmond are nervous."

"I'm diggin' trenches and buildin' bulwarks to try to keep them all safe." Jed smacked Jack's shoulder. "How are you, kid? You getting enough to eat?"

"No," Jack said begrudgingly.

Kellie brightened, tilting her face up to Jed's. "I brought some dinner. Can you eat with us?"

"Sure. I think they just want us inside by the time it gets dark. They don't really treat us like prisoners, but the officers can't afford to lose us, either," he said. "I need to wash up, though."

Kellie got a picnic basket from the wagon, Jed washed his face and hands at a pump in the yard, and the four siblings took seats on the stone wall. Jed loped his free leg over the wall and sat straddling it, reaching to take the basket from Kellie and help her up. She handed out chicken legs, cold beans, and cornbread, and her two younger brothers looked at her like it was Christmas day.

"Chicken! Where did you get chicken?" Jack's eyes popped and he grabbed a leg.

"From the boardinghouse. I bought it from the proprietress and helped her cook it this morning." Kellie smiled and handed him a square of cornbread.

A lieutenant came out of the warehouse looking for Jed while they were eating, and Jed waved at him across the yard.

"I'm not goin' anywhere," he called, which seemed to satisfy the officer, who sat down on the front step and lit a cigar.

Justin held his chicken leg and viewed the scene in front of him—Kellie, Jed, and Jack sitting together eating dinner. It all felt too good to be true, but there was no doubt these people were his real siblings.

"Okay, who wants to go first?" he asked. "I want to know where everyone's been and who you lived with growing up and everything that happened since you were all taken away."

"Why don't you go first," Jed countered back, "and tell us about what happened before that and who our parents were and how they died."

Jack took a drink from his canteen. "Let's just tell the short versions today since we don't have a lot of time. We can hear the whole story later, and I didn't even know I ever had parents two months ago."

Justin agreed and began at the beginning, briefly telling what he knew about Henry and Sinead, where they came from, how they died, and what he remembered from the first seven years of his life in Grayson County.

When he finished, Kellie took over.

"I was sent by train to Baltimore to live with Pa's sister Elizabeth," she said. "She was single at the time, but she got married a couple of years later and had a daughter of her own. I was always taken care of, but I wasn't close with them. Nathan came along shortly after I was out, and we got married when I was seventeen. I haven't seen Aunt Elizabeth since I got married, and I know she doesn't mind, either. Nathan and I were married for a year before the war started and he joined up, and he knew I always wanted to find you all. He thought of the army rosters and encouraged me to begin looking for you. After he was killed at Bull Run, that's what I've spent all my time doing."

She turned to Jed and Jack. "Both of you were in North Carolina, so I assume you were with Ma's relatives? I understand that Elizabeth was Pa's only living relative."

Jed and Jack looked at each other and shrugged, their faces indicating that they had no idea.

"I lived with Uncle Richard and Aunt Meg when I was little, but I never knew how they were related to me," Jack replied.

"Did either of them have an Irish accent?" Justin asked. "Ma came over from Ireland with her family, but Pa was born here. And her last name was Kellie."

Jack thought about it for a minute. "Yeah, I guess that's Richard then, because that sounds right. He must have been her brother. Meg died when I was little so I don't remember too much about her. Richard didn't know how to take care of a kid and kicked me out a few years later so I just made it on my own ever since." He glanced around. "I think I've done alright for myself."

"Did you ever go to school?" Kellie asked.

Jack shook his head. "Not a single day. I got to be free and do whatever I wanted while all the other kids were tied up."

"Me neither," Jed put in. "I liked being free too, at the time. Now I wish I could read, though."

"Where did you live in North Carolina?" Justin asked. "Were you both in Raleigh?"

"I was," Jack said, at the same time that Jed answered in the negative.

"I grew up closer to Asheville," he said. "I don't know how I got there, but I don't think I ever knew any of my relatives, or if I did, they passed me off. The only people I remember livin' with was a family that I ran away from pretty young."

"You don't know who they were?"

"Nope, and I don't want to. I only know they had no business having children."

Jed seemed to think the conversation was over, so the others didn't press further. He took a few more bites of his food, then added, "I joined the cavalry last summer, but had a streak of bad luck this year that ended me up here." He looked up. "I don't mind the work, but I heard Stuart's ridin' around the entire Yankee army right now, and it's beastly to be missin' that."

"Where did you hear that?" Jack demanded, and Jed cocked his head.

"I hear things. Seems like it's going to be a big one. Rumor is that Lee even summoned Jackson down from the Valley."

"Are you serious? I haven't heard any of that. Everyone gossips in the infantry but no one knows anything," Jack complained.

Jed wiped his hands on his pants. "I'd be careful if I were you, and I think Justin and Kellie should get out of here as soon as they can. I'm not scared of McClellan because God knows he doesn't know what he's doing with Lee, but Richmond isn't gonna be a safe place to be next week."

Justin turned to Jack. "Have you thought about getting out?"

"Out? I'm not desertin'. I've been through worse than this," Jack said firmly.

"Not deserting. Proving that you're underage and don't have a right to be here. Jed's going to be out in August, and the rest of us are free. And we'll just be sitting around together worrying that you're getting yourself killed."

Justin straightened up. "Think about it, if there's a big battle coming, we don't want to lose you now."

Jack looked pensive, but Jed cut it again. "If you're goin' to decide to get out, you should decide soon, 'cause Justin and Kellie shouldn't be waitin' around here for you to make up your mind."

"Jed, you're not that safe here either, and you can't run very fast with that thing on your foot if Richmond falls," Justin reminded him, but Jed waved his hand at him.

"I can take care of myself. And Richmond isn't going to fall anyway, especially not if Jackson's comin' in. McClellan isn't going to outsmart him, that's for sure. That doesn't mean there won't be shellin', but I'm not worried about myself."

"Well," Jack said, taking a deep breath and looking at each of his siblings, "If I get out, what are we gonna do then?"

Everyone was silent and surveyed each other for a minute, contemplating the question.

"I mean," Jack went on, "If I get out, I want there to be family and home-cooked meals and a bed and stuff."

Jed readily nodded in agreement, and the two younger boys looked to their older siblings.

Kellie took a deep breath. "Okay," she said, "I think so too." She turned to Justin, thinking out loud. "I have the house, but I could sell it. We don't have to live in Baltimore unless you want to; we could go back to Grayson County or something."

"You don't want to live in Baltimore?"

"Not really," she admitted. "There's nothing for me there. What do you want, Justin?"

Justin took off his hat and ran his fingers through his hair. "I want what's best for everyone, honestly. But if I got to choose my ideal, I would live in Chicago, and I would have all of you with me."

"Really?" Jack exclaimed. "Everyone wants to be together?"

Without hesitation, all three siblings reacted affirmatively.

"I've been dreaming of this for years," Justin said. "As the oldest, I've always wanted to take care of all of you, but I didn't even know if you were still alive. I have a good job in Chicago, some really great friends, and a flat. It's not big; it's about the size of Kellie's house, but we can live there until we get a house. It would be a dream come true to bring you all back to Chicago with me."

"Wouldn't have to worry about the war up there," Jed added. "May be Yankee territory, but food and supplies are probably easier to get up there than down here."

"I would think so, although I haven't been up there for the past year to know how things are," Justin said.

Jack shook his head in wonder. "I still can't believe I have a family. My very own."

"I knew, but I thought it was a dream," Jed said. He glanced at Kellie. "I think I always knew about you, but it wasn't real. I had this pretty sister with black curls and blue eyes in my dreams. Somewhere deep inside me knew that, but I thought it wasn't real."

Kellie scooted closer to him and leaned back so her head rested on his chest. "I'm quite real, and I've been praying for you for the past fourteen years. God is so kind to give you to me again."

It was becoming dusk, and everyone knew that Jed was going to need to head in soon. Kellie began packing up the scraps from dinner, and Jack stood up and stretched.

"I know you all want me to quit now, but it don't feel right to quit before this battle. I'm no coward," he said, as his siblings stopped and looked at him. "I think I should stick it out to see my regiment through this thing."

"I can't blame you. I wouldn't leave right now either if it was me," Jed spoke up. "But if Justin and Kellie go back this week, how are you gonna get yourself up to Baltimore when you're done bein' a hero?"

"I'd be the same way too, but my concern is that we don't know where the army will be in a month. You could be up in Washington or out in the mountains or who knows where, if you survive. It could be a lot more difficult to find you than it is now," Justin pointed out.

Jack looked at Jed. "Are you gonna meet us up in Baltimore in August? And we'll all go to Chicago together?"

"I think it's probably best," Kellie said. "We can stay there and sell my furniture and get everything packed up and head from there. I don't think we would come back down here before then."

The lieutenant was at the barracks waving for Jed to head inside, and he stood up.

"I could wait and come with Jed," Jack suggested.

"No!" all three of his siblings exclaimed together.

Jack kicked at the dirt. "Good for me. I made my own decisions for fourteen years, but now I have the lieutenant, the captain, and the colonel all here tellin' me what to do."

Kellie laughed. "I'm the colonel, right? Jack, you can come when you want and we understand why you don't want to leave right now, but it makes sense to come while Justin and I are here and Justin has the documents. And you're still alive."

"I'm goin' in now, y'all finish arguin' and let me know what you decide and when you're headin' home," Jed said. Kellie gave him another hug, and he looked around at them. "This is really great," he said. "A really great thing."

"Goodnight, Jed, we'll see you," Justin said, and they went their separate ways.

In the end, Jack didn't make his own decision any more than his siblings did. Justin met with Colonel Garrett to discuss Jack's actual age and let him know that Jack would not be fulfilling his two year commitment. He hadn't even finished talking, and even before he was able to mention that Jack was willing to stay on for another month or so, the colonel had written *Discharged* on Jack's paperwork, and that was that.

Jack was understandably disappointed in his sudden discharge, since his comrades were the first real friends he had ever had and he had become close with them. Worse, he felt like a heel for leaving right before a battle and with no warning. But as with everything in the army, he had no control over the situation and had to accept it and then try not to let on to Justin and Kellie that he was actually feeling a bit emotional about leaving.

Kellie took a sack of food to Jed that evening and hugged him tight. She, too, found it difficult to leave him after only having so briefly known him, but he was adamant that his siblings leave Richmond as soon as possible. He promised her that he would find a way up to Baltimore the second that he was available to come and that she needn't worry about him.

So it was that Justin and Kellie left Richmond after four short days in the Confederate capital, with Jack in tow. Two days later, Stonewall Jackson's army arrived from the Shenandoah Valley and the Seven Days Battle began. The fighting was fierce and bloody, but Richmond remained standing, and a week later, McClellan and the Yankee army were retreating toward Petersburg less 16,000 casualties.

Morale was high in Richmond, even as the Confederate wounded began pouring in to the hospitals and every available bed in the city. General Lee took a breather before he took the opportunity to push his high spirited army north. The 5th North Carolina had been heavily involved during the battles and although now they were left to guard Richmond, all of Jack's siblings were grateful that he was no longer in danger.

Back in Baltimore, Justin found letters waiting for him from Chicago. He had sent a quick letter to Luke upon arriving at Kellie's the first time, but now realized that he hadn't written back to Rebecca at all since he left Kentucky. He immediately took the time to send full letters to both of them as well as to Robert and the Wests, catching them all up on the news of his family and the decision to bring everyone back to Chicago with him.

He wrote to Mrs. Katz to let her know to expect his return, and requesting work be done in the apartment to divide the one big open room to include two small bedrooms and have additional beds delivered before the Youngs' arrival. He included some advance money, then took a job at the docks in Baltimore to help fray the pending costs of transporting his family to Chicago.

Before Kellie began packing a trunk to take with her and selling the rest of her belongings, she headed to the dry goods store for a few rolls of material and got busy making pants, shirts, vests and jackets for her two younger brothers. New boots were also in order, since the ones Jed was wearing he had taken off a dead man and didn't fit properly, and whatever Jack had on his feet had long since resembled shoes. She wished she had thought to take Jed's measurements, but she did the best she could—he was at least three inches taller than Jack and a good two inches wider in the shoulders—but Jack's clothes she tailored, with an extra bit of space for the weight she intended for him to gain.

Jed left Richmond on August 21st and hitchhiked his way to Maryland with General Lee on his heels, arriving four days later. With the money from the sale of the house, horse, and wagon, Kellie helped Justin purchase the four train tickets from Baltimore to Chicago, and packed the rest of her money away privately for when it would be needed.

On the day before the Second Battle of Bull Run in Virginia, Justin, Kellie, Jed and Jack Young boarded a train bound for Chicago and a new life together.

-9-

August 28, 1862

The train lurched around a curve and Justin's eyes flew open. It was hot in the passenger car, and he had fallen asleep to the rhythmic clacking of the train over the rails. Kellie's head leaned on his shoulder and she was apparently still dozing, since she didn't move now. Jack sat directly across from Justin in the window seat, and Justin saw that he was gazing out the window watching mile after mile of wheat and cornfields go by, peppered with dozens of towns along the way.

They had given Jed the aisle seat across from Kellie for the sake of his long legs, but even still he hardly looked comfortable, and was having poor luck sleeping. Once he'd joined his family, Jed had cleaned up and gotten a shave and a haircut, looking tidier than they had seen him in Richmond, although he still kept his hair longer than Justin's and had already begun growing another beard.

"Do you want to play whist?" Justin whispered, pulling his cards out of his pocket.

Jed yawned and turned to join in as Jack perked up. "Sure, if you don't mind losin'."

Justin opened the pack and began dealing the cards loosely with his right hand to minimize moving the arm Kellie was on. "Losing? I don't usually lose whist."

"Mmm, better watch him dealing there," Jed warned as he picked up his cards and looked at them.

They were a few rounds in when Kellie woke up, blinking her eyes and watching the game without moving at first. Justin was actually doing poorly; Jack had won the first round and Jed the second, but since he kept getting dealt poor hands, he couldn't get a leg up.

"Oh, that's really bad," Kellie said, looking over his shoulder at his cards.

Justin turned at the sound of her voice. "Good morning. Did you have a nice nap?"

Kellie swiveled her aching neck. "I suppose so, but I'm stiff now. Deal me in the next round."

"Sure, with four in we'll play pairs."

Jed won the current round and picked the cards up to shuffle them as Justin took a deep breath. "I wanted to give you all some idea of what to expect in Chicago, and answer any questions you have so that the transition can be as smooth as possible."

Jed began to deal the cards, but Jack looked at Justin expectantly, and Kellie nodded for him to continue.

"Well, first of all, I live in a neighborhood that is mostly Irish and German immigrants. The apartment is above a bakery owned by Mrs. Katz, who goes to my church, and she takes pretty good care of me. I've sent ahead a request to add some bedrooms in the place so we'll have one and Kellie can have her own room. As I've mentioned, I work at the lumberyards on the Chicago River, only about a mile from the flat." Justin described the Dinsmores, church, and everything else he could think of that would be helpful for his family.

"I do expect us to all go to church together every Sunday," he added. "I know we aren't used to each other and our individual habits, and it may be an adjustment to get used to a new place and really, to each other. But going to church is important to me, and that is one thing I am going to ask of you all. Another one is that I don't want alcohol in the house."

No one replied, but the look on Jack's face told Justin that he wasn't too keen on this restriction, but Jed was expressionless as he met Justin's eyes.

"Tell me about the stores and where I will get food and supplies," Kellie asked, and Justin complied.

"Are you going to cook for us?" he asked.

"Of course." Kellie looked surprised. "I expect to keep house."

"I didn't want to presume. I can cook too, if you ever need a break, and we can all help with the chores, hauling water and firewood and so on."

"You can cook?"

Justin set his cards down and looked patiently at his sister. "I learned how in the orphanage, and I have been cooking for myself since I've been in Chicago. I make very good pie, actually."

"Well, I'm impressed," Kellie admitted.

"Do any of you snore?" Jack asked. "I might have to reconsider this if any of you do."

Jed slapped his knee. "It can't be any worse than in the army, and we'll have actual beds so you can be comfortable while you're listening to it." Jack snorted and then realized that Jed was serious.

Jed turned back to Justin and Kellie. "Actually, I've never slept on a bed before so I don't know if it's more comfortable. Is it?"

"Never?" Kellie was aghast.

"No," Jed replied, not sure why she didn't believe him.

"I think they're more comfortable," Jack said. "You never told us where you lived after you ran away from that family. What did you do to survive?"

Jed picked up his cards again. "I guess I just lived here and there on my own. I don't remember."

"I'd rather live with people," Jack said. "I don't like being alone."

Jed shrugged and looked at his cards as if he wanted to resume the game.

"Doesn't bother me," he said. "It's your turn, Justin."

Justin played his card and glanced at Kellie. "You said that you weren't close with Aunt Elizabeth. What kind of people were they?"

Kellie laid her card down. "They weren't bad people, and we got along fine before Aunt Elizabeth got married. She wasn't very attentive, but I was a big girl and managed. But after Henrietta was born, she and her husband doted on her and then the difference was painfully obvious. I was nine when she was born, and I was old enough to know what was going on. She was their daughter and I wasn't, and it was always made clear that they thought they were being charitable by keeping me alive." Kellie drew her next card, and Jed took his turn.

"I think they were mean," Jack stated. "They should have been nicer to you."

"I can't complain; I did live comfortably and always had something to eat. I was starved for love, though. I found some in church and it drew me to God. He always met my needs and then brought me Nathan so I was able to leave them and live with someone who loved me for the first time."

"How did you meet him?" Justin asked.

"At a party. He was from Bethesda, and his cousins were our neighbors in Baltimore. He was visiting them when he came to a ball I was at, and the first time we met, he danced with me almost the whole evening." Kellie laughed. "I was pretty tired that night. I don't usually dance that long."

She looked at the card Jack put down. "Seriously Jack, you're going to lose us this game."

"I can't help it!" Jack exclaimed. "Jed gave me the worst hand."

"Then you shouldn't have bid so high," Kellie retorted.

"Sorry. Did Elizabeth give you a hard time about Nathan?"

"Not at all. She was happy to get rid of me to the first person to come along. I was just lucky he was a good one."

Jed glanced up from his cards at his sister. "I'm sorry he died."

"Thank you, Jed. Me too."

"Did you always go to church?" Justin asked, taking his turn and watching Kellie lay her card and take the trick.

She nodded and led off again. "That was the best part of my life growing up. I'm thankful for that."

Kellie looked at her silent younger brothers across from her as they studied their cards and took their turns, wondering what kind of pain they had been through in their lives and what scars they carried with them.

Jed had shared almost nothing about his life and did not seem interested in making any effort to think about it or remember his childhood, if you could even call it that. Did he ever get to play and be a child without having to worry about where his next meal came from or who would take advantage of him next?

And Jack was so intent on making sure everyone knew that he could take care of himself, she couldn't help but wonder what she would find if she peeled back the layers and found out what his heart really held beyond what he wanted people to see. At least Justin had been taken care of as a child and grew up in church and school, and she didn't have to worry about him.

Kellie figured that with Justin there, together they could really make a difference in their younger brothers and help them recover from whatever it was that they had been through in their formative years. She had stopped paying attention to the game and suddenly realized it was her turn and laid down her last card.

Justin and Jed easily won the game, and Jed picked up all the cards, stretched, and handed the deck to Justin as if he was done. It turned out to be a natural time to take a break, as the train pulled into a station a few minutes later and the Youngs disembarked to quickly get some supper before it continued on its way.

After the train left Cincinnati the next morning, Kellie pulled her Bible out and tried to read it although she found it difficult to focus on the words with the movement of the train and the stale, stuffy air. She found her eyes wandering every few minutes and kept trying again to read. Jack was next to her now, and she realized he was looking at the words over her shoulder.

"Do you want me to teach you how to read?" she asked softly.

"Would you?" Jack looked at her in wonder.

"Of course."

Jack reached into his pocket and pulled out a crumpled piece of paper.

"This is the first thing I ever really wished I could read for myself," he admitted, and Kellie realized that it was the letter Elisan had given him from her. She smiled.

"Do you know what it says now?"

"Only some of it. I forgot some."

Kellie took the letter, unfolded it and read it to him again, cocking her head close to his so that he could hear over the clatter of the train. When she finished, she folded it up and handed it to him.

"Was this the first one you got? I sent you a letter before but I didn't know if it got through."

Jack shook his head. "I didn't get any others."

Kellie turned to Jed. "How about you?"

"No, I didn't get any. I didn't stay in one place very much, though."

"I can teach you how to read too, if you want," Kellie said.

"I was thinking about that," Justin cut in. "If Jed and Jack took some time to get an education now, then after a while you both would likely be able to get better jobs than without it. I think I make enough at my job to support all of us right now, since my rent is quite reasonable, and I had enough to put some away before when I was on my own. It depends on if you're up for teaching them, Kellie," he added.

"Yes, I definitely am up for it." She looked from Jed to Jack. "If you want, I can teach you to read and write, and some history and math. Justin's the real math teacher, though."

"Don't sell yourself short," Justin said. "It takes a lot of math to run a home, with all the economics, baking, and sewing. I can lend a hand where you need me."

"Justin's right that if you learn these things now, you will probably be able to get better jobs when you're ready for it," Kellie agreed.

Jed looked at Jack, and Jack looked at Justin. "So we can just have school and we don't need to work? Are you sure?"

Justin waffled before responding. "I can't honestly say for sure yet, but if I pick up my old job like I'm planning to and figure the math, I think we will have enough. I would really like for you two to be able to take a break and not have to worry about working for a while."

"I don't mind workin', but I would like to learn to read," Jed said, and Jack nodded.

"Have you thought about what career you would like to have?" Justin asked.

"I never thought I'd get much choice," Jack said. "I always did whatever I needed to make a dollar, so I never thought about what I would do if I could choose."

Jed twisted his mouth wryly. "The cavalry was the career I wanted. I don't think I want a job where I have to be in a building all day."

Justin laughed and shrugged. "I understand. I think I'd prefer that type of job myself, but here I am working at the docks. Although I never would have thought of it as what I always wanted to do, I like being part of something big. And I think that after a while, I could get promoted to foreman and then it will be better pay. I can hope, at least."

Justin realized that he was rambling and stopped. "The point is, it's good to know what you'd like to do, but it's also a good idea to keep your mind open to something you may not have thought of."

"Whatever I do with my life, I want it to be off this train." Jack sighed and looked out the window. "When's the next stop?"

"In an hour," Jed said. "If everythin' stays on schedule, we'll arrive in Chicago tomorrow morning."

Kellie turned to Justin. "What will we need to do when we arrive?"

"I heard there's beds, and that's all I need," Jack said, stretching.

"We'll need to get supplies. I can take you home first and you can decide what you need, then we can go to the store, haul water to clean up, and get firewood. There's usually a boy who comes down the street selling it every morning." He chewed his lip. "We'll have to see what things are like at the house. I should message Luke ahead to let him know we're coming so he can check on it."

"I have the money from my house to help get us set up," Kellie said.

"I don't want to use your money if I can help it," Justin replied. "That's yours."

"Don't be ridiculous. Why would we use your money and not mine? It's just as good." Kellie closed her Bible. "That's what it's for, making a home together. I wish Pa and Ma could see it."

"I really don't remember them," Jed said. "Can you tell us all you remember about them?"

"I can try. Justin probably remembers a little more, and a lot that I remember about Ma was her being sick in bed."

Justin nodded. "She didn't ever get her strength back after Jack was born. Mr. Campbell told me that she used to frequent the hot springs, so I think she was never very strong to begin with, and then she had all of us."

He and Kellie took turns telling stories that they remembered from their early years. They told about their pa singing to them by the fire in the evenings with his rich baritone voice, of Christmases in the cabin and the hard rock candy they would get and suck on all morning. They remembered the little clothes their ma would carefully stitch and fit on them, fussing over every little pleat and hem and how attentive she was to each of the children individually. Their stories helped to pass the second day on the rails as they made their way up through Ohio.

The four passengers could not have been happier when the train pulled into the station in Chicago the next morning and they disembarked, dirty, stiff, hungry, and exhausted from two and a half days of little to no sleep. Jed and Jack immediately left to find the lavatory, and Justin stopped with Kellie to wait for her trunk. They had barely gotten their bearings when Luke rushed up and grabbed Justin by the shoulders.

"Luke!" Justin exclaimed, quickly hugging him. "Boy, is it good to see you." He reached back and pulled Kellie beside him. "Luke, meet my sister. Mrs. Kellie Burns."

Luke bowed and kissed her offered hand. "Mrs. Burns," he said. "It is such a pleasure to finally meet you."

"The pleasure is mine," Kellie responded cheerily. "And please call me Kellie. If Justin considers you his family, then you are our family as well." Having passed the anniversary of her husband's death, Kellie no longer wore a veil over her face outdoors, and Luke was struck by her bright blue eyes, just as Justin had been.

"The same goes for you."

Luke looked up as the two younger brothers joined them, and Justin proudly introduced them to him.

"You all resemble each other so much," he said, shaking their hands warmly before turning to Justin. "I told the superintendent that I would take a break when you arrived. I have the carriage here so I can take you all home."

"Really? You didn't have to do that. Thank you." Justin saw the porter bringing Kellie's trunk, and gesturing to his family, followed Luke to the waiting carriage.

"I can't tell you how glad we all are that you decided to come home," Luke told Justin as they walked together, Kellie on Justin's arm, gingerly lifting her skirt over the muddy ground. "You really had me worried there when you stayed in Kentucky all year and then went to Maryland. After ten months, it sure is good to see you."

"Tell me about it," Kellie said with a laugh. "I had to wait fourteen years. He grew a beard during that time."

"Oh, he grew that since the last time I saw him, too," Luke told her, and his heart swelled at the sight of Justin's sister hanging onto his friend's elbow.

"You didn't tell me it was new." Kellie looked at Justin, eyebrows arched.

Justin rubbed his facial hair. "I had to look the part of a mathematics teacher," he explained. "Then I kept it to look like the oldest brother," he added with a wink.

"I might forget myself and start calling you sir," Luke teased. "You look so dignified."

Once the trunk was loaded and everyone was inside the carriage, Luke picked up the reins. "Straight home?"

"Yes, please. I'll stop downstairs and get lunch from Mrs. Katz," Justin replied.

"She's so happy you're coming back. I think she's missed you."

When they arrived at the bakery, Kellie followed Justin into the shop, while Jed and Jack waited outside with Luke, taking in the sights of their new neighborhood. He pointed out the livery and some of the buildings within view as well as the pump where Justin got his water.

Inside the bakery, Mrs. Katz had Justin and then Kellie in a large hug. She was normally an all-business director in her little domain, but the little German lady had a weakness for Justin. She loaded both of their arms with loaves of bread, rolls, and even a cake, wouldn't let them pay for any of it, then waved for them to follow her outdoors and up the flight of stairs.

Justin knew that the addition of bedrooms in the back of the apartment would cut the size of the single large room he'd had before, but stepping into his newly renovated flat with his three new roommates, he was not prepared for how tiny it now felt. To his right inside the door was the wood stove and kitchen cabinets, and straight ahead was a table with four wooden chairs, which he was now glad that he had bought for when the Dinsmore siblings came over for cards and coffee. Next to the table to his left in front of the fireplace was his single couch, which now took up most of the remaining space before the bedrooms, a larger one on the left side on the back wall and the smaller one on the right.

He and Kellie set their armloads of food on the table, and Kellie unpinned her hat while she surveyed the room. She handed Jed and Jack each a loaf of bread wrapped in brown paper and turned toward Justin.

"I had the windows open to air it out when I heard you were coming. The Richardson brothers did the rooms and built the beds," Mrs. Katz was saying. "You know them from Pine Street, and church. They left a bill here for the rest of the work." She indicated a paper sitting on the table and headed into the bigger bedroom, adding, "I figured you would need extra sheets and pillows to go with the beds, but I couldn't get blankets in time."

In the boys' windowless room, three wooden beds lined the wall with no other furniture. Folded sheets sat on the foot of each ticking covered mattress, along with a pillow.

"I have my wedding quilt," Kellie said, peeking into her tiny room.

"Thank you, Mrs. Katz. I wasn't expecting you to do all of that," Justin said gratefully. He opened a small steamer trunk next to the couch, in which he had packed up all of his personal belongings before leaving, in case Mrs. Katz ended up needing the flat for someone else while he was gone. Folded on top was his own quilt, which he pulled out.

"Does your family have two we can borrow until we can get some?" he asked Luke.

"Of course. I can bring them over tonight," he said. "Let me help you carry Kellie's trunk in now, and then I'll head back to work."

While he and Justin left, Kellie got busy putting the sheets on all the beds and Mrs. Katz returned to her shop.

"Can you give me a hand?" she asked Jed, who quickly jumped in to help, and in short order the beds were made. Kellie stretched Justin's quilt over one of them, and Jack lay down on another with a contented sigh, munching on his loaf of bread.

"Take your boots off, Jack," Kellie told him before disappearing into her room once Justin and Luke had deposited her trunk at the foot of the bed. Next to her bed was a tiny lamp table with a candlestick, and beyond her bed, the trunk filled most of the leftover space, leaving only about six inches before the wall. She finished making her own bed while out in the living room, Luke handed Justin a pail of soup from the carriage.

"Rebecca sent this for your supper," he said. "Everyone is anxious to meet your family. When do you think you can come over?"

Justin took the soup, eyes wide, and set it on the counter. "Tell her thank you from us. I'm not sure; we're tired and need to get things in order today. Can we come for dinner tomorrow?"

"They will be pleased to hear it," Luke said, turning to the door. "I'll bring over the quilts tonight. Oh," he added, reaching into his pocket and handing Justin a small paper bag. "This is from me, just to get you through to morning."

Justin opened the bag to find freshly ground coffee, and a huge smile took over his face. "You're the best. I needed this!"

Luke slapped him on the back and headed down the stairs, and Justin turned to look around at what needed to be done. It appeared as though the apartment had been cleaned; he wasn't sure whether it was by the Dinsmores or Mrs. Katz, but it was a nice touch. He took off his hat and ran his fingers through his hair as Kellie came out of her room.

She peeked into the boys' room, then grinned at Justin. "The boys are both asleep."

"Are you serious? They must be tired after the train ride." Justin turned to start a pot of coffee and realized he needed water. "Do you want to get some rest too, then we can go to the store later and unpack."

"That might be nice," Kellie said. "I'm pretty stiff right now."

Justin took a pail and left for water. Upon returning, he started the coffee and sat down at the table, picking up a roll to eat. Kellie joined him at the table and together they began making a list of what was needed for the house.

"I'd like to get a couple of armchairs," Justin mused, looking around. "Now that there are four of us, so we can sit around in the evenings. I don't know how much they cost, though. I'll swing by the furniture store tomorrow and order them."

"I need slates and a reader for lessons," Kellie said, jotting with a pencil on the back of the carpentry bill. "Blankets, beans, flour . . . "

"Coffee," Justin added.

Kellie laughed. "Of course, coffee."

Justin went over to his trunk and began unpacking, setting out candlesticks and a stack of books as he and Kellie continued listing items. He examined the clothes he had packed away and put them back in the trunk. "We can move this to the bedroom when the boys are up," he said, straightening up.

Kellie poured the hot coffee into two mugs and handed him one, then scouted out the kitchen, opening cabinet doors to inspect the dishes and pots.

"You're pretty well supplied here," she noted with surprise.

"I told you I liked to cook. Put eggs and cream on the list. I want to make a pie to take to the Dinsmores' tomorrow."

Justin took a sip of the coffee and audibly sighed. "That hits the spot," he said with satisfaction. He sat down on the couch and put his feet up on the coffee table to drink his coffee. When Kellie looked over a minute later to ask him a question, he was sound asleep.

-10-

It was midafternoon before Jed wandered out into the living room, saw the coffee pot on the table, and helped himself to the remainder of the coffee, waking Justin on the couch. Justin yawned and stretched, feeling refreshed and ready to get to work as he dropped his feet to the floor and sat up.

Before long, the four siblings headed out to explore the neighborhood dry goods and grocery stores, taking their time together and enjoying each other's company and the fresh air. Once they had gathered all the supplies they needed, they headed home to Rebecca's supper. The August sun was still high after they ate, so figuring she had plenty of time to unpack before bed, Kellie moved to her bedroom to get to work.

"I thought I'd head out for a bit to explore, if y'all don't need me for anythin'," Jack said, standing up from the table.

Jed looked up. "I'll join you. Do you have some money? I don't have any."

"A little," Jack said. He turned to Justin. "Are we gonna have spendin' money if we aren't workin'?"

"I can make my own spendin' money. I just need a bit to get started," Jed stated.

Justin stood up and dug in his pocket. "I guess we can work something out for an allowance," he said, handing Jed the few coins he had on him.

"Thank you. I'll pay you back." Jed reached for his hat, and before Justin could tell him that he didn't need to repay him, he followed Jack out the door.

As the door closed, Justin turned around and saw Kellie standing in the doorway of her room with her head cocked to the side.

"Why did you give them money? They're just going to go drinking."

"They are?" Justin realized he hadn't really thought about what his brothers wanted the money for, and he hadn't known that the fifteen-year-old drank. As far as Justin knew, Jack hadn't done such a thing in Baltimore.

Kellie didn't bother to answer as she came to clear the dishes and spread her lace tablecloth on the plain wooden table.

"I can't really blame them after the trip," Justin said, but Kellie shook her head.

"You shouldn't encourage it. Jack's just a kid, and you're probably the first good influence they've ever had."

"I didn't encourage it. I don't think I can tell them they can't go out in the evening, though. They're not used to that kind of restriction." Justin stood up and opened the cabinets to begin putting the new supplies away.

Kellie didn't look convinced. "You don't have to fund it, at least," she finally said. "You don't drink, do you?"

"Not at all," Justin replied, stopping to look at her.

Kellie poured water into the wash basin for the dishes. "That's good. I think we have an opportunity to help the boys get their lives on a solid footing and become good citizens. Neither of them had anyone raise them or teach them anything. It's amazing that both of them have turned out as mannered as they have."

"I completely agree," Justin said, taking a seat and leaning back in his chair. "I just don't think that hitting them with a bunch of rules they aren't used to the first week is the way to go about it."

Kellie picked up another dirty bowl and rinsed it. "Maybe so, but you don't want to set a precedent now that you'll have to undo later, either." She glanced over at Justin. "What do you make of them?"

"What do you mean?"

"I mean that they hardly talk about themselves or their lives or what they've been through. We know almost nothing about them. Do you think Jed really forgot everything, or do you think he just doesn't want to talk about it?"

Justin rubbed his neck. "I believe him. He's so precise in everything else he says. He made that one comment about the family he lived with, it makes me wonder what they did to him. I think he's chosen not to think about it for so long that he's trained his memory away from it."

Kellie stood motionless at the dishpan. "He's so serious," she murmured. "He never teases or laughs. Jack does, though."

"Jack does." Justin inhaled. "But I don't know about him either. He's different. Sometimes I get the feeling like it's all an act for him. I could be wrong, but he seems intentional about what he wants us to see. Not with Jed. I think Jed's a straight shooter."

Kellie nodded thoughtfully and turned back to her dishes. When she'd finished washing, she sat down on the couch.

"Come sit with me," she said. "I'm ready to take a break."

Justin was happy to oblige, and picked his Bible up from the mantel. Kellie leaned in close as he opened it and began to read aloud. In that moment, nothing in the world could have felt more perfect to him. His heart was full of wonder that he was sitting in his own home with Kellie snuggled up next to him, and she was here to stay. What more could he possibly want?

A few minutes later, a knock came at the door, but before Justin could stand up, Luke opened it and poked his head through.

"Am I still allowed to do this?" he asked cheerily.

"Come on in," Justin said, coming to his feet and taking the armload of quilts Luke handed him.

"I'm sorry I'm so late. I got tied up." Luke looked around. "Jed and Jack are out?"

"They are. Thanks for bringing these. Have a seat and stay a while."

Justin stepped into the bedroom with the quilts as Kellie stood up. "Can I get you some water or piece of cake? Or a cup of tea?" she asked Luke.

"Oh, no thank you," he began, then stopped. "I mean, you are queen of this estate now, so you may rule how you wish, but I've never been waited on here before and I don't expect you to start now," he finished with a grin.

"I'm afraid Luke is used to fending for himself around here," Justin admitted as he reentered the room and they took their seats on the couch again.

Luke pulled up a chair from the table. "I can stay for a few minutes, but I shouldn't make Rebecca jealous, since she has to wait until tomorrow to see you," he said. "When are you starting back at work?"

"I thought I'd go down there in the morning and talk to Mr. Brewster to make sure I can get my job back. Hopefully, I can start Monday." Justin asked Luke about church, work, and his family, and he and Kellie told about their long train ride and the events of the past few weeks.

Eventually, Luke stood up to go, already having stayed much longer than he had intended, and Justin joined him. "It sure is something to see you two together," Luke said. "It all happened so fast."

"I can hardly believe it myself. So many variables could have come in our way and prevented it, but God opened every door and here we are. It's a miracle," Justin said.

Kellie looked at Luke with raised eyebrows. "I'm still flabbergasted by all that Elisan did to make this possible. I'm not sure this would have happened without her. What did your family think of her going down to Virginia like that?"

Luke laughed, his hand on the doorknob. "To be honest, we didn't find out about it until after it happened. If I'd known about it, I would have been on the next train down there, to accompany her myself. I think it only could've ever been her, though. It was as if she was born for that moment, so I can't say any of us were terribly surprised."

"Well, we will always be in her debt," Kellie said.

"It'll sure be fun when she gets back in October and can see this for herself. Thank you again for the quilts," Justin said, and Luke bid them goodnight.

Justin and Kellie stayed up late together until Jed and Jack came home, tromping up the stairs long after dark. Jed reached his hand in his pocket and handed Justin the same amount of money that Justin had given him earlier.

"You didn't need it?" Justin asked, looking up with surprise.

Jack laughed, and Jed sat down to take off his boots. "I did use it. Thank you for the loan."

"He played poker all night," Jack explained in response to the confusion on Justin's face. "I don't think the fellas down the street took too kindly to a Johnny Reb hustlin' them on a Thursday night, though. We might need to find a new spot after tonight."

Kellie looked at Justin in horror, as if she expected him so say something against the idea of the boys gambling, but he didn't know what to say so remained silent.

"I just made a bit of spendin' money is all," Jed defended himself. "I'll go easier on them tomorrow, or they won't ever play me again. Nice spot though, and the drinks were cheap."

"Well, I never got so many dirty looks in my life. They didn't seem so friendly once we started talkin' and they heard our accents," Jack grumbled.

Justin saw Jack put his hand out to lean against the chair, and miss. "Jack, how drunk are you?"

"Just a little bit drunk, honest. I hadn't had anything 'most all week. I'll be alright."

"I won't have you getting drunk. I have a good reputation in this neighborhood, and I intend to keep it that way," Justin said in indignation. "By morning, everyone this side of town will know about you two carousing."

"Aw, we weren't carousing, Justin, take it easy," Jed said, standing up and patting Justin on the shoulder on his way to the bedroom. "I kept Jack outta trouble. It'll be fine."

The look on Kellie's face told Justin that she did not think any of it was fine, and she wanted him to do something about it.

"Thank you very much, I don't need anyone keepin' me out of trouble," Jack called after Jed.

"Go to bed, Jack," Justin said. He handed Kellie a candlestick. "Goodnight, Kellie. I'll talk to them," he promised, quiet enough that Jack couldn't hear. "Right now they just need some sleep." He kissed her cheek, picked up the other candle, and followed Jack into the bedroom.

At six o'clock sharp the next evening, Justin knocked on the Dinsmores' door with his siblings by his side and a lemon meringue pie in his hand. Luke answered the door, and once they had removed their hats, ushered them into the drawing room to meet his father and Titan.

Rebecca entered the room just before they did, and stood by her father in her favorite mauve silk dress with coat sleeves and a gold watch chain looping to a pocket at the waist of her bodice. Her head was bare, but her brown hair was sleekly rolled over her ears and pinned perfectly at the nape of her neck. She was pretty enough, if not somewhat nondescript, with hazel eyes and a trim waist that she didn't make effort to maintain, and stood the same height as Justin.

Reverend Dinsmore's hair and impressive beard were graying, and he was not as slender and fit as he had been as a younger man, but his eyes were gentle and friendly, and immediately made guests feel comfortable and at home in his presence.

Titan was twelve now, and he had recently had a growth spurt that gave his mother a full time job keeping him properly clothed since he had nearly overtaken Luke in height. He was lanky and blonder than his siblings had been at his age, and had trouble remembering to do things like tuck in his shirts, button all of his buttons, and tie his shoes, but thankfully he was the youngest and had three or four people in the house to fuss over him and keep him presentable.

"Mother will be done shortly," Rebecca reported to the reverend as the door opened, and Justin came in with his sister on one arm and the pie in the other. Rebecca could see immediately that Justin was happier than she had ever seen him; he was glowing with joy, and her heart gave a little flip to see his familiar gray eyes again.

As Justin turned to greet Reverend Dinsmore, he handed the pie to Rebecca, and proudly introduced Kellie and his brothers to the reverend, Rebecca, and then Titan. In the activity of the introductions, Justin never stopped to give Rebecca more than a passing glance, but she watched him and waited.

When he presented Kellie to her, she gave him the pie back so that she was free to give Kellie a hug.

"It thrills me to meet you," Rebecca told her earnestly. "Justin has been hoping for this moment as long as we've known him. Thank you for loaning him to us for the past several years."

Kellie smiled merrily. "I should be thanking you, for taking care of him for me all that time. It feels like I'm meeting his other sister."

Luke gestured to the pie in Justin's hand. "What's this, old boy?" he asked. "You really are unbelievable, showing up with a pie like this."

Justin held it up with feigned innocence. "I don't know what you mean. I was in the mood for pie this week since I hadn't had one for a while."

"I've been in the mood for pie for the past two years, since the last time you made one, to be exact," Rebecca said with a grin. "Does this mean you've forgiven her after all she's done for you?"

Luke eyed Justin dubiously. "I'm not sure this means Elisan is forgiven, if he's showing up with a pie when she happens to not be here."

"Is there a story here that we don't know about?" Jack asked curiously.

Rebecca shrugged. "Oh, I don't know. It's only that the last time Justin made a pie, it somehow ended up in his face, and since then he apparently hasn't been in the mood for it. Until today, when Elisan happens to be on the other side of the world."

"Three hours," Justin cut in. "It took me three hours to make that pie. But," he added, his voice softening, "I don't know what making a pie today has to do with Elisan. I don't see her anywhere."

"Nope," Titan said, almost under his breath. "No Elisan, just a pie. And about two inches of meringue . . . " His voice trailed off as the others laughed.

"I think I'm done talking about the pie. A fella can't make a pie around here without getting ribbed about it," Justin said good-naturedly, handing the pie back to Rebecca. "With this kind of abuse, I might have to rethink making one next week."

"Why on earth did Elisan put a pie in your face?" Kellie asked, but just then Mrs. Dinsmore came in and Justin was saved from answering by introducing his family to her before they all headed in for dinner.

Justin was clearly in his element with both of his families together in one place once again, missing only Elisan. He talked and laughed, engaging with everyone present, keeping Kellie at his side as he stayed attentive to her and her needs throughout the evening.

"Did you talk to Mr. Brewster today?" Luke asked at dinner, and Justin responded in the affirmative.

"I'll be back to work on Monday like I'd hoped," he said. "I'll be able to get several months of work in before winter comes and things slow down."

"Mr. Brewster likes you," the reverend said with a smile. "When your family gets your new routine figured out, will you still include Friday night dinners with us?"

"Are you sure?" Justin asked, looking at the reverend and then his siblings. "There are a lot of us now."

"Of course we're sure! Friday nights have been too quiet without you, and we would love to make you all part of our family," Reverend Dinsmore said.

Kellie smiled back at Justin, so he replied, "Well, then, we would love to. It's good to be home."

After dinner, Luke invited Jed to a game of chess, and Justin sat on the settee next to Kellie in the drawing room, visiting with Reverend Dinsmore. When the evening ended, he left with his family without having made any effort to be near to, converse with, or even glance at Rebecca, as if the special history between them had been obliterated. He'd talked to her in the group, but nothing about his demeanor gave her a hint that she meant anything more to him than one in a group of friends.

Her heart couldn't help but ache when she went to bed, even as she attempted to give him the benefit of the doubt in her mind, but it hurt. His letters had become fewer and shorter as time went on, and now he had completely forgotten her, for all appearances. The only thing there was to do was wait to see what would come of it, but it took her a long time to fall asleep that night.

On Sunday morning, Justin had his family up and ready for church on time. Although Jack had a headache from another night out the night before, he knew enough to not complain about having to get up early, since there was no question that Justin was dead set on everyone being at the service and Kellie was backing him up.

"You need to wear your vest under your jacket," she told Jack, despite the fact that it was a hot August day. "And comb your hair."

"Yes, Colonel," Jack replied a bit saucily, feeling rather patronized to be told how to dress.

Still, he and Jed turned heads looking sharp and handsome as they followed Justin and Kellie up the aisle of church later that morning. They began to panic the further up the aisle they walked, until with great horror they beheld the front pew where Justin stopped, realizing that he actually intended for them to sit there.

"What are we doing up here?" Kellie hissed to Justin.

"I always sit here," Justin replied innocently, indicating the Dinsmores' row. "There's plenty of room. Rebecca sits at the organ, and Elisan isn't here."

"Can we not sit further back a bit?" Kellie asked, self-conscious of the entire church watching them, but Justin didn't budge.

"The next dozen pews or so belong to other families. If we don't sit here, we'd have to sit in the back."

"Sittin' in the back is fine," Jed suggested brightly.

Justin sat down next to Luke. "We can sit here," he stated, and his siblings dropped into the pew next to him.

Before Justin showed up at the train station on Thursday, no one in church had known that he was returning except for the Dinsmores and Mrs. Katz. By the time his family took their seats at the front of church on Sunday, however, everyone knew that he had, that his brothers had spent two of the last three nights at the saloon, and which church members had been there as well to see them. It was convenient for all that Justin sat in the front, so they didn't have to crane their necks to get a good look at his strapping brothers and widowed sister, and were able to whisper amongst themselves without Justin's knowledge.

Rebecca played the prelude, and the congregation stood to sing. Jack had heard one or two of the hymns before, having attended chapel in the army and church in Baltimore, but he didn't know them and couldn't read, and Jed had never even heard them. Reverend Dinsmore had made a warm first impression on them at dinner Friday night though, so even though the sermon made little sense to them, both made an effort to listen to what he had to say.

They were less enthusiastic that evening, however, when Justin expected them to all sit together at home and listen to him read the Bible. Since they'd already been to church that day, they failed to understand the point of additional religious activity, despite the fact that they had nothing else to do.

"I think it's good for families to read together," Justin said. "We can discuss what we read and it will help us grow together. It doesn't have to be me, though; hopefully soon we can all have turns doing the reading."

He figured that he would begin in Genesis, since it was apparent that Jed and Jack had never been taught basic truths about God before. After he read the first chapter, he reverently closed the book and stood to put it back on the mantel.

"You believe that?" Jed asked mildly. He lit a pipe and leaned back in a new armchair, puffing smoke.

"Yes, I do," Justin said, turning towards him.

"I don't," Jed countered. He spoke honestly, not combatively, and Justin recognized it as an opportunity to hear his brother's heart.

"Why not?" Justin took his seat again, genuinely interested in the answer.

Jed tapped his pipe. "I don't believe in God. I think He doesn't exist, and people made the idea of Him up."

"What about His existence do you find hard to believe?" Kellie asked.

"Well, all of it," Jed said. "I've seen enough situations where if He existed, He would have been there. But He wasn't. And all the things that people say God does can be explained in other, more logical ways."

Jack looked bored with the conversation, but Justin was glad to see Jed feeling comfortable enough to share his views. "I wouldn't mind talking to you more about those things, and want you to know that I'm not here to make you change your mind. Personally, I've seen Him do things that make His reality in my life unmistakable, and I can only hope that one day you'll see Him in your life too."

Justin shifted and pulled his foot over his knee. "The Bible says it's the living Word of God, so why don't you see what it has to say. We can talk about any parts that you want to, and after you've heard it for yourself, then we can each decide what to believe about it."

Kellie nodded in agreement. "I've seen God in my life too. I think even when things in my life were the most difficult, I could still choose what to see. I could choose to see the things that weren't right and the injustice, or I could choose to see how God was carrying me and protecting me. When I chose to look to Him and follow Him, He opened my eyes even more to His presence and became even closer to me, and I realized that we see what we have eyes to see. God doesn't force Himself on anyone. I agree with Justin; if you've never read the Bible before, perhaps listen to it first before you make your decision about Him."

"I don't think that I'm very interested to know what a fake religious book has to say, or if God exists, that He's the type of being that I want to know." Jed stood up and stretched. "I'll listen if you want me to, but it seems pointless."

"Genesis gets pretty interesting and it has a lot of action so I think you'll find it engaging," Justin added. "I would love to read it to you, and after Genesis we can see if you want to continue or not."

Jed didn't say anything, but he nodded, got himself a drink of water, and began to prepare for bed, so the conversation ended.

Justin reminded himself not to push too hard at the beginning since Jed seemed like he was someone who would open up in his own time, and there was no rush to force it. Building trust with his brothers was his highest priority for the first weeks and months; once he had that foundation established, then other things could follow.

He stayed on the couch while the others got ready for bed, thankful for the quiet. He hadn't had a moment to himself since before leaving Baltimore, and was already feeling the need for space to think. If nothing else, God would be stretching him through this experience with his siblings, he thought, fearful of his ability to adjust to the constancy of it all. Kellie seemed to have faith in him to lead his family, and he couldn't, he wouldn't let her down.

Justin felt the weight of the world as he stood to prepare for bed and his return to work early the next morning. He tried to pray as he drifted off to sleep, but his thoughts were scattered and he felt like his heart wasn't where it should be. Justin hoped and prayed that leading his family would get easier over time, but it was starting out harder than he had expected.

"Kellie, did you take my shirts?"

Kellie looked up from the tub she was bent over on the kitchen floor to see Jack come out of his bedroom in just his trousers on Monday morning two weeks later. She almost started in shock at the sight of him, but managed to control her reaction before he noticed. She had never seen him bare-chested before, and was horrified at the scars of varying types and degrees covering his chest and arms.

"Yes, I'm sorry, Jack, they were all dirty and I thought since we weren't going anywhere, I could wash them all today," she said, trying not to stare at the disturbing sight in front of her. "Did you need one? I think Justin has some extras."

"Naw, it's fine." Jack sat down at the table, which had been pushed back against the wall to make room for the washtubs, and picked up a piece of bacon she had left him from breakfast.

"There's some coffee, too," Kellie said, squeezing out the shirt she'd been scrubbing and setting it on the wringer as Jed entered the front door carrying an empty basket. "Can you get me your sheets when you're done eating, Jack?"

Jack nodded, but Jed headed to the bedroom himself. "I can grab them," he said.

Kellie stopped and stretched her back, considered protesting, but decided to bite her tongue. Jed was always quick to help around the house, and he'd been up hauling water and hanging laundry out back for over an hour already. She wasn't sure if Jack was lazy or if he just didn't need to help as much since Jed took care of everything, and she could tell that Jed needed the physical exertion. He apparently wasn't used to sitting around doing lessons, and she often felt like the former cavalryman was like a caged animal in the apartment all day.

Jack stood up and poured himself some coffee, displaying for Kellie scars on his back as well. "Are we doing lessons today?"

"You can get started on your letters if you like. I'll be done in a little while, but we can always do some after lunch too. I just wanted to get the laundry drying as soon as possible."

Kellie moved to the wringer and after carefully running each piece through, tossed it into the basket for Jed to hang. She wanted to ask Jack about his scars, but wasn't sure how he would take the question from her, and Jed didn't seem to show any reaction to them.

"I think we can get done before lunch," Jed said, dropping Jack's sheets on top of the pile beside the washtub. "After all, Jack's still having breakfast, so he won't be ready for lunch for a while, and I think these sheets are the last thing to wash."

"If that's what you want to do." Kellie wasn't sure why neither of the boys could ever be convinced to continue their lessons after lunch when they had nothing else to do with their afternoons, but at least they were predictable. They had settled into a routine lately; mornings were for lessons, and after lunch she took care of the house and cooked supper, but both Jed and Jack seemed to struggle to fill their afternoons. Dinner was served every day when Justin arrived home, and she always looked forward to spending her evenings sewing on the couch next to him.

She started on the sheets while Jed headed out the door with the full basket, and glanced back up at Jack, who was eating quietly at the table. She wondered if he would ever be willing to open up to her and tell her about his past and his scars, but she thanked God silently that he was safe now. She was here to take care of him, and she would make sure he didn't have to worry about ever getting more in the future.

-11-

September 18, 1862

A knock came on the Youngs' door after supper one Thursday, and Justin opened it to find Luke and Rebecca on the step.

"We're just going on a walk down to the lake, and wondered if any of you would like to join us," Luke said.

It was finally cool enough in the evenings to be comfortable for exercise, and Kellie was game for getting out of the house. Jed and Jack already were preparing to head out for the evening on their own, so Kellie convinced Justin to join the Dinsmores. Justin hoped that Kellie and Rebecca would become friends and was pleased for the opportunity for them to be together, so he fell into step with Luke. He barely had time to connect with Luke anymore when there weren't others around, and both of them were hungry for the chance to catch up, even after a long day of work.

"How are things with your family?" Luke asked. "I've been wondering how everyone is adjusting."

"Mostly good," Justin replied. "We're enjoying learning about each other and being together. It still feels unbelievable sometimes, but every day when I come home from work, they're all there and a hot dinner is waiting. I'm a little concerned that we're putting too much on Kellie, though. I don't think she's very strong; she said she gets sick a lot like our mother did, and now she's suddenly caring for all of us. I do as much as I can to help in the evenings, since I don't want to put too much on her."

"I can always tell how happy she is just to be with you," Luke said. "She thinks so highly of you."

Justin grinned and continued. "The boys are having a rougher time though, since this is all new to them. Neither of them grew up with anyone caring for them, teaching them, or taking them to church, so there is a lot that they are adjusting to at once. It makes it worse that they're Confederates and aren't making friends."

"I was wondering about that. I saw that Jack had a bit of a black eye."

"Yes, it's getting better now but he got into a fight at the saloon the other night. He and Jed go out and drink once or twice a week; Kellie wants me to stop them but I don't think I can."

"Mmm." Luke looked thoughtful. "I can't blame you. I don't know what I would do in your position."

"Anyway, Jack gets drunk sometimes. Jed doesn't. He mostly goes to gamble, and it seems like he's made a good bit of money, but it doesn't make them any friends. And you know no one at church will have anything to do with them."

"I've noticed that," Luke said. "I'm sorry to see it."

"I hope it gets better for them, because I feel badly about bringing them here if everyone is going to look down on them." Justin sighed. "I read the Bible to them in the evenings, and they don't like it. They still sit there, but I can tell they're not listening, and Jed told us that he doesn't believe in God. I think he's been through things in his life that he feels like God should have prevented."

"Don't tell yourself you shouldn't have brought them here. They may not have friends, but they've never had family before, and they have that now. They probably need someone to show them God's love for the first time," Luke said. "I will pray that as you read His word to them, that their hearts will soften towards Him."

"Thank you. I appreciate you praying. Even Kellie had a rough upbringing, and they've all been through a lot. It's challenging since everyone has survived for years on their own and now we're needing to figure out how to get along and live with other hurting people. I'm tired when I get home from work, but Kellie needs me to talk to her every day and I'm not used to having to talk every evening. I also need to try to connect with Jed and Jack somehow. I think it will take a long time for everyone to heal, but at least I finally get to help them. So your prayers mean a lot to me."

"Anything, Justin," Luke said earnestly. "If you need anything, or just to talk through things, I'm here."

Justin glanced back at Rebecca and Kellie engaged in conversation, and turned back to Luke. "Can we do this regularly? I think it might be good for all of us."

"Sure," Luke said with a grin. "I'm glad you decided to come out tonight."

They reached the lake then, where a cool breeze felt inviting at the end of a hot summer. Justin paused to watch the water lap against a low stone wall and the seagulls peck on the ground nearby. A path ran beside the lake and a few benches were scattered along it, but the closest ones were occupied with young lovers out enjoying the evening. So after a few minutes taking in the scene, they turned and headed back to the apartment.

Several more days passed, and Justin had still not spoken to Rebecca more than the polite conversation that social situations dictated, and every day the hurt she felt intensified. When their eyes met, she saw only an impenetrable wall and he would move on like nothing had happened. He didn't even give her the attention he used to as her adopted brother anymore, and she missed him. Only once, at church, had she glanced up and caught his eyes watching her tenderly before he quickly looked away.

She lay awake in bed at night sometimes thinking about it, consoling herself with the knowledge that he was never cold or unkind to her. His friendliness carried a vacancy though, rather than the warm understanding that had been between them before he had left home. She continued to patiently bear up under the hurt and confusion as she gave him time to adjust to his family.

Unbeknownst to her, Justin had been looking for an opportunity to talk to her, and he finally found it one day when he stopped in the church to see the reverend for a few minutes after work. Rebecca had just finished practicing the organ for Sunday when he came through the sanctuary on his way out and he turned her way when he saw her.

"Hi," he said as he approached. "Do you have a few minutes?"

Rebecca's heart raced, but she calmed herself. "Sure."

"Walk with me?"

"I'd love to." She left her sheet music at the organ, picked up her hat, and pinned it on as she followed him out of the church.

Out in the fresh air, Justin walked slowly. "I've been wanting to catch you alone," he began, glancing over at her. "We should talk."

She ducked her head to indicate that he should continue, so he turned back to the path in front of him and shoved his hands in his pockets.

"Everything in my life has changed lately, and I've been trying to adjust to it and help everyone else adjust too." He chewed his lip before continuing. "I've taken on a big responsibility by bringing my family here. But it's such a gift from God to have them again. It's more than I had ever dreamed possible."

Rebecca ambled along beside him. "I know it's what you always wanted. I'm truly happy for you. And for us to get the chance to know them as well." She smiled at him, but he kept his gaze in front of him and didn't notice.

"I've made promises to them," Justin said, somewhat abruptly. "I've committed myself to take care of them, especially Kellie. She's been alone since she lost her husband, and I have a responsibility to her now."

Justin stopped walking and turned his body towards Rebecca. "I don't want to ever make her feel like a burden to me, because she is the biggest answer to prayer in my life. It's my privilege to be able to care for her. But you should know that."

Rebecca watched his face and waited. He was having trouble making eye contact, and he kicked at the ground, moving restlessly around for a minute. Eventually, he stopped and looked up at her, his eyebrows tightened together.

"Don't wait for me, Rebecca," he said. "It could be years before I'm at a point where I can think about my own family, and I won't do that to you."

Rebecca's whole heart fell. Ever since he had arrived home a different person around her, she had wondered how he perceived the situation and whether once things settled down at home, if he would still have room in his life for her. But now her worst fears were confirmed; she was being edged out.

"Does it have to be one or the other?" she asked softly, pleadingly.

Her voice was like a knife to his insides, but with great effort, his face remained stoic. He had to be firm; he had to make a clean cut to set her free. If he wavered, she might not take him seriously, and in the long run, that would hurt her even more. Never in his life would he have wanted to do anything to hurt one of the Dinsmores. They were like flesh and blood to him. But his siblings actually were his flesh and blood, and he had a duty to them, and there was only one of him to go around. He heaved a sigh, looked her in the eye, and paused before responding.

"I have to put my sister first right now. And I can't—I won't—give my wife a shared position or string along someone I love through years of uncertainty."

Rebecca didn't respond, but she didn't flinch or cry, either. She swallowed her emotions and looked past him into the street, unmoving.

"Please understand, Rebecca. I want you to be happy and to find someone who can give you all of himself. You don't deserve a half-hearted love. And I can't be that person for you. I don't know if I ever will be able to be." His voice had softened and he looked at her with tender eyes. "Please don't wait for me."

Rebecca nodded numbly and stood rooted to the ground, her expression emotionless. She wanted to entreat him to reconsider, to remind him that she didn't need much, even a piece of him would be better than nothing at all. But she said nothing and nodded so he would go away, so eventually he left her.

She turned and hurried back to the house, tears falling. How could she make him change his mind? How could she make him see that she would wait forever for him, because she loved him and always would? How could she help him understand that she couldn't imagine ever loving anyone else?

She desperately wished that Elisan was home, because as it was, there was no one she could talk to. As Justin's best friend, Luke was not an option to be a confidant on the issue; she wasn't sure that she could convince him not to talk to Justin about it if he knew.

She felt childish, but wished Justin hadn't said anything at all. How could he look her in the face and tell her that he had no room for her when he had never found the courage to start a proper understanding with her in the first place? Why did this have to happen when Elisan was still away? Why?

But deep inside, she knew that she was mostly angry at herself. She was angry because if she was honest, she had known all along, since before Justin came home. She knew that his family was going to come first to him, although she hadn't been sure whether he would say anything to her about it or not; in the end it didn't really matter. What mattered was that she had been unable to stop loving him, even though she knew she was going to get hurt, and had stubbornly refused to think down that path.

Rebecca stopped on the front step of her home, breathing heavily and wanting to sob, but she controlled herself. She stood for several minutes gathering her composure, then took a deep breath and entered the house to face her family as if nothing was wrong.

Justin had to drag his heavy feet up the stairs after work a few days later, more exhausted than usual from the long day. The room was quiet when he came in, and the table empty. Kellie was nowhere in sight, but Jed was in the kitchen and turned around when Justin entered.

"Hi," Jed said, and Justin greeted him back as he glanced over and saw Jack on the couch whittling silently away. Jack had recently taken up whittling for the first time, and these days the apartment was covered with little carvings of gradually increasing skill level and shavings on the floor, but Justin was glad that Jack had the chance to try such things now.

Jed grabbed a hunk of bread from Kellie's bread basket and took a bite.

"Kellie left this for you," he told Justin, holding up a plate of potatoes and cabbage. "She cooked a while ago and then went back to her room."

"Is she okay?" Justin sat down at the table to pull his boots off.

"I don't know. She said she's fine, but I don't think she is. She's been in her room a lot today and she was crying a lot. She even cried when we had trouble with our letters this mornin'."

"She cried when *you* had trouble with your letters," Jack cut in from the couch. "I didn't have trouble."

Jed turned back to Justin. "Well, I dunno what's wrong, but I'm worried about her."

Justin set his boots aside and stood up to wash his hands. "If she said she's fine, then she is. I'm sure she'll be back to normal tomorrow."

Jed stood in the middle of the room, obviously dissatisfied. "She did this once last month too. I don't know what to do for her."

Justin could see that Jed was actually upset, and he realized that his brother had no clue what was going on. Since Jed seemed to like things to be upfront, Justin knew the best thing to do was just to tell him the truth. He picked up his plate of food and walked over to where Jed stood.

"It's just her monthly, Jed," he said in a low voice.

Unfortunately, this explanation did nothing for his brother.

"What do you mean? This happens every month?"

"Yes," Justin told him patiently. "It happens to all women. She's fine."

He sat down at the table and started to eat, but Jack was laughing at the look on Jed's face.

"All women do this every month?" Jed was incredulous. "Why?"

"Good grief, Jed, haven't you ever been with a woman?" Jack chortled, and Justin's eyes darted to his face, appalled at the question.

"I never even spoke to a woman until Elisan," Jed muttered.

"Are you serious?"

Justin had learned in time to not ask Jed that question, but Jack kept forgetting that Jed was always serious, even when the strangest things came out of his mouth.

"Not since I was little. I avoided them."

"Have you ever been with a woman, Jack?" Justin countered back, assuming that Jack wouldn't have asked Jed the question if he hadn't done it himself.

Jack shrugged and deflected the question. "I know enough to know when a woman is crying and says she's fine, to leave her alone," he said with a snort.

"Well, they don't talk about these things in proper company, Jed," Justin said. "And you shouldn't talk about being with women either, Jack. It's inappropriate and shouldn't be discussed."

Jed looked at Kellie's door. "You really think we should leave her alone? What if she needs somethin'?"

"Really, Jed. If she wants to be alone, we should leave her be," Justin said gently.

"I hate to see her upset, and you know she always likes to talk through things." Jed ignored his brothers, and walking over to Kellie's door, knocked softly. "Kellie? It's me. I was wonderin' if you needed anything."

To his surprise, Kellie opened her door a few seconds later, her shawl pulled tight around her shoulders.

"Thank you, Jed. I don't need anything." She looked past him and saw Justin eating at the table. "Oh hello, Justin, welcome home. I'm sorry about dinner."

"It's okay, you get some rest," Justin said. "Can you give Jed something to do though?"

Kellie pursed her lips in an attempt to hold back a smile. "Actually, I could really use a cup of water, if it's not too much trouble. Now that I think about it."

Jed retrieved the water and brought it back to where she stood in her doorway.

"Thank you."

"Let me know if you need anythin' else, okay?" Jed reached down and pulled her into a tight hug. "I love you."

Kellie burst into tears and stood holding her cup while Jed gave her the first hug he had ever initiated in his life. He let go quickly and stood uncertainly, wondering what he had done wrong.

"Thanks, Jed," Kellie said through her tears. "I love you, too, and it means a lot to me."

When she saw that he was reassured, she bid him goodnight and went back into her room, where she sat on her bed and cried. To hear Jed tell her he loved her touched her deeply, and the moment didn't go by unnoticed by Justin at the table, either. He remembered what Luke had said when he confessed his regret of his brothers' lack of friends. "*They have family now . . . they need someone to show them God's love.*" Seeing Jed soften with Kellie was special, and Justin knew that they were making progress. Jed had family now, and Kellie did too, for that matter, Justin thought. And a family's love is forever.

-12-

Elisan returned in October to great fanfare and celebration. Her family was relieved to have her back, for even with three siblings still at home, without Elisan it felt painfully quiet. The evening after she arrived, she was anxious to call on the Youngs and bring them their souvenirs, and petitioned her siblings to join her. Rebecca excused herself, claiming to be tired and intending to retire early, and Titan had to work on his studies, so in the end only Luke escorted Elisan to the apartment. She gaily hugged Justin and each of his siblings as if they were her family and looked around the room.

"It sure is smaller in here now, Justin. But I like it. It feels like family now, not bare and empty anymore."

Justin smiled. It did feel like family, for better or worse, and with Elisan home, everything felt a bit more complete. Even Jed brightened to see her and listened attentively as she told of her travels and the things she saw.

"They have ever so many colors of aniline dye now. You should see how brightly colored the dresses are in Paris," Elisan told them, her eyes sparkling. "I came home with a trunk full of clothes, and I had to make Aunt stop buying more things. I think having me there made her feel young again and she made me get all the things she wanted for herself. But I'll give half of them to Rebecca. I got her the prettiest silk bonnet, just wait until you see it on her." She looked at Justin expectantly, but Justin appeared to not be paying attention.

She handed out her gifts then, silk cravats for the brothers and brightly colored silk handkerchiefs for Kellie. "I know you can't carry them now," Elisan said, "but they were so pretty, I couldn't pass them up and I thought you could still use them at home." Kellie thanked her for her thoughtfulness and gave her a hug.

"There's one more thing," Elisan added, reaching into her satchel. "I couldn't help but think of you, Justin, because the coffee in France was amazing. But then I went to Rome and had Italian coffee." She presented him with a paper bag of coffee beans tied with string. "I can show you how they make it there. It's the best coffee I've ever had; you simply must try it."

"You've really spoiled us, Ellie," Justin told her, eyes wide. "I can't believe you brought us anything at all."

"I really couldn't help it. I missed everyone so dreadfully while I was gone, I know I could never live away from here," she said.

"We both have our families back now." Justin leaned back in the couch to wrap his arm around his sister, grinning at Elisan. "A family's a hard thing to miss, isn't it?"

It didn't take Elisan long to become cognizant of how much things had changed since she had last been home. Shortly after her return, she turned to Rebecca from her seat at the vanity as she brushed her hair before bed.

"What's happening between you and Justin?"

Rebecca dropped her eyes, plopping down on the bed. "Nothing. Nothing is happening between us," she replied honestly.

"The way the two of you avoid each other is as obvious as it is painful to see," Elisan continued. "I can't even tell whose fault it is since you both put so much effort into staying on the other side of the room from each other."

Rebecca exhaled softly. "Ever since he returned, he's been different around me. Then a few weeks ago, he told me that he needs to make his family his priority now and that I shouldn't wait for him."

Elisan stood up with fire in her eyes. "A few weeks ago? But he's been back since August."

Rebecca shrugged. "I don't think he wants his family to know, so he had to talk to me when they weren't around. I have to try to avoid him, Elisan, it's the only way I can survive. I can't get over him when he's always around like this. But I don't want to get over him; I'm in love with him."

Rebecca began to cry, and Elisan moved to her side, muttering, "I'm going to punch him in the face."

Standing by the bed, she pulled Rebecca in close as she sobbed into the folds of Elisan's dress. "It hurts so much to be around him because he acts like he doesn't even see me, but I love him so much, I don't want to let him go."

She wiped her eyes on Elisan's skirt. "It's only ever been him, Ellie. I could never love anyone else. If he won't marry me, I would honestly rather stay single."

Elisan held Rebecca and rocked her gently as she tried to calm her anger. "You're the most eligible young lady on the west side, Rebecca. If you don't act like things are normal, every mother in church will notice and the vultures will start landing, and you're going to have to figure out what to do with all of the callers."

"I know," Rebecca said, drawing a wavy breath. "I would die if I started having callers. I don't know what to do, Elisan. I always wanted him to find his family, but not now, not like this, not without me." She rubbed her forehead with her fingers and sighed again.

"Does anyone else know?" Elisan asked, meaning Luke.

"No. You were the only person who would understand."

"I understand that Justin is going to get a black eye," Elisan retorted fiercely. She took a deep breath and tried to calm herself down. "Everything is so new for him right now. Maybe after he's lived with his family for a while, he'll be ready to reconsider."

"I can only hope so." Rebecca's shoulders slumped. "He made it sound like he would have to care for his sister forever, but it's hard to know. I can't help but wait for him, because I don't think I can stop loving him." She stood up and pulled the covers back on the bed before climbing in.

"I'm really sorry, Rebecca," Elisan said, climbing in next to her. She blew out her candle and sat stroking her older sister's hair until she fell asleep.

"Jack has really been filling out his clothes these days."

Standing next to her in the Dinsmores' kitchen, Kellie smiled at how happy Elisan sounded about her observation. "He does love to eat," Kellie replied, slicing into another apple. "He was excited about me putting up apples with you today. I think he's hoping for an apple pie this week."

"We can make him one, then," Rebecca said, turning around from the stove to empty Elisan's bowl of chopped apples into the pot she was stirring.

"Well, I think the weight he has gained just accents his striking features even more. You've been doing a good job on him, Kellie," Elisan said, and Kellie sighed with satisfaction.

"I'm a rather simple cook, but I don't think that he's ever eaten properly in his life. I wish I could convince him to dress properly, though," she added, and her friends laughed.

"We know how younger brothers can be about that," Elisan said. "And I saw Jack biting his nails leaving church yesterday. I was thankful for your sake that you were talking to Rebecca and didn't notice."

"Oh, goodness! I've told him so many times not to do that. At least Justin always helps when I'm trying to convince the boys to behave in proper company. I don't know what I would do without him." Kellie wiped the perspiration from her forehead with the back of her hand in the hot room, but her voice was light and affectionate.

"I can tell you're making a difference in them, though," Rebecca put in encouragingly. "Both of them seem more comfortable at the dinner table, and they knew the words when we sang *Amazing Grace* on Friday night."

"Yes, I've been trying to teach them the words to the most common hymns so they can sing at church, and it was sweet to hear them the other night. I was actually rather surprised by that, because neither of them have been putting as much effort into learning the hymns as they have into the rest of their lessons. I didn't know that Jed had such a nice voice."

"He does," Rebecca said. "How have the rest of their lessons been going? Are you just teaching them to read, or other things as well?" She reached for the sugar canister and measured some into her pot.

"We do a few other things, like memorizing multiplication tables and the Declaration of Independence, and I read poetry to them after lunch every day. It's actually going fairly well, I think," Kellie said, finishing her apple and reaching for another. "Some days I have to work hard to keep my patience with them, and other days they have to work to keep their patience with me, but . . . I love them so much, and I'll never stop being grateful to be here with them."

Elisan glanced over at her. "So it's not too overwhelming to suddenly find yourself caring for three men?"

"Oh, it's a lot of work." Kellie grinned back at her. "But they're my brothers, so no, not too overwhelming. I think we're getting used to each other, and they're all terribly sweet. I could go on about each of them. Justin, for example—he'll sit all evening untangling my yarn and asking questions, just listening to me talk while I knit. I've hardly ever met anyone as attentive and thoughtful as him."

Elisan felt Rebecca stiffen next to her, and quickly turned to hand her a bundle of cinnamon sticks so that she could see her face, but it showed no shade or tightness, and Elisan was envious of her ability to hold herself together. She was starting to get used to seeing the mask on Rebecca's face, but for all the sadness seeing it brought her, she was always impressed by it.

As she had predicted, the mothers at church had been quick to catch on to the fact that Justin was no longer calling on Rebecca, but Rebecca successfully avoided making eye contact with their sons when they tried to catch her attention, and none of them had produced the courage to actually call on the icy pastor's daughter, to Elisan's relief.

"You're all still coming picnicking with us this Sunday afternoon, if it doesn't rain?" Rebecca suddenly asked, and when Kellie responded in the affirmative, the conversation turned to their plans for the picnic baskets.

"We used to eat soft shell crabs on picnics in Maryland," Kellie said. "I haven't had any crab since moving here, but it was always Nathan's favorite."

"I never had crab before I went there, and I can't say I got used to it, but the plethora of seafood in Baltimore was fabulous," Elisan said.

"I'd never had pork sausage or sauerkraut before coming to Chicago, either. Mrs. Katz gave us a sausage with apple in it last week, and it's one of the best things I've ever had. Oh, Rebecca, that's smelling so good."

Kellie leaned over to smell Rebecca's pot, reminding herself to stop talking so that she could learn from what Rebecca was doing, and turned her focus toward the bubbling apples.

Rebecca continued accompanying Luke two or three evenings a week to the apartment as long as the weather permitted, looking for company on their evening walk. She took great pleasure in Kellie's acquaintance, and it gave her extra time with Luke on the way to and from the apartment, so she found the discomfort of seeing Justin usually allayed. When Elisan came along, she helped Rebecca avoid getting stuck next to Justin as the pairs fell into place, but whenever it did happen, Justin would saunter along easily, casually asking about her week and never really telling her anything about his.

"I've started volunteering at the orphanage," she told him one day. She had been waiting to tell him, and was actually glad that she got the chance. "I go on Tuesdays for a few hours and teach piano lessons to about five or six of the children."

"Really? That's fantastic, Rebecca." Justin looked truly pleased, and it made her heart skip a beat to have the pleasure of making him happy.

"I love it. I get individual time with them at the piano, and sometimes during the lesson we end up talking and I can get to know their little hearts. They're so precious."

Rebecca didn't tell him how she was gaining better insight into him as a result of hearing the orphans share their stories with her, or that she kept seeing him when she looked in their eyes. For many years, she had taught piano lessons to children at the church for income, but she'd been looking for ways to use her gift to help those who otherwise would never have the chance to learn music. She wondered why she hadn't thought of the orphanage before.

"I'm sure it means so much to them," Justin said. "Music is a tremendous gift, and they'll have that forever."

"Thank you." Rebecca looked up and her eyes met his for a moment before she turned back to watch where she was walking and tried to breathe again.

Justin didn't say anything and she wondered what he was feeling, but then he coughed and changed the subject. "Kellie's birthday is next Friday, and I was wondering if you could make a cake for dinner that night, if it isn't too much trouble. If I make it, it won't be a surprise."

"I would love to." Rebecca swallowed, trying to clear her head, and then smiled at him. "Thanks for the heads up. We can plan something to make her day special."

"I appreciate it."

Justin remembered then that he hadn't talked to his siblings about their Christmas plans yet, and he fell silent as his mind wandered off to the upcoming holidays, wondering what he could afford to do for them. He had been finding that his family cost far more than he'd expected, and had even talked to Mr. Brewster about ensuring that he could work every Saturday instead of the occasional Saturday like he did before. Although river traffic mostly ceased in the winter, the trains still ran their usual routes, and since the full number of stevedores weren't needed through the winter months, he'd been working harder than ever to make himself indispensable to his foreman and manager.

Realizing that he was being poor company, he politely asked Rebecca to tell him about her students and listened to her talk all the way back to the apartment.

Kellie's birthday came, and her brothers doted on her all day, beginning with the breakfast Justin got up early to make for her and served with a cup of Elisan's Italian coffee. It snowed overnight and stopped late morning, so after lunch Jed and Jack humored her by going out for a walk to see how beautiful the city looked under a clean white blanket. Kellie walked between her brothers, tromping arm in arm over the snow and breathing in the icy air, noses turning pink in the chill. As they passed the Catholic church, they saw several people ice skating on a small pond next door and stopped to watch.

"That looks fun," Jack said wistfully. "I've never skated before, but I'd love to try sometime."

"It does look fun," Kellie said, leaning against a wood rail fence. "It's harder than it looks, though. We should do it together sometime."

Even Jed looked interested. "It usually didn't get cold enough in North Carolina for the ponds to freeze, and when it did, I never had skates," he said. They stayed until their faces were frozen before heading home to mugs of hot tea.

Kellie cried happy tears that evening when Rebecca brought her birthday cake out and everyone sang to her. She clasped Jed's hand and leaned on his shoulder as she looked around at the faces of her friends and family.

"When I was alone on my last birthday, I would never have dreamed that this year I would be here with all of you, celebrating with people that I love," she said. Jed kissed her hair and squeezed her tight, and joy flooded her soul.

Justin broached the subject of the upcoming Christmas holiday for the first time with his family at dinner the next week. "We're invited to the Dinsmores' for Christmas dinner, but I thought it would be special if we spent Christmas morning with just us at home. I don't think we need to exchange gifts, but we can get a Christmas tree and have a nice breakfast together."

"Can we please? I've never had Christmas before," Jack exclaimed, and Kellie could have cried at the childlike look on his face.

"I can make some gingerbread and Christmas cake," she said. "And we can make popcorn to string on the tree."

Jed perked up then, and Justin grinned. "I did that just last year at the orphanage, and it would be fun to do together."

Before the candlelight service at church on Christmas Eve, they set up a little tree in the corner of the apartment. They all wanted something bigger, but the apartment was cramped enough as it was, so they bought the smallest one that the peddler had. Once the tree was all decorated with popcorn, cranberry strings, bows and candles, Jack insisted on hanging their stockings on the mantel.

"You can if you want, but we said we aren't doing presents," Justin laughingly reminded him.

Nevertheless, when they woke up the next morning, all four of them had presents for each other, to the surprise of them all. Kellie had put little packages under the tree with warm scarves and mittens that she had knitted for her brothers, and their stockings were bulging. Justin's, Kellie's, and Jed's had little carved animals that Jack had whittled, and all four stockings had oranges from Justin as well as the very same rock candy that they'd had for Christmas as children in Kentucky.

Kellie's eyes sparkled as she unwrapped hers and sucked on it. "I haven't had this since I was five! It tastes exactly as I remember it."

"Are you going to make it last all morning, the way we used to?" Justin teased, smiling fondly at her.

"I sure am."

"I didn't have a nice package for my gifts," Jed told them, setting a wooden crate on the table. Justin's eyes grew wide as he looked inside and found four pairs of ice skates.

"Jed! How in the world?" he exclaimed, pulling one out and looking it over.

Jed grinned and shrugged. "I've been puttin' some money aside. Do we have time to go after breakfast or do we have to wait until later?"

"I think we'll have time," Kellie said. "We don't have to go to Dinsmores' until two." She wondered if Justin noticed how happy Jed looked, since it was the first time she ever remembered seeing a full smile on his face.

Jack, too, beamed with excitement, finding that Christmas did live up to his dreams, and he was grateful to not be camping in the Virginia snow like he had the previous Christmas.

Justin put the coffee pot on and helped Kellie make a breakfast of biscuits, ham and eggs. When they had stuffed themselves full and were lounging around the room, Justin leaned back in his armchair and read the Christmas story aloud from his Bible. Although Jack had learned the story for the first time in the army, there was a lot that he didn't understand about who the Holy Child was and why the story unfolded as it did. Jed had never heard it before and sat smoking his pipe while he listened. Justin took a few extra minutes to explain Jesus and His birth to them, but he didn't want to preach, and put it away when they stopped asking questions.

"Let's go skating," he said, standing up and stretching, and soon they were bundling up to go out.

The perfect day ended with them gathered in the Dinsmores' drawing room, singing carols together as Elisan played the piano.

Veiled in Flesh the Godhead see, Hail the incarnate Deity!
Pleased as Man with Men t'appear,
Jesus our Emmanuel here.

As Kellie sang the words of her favorite Christmas hymn, tears streamed down her cheeks. When Justin looked over and saw it, he found himself tearing up as well, and stopped singing to take in the moment. The look on his face as he sat in deep contentment with tears in his eyes was too much for Rebecca, and before she could manage to get her mask into place, she too had started crying, for an entirely different reason. Thankfully, no one could read her thoughts, and she turned her attention to the next verse.

Mild He lays His glory by, born that man no more may die,
born to raise the sons of earth,
born to give them second birth.

For all the pain she felt in letting Justin go, she never stopped having the deep-seated joy of knowing that the Creator of the universe humbled Himself so that He might make her heart His home. He never stopped loving her, and there was always enough of Him to go around.

Let every heart prepare Him room, she thought, the emotions that she usually kept so carefully bottled up flowing freely, and as she bowed her head and tears dripped from her nose, she felt her heart flood with the love of her Savior.

-13-

January 17, 1863

Kellie had just gone to bed on a cold night in January, and Justin was beginning to move in that direction when he heard his brothers coming up the steps outside. He could hear them talking in low voices and their footsteps were irregular as they stopped a few times and started again, so he waited for them to enter to find out what was going on.

Jack came through the door first, peering into the dark room and seeing Justin as he held the door for Jed, who was apparently reluctant to enter. Even in the darkness, Justin could immediately see that there was a problem. He held his candle higher, exposing the bruises and blood on Jed's face and hands. Jed held a handkerchief to his nose and his eyes were like a storm cloud, only a shade darker than the look on Jack's face.

Justin didn't even know where to start, but he figured that he would be told what had happened eventually anyway, so he stood mutely, looking at his brothers as they looked at him. Jack plopped into a chair and started to take off his boots, throwing them angrily on the floor.

"Ghastly bunch of Yankees down there," he announced in Jed's defense.

"What on earth happened?"

The three brothers turned to Kellie's bedroom door at the sound of her voice to see her in her robe, her curls falling around her shoulders. She came into the room, lit the lantern on the table, and moved to the pail of water.

"Bloody Yankees picked a bloody fight," Jack said hotly.

"And we couldn't just walk away?" Kellie pulled a chair out at the table for Jed and looked at him expectantly, so he sat obediently as she began patting at his face with a damp rag.

"Apparently not. And now we're expelled from O'Brien's and have to go down to Bridgeport to get our liquor, which means we'll have to walk further and it's bloody cold outside," Jack said, revealing his true feelings on the matter.

"Shut up, Jack, and quit your whinin'," Jed snapped, wincing at Kellie's dabbing. He gently pulled her hand away from his face and took the rag from her hand.

"I'm fine, Kellie," he said, but even that movement was stiff and slow, and Justin saw that he was babying his tender right hand.

"This isn't fine! This is worse than the black eye that Jack came home with, and you were kicked out of the establishment? When will you two learn?"

Jed scowled darkly at Kellie. "I didn't throw the first punch. And Jack was no help at all. So much for having family when you need them."

"I was tied up, and it was a stupid fight anyway," Jack said. "I can't believe you got us kicked out like that."

Jed swung at Jack with his other arm, but Kellie blocked him and pushed him back down in his chair. "Tied up? That tramp was more important to you than your own brother?"

"My brother, the one who ruined my night and ruined my right to ever go in O'Brien's again? I don't need that kind of brother," Jack shouted.

"God, Jack, you only ever care about yourself! Who cares about that slut and whatever kind of night you were going to have with her! You were just going to throw her by the wayside before mornin' anyway!"

"That's enough!" Justin thundered, afraid that Kellie was going to need her smelling salts by the way she looked. "This is despicable, and I'm ashamed of both of you! I told you that my reputation in this neighborhood is important, and that carousing is forbidden, and look at you two right now. Running around with whores and getting into fights?"

Jed stood up and towered over Justin. "I told you, I didn't start the fight."

"Then why were you the one who was kicked out? And Jack with you?"

Jed jutted his jaw out. "Because our street is the only one in the seventh ward with blasted Republicans who were all toastin' President Lincoln and the damn Emancipation Proclamation and I wouldn't participate. I'd bet no one down at O'Malley's would ever make a row over such a thing."

"Oh, God," Kellie moaned, covering her eyes.

"I wouldn't call that 'not participating,'" Jack contradicted. "Standin' up in a bloody Yankee saloon and cursin' Lincoln is not the smartest thing I've ever seen done, and you knew O'Brien's a Republican."

Justin choked. "Well, it saved me from being the one to punch you in the face," he gasped.

"Oh honestly, Justin, you aren't helping anything," Kellie returned sharply.

"I'd probably make more money outside of this ghetto anyway, and O'Malley's a real Irish Democrat. I woulda been going down there all this time if I didn't have to drag your lazy hide around with me, Jack."

"And cross the river to Bridgeport every day? Are you kidding me? If you just learned to shut your damn mouth, we woulda been fine. How are you gonna pay for all the broken glasses and furniture, anyway?" Jack said before Justin could tell Kellie that there was nothing he could do to help this situation anyway.

"I'll figure it out." Jed gingerly touched his nose. "I think it's broken. I don't think it's fair for O'Brien to make me pay for everything. He's never liked me and is just trying to get back at me."

Justin squinted at him. "How much is he making you pay?"

"It's none of your business, I'll figure it out," Jed grunted at the same time that Jack replied, "Twenty dollars."

"Twenty dollars?!"

"Twenty dollars AND I have to start walkin' two miles every night because of him."

"You don't have to walk any miles, because you're going to start staying home at night," Justin countered hotly. "You're not going anywhere until you learn how to behave in public."

"Oh, please." Jack stood up, glaring at Justin. "You aren't my father, and you can't tell me what to do." Throwing some choice words at Justin, he stomped towards the bedroom.

Kellie got up with a loud sigh and followed so that she could speak to him alone and tell him that fifteen-year-olds ought to stay away from ladies of the night and that he needed to be more respectful to Justin.

Jed stood at the counter, carefully washing the blood off of his hands in the wash basin.

"I could have told you that this would happen," he said to Justin. "I was attacked tonight, and when I come home, all I get is condemnation from my family without an ounce of understanding."

Justin crossed his arms and looked at Jed through slitted eyes. "Look, Jed, we're sorry you got hurt, but you need to take responsibility for the consequences of your own actions. Put some effort into trying to become a decent citizen, will you? Then these things won't happen to you."

"I'm a citizen of a different country," Jed retorted. "I just live here."

He headed towards the bedroom and turned around before going in.

"It's Jack you need to worry about, if only you knew what he does at night. He makes me look like a saint."

"Neither of you are looking particularly saint-like tonight," Justin called as Jed left the room.

Kellie came out after Jed went in, stopping by Justin on her way to hers. "That was badly handled," she said, and Justin threw his hands in the air.

"What do you want me to do with them? They're grown adults and Jack is right, I can't tell him what to do."

"Well, someone should," Kellie snapped back. "He's not a grown adult. He's just fifteen and he shouldn't be around those types of people. He's been coming home completely drunk more and more often, and twice now he didn't even come home until nearly morning. You need to talk to him more while he's still young, before it's too late."

Justin shook his head and sighed. "I can talk to him until I'm blue, but I don't think it does any good."

"It does. You're his brother, figure something out."

Kellie brushed past him and stalked off to bed, leaving Justin reeling from the evening alone.

Figure something out? Who did she think he was? He was just a stevedore at the docks, who'd lived alone for most of his adult life. What did he know about what to do with fifteen-year-old drunk Confederate orphans? He felt clueless as a leader, and on top of that, struggled under the onerous time he was having balancing the budget. He was working the longest hours Mr. Brewster would give him, but keeping the family fed was expensive and costs were rising due to the war. They flew through sacks of potatoes and flour at astounding rates and burned a shocking amount of firewood. Adamant about keeping money woes from them, he had started eating less himself, making it difficult to sustain his strength during the day. His boots wore through from being on his feet all day, and he couldn't afford to replace them while his brothers' boots sat shiny and unused at home until they went out in the evenings, and they ate until their bellies were full and then some.

The stress of it had become so consuming that lately, he'd found himself unable to open up to Kellie without risking letting on to this major burden he was bearing. And now, what he was doing for his brothers wasn't enough, either. Justin sat at the kitchen table running his fingers across his forehead, thinking and praying until late into the night.

Although none of the brothers felt particularly sorry for their part in the previous night's brouhaha, they all apologized to each other at dinner the next day, and nothing more was said on the matter.

Kellie woke up on Sunday morning feeling under the weather and came out of her room only to tell Justin that she wouldn't be going to church.

"I'll stay with you," Jed said. "I'm not goin' to church lookin' like this anyway."

On any other Sunday, Justin would have pushed him, but Jed really did look terrible, and it made sense to have him stay with Kellie.

"I wish I didn't have to go," Jack muttered as he started down the block with Justin.

If Jack didn't feel the need to grumble so often, perhaps everyone would pay more attention to him, Justin thought as he turned to him. Before he could open his mouth, Jack continued.

"Everyone is so nasty there, the way they snub Jed and me, and we have to sit up front where they can look down their noses at us as we pass."

"You know there are plenty of Confederate sympathizers in the city and even a few at the church, don't you?" Justin asked. "I think the church people snub you more because they know where you were Friday night and maybe only partially because you're a Confederate. You'd get on with them better if you had decent morals."

"I don't care to have the kind of morals as people who look down their noses at other people," Jack responded, and Justin actually thought that he had a good point.

"They aren't all like that. The Dinsmores aren't like that, and the Hennesseys and Katzes aren't, either," he reminded Jack. "I do wish they all treated you with respect, but in the meantime, you might have to work harder to earn it."

"In the meantime, I wish I didn't have to go," Jack said and sighed. "Jed hates it worse than I do."

Justin didn't know this, because Jed hadn't said anything more on the subject since the first Sunday, but he wasn't going to back down.

"Just do your best to ignore the rude ones, and listen to the sermon. That's what we're really there for anyway, and if there are things you don't understand from it, you can ask me about it later. There's not much in life that matters more than what you hear from Reverend Dinsmore on Sundays," Justin said, tugging his coat tighter against the chill as they neared the church.

Kellie grew worse as the day progressed, and by evening, she was running a fever and suffering from a headache and stomach pain. Justin made her some tea, and she insisted that she would be better by the morning if she had a good night's rest. When he checked on her first thing in the morning, however, she was no better, and he informed his brothers that he would be fetching the doctor on his way to work.

"I'll take care of her," Jack assured him, glancing worriedly at her door.

Justin had trouble focusing on his work all that day, anxious to return home and hear what the doctor had said. When he finally walked through the door that evening, he found Jed in the kitchen scraping potatoes out of a burned pan.

"How's Kellie?" he asked, heading to the wash basin.

Jed scowled at the pan in his hand and dropped it with a clatter on the counter. "The doctor said she probably has typhoid. Jack's been with her all day and said that she's quarantined so he's the only person who can take care of her."

Justin's eyebrows arched. "Since when did Jack become an expert on typhoid?"

"Since today, apparently. Dr. Ricketts gave him some medicine for her and told him how to administer it and all, and Jack is very serious about his job."

Justin bit his lip and the news sank in as fear rose in his throat. He approached Kellie's door and finding it ajar, gently pushed it open. Jack was by Kellie's side, as he had promised, patting a wet rag on her forehead. He looked up when the door squeaked.

"Hi there. How are you doing?" Justin asked, noticing Kellie's eyes were open.

"I'm alright," Jack said. "It smells like somethin' burned, though."

"That would be dinner. Hi Kellie, I'm sorry you're sick."

Kellie smiled faintly and shook her head on the pillow. "I'm sorry for getting sick."

"The doctor said it's contagious, so you shouldn't be in here," Jack said. "I need you to make her some broth, and I'll tell you how he said to make it. I don't trust Jed, because I can smell what he did to my dinner out there."

Despite his long day at work, Justin obediently made Kellie's broth and then turned his attention to dinner for his brothers, so it was late and he was exhausted when he finished and fell into bed.

The next evening, he stopped by the Dinsmores' on his way home. When Luke answered the door, Justin took a step back down the stairs.

"I just came to let you know that Kellie has typhoid. The doctor said it's contagious and she's quarantined, so we won't be coming to dinner this week."

"I'm sorry to hear." Luke's eyebrows knit together, noting how tired Justin looked. "Do you all need anything?"

"I don't think so, since the doctor seems to have given Jack everything that she needs. Thanks for offering, though."

Justin's feet dragged and he yawned on his way up the stairs into the apartment, but he didn't smell anything burning this time. He found Jack still guarding Kellie carefully, and ate Jed's undercooked and oversalted potatoes gratefully.

It wasn't until Kellie was asleep that Jack came out to eat, and his face fell when he saw his plate of food. "Can't you cook again, Justin?"

"No. I worked all day, and I'm tired. It won't kill you."

The withering look that Jed was giving Jack from across the room did look like it might kill him, however, so he choked down his potatoes with all the drama he could muster.

Justin checked on Kellie from the doorway, heeding Jack's instructions not to go any further. "How are you?" he asked her when he saw she was awake again, not knowing what else to ask. "I'm praying for you."

"I'm fine, Justin," Kellie replied softly, her cheeks bright pink against her white pillow. "I've had typhoid before, you know."

"You have?"

"Yes. It doesn't feel as bad this time." Kellie wasn't exactly sure how it felt compared to the last time she'd had it, six years prior, but if there was anything she could say to ease Justin's fears, she would. "Jack's been taking good care of me."

"How long does it last?"

"I don't know. A couple weeks, maybe. Can I have a drink?"

Kellie licked her dry lips, and Justin turned around to find Jack. "Can you get her a drink, Jack?"

"Yep," Jack said, pushing back his plate and standing up. "It's about time for her medicine anyway."

"Justin, all of my clothes will need to be washed, but I don't want you to do it yourselves. Mrs. Brown down the street does laundry, and I'll pay for it," Kellie said as Jack came with a cup of tea to give her with her medicine.

Justin stepped back to make room for him, and assured Kellie that he would take care of her laundry the next day. "And please don't worry about who will pay for it. Have a good rest," he said, turning back to the kitchen.

The table and counter were covered with dirty dishes, which Justin found truly astonishing considering how simple dinner was. Jed was on the couch with his feet up, smoking his pipe. With a sigh, Justin rolled up his sleeves and started a kettle of water on the stove for the dishes, determined to get up early in the morning to make everyone a big breakfast and get Kellie's laundry to Mrs. Brown.

He could barely move his aching body on Wednesday night when he came in the door, and his heart sank to find the kitchen clean and Jed on the couch again. Thinking that he would have to make supper, he set his lunch pail on the counter before he noticed a pot of soup on the table.

"Where did this come from?" Justin asked, lifting the lid and peering inside. The aroma that greeted him told him that Jed wasn't the one responsible for it. He closed his eyes and breathed deeply.

"Rebecca brought it by earlier, and she said she'd have more for us on Friday," Jed said.

"God bless Rebecca." Justin sighed with relief, grabbing a bowl and sinking into a chair at the table.

With Rebecca's soup three times a week and Jed's barely edible concoctions for dinner the other days, the Youngs survived Kellie's confinement, but everyone was relieved when she began building up strength again. She had stayed conscious through the fever and remained alert except for when she was sleeping, so her case was not nearly as bad as Justin had feared. By the end of the second week, she was sitting up in bed and Jack practiced his reading with her to pass the time.

"Don't let her do anything," Justin warned his brothers, stabbing his fork into a crunchy potato at dinner. "Not until she's completely well, and I mean completely."

"I can't eat too much more of this." Jack scowled at his plate, and Jed could have taken him out right then and there.

"Have you ever been grateful for anything in your life, Jack?" Jed growled.

"I'm grateful for Rebecca's soup. That woman can cook."

"You have a lot of nerve to complain about my cookin' when you haven't lifted a finger to help around here all week. You got the easy job, takin' care of Kellie, where you can just sit there and talk to her all day and leave everything else to me. I'd like to see you try to cook."

Jack stood up and stretched. "I don't see why you think you deserve to get credit for this," he scoffed. "A dog can cook better than that."

Jed did swing at Jack then, and Justin quickly stood and grabbed at him.

"Calm down. Kellie's getting better, and hopefully we'll be back to normal soon." He gave Jack a dirty look before turning back to Jed. "Your food is better than nothing, and with some practice, you'll get better. I, for one, appreciate you cooking for us."

Jed was still offended at Jack, but appeased for the time being, slunk off to the couch. It didn't matter anyway, because by the next morning, Jack was sick himself, tossing in bed with a fever when Justin woke up.

"Please make a bed for him on the floor of my room," Kellie said when Justin poked his head in her room to tell her. "I was sitting with him anyway, so

I should be the one to sit with him now, since I already have it. I don't want you or Jed to get it, and I'm nearly well."

Justin agreed that it was logical, so he got Jack moved onto Kellie's floor. Before work that morning, he took Jack's laundry to Mrs. Brown and stopped by Dr. Ricketts' to ask him to bring more medicine to the apartment.

By the second week of February, Kellie had recovered completely and Jack was on the mend, although she kept him quarantined in her room for another week. She was as grateful to be back in the kitchen as her brothers were to have her there, and it felt good to resume her normal chores. She'd missed Justin and Jed while she was sick, and after the altercation in January had determined to put in the effort bridge the distance she felt growing between them all.

When Jed started sitting at the table to watch her cook dinner in the afternoons, she let him rather than fussing at him for being underfoot, and relished his company. Perhaps compounded by the fact that Justin was unwilling to open up to her anymore and Jed's quiet, thoughtful spirit was one that she could understand and relate to, she found that Jed was the one of her three brothers that she got on the best with. His straightforwardness made him easy to communicate with, and he was quick to apologize when he stepped out of line or displeased her.

One afternoon she sat peeling potatoes next to him, chatting about the boarding school she had gone to when she was a girl, and casually reached over and handed Jed a knife. He looked at the knife in his hand and looked at Kellie.

"Put your hands to use," she suggested with a smile.

"I don't do a good job at this. When you were sick, I couldn't get it right and made a mess of it."

"Here, I'll show you," Kellie said, reaching over and showing him how to turn his wrist and hold the potato so the knife gently skimmed the peel off.

"It's the same with carrots?" he asked, watching her and making effort to imitate her movements.

"Carrots are a little harder since you have to hold them differently. I'll show you in a minute."

Jed didn't look pleased. "Aw Kellie, I help you how I can, but this is women's work."

"It's no such thing. All people eat. Besides, cooking is a good skill to have, and you never know when you'll need it," Kellie replied merrily. "You're sitting here anyway, so make your hands busy."

She had a point; sitting still was not something that Jed did a good job of handling, so he reluctantly picked up the knife and continued working on his potato. The next day she showed him how to chop onions, and as she gradually taught him how to cook, she gave him space to think and to talk if he wanted to.

With his hands occupied, his tongue loosened little by little, and Kellie found herself given access to sacred halls in his heart that he had never let anyone into before. Once in a while she ran into inner rooms that remained locked, rooms to which he had apparently long since lost the keys, but she always backed off at that point and never made him feel uncomfortable about it.

She learned about friends that he had made before the war that walked all over him, and about the dog he had for three years that he gave food to before he'd eat himself. As the months went by, she eventually gathered that his fear of women came from the mother of the family he had lived with, although he never told Kellie what the woman did to him.

"I don't know why it was different with you," he admitted to her. "The moment I laid eyes on you for the first time, I knew you were safe, and that was the first time I had ever been around a woman without feeling terror rise up the back of my neck."

Kellie was pleased to give a positive report on the boys' education to Justin on the first warm evening in April as she hung on his arm, trailing behind Luke and Rebecca on their evening walk.

"Jed's writing is really looking legible these days," she said happily. "I think he's finally getting the hang of it, and he almost has the Classifications of Living Things memorized. He works hard and is really dedicated to his studies."

"I never see him read anything myself, so that's great to hear," Justin said as they paused behind their friends to let a buggy pass.

"No, when their lessons are over, he won't touch a book for the rest of the day. It seems to take quite a bit more effort for him than Jack. Jack has been picking everything up so much quicker, and he actually enjoys it."

"I saw that Jack was reading King Lear the other day."

Kellie smiled and nodded. "The way that he likes to poke fun at people made me think that he would appreciate Shakespeare, and he does. I've given him some passages of Shakespeare's plays to memorize, and sometimes we perform them after lunch." She gave a little chuckle and added, "Jed doesn't seem to understand any of it. But Jack's been doing so well. His penmanship is neat and tidy and he can read almost as well as I can. Did you know that he sent some letters to his friends in the army?"

Justin shook his head.

"He hasn't gotten any responses, though, so I don't know if his letters are getting through the lines." Kellie and Justin had the same thought that it was possible that Jack's friends in the 5th North Carolina may not be still alive, but neither one felt the need to vocalize it.

"I really do feel sorry for Jack." Kellie sighed, squeezing Justin's arm tighter. "He lies around on the couch reading or whittling every afternoon, but I think he's the type of boy who would love to have a group of buddies to run around with. I actually think he seems to be a bit depressed about it."

Justin shrugged and looked down at Kellie. "But he goes out at night."

"He goes out at night, yes. I don't know what makes the two of them still want to go out like that when they're treated so poorly. I've been thinking about it, and I wonder what it is that they're looking for."

Kellie wasn't sure whether Justin was aware of the severity of Jack's hangovers, or how her school mornings were disrupted from time to time, since he was always at work when Jack was throwing up and needing her to patiently clean up after him. Rather than finding it annoying, Kellie's heart twisted in compassion towards her baby brother, and she was thankful that he had her there to care for him when it happened.

"I don't think that Jack intends to drink as much as he does when he sets out in the evening," she said softly. Justin's eyebrows rose questioningly at her, so she continued. "I think he's looking for something—companionship, perhaps—and when he doesn't find it, ends up drinking more than he means to."

Justin looked thoughtful but didn't reply, so they walked quietly on, each pondering what Kellie said. Kellie didn't tell Justin that of her brothers, he was actually the one that confused her the most. Things had started off so well between him and her, and as the other Christian in the family, she had expected more from him. Yet all of her probing had failed to produce a satisfactory theory for why he had become so quiet lately, except perhaps that he was just tired from work. She prayed about it as she walked, asking God to show her what was in Justin's heart and how she could help him reach the potential of the leader she knew he could be.

-14-

April 22, 1863

Justin fell asleep on the couch one evening a few weeks later after struggling to keep his eyes open through dinner, even as he felt Kellie watching him closely as he ate. When he woke up, Jed and Jack were out and Kellie was knitting in the armchair next to him. He stirred and she glanced over when he moved to sit up.

"We need to talk."

Justin groaned and rubbed his eyes, leaning forward with his elbows on his knees.

"I paid your bill at the grocer today," Kellie said without taking her eyes off of him.

"What?" Justin dropped his hands and stared at her as anger rose in his chest. "I told him that he was to discuss my account with me, and only me. I made that clear."

"I couldn't get groceries today, Justin. We wouldn't have had supper tonight. I needed food and I was getting upset, and he finally told me the truth, which would have been a lot easier to hear from you a long time ago."

Justin didn't say anything, pressing his fingertips together with his eyes on her moving needles.

"Will you tell me what is going on?" Kellie asked.

Justin wanted to talk to her, but he was at a loss to know where to begin, let alone end. His mouth froze as his mind raced on and on.

"Okay then," Kellie finally tried, taking a deep breath. "Why don't I tell you what I think is going on, and you tell me if I'm right or wrong?"

Justin didn't move.

"I think feeding your family, including two grown brothers, is more expensive than you figured it would be, and I think that you're afraid of us finding out because it will hurt your pride."

Justin bowed his head and ran his fingers through his hair.

"Justin, you know we would all be happy to help. No one ever expected you to do this by yourself. Not even a week ago, Jed asked you if he could get a job and you turned him down, and I don't understand how you could do that when you knew about this."

Justin lifted his head and looked at her. "I want him to get an education, Kellie. It's for his own good, and I did my best to communicate that as gently as I could. At least a year."

"Is that all that it is, really? He can study in the morning and get a side job in the afternoon. You don't understand how much he needs to get out of the house. He has so much energy and he's never been caged up like this in his life. It's making us all crazy." Kellie paused her knitting.

It wasn't all that it was to Justin, but he didn't know how to explain how much he also wanted his brothers to have a respite from work that they were never afforded as children. He'd never intended to make them miserable, but since they had been robbed of their childhoods, he had wanted to give them time to have leisure before they had to be adults. But here he sat, having failed. He had toiled day after day working long hours at the lumberyard to make himself be enough for them, and he wasn't enough, and he had wanted to protect his family from the burden of his financial struggles, and he had failed at that too. He had done everything he could do and it wasn't enough, and he struggled to face Kellie and admit it to her.

"Well, never mind about Jed," Kellie continued. "He took a job at the livery this afternoon anyway." She stretched out her yarn and picked her needles back up.

"So you don't care that he undermined my authority?"

"I care that you've been hiding things from me and pushing me away." Kellie's eyes filled with tears as she fingered the material in her hands.

"Don't cry, Kellie," Justin said, and took a deep breath. "I'm sorry."

Kellie pulled out a handkerchief and dabbed at her eyes and Justin could have killed himself. He looked at Kellie, longing to give her what she wanted and open up to her, but he couldn't form the words. Finally, he hoarsely admitted, "I don't know what to say, and that's the most honest thing I can say right now."

Kellie looked at him for a long minute, her eyes softening. She rose, set her knitting down on the coffee table, and knelt on the floor beside him, resting her arms on his knee and tilting her face up.

"You're killing yourself, Justin," she said softly. She reached over and fingered the frayed cuff on his sleeve, and he saw how shabby he'd been looking lately. "Please let us take care of you too. It's what families do."

Justin looked at her mutely and then nodded, closed his eyes, and leaned down to rest his head on her curls.

"I'm sorry for making you feel poorly about it," Kellie whispered. "I know you've been doing your best."

"You don't have anything to be sorry for, Kellie. It's not your fault."

Kellie exhaled slowly. "I wish you could talk to me about it."

"Me too."

He wanted her to know that he had waited fourteen years to take care of her, and now that he had the chance, he found that he was unable to do that, the one thing he had always wanted more than anything, and she'd had to bail him out. And he wanted her to know that he had tried to prevent her finding out how miserable of a failure he was because he didn't want to hurt her, but she had found out and been hurt by it anyway. And he wanted her to know that he would always protect her from anyone who hurt her, even if it meant keeping himself from her. But there was no way to say these things to her, so he sat resting his head on hers, stroking her hand on his knee, hating himself.

"You think it will be good for Jed?"

"Mmhmm, I do. He really misses the cavalry, so at least he'll be able to be around horses again. It won't be the same without having him help me with dinner, but he needs the space."

Justin sat up again so he could see her face. "He's a good kid. You've been getting close with him, haven't you? If you think it will be good for him, then I won't give him a hard time about it."

"Thank you." Kellie stood up and kissed his forehead. "He's starting to open up. Tiny bits, little stories here and there. I want to give him everything he needs to flourish, and Jed is someone who can't sit at home. It's suffocating him, Justin."

Jed and Jack's boots sounded on the steps just then, so with a sweep of her hand across Justin's shoulder, Kellie stepped back to her knitting.

In July, General Lee suffered a crushing defeat in Pennsylvania at Gettysburg, and the reports from the largest battle of the war to date sent shock waves through the nation. The remustered 23rd Illinois Infantry, 1st North Carolina Cavalry and 5th North Carolina Infantry were all engaged during the three-day conflict, and the thought that all three of the Young brothers would have been there fighting against each other had they remained enlisted turned Justin's stomach. On their walk that Saturday, they passed crowds of people gathered at the train station waiting for casualty lists, and Justin was grateful that his family and closest friends were safe and he could continue on by. As far as his family was concerned, the war was over, and even the draft talks didn't affect them since they had already served.

The second anniversary of Nathan's death fell on the day before Justin's birthday in late July. Although in general, Kellie felt less fragile about her husband's death as time went on, the actual anniversary of the day was still tender. She let her family know that she needed space that day, and they respectfully gave it to her. Her brothers gave her hugs and told her they loved her, and Justin cooked a late supper after work so she was free to spend her afternoon alone at the lake thinking, journaling, and praying.

She sat on a bench overlooking the water and found herself thinking about the progress she was making in the relationships she was building with each of her brothers. Since finding out about Justin's struggles paying the bills, the shadow between them had lifted, and Jed's contributions to the family's expenses had made a noticeable difference in Justin. Once again, he had energy to put into his family, and Kellie felt that his trust in her was strengthening again.

Slowly, steadily, she was learning to listen to her brothers and love them, and little by little, she saw walls coming down in their hearts as they each in their own way let her in. Although she didn't see the same kind of progress in their relationships with each other, she felt hopeful for the difference that love was making in their lives, and her spirits were higher than they had ever been.

Caring for her family consumed so much of her daily thoughts and energy that after she'd taken the time to fill several journal pages about them, her mind was free to return to her reason for being there. For the next hour and a half, Kellie took the time to grieve and honor her late husband, remembering the tender love they had shared and thanking God for the role Nathan had in her life and in the reunion of her family.

The next morning, Kellie put her grief aside once again and was ready to celebrate Justin's birthday with all the gusto of the day. At his place at breakfast was a box with new boots in it, a gift from his three siblings together. Kellie was relieved to have found a way to provide this need for him without sacrificing his pride, and Justin was grateful.

"I invited Luke, Rebecca, and Elisan to dinner tonight," she told him as he tied his boots on before work. "I should have had Rebecca cook your birthday dinner, though; she's such a better cook than I am."

"Nonsense," Justin said, standing up and kissing her hair. "That will be fun, thank you. I'll look forward to it."

At the Dinsmores', however, Rebecca was struggling deeply with the innocently extended invitation. She was quiet and tense most of the morning until Elisan got her out in the garden after lunch and begged her to unload what was bothering her.

"I really don't want to go tonight, Ellie," she admitted from under a wide brimmed straw hat as she knelt weeding across from her sister. "It's one thing to have to be in the same group as him in every social situation and have him for dinner every Friday and see him on the front pew every Sunday, and have him ignore me the entire time. I can put on an act and hold myself together through a great deal, but going in his home and honoring him by celebrating his birthday feels like more than I can bear. It's not that I don't wish him the best—you know I do—it's just that I have to do it while he looks past me and I'm invisible to him."

"I wish I could do something for you." Elisan leaned back on her heels. "It would be so awkward if you excused yourself again, since just the three of us were invited and you've been saying you're not feeling well so much lately. If Justin's siblings don't catch on soon, Luke surely will."

"I know." Rebecca's shoulders dropped and she knew she had to start the hard work of mentally preparing for the evening. "I don't know what's wrong with me. It's been almost a year of him treating me like this and I still haven't gotten over him. Rather than getting used to it, the pain is compounding. My heart still beats fast when I see him, and I can't make it stop even after all this time of him rejecting me. It's ridiculous, Ellie."

"It's not you he rejected," Elisan said, slowly and pointedly. "I think Justin knows that he would have been lucky to have you. He rejected marriage to anyone, and don't you think that he is denying himself too—not just you?"

Rebecca knit her eyebrows together. "But he doesn't seem bothered by it. Don't you think he's happy?"

"No, I don't," Elisan replied, her eyes widening. "Have you seen him lately? He's aged five years and always looks like he's carrying the weight of the world. He's not carefree anymore the way he was with you."

Rebecca pondered this, but it was hard to see Justin over the wall he had erected between them. "I still don't think he misses me, though, because I would notice if he was pining. I can't blame him; he hasn't done anything wrong, but I'm still giving him space in my heart to hurt me. The problem is that he told me not to wait for him, and if I'm still hurt a year later, it's my own fault. How can you stop loving a person when you're going to their birthday dinners?"

"And you don't want to try giving one of the other men at church a chance to see if they could turn your heart?"

"Oh, no, I couldn't," Rebecca insisted with a shake of her head.

Elisan looked at Rebecca straight on. "Well then, maybe you need to think about talking to Justin," she said softly. "If there's nothing else to it, perhaps you should let him know. See if he'll be willing to talk about it and reconsider."

Rebecca fell silent, trying not to dismiss her sister's input without giving it some thought, but she couldn't imagine herself talking to Justin, either. She wondered how much she would have to be hurt before she would be willing to add to the burdens he was already carrying.

She joined Luke and Elisan at dinner that night and made it through the evening without crying, despite having trouble breathing all evening with Justin in close proximity and the center of attention. Jack showed her his carvings, and she took great interest in them as a distraction. Later, she washed the dishes for Kellie so her friend could give her attention to her brother and organize a game of cards. There was an odd number of people anyway, so it gave Rebecca an excuse to bow out of the game, and she dawdled at the dishpan.

When Justin bid each of them goodnight later, he looked at her and thanked her for coming, but she couldn't smile or say anything in response, nodding mutely around the lump in her throat. She later felt that it was rude, but as usual, Justin didn't notice anyway. He'd had a good day, and he gave Kellie a hug and thanked her before heading to bed.

"You've done so much for all of us. I'm thankful that we're able to spend your birthday together," Kellie said. She smiled admiringly up at him and kissed him goodnight.

August 19, 1863

For the next several weeks, one day was much like the next and time passed without any noticeable shift or alteration. Justin went to work; Jed and Jack studied in the morning, and Jed went to the livery in the afternoons while Kellie cleaned and cooked and Jack lounged around. There were no looming storm clouds, no observable troubles brewing. So when Justin got home from work on a Wednesday night in August, he had no indication to expect anything to be awry until he walked through the door.

The first thing he noticed was that Jed was sitting at the kitchen table, which was unusual since Jed usually arrived home after Justin did. Kellie was at the stove frying salt pork, and her face was red, wet, and swollen.

Justin set down his lunch pail on the counter and looked from Kellie to Jed and back at Kellie again, noticing Jack on the couch whittling in the meantime.

Kellie looked at Justin and nodded her head toward Jed without saying anything, so Justin looked back at Jed and waited.

"I'm leaving," Jed said.

-15-

Justin froze and blinked at Jed, not knowing which question to ask first as Kellie sniffled behind him.

"Where?" he said after a pause.

"To rejoin the cavalry and finish the war."

The Confederate cavalry, of course, Justin thought. The enemy.

"And then?"

Jed exhaled and shrugged. "I don't know, I guess we'll see."

Justin really didn't want to know Jed's reasons why, but he knew he had to ask, so pulling out a chair, he sat down and did.

"Well, I never thought this was going to be permanent," Jed said with a little wave of his hand. "We tried it out, but now it's been a year and I'm ready to go back and finish what I started with the cavalry."

Stunned, Justin wondered where this was coming from and what he could do to change Jed's mind.

"Actually, I did think that families were forever. Not necessarily this living arrangement in this particular house, but I didn't think we were an experiment we were simply trying out."

Kellie set dinner on the table and sat down without calling Jack to the table, and Jed dove into the food without waiting for prayer.

"It's not like we're a normal family," Jed said, serving himself. "We don't even know one another, and you have to be honest, it hasn't been working out that well."

"How can you say that?" Kellie exclaimed, tears falling. "Don't we mean anything to you?"

Jed sighed and looked at her. "You know I love you, Kellie. But that doesn't change the fact that I obviously don't belong here."

"But you do belong here! If you don't belong where you love and are loved, then where do you belong?" Kellie obviously didn't understand, and Justin could have punched Jed in the face for making her cry.

"I belong where I can be me, Jed Young, and don't have to pretend to be someone else. Where I don't have to make apologies for the choices I make with my life, and where I don't have to look a certain way to be presentable to your friends. I belong where I can believe what I believe about the universe without being forced into something else, and where I can be a man again."

Kellie was too upset to respond to Jed's mistaken opinions and sat sobbing.

"Jed, I'm sorry you see things that way. If you have problems with the way things are, we can talk about it and make adjustments if we need to. You don't have to leave," Justin said, impressed at how well he kept his voice level.

Jack swore from the couch and got up to get a bandage for his bleeding finger, dropping his knife and carving with a clatter on the floor.

"I'm not going to waste my time trying to speak where I'm not heard," Jed said, taking a bite and chewing it. "You're used to things being a certain way around here and being king of your castle, and I don't see where there's room for me in it. I'm not sure what you were trying to do here, but I didn't come all the way up here to be an ornament for you to show off in church every week. I've made my decision, and I'll be leaving in the morning."

"In the morning?" Kellie gasped as her face drained of color.

Jack took his seat at the table and filled his plate without a word or making any eye contact. Justin was quite hurt by Jed's assumptions about him, and sat with a still empty plate, struggling to reach beyond his hurt to set the record straight.

He looked at Jed sincerely and with great effort, said, "You're our brother, not my trophy. I don't see you like that, and I'm sorry for making you think I do. Please don't go. I never intended to treat you like less than a man or less than my brother."

"Well," Jed said, looking back at him, "then you failed."

Without another word, Justin pushed back from the table, stood up, and left out the front door as Kellie and his brothers sat listening to his boots thud down the stairs.

Justin stood inside the doorway at the foot of the stairs, doubled over as if he had been punched in the stomach. He tried and failed to collect his thoughts or make sense of what had just happened as he stood leaning against the wall, gasping for breath. As soon as he could move again, he started walking and didn't stop until he arrived at the Dinsmores' home.

He let himself in the front door and found the family seated at dinner, where he took an empty seat beside Elisan.

"Justin! What's wrong?" Luke asked as Rebecca quickly stood up to get him a plate and fork, but Justin didn't reply. When Rebecca gave him his food, he picked up his fork and started eating although he felt like throwing up and no one else in the room was eating with him.

"Justin," the reverend said quietly but firmly, "We love you, but you may not come in and disrupt my family dinner and give us all indigestion like this without letting us know what we can do for you."

Justin looked up and froze, then quietly set his fork down and looked around at his friends guiltily.

"May I speak with Luke, please?"

"Certainly," Reverend Dinsmore said, so Luke rose and led Justin into his father's library, closing the door behind him.

Back at the table, Elisan murmured, "He's madder than when I put the pie in his face."

"You think he's mad? At Luke?" Rebecca asked, but Elisan shook her head.

"No one could ever be mad at Luke; he must be mad at his family. Did you see his face?"

Of course Rebecca had, and had seen how upset Justin was, but didn't translate it as anger.

"It's how he looked when he stalked away with the pie in his face, except more so," Elisan added.

"I wonder what's wrong," Rebecca murmured, her heart breaking.

Justin slumped into the armchair by the fireplace as Luke turned around from the door.

"Jed's leaving," Justin said, and Luke stood looking at him, as stunned as Justin had looked at Jed.

"Why?" Luke moved to the other chair and took a seat.

"According to him, because I'm a failure," Justin said dejectedly, and Luke stared at him.

"He said that?"

Justin nodded.

"Good God. I'm so sorry, Justin."

Justin sat morosely and didn't say anything.

"What are you going to do?" Luke tried, and Justin heaved a sigh.

"I don't know. I feel like I've been slapped in the face and I'm seeing stars right now and trying to figure out which way is up. Does your pa have an extra Bible I can give him?"

"He does," Luke said, looking up at the reverend's bookshelves. "You're just going to let him go?"

"I don't know what else to do, Luke. He's leaving in the morning, and he said his mind was made up."

Luke took a minute to think, then stood up and pulled a small Bible off the shelf. He handed it to Justin, who took it and sat as if in shock, making no movement to go.

"I'm going to get us some tea," Luke said after a moment, and stepped out of the room.

In the kitchen, he found the reverend talking to Rebecca, who was pouring water into the dishpan. She quickly dried her hands and put on a kettle to boil when he asked her to.

"What's wrong with Justin?" she asked in a hushed tone.

"Jed's leaving in the morning, and he's really upset. I think Jed said some hurtful things to him and is blaming him," Luke said.

"Oh no!" Rebecca exclaimed in a whisper.

"He asked for a Bible to give Jed," Luke continued, turning to his father. "I'm sure it's not a problem."

"Not at all."

"Can I talk to him?" Rebecca asked, her eyebrows furrowed in concern, and Luke shrugged.

"I don't know. You can try if you like."

Leaving Luke with her father to watch the kettle, Rebecca walked to the library and quietly opened the door. Justin was motionlessly looking at the empty fireplace when she entered and came near.

"Luke said that Jed is leaving," she said, kneeling on the floor next to his chair. Justin quickly looked up when he heard her voice and saw who it was.

"Yeah," he whispered, hanging his head again.

"I'm so sorry."

"Thank you." His hand dangled off his knee and she wanted so badly to reach out and touch it, as inappropriate as it would be and as much as she knew that he would not receive comfort from her. She felt his sadness deep in her soul.

"Well, I wanted to let you know that I cared," she finally managed.

"Thank you."

Luke came in with the tea, and Rebecca stood up.

"You don't have to go," Justin said, and as tempting as it was to take him up on the invitation, it was too difficult to stay, so she gently brushed his shoulder with her hand as she moved away.

Luke handed Justin his mug and sat down, alone once again.

"What do you need?"

Justin shook his head. "I guess time. I need to figure this all out."

He leaned forward and buried his face in his free hand and Luke sat wordlessly, feeling unprepared to help Justin through this trial.

"I don't know if I'm more hurt or angry," Justin finally said. "I've never been so hurt or angry, and I can't figure out how he could do this to Kellie when she was getting so close with him."

"Do you think he's running from something?"

"I don't know. I don't know very much about him or his past to know, so it's possible." Justin rubbed his eyes and lifted his head. "I haven't had enough time with him, and I always thought I'd have more time later, because I work so much and he went out in the evenings a lot. I should have tried harder, but I didn't know."

"Mmhmm," Luke murmured, taking a sip. "I guess we never know how much time we really have."

Justin stood up and set his mug down. He paced the floor, ran his fingers through his hair, and slouched in the chair as Luke did his best to listen and comfort as time passed. It was late when he finally went home, and Luke went to bed, worn through from the emotionally exhausting evening.

When Justin arrived home, he found only Kellie waiting up for him.

"Where have you been?" she demanded in a whisper, standing up from the couch as he came in with the Bible in his hand.

"I went to the Dinsmores'."

Kellie swallowed hard, obviously unhappy. "This is your last evening with Jed, and you just left," she accused, and Justin stared at her.

"I needed to talk to Luke, Kellie."

"You're not the only one in this family. There are other needs besides your own," she hissed back at him.

Justin rubbed his forehead with his fingers, feeling like she was being unfair to him after the way Jed had attacked him at dinner, and he didn't apologize.

"Yes. I'm here now."

Kellie sighed, frustrated with the realization that he couldn't see past his own pain.

"Do you want to talk about it?" she asked, hoping that he did, but Justin shook his head.

"No, I'm tired and talked out," he replied numbly, and rubbing her arm, turned toward bed.

Kellie watched him go, tears falling. "I need you," she cried softly after his door closed. "I just need you."

Jed was up early the next morning, getting ready to leave for the train station before Justin left for work. Kellie fussed around him, making him eat, packing him food, and ensuring that he had everything he needed.

"I wish you'd told me earlier," she complained to Jed. "I would have made you some new shirts and socks, but now I don't have time, and I don't think you have enough."

Jed and Jack were both quiet as they ate, but it wasn't that unusual for either of them in the mornings. Justin came out of the bedroom dressed for work and picked up a biscuit off the table, which he ate without sitting while he drank his coffee.

When Jed stood up from the table, Justin reached out and stopped him. "You don't have to go," he said quietly. "It's not too late to change your mind. You're wanted here."

Jed looked at him but didn't reply, so Justin handed him the Bible.

"I know you don't want this or believe it, but it's true, Jed. Every word of it. And one day you'll realize that you need it, and I want you to have it when that day comes."

Jed took it, pausing awkwardly before sticking the Bible in his open knapsack next to the food that Kellie had packed for him, and closed the flap.

Kellie came over with writing paper and stamps for him, and he opened the knapsack back up and put them in the front cover of the Bible.

"Please write," she begged. "Please let me know that you're alive, and please come back to us after the war is over." She wrapped her arms around him and hugged him tightly, and he rubbed her back and kissed her hair.

"I love you," Jed told her, and she said, "I love you too."

He clasped Jack on the back and told him to stay out of trouble, and with a nod to Justin, picked up his knapsack and hat and left.

-16-

Kellie cried on and off all that day, and by the next day, she had made herself sick and was bedridden for the next two weeks. Jack stayed by her side and gave her excellent care, but he didn't do any chores, so Justin had to do all the cooking, dishes, and hauling firewood in the evenings after work. He was exhausted and mentally worn through, but he didn't have any choice but to keep going.

Soon after arriving home and tackling his responsibilities, Justin would often look up to see Jack preparing to leave, and he usually stayed out until after Justin was in bed. It was infuriating, and although Justin put a great deal of effort into being patient, the more exhausted he became, the less emotional energy he had to handle it well. As time passed and each of the siblings struggled to figure out their emotions after Jed's departure, Jack grew only more churlish and combative towards Justin.

The first night that Kellie was well enough to eat dinner with the boys again, Justin moved to retrieve his Bible from the mantel after the meal. He was heading back to the table when Jack stood up.

"Where are you going?" Justin asked, his tone harsh.

"Out." Jack picked up his boots and carried them back to his chair.

"Out where?"

Jack stopped and looked at Justin. "Out out."

Needled, Justin pressed further. "Why won't you tell me where you're going?"

"Because," Jack said as he sat down and pulled his boot on, "It's not your concern, and I don't have to."

"I am concerned, actually. We're going to read now, so you aren't going to go anywhere."

Jack tied his boot and pulled the other one on. "Go ahead and read, but I'm not going to sit through that."

"Yes, you are. This is my home, and in my home we read the Bible together every night."

"Okay. That's fine," Jack replied belligerently. "I said you can read, but you can't make me stay, and I'm not going to."

Justin stood blinking at Jack as Jack rose and passed him on his way out the door. It clicked behind him, leaving Justin in the stunned silence with Kellie. Without making eye contact with her, he sat down at the table and began to read aloud.

The following week, Justin came home to find Jack whittling on the couch with shavings all over the seat and floor. Jack had decided to make himself a chess set since his skill at the game had been improving, but as usual, didn't seem to feel any need to be tidy about his work.

"Are you going to clean that up?" Justin asked before even offering a greeting.

"Not planning on it," Jack said without looking up from his project.

"Well, plan on it then, because you aren't going to leave that for Kellie to clean up." Justin set down his lunch pail on the kitchen counter and rolling up his sleeves, turned to wash his hands.

"It's not bothering anyone," Jack replied lazily.

"It's bothering me, and I want you to clean it up. You can't trash my house like this."

Jack glanced up at Justin for the first time but still didn't move. "I can leave then so you can have your clean house," he said, waiting for a reaction from his brother.

"You will do no such thing," Justin said testily. "You need to man up and start pulling your weight around here. Kellie doesn't need to have a big baby to clean up after; that's not her job."

Jack sat up and set down his carving. "I don't think you're in any position to tell me what Kellie needs, when you make her cry so often and never take the time to ask her what she needs. I don't believe you have a right to think of yourself as her spokesperson."

He stood up, swore under his breath at Justin, who stood silenced in the middle of the kitchen, and disappeared into the bedroom. Clenching his jaw, Justin grabbed the broom and swept up the shavings himself.

October 13, 1863

Kellie excused herself from the table one evening after Justin and Jack had bickered all through dinner, and leaving the dishes behind, headed out for her evening walk alone. She'd been gone nearly twenty minutes when Luke arrived and knocked on the door.

"Rebecca couldn't come tonight, so it's just me. Are you and Kellie coming for a walk?" he asked when Justin answered the door.

"Kellie already left," Justin said. "I think I'm staying in tonight, but maybe you'll run into her if you go."

So Luke left and sauntered along their usual route until he spied Kellie in the distance, seated alone on a bench overlooking the lake. She didn't see him coming up behind her until he rounded the bench, and he was taken aback with the realization too late that she was crying. She saw him and quickly straightened up, dabbing at her wet face with an already damp handkerchief balled up in her hand.

"Don't," he said, putting his hand out to stop her. "I didn't mean to interrupt you. Please, you don't have to act differently around me."

He sat down next to her and leaned forward as she continued to wipe her eyes and sniffle. Kellie didn't say anything, so Luke asked, "What's wrong? Would you like to talk about it?"

Kellie looked at him and shook her head.

"I'm sorry," she said with a sniffle. "I really shouldn't. I'll be fine." But as she sat watching the gentle ripple of the water, her tears started to flow again.

Luke thought for a moment. "You don't have to talk to me if you don't want to, but I just wanted to let you know that whatever gets said to me is never repeated. Sometimes folks will just talk to me because it helps them understand the problem better. But it's your choice."

"It's not that. I know you wouldn't repeat it," Kellie quickly assured him, wadding up her handkerchief and swiping at her nose. Finally she added, "It's just that you're his best friend."

Luke sat up and exhaled. "Justin." What was he doing to make his sister cry like this?

Luke joined Kellie in watching the water while he tried to think of what to say. "I've known Justin a long time. Perhaps I can help you understand him. Or maybe just having someone to talk to will help you feel better." He glanced over at Kellie. "My opinion of Justin or of you won't change, but if there's some way I can help, I'm happy to do it."

Kellie started crying again, and it was a few minutes before she could calm herself down enough to talk. Luke waited patiently, his heart hurting to see his friends in conflict with one another.

"I don't want to gossip, Luke, not about my family. But the fighting has gotten so bad lately," she finally admitted through her tears.

"Justin?" Luke felt a stinging shock. Justin had not been himself lately, but Luke had never known him to be the type of person to fight with anyone.

Kellie nodded, sniffling. "And Jack."

"Why?"

"Jack's so difficult to live with these days. He's pushing back against everything." She heaved a sigh and folded her hands. "I can usually deal with it, and we get on okay during the day. But he knows how to agitate Justin and get on his nerves, and lately, Justin has been reacting poorly to it."

She sat watching the water for a moment, and Luke didn't say anything, so after a pause, she continued.

"I don't know what Jack has been through in his life, or what his childhood was like, but it wasn't easy. I know it's left him with a lot of scars that he still won't even talk to me about. So I try to see past what he wants me to see and love him as best as I can. Once in a while it seems like I break through to him a little. But he doesn't let Justin see that side of him; he's just rude and disrespectful to him and tries to pick fights. Usually, he's successful."

Kellie drew a wavy breath, looking down at her hands. "It's been so awful lately with all the shouting and hateful things they say to each other. I had to get out of the house."

She started to cry again, and Luke wished he could wrap his arms around her like he would have done for his sisters.

"Have you talked to Justin about it?"

Kellie shook her head. "I mean, I've tried. But not lately." She exhaled, and Luke's eyebrows furrowed.

"What is it?"

"Justin has stopped talking to me about anything, and lately I have been trying less and less to make him." She looked up at him, the ache in her heart plastered all over her face.

"Why?" Luke was bewildered, realizing the tragedy it was to both of them.

"I don't know," she whispered, and fell silent again.

Eventually, Kellie looked up. "When Jed left, I think it hurt each of us tremendously for different reasons. And I think Justin is very hurt right now. I've found that when things are painful for him, he shuts everyone else out, and I wonder if that's how he trained himself to deal with pain throughout his life."

She turned back to watch the water softly lap at the stone wall, giving Luke a minute to think through everything she had said.

"I remember how upset he was the night he found out Jed was leaving," he offered. "He came over and spent a while at my house."

"I know," Kellie said shortly, and the look on her face told him how she felt about it.

"Oh," he said, sucking in his breath as understanding dawned. "You didn't like that."

Kellie struggled to know what to say. She hadn't meant to be so abrupt, but it had just come out.

"No, I mean, I'm glad he has you. He needed you and it meant a lot to him."

Luke waited for her to tell him the truth. She sighed.

"It's nothing, Luke. I'm being selfish and it isn't fair to him."

"You wanted him to stay. That isn't nothing."

Kellie bowed her head. "We were all battered and crushed that night. And I wished he would have stayed so we could have . . . strengthened . . . each other. And grieved together." Tears slipped down her face again. "I wanted him, and I was jealous that he had somewhere else to go. He has another family, and he didn't need us like I needed him."

"I'm sorry, Kellie," Luke said. "I had no idea. But we're not family for just him. The relationship we have with him is extended to all of you. But I understand that you needed him, and I'm sorry I didn't see it at the time."

"Don't be sorry." Kellie tried to wipe her eyes again, but her handkerchief was soaked, so Luke reached in his pocket and handed her his.

"I didn't tell you to make you feel bad about it; you did nothing wrong. Now you see that Justin isn't the only one at fault, when I'm this selfish too." She dabbed at her face with his handkerchief. "We're all tense and distrustful lately, and I don't know if we can get back to where we need to be."

She turned a teary face to him. "I'm scared for my family and what will become of us. And I love them so much, Luke. I can't bear the thought of losing them again."

"What do you think you—and they—need?" Luke asked, leaning forward to rest his elbows on his knees.

"Jack needs to find Jesus." Kellie answered without hesitation. "He needs to heal from whatever it is he's keeping hidden from us. And Justin and I . . . actually, we all need Jesus," she finished with a sad smile. "There is so much hurt in our family and we need to learn how to love each other through it. Right now it feels like I am the only one who wants to put in the effort to do that, and that's hard. Jed is gone, Justin is withdrawing, Jack is attacking, and I am becoming weary."

She bit her lip for a moment before continuing. "God is my strength, and He has always been faithful to me. So I can't quit even though it's hard, and I will continue to love my family and pray that He will restore all of our broken pieces." She looked up at Luke. "Pray for us, okay? I don't always love very well, and I can't save my family anyway. Only Jesus can."

"Yes, of course," Luke said, meeting her gaze. "You know I'll do that, and whatever else I can. Would it help if I tried to talk to Justin?"

Kellie shook her head vigorously. "No, please don't. I don't want him to feel betrayed by me talking to you about him."

Luke looked at her dubiously, convinced that he could have managed it in a way to make Justin feel unthreatened, but he didn't say so.

"I won't then." He continued to hold her gaze, and whispered, "I'm glad you told me, Kellie."

She didn't answer, so after a moment, he changed the subject.

"I noticed you're out of mourning now."

Kellie still wore her plain black crepe dress with black buttons, but her cuffs and collar were cream now, and she had a gold locket pinned at her Adam's apple. Instead of her black bonnet and veil, she sported a new straw bonnet lined in green velvet with green and navy ribbon that made her blue eyes pop.

"Yes. It was actually two years back in July, but I've been slow to get new things. It just hasn't been important."

"Do you still think about Nathan every day?"

Kellie nodded. She had stopped crying, and folded Luke's handkerchief back up. "It was hard to lose him, but mostly I'm grateful for the time that I did have him. I am incredibly blessed to have had him in my life. So I don't wallow when I think of him." Her lips turned up at the corners contentedly and Luke was fascinated by her perspective.

"What was he like?" he asked curiously. He'd never talked to Kellie about Nathan before, and Kellie seemed eager to share about him.

"He was boyish, playful. Amazingly kind and caring. And he really loved me a lot. We were only together just over a year before he left, and I know our love was never really tested, so all I have are happy memories. Because of him, I was able to leave the family I grew up with, and he was the one who had the idea that I may be able to find my brothers in the army rosters. I may not be here today with my family if it wasn't for him."

She wrapped her arms around herself and hugged her chest. "God has been so good to me to bring me here. So even though it's hard, I want to do my best with what He has given me, and I want to love my family well." She looked at Luke sheepishly. "But sometimes I need to get out of the house and come have a good cry."

"It sounds like things have gotten pretty serious though," he said as he stood up and offered Kellie his hand. She took it, and they began to walk back with her on his arm, talking comfortably together.

"Thank you for listening," she said, turning her bright blue eyes up to him, and he smiled and squeezed her hand on his arm.

"See, it wasn't so bad. Actually, I would be grateful if we could do this again sometime, so I can hear how things are going and how you are doing," he told her.

"I appreciate that, truly."

They reached the flat and he let her go, sticking his hands in his pockets.

"Take care, Kellie. You know I'm praying for you."

She thanked him again, and headed up the stairs.

Luke walked home deep in thought, praying and thinking through everything he had just heard. When he got home, he peeked into the drawing room and saw Elisan reading aloud to their parents. He bid them goodnight before heading up to his room.

At the top of the stairs, he stuck his head in his sisters' open bedroom door, where Rebecca was seated at the vanity patting some ointment on her hands. She turned when she saw him in the mirror.

"Did you have a good walk?" she called after him, so he came into the room and sat on the trunk at the foot of the bed.

"I did," he said and hesitated.

Rebecca could see that something was on his mind, so she waited.

"What would you think if I fell in love with Kellie?"

"Oh!" Rebecca exclaimed in surprise. His question came completely out of the blue and with all the transparency of their relationship of trust. She looked at her adored older brother, sitting on her trunk with innocence in his eyes, and in that moment she didn't think she could love him any more.

"Are you?"

"No, not yet. I think it would be pretty easy to do, though. I just got to thinking that it could be a good idea, and I was wondering what you thought."

"She is out of mourning now," Rebecca said slowly. "Honestly, I think she would be really good for you. Her faith is solid, and she's a compassionate person like you. She's mature and not dramatic like the girls at church."

Luke sat pondering for a few minutes. "The Hennessey girls aren't like that, but I've never felt that their personalities were right for me."

"Me neither. Has Kellie given you any indication that she would be interested?"

Luke shook his head. "She hasn't given me anything, no. But I don't think she would be against it. I'm more uncertain about what Justin will think."

That was the hot question, and Rebecca had already wondered it too. Justin seemed so volatile lately, and a misstep in a matter like this could be costly. Rebecca shook her head.

"I have no idea. He's been really unpredictable these days; it's hard to say how he'll take it."

"I've been friends with him for a long time," Luke said, thinking out loud. "I think if nothing else, he still respects me and will take me seriously. And he knows that I would not intentionally hurt anyone. But I don't know if he'll feel like he's losing her or be uncomfortable with a new kind of relationship with me."

"No matter what happens, it would change things between our families. It seems like a pretty big risk." Rebecca cocked her head. "Unless you're very sure about it."

"I actually think it could be good for all of us," Luke admitted confidently. "There is opportunity to strengthen the bond between our families and put me in a position to be more of an asset to them. If Kellie and I were together, I believe we could be a strong unit that would have more of a positive impact on all sides."

He waved his hands animatedly as he talked. Luke had made his mind up in the course of the short conversation, and was growing more excited. "You're right; it would almost certainly change things between him and me, though."

Suddenly, he stopped and looked at Rebecca. "Weren't you and Justin starting to fall in love before the war? What happened between you?"

Rebecca's face turned pink and she smiled, shaking her head. "Never mind, Luke. It doesn't matter now. Tonight is about you and Kellie."

Thankfully, Luke was too caught up in the thought of Kellie to give much concern to Rebecca's answer. "Well, maybe something will come of it yet. Anyway, I think I'll let Justin know I'm interested, and see how he reacts."

His eagerness made Rebecca's heart leap, but she had a nagging fear that Justin would not take kindly to the idea of Kellie turning her affections to his best friend. She listened to Luke prattle on for a few more minutes, and then shooed him off to bed.

She sat looking at her reflection in the vanity, astounded by the speed of his revelation and decision making. And in the back of her head, the thought crept in that made her heart flutter. If Kellie was taken care of, then Justin would be free again. And if Justin was free again, her long buried love would have the hope of new life. Now she just had to manage to not get ahead of herself—and somehow figure out how she was going to get any sleep that night.

-17-

Luke thought and prayed over his new idea for the next couple of days while he looked for an opportunity to speak to Justin. These days, they didn't necessarily have private time to talk, and he didn't want to bring it up when they might be interrupted. With his parents and Rebecca on his side to ensure everyone else stayed entertained in the drawing room, he was able to retire to the library after dinner on Friday night with only Justin.

"How have things been at home? I haven't had a chance to catch up lately," Luke said, settling into one of the large leather chairs by the fire. Justin took a deep breath and let it out, falling into the other chair and leaning forward to watch the flames in the hearth.

"I guess I'm pretty tired when I get home every night. Kellie has been pulling most of the load at home, but she's been healthy lately so we've been making it." He let out his breath. "I keep hoping I'll get one of the promotions at the docks. If I could get a foreman position, it would help so much. We could really use the extra money and the job wouldn't wear me out quite so much. But they haven't been in a hurry to move anyone up, so I don't know."

He had skirted the real question, and it wasn't unnoticed by Luke, who replied despite himself. "I heard about the Williams stevedores going on strike. Do you think Danford's will, too?"

"I don't think so," Justin replied steadily. "We're all watching it closely, of course, but we already make twenty-five cents a day more at Danford's than the others do. It's not much, but between that and Mr. Brewster being the manager, I don't think the Danford men will strike." Justin didn't mention that he wouldn't go on strike anyway, since he couldn't afford to miss even one day of work.

"I do hope you get moved up soon," Luke replied, pausing before veering back to the subject of Justin's family. "How has everyone been doing without Jed?"

Justin fingered the chain of his pocketwatch and stared at the flames licking the logs.

"It's not what anyone wanted to have happen," he finally said. "I wish he hadn't hurt Kellie like that. He made his own decision, though."

"I've been thinking about her. I know she had gotten close to him, and it must have been hard for her to lose him."

Justin didn't say anything or look at Luke, slumping sullenly in his seat.

Luke was struggling; he was looking for a lead-in to talk about Kellie, but Justin wasn't helping him out. He wracked his head but no ideas were coming, and for the first time that he could remember, Luke actually didn't know what to say. Eventually, he came to terms that there was nothing else to do but dive in.

"Justin, I'd . . . I'd like to talk to you about calling on Kellie."

Justin started and his eyes darted to Luke's face.

"You?"

Luke sighed and nodded. "Yes, I've been thinking about it, but I wanted to see how you felt about it before I did anything."

Justin sucked his cheeks in and appeared to be looking past his friend at nothing in particular. "You're asking my permission?"

"Do I need to? I'm asking as a friend to know what you think of it."

Justin shook his head. "No, you don't need my permission. I'm not her guardian."

Luke waited and let Justin process the request.

"If anybody hurts Kellie, I will murder them."

Luke tried not to laugh, but hearing Justin say that to his best friend was just funny. "If anybody hurts Kellie, I'll help you dispose of their body."

Justin chuckled and visibly relaxed. "Do you love her?"

It was the same question Rebecca had asked, and it was a legitimate one to raise. Luke took a deep breath and leaned forward in his chair.

"No, not like that. Loving someone is a choice, though, not something that happens to you. I didn't want to make that choice until after I had talked to you, since my friendship with you still comes first."

He rubbed his palms on his knees. "I'm not sixteen, Justin. I've thought about it, and I think Kellie and I would be good for each other. I don't know what she thinks about me yet, so I would take things slow to get an idea if she would be interested before I say anything to her."

Justin's brow furrowed pensively. "If you say something and she isn't interested, it would make things awkward between our families, and that would affect everyone."

"I know. It would be a risk we would all be taking, I guess, but like I said, I would be delicate about it."

Straightening up and looking at Luke, Justin responded truthfully. "I'd give you my right arm, Luke. I'd give you both of my arms, if you needed them. Kellie is like both of my arms and both of my legs to me, she means more to me than anything in the world, and you're the only person I know who would be deserving of her. If you wanted to call on her, or marry her, and she does too, then I would be happy for both of you."

Luke's face broke into a full grin then. "Thanks, man," he said, and Justin nodded.

A minute later, Luke added, "It might be some time until I say anything to her. Do you want me to let you know when I'm about to?"

"You don't have to, unless you want to."

Luke turned back to the fire and as the silence took over, he began considering what his next steps would be with Kellie.

Across from him, Justin's mind raced. There was no one else he knew that would be capable of handling a situation like this as delicately as he knew Luke could. Justin trusted Luke, and he didn't want to press further and risk offending his best friend by his interrogation. He pondered what a relationship between

Luke and Kellie would look like and how it would affect their families, especially his. If she got married, there was no doubt that Jack would leave, since there was no reason for him to stay on with just Justin the way things were. He wondered if Jed would ever return, and what the future held for their family. Jed was right; they had tried the experiment of living together, but the situation wasn't sustainable forever, and Kellie deserved to be with someone who would make her happy. He hadn't been doing a good job of taking care of her lately, but Luke would. In the end, Justin knew that Kellie would be in good hands with his best friend.

December 5, 1863

Justin made an effort to give Kellie a nice birthday, and she noticed and appreciated it. It fell on a Saturday, so he took the morning to bake a small cake and gave her money to get some new things for her wardrobe, since he had no idea how to pick anything out for her. If he was honest, he didn't know what she liked since she hadn't worn anything but black crepe since he met her and he wasn't even sure what her favorite colors were.

Jack actually helped with the dishes and brought in firewood without being asked, but he had a bigger gift planned. After lunch, he sat her down and performed what he knew was her favorite Robert Browning poem, *The Last Ride Together*, which he had memorized just for her. Kellie sat listening with tears rolling down her cheeks as she whispered the words along with him.

My last thought was at least not vain:
I and my mistress, side by side
Shall be together, breathe and ride,
So, one day more I am deified.
Who knows but that the world may end to-night?

Curled up with a blanket on the couch after supper the following week, Kellie asked Justin for her Bible, which she had left on the table. As he lifted it, a sheet of paper fell from inside the flap of the Bible, but when he bent down to pick it up, he stopped short.

Dear Kellie, he read in large childlike letters at the top of the page, and his eyes quickly swung down to the bottom. *Love, Jed*

Justin looked at the paper and his heart froze. For the space of several seconds, he stood holding the paper without reading it.

"You heard from Jed," he said flatly, glancing up at Kellie.

"Yes." Watching him, she reached out her hand for the paper.

"Why didn't you tell me?"

Kellie didn't answer right away as she slid the letter back into her Bible.

"I didn't think you'd want to know."

"Why wouldn't I want to know that my brother has been in contact with us?"

"With me," Kellie corrected. "The letter was to me."

Justin stood like a statue, blinking at her. "I don't have to know everything he said to you, but I would have thought you would have told me if you heard from him and knew he was still alive."

"I had no reason to believe you cared that he was still alive," Kellie said.

"What are you talking about? He's my brother! Of course I care," Justin declared, feeling affronted by her assumptions about him.

Kellie swallowed in annoyance. "You haven't talked about him since he left, and when we talk about him, you change the subject. I didn't think you would be happy about me being in contact with him."

"So I'm not part of the family anymore? I would have expected to receive the basic respect of being included in the family news, and I don't know why you think these things about me. I don't hate Jed any more than you do."

"I don't think you have any right to get irritated with me for not telling you. You don't tell anyone else anything, and I don't believe I'm required to report all of my correspondence to you," Kellie said tightly.

Justin stared at her, then turned on his heel and headed for the door.

"You always leave when you get upset, Justin. We can't work through anything when you always leave." Kellie's voice rose as Justin turned the handle.

"I can't think in here!" Justin exclaimed, and shut the door after himself.

Kellie sat with the Bible on her lap, not reading it, her head exploding with frustration. She had never gotten into a real fight with Justin before, and it stung, as well as scared her. What was going to become of all of them if they couldn't speak respectfully and honestly and trust each other?

After a while, she rose and peeked out the window, expecting to see the empty street, but was surprised to see Justin down below. He was pacing the frozen sidewalk in the frigid December air without his coat or hat, his hands shoved in his pockets. Occasionally he stopped and ran his fingers through his hair or rubbed his forehead, but he kept pacing for quite a long time. As she watched him, Kellie's heart softened, glad to see that he had not run off to Luke's again, although she had reason to believe that if he did that anymore, Luke would just send him back home.

When Justin opened the front door much later, he was quiet and mellowed, his nose and ears bright red from the cold. Kellie wordlessly handed him a hot cup of tea that she had already prepared, knowing that he would need it, and he came and stood in front of the fire to sip it.

"I'm sorry," he finally said in a low voice as he began to thaw. "I'm sorry that I gave you the impression that I don't care about Jed. I do care, quite a bit." He stopped to take a sip. "You're right, you aren't under obligation to report your correspondence with me, but I would like to know when you hear that he's alive and if he's well."

Kellie heaved a sigh. "I didn't mean to be disrespectful by not telling you. I only didn't want you to be angry at me for writing to him."

Justin almost turned and ended the conversation, but stopped.

"To be honest, I'm offended that you think that I'm that kind of person," he told her sincerely, and although she still felt like he had given her reason to think so, she was also appreciative of him expressing his emotions to her. It was such a rare occurrence, she didn't argue further.

"I'm sorry, Justin. I was wrong."

Justin nodded acceptance, then put his mug in the kitchen and went to bed.

By Christmas, Luke was ready to broach the subject of courtship with Kellie, but he chose to wait until after the new year so that the holidays wouldn't be marred should she be opposed to his advances. It was difficult to wait, because no one in the Young family put any effort into pretending like they felt like celebrating the holidays, and Luke wasn't in a position to offer the comfort that he wished he could to Kellie. Justin didn't even get a tree, though he quietly hung their stockings on the mantel for the candy and oranges everyone knew he'd gotten again.

Kellie sat in the Christmas Eve service holding her candle in the darkness with tears streaming down her cheeks, and Justin squeezed her hand, knowing that she was missing Jed and dying inside to see her so devastated.

When they got home that night, Jack went to bed without a word, and Justin stopped Kellie before she disappeared to her room.

"Come here," he whispered.

He pulled her close and just held her, not saying anything for a long time, because as usual, he didn't know what to say but he needed her as much as she needed him. So he held her, and they hurt together in the silence.

"Jesus came for all of this," he finally breathed. "He came for all the hurt and sadness and He redeems it, He makes it new. He makes us new. The gospel is still true, Kellie. It never stops being true."

Kellie nodded, the wet spot on Justin's shirt growing from her tears.

"But what about Jed? He doesn't know Jesus," she cried, and Justin didn't know how to respond.

"He has the Bible, and he knows how to read. There's always hope."

Christmas is about hope, Justin thought. The hope that the little babe in the manger brings to the hurting world every year, because every year the world needs Christmas. And this year he and Kellie needed it more than ever, the reminder that God became man and He lived among them and took on all the pain, the reminder that He came to redeem it and one day make all things new.

Jesus didn't come among festive celebrations in brightly lit extravagance. He came in the cold dark quiet to the lower west side, so to speak, to cramped quarters where hurting hearts looked to Him and believed that God truly is good, and that Jesus is His tangible expression of deep love. Justin leaned into the truth, reached out for a glimmer of hope and grasped it and held on for all he was worth, because he needed Christmas, and true Christmas never disappoints.

-18-

January 20, 1864

"Deacon Hennessey is under the weather this week," Reverend Dinsmore announced, turning to Elisan at the breakfast table one morning in January. "Do you think you could help me at the camp today?"

The reverend had been visiting Camp Douglas, a Union prison camp on the south side of Chicago, since October. His most faithful deacon, Mr. Hennessey, joined him taking supplies to the inmates and holding Bible studies in the chapel every Wednesday morning, and they continued their mission of reaching out in love to the prisoners throughout the winter.

None of the rest of his family had ever accompanied them, but Elisan had read in the newspaper that the camp was a point of concern to residents of the surrounding areas; the noise, smell, and disease were bad enough, but the fear of escaped convicts roaming the neighborhood was another, and the residents did not feel safe living in such close proximity to so many Confederate soldiers. Many in the church even questioned the reverend's decision to spend such a large amount of resources on Confederate prisoners when there were so many other, more deserving, citizens of the city in need of aid. Nevertheless, he continued to go, and Elisan appreciated his dedication and willingness to love the most unlovable.

Her eyes widened with surprise at his request. "Me? What would you need me to do?"

"Mostly pass out the food from the crates. I would like to spend most of my time in the chapel, if possible. There are a few men there that I've been teaching who have been leading Bible studies throughout the week, and I don't want to take my time from them. If you finish that, there are usually some who want to dictate letters to be sent for them. They closed the sutlers and sale of paper and stamps to the prisoners last month, so many of them appreciate that especially."

Elisan almost asked her father if it was safe for her to be there, but she stopped herself at the irony of the question when she had been the one who had traipsed into an actual Confederate camp. If her father asked her, then she knew it was because she could and would be of help, and furthermore, he knew that she of all people had more of a soft spot for Confederates than nearly anyone else at church. Who else should he possibly ask but her?

So after breakfast, she put on her gray work dress and warm stockings while Titan helped the reverend load crates into the wagon, coming out into the frigid cold in her heaviest wool cape, bonnet, and thick mittens. When Titan finished, he headed off to school and Reverend Dinsmore helped her up into the wagon.

He took vegetables and fruit to the camp every week out of sheer generosity, as the Confederate prisoners received far better rations than Union soldiers received in Confederate prisons, but it was still prison food, and the reverend had seen that scurvy was a problem nonetheless.

"There's a square in the camp where the chapel, post office, and sutlers are, and I pull the wagon right up by the chapel. The chapel belongs to the YMCA, and there are services there on Sundays, but they let us use it on Wednesdays. There are three young men who have been of great help to me in the ministry, so I spend some time discipling them and praying together. I'm sure you'll be fine, as the place is well guarded, but you'll know where to find me if you need me," Reverend Dinsmore said as he drove along. "I'll need you to unload the crates and distribute the vegetables to whoever comes. When you finish, the men who want their letters written will be waiting in the reading room next to the chapel."

"Does the YMCA do anything to help the prisoners? Or any other churches or organizations?" Elisan asked, and her father nodded.

"I work closely with the post chaplain, Reverend Tuttle, and there's a relief society that comes on Saturdays, but there are so many prisoners that no one group can help everybody. We all just do what we can, and my main purpose is discipling the men who lead the Bible studies. There are far more men there than Reverend Tuttle can shepherd alone."

Elisan found the camp as her father described it. Her presence turned heads as quickly as she had feared it would, but she was more used to it this time and felt safe with him near. In the square, he alighted and began helping set her up for her work. She was bent over a crate of carrots when she was shocked to hear her own name.

"Well, if it isn't Miss E-liiii-suuun Dinsmore," a southern accent drawled, accenting the long 'I' of her name slowly.

Elisan straightened up, flabbergasted, to find Pick sauntering towards her. He appeared far less elegant than the last time she had seen him, his uniform torn and shabby. He sported a scraggly beard that had replaced the whiskers, but he removed his kepi and bowed low and dramatically. He'd obviously lost weight since she met him, and it made him look lankier and taller than she remembered.

Elisan bristled, feeling the indignation from their last meeting crawl up the back of her neck. Glancing around, she looked for a place to hide but didn't find any.

"Pick," she said politely when he stopped before her.

He held his hat in his hand, showing off a headful of thick, wavy straw-colored hair, and his brown eyes danced.

"I can't believe I didn't put two and two together," he said, indicating her father. "I suppose I never imagined that a man of such a calm and gentle disposition would have a daughter as fiery as yourself."

Reverend Dinsmore's merry laugh rang out, but Elisan glared at Pick peevishly.

"In case you don't recall, one of us displayed propriety the last time we met, and your mother is the one for whom I am horribly embarrassed," she retorted.

Pick crossed his arms and grinned obnoxiously at her. "Still all high and mighty, with your Yankee spunk. You know, you haven't changed one bit, so I can only assume you haven't been married."

Elisan stared at him, agog at his nerve. "I don't believe my marital status is any of your business. I came to help my father, not to have a reenactment of our last visit." Elisan turned towards the crates.

"Here, let me help you." Pick reached over her for the crate she was about to pick up, and she was tempted to stomp on his foot.

"I can pick up a crate, thank you," she growled.

Reverend Dinsmore set down the one he was holding and turned to Pick. "Sergeant Thomas, if you can finish helping Elisan, I'll go ahead and get started in the chapel."

"Certainly. I would love to be able to catch up with an old friend," Pick replied cheerfully, and Elisan muttered, "We aren't friends." With horror, she watched her father walk away, leaving her alone with Pick.

"Well then," Pick said, far too happily, "Let's get started. You know, I've never met anyone named Elisan before."

Elisan gave Pick a side eye. "I can assure you, I've never met anyone named Pick before, either," she returned saucily.

"It's short for Pickens," Pick announced, even though Elisan didn't ask and didn't care. "Pickens Thomas. I'm named for my mother's old butler that my grandfather kept when she was growing up in England. Isn't that a hoot? I never met him, of course, but apparently he was always a good friend to her when she was a little girl. I always thought it was terribly funny."

"Is anyone else from the 5th North Carolina here?" Elisan asked, changing the subject. "How did you end up here, anyway?"

"I was captured at Bristoe, but the Yank generals didn't really make us privy to their decision making process," Pick said. "There's a few of us here, but I don't think you knew anyone else. If you're looking for Sergeant Blake, he's dead."

Elisan's hand flew to her mouth. "He is? I'm so sad to hear that."

"Yup." Pick nodded. "He was killed at Chancellorsville, and it was ghastly. He never saw the bullet that hit him, but it was really awful. It just wrecked his brother Charlie. He saw it happen and hasn't been the same since, and after a while the army just sent him home because he wasn't good for anything more."

Elisan stood sorrowfully, taking in the news. "He kissed me," she murmured distantly.

Pick's lips turned up into a smile. "He sure had a way with ladies. I'm afraid to tell you that he kissed a lot of pretty girls in the army. But he was a good man, Tom, always real respectful. He never took them to his tent like everyone else did."

Elisan assumed that "everyone else" meant Pick himself, but she didn't say so. "He was a good man," she said softly. "I'm sorry to hear he's gone."

"Lots of good ones are gone." Pick paused, standing quietly.

"I never did understand how he could be friends with you and why his good manners didn't rub off on you. You should learn a thing or two from him," Elisan continued.

Pick looked at her for several seconds, and her eyes dropped under his gaze. After a minute, he grinned at her. "Actually, I converted last year, and I'm not that way anymore," he admitted. "You may be surprised to learn that I meet with your father every week, and he's waiting for me in the chapel now, when we finish this."

Elisan couldn't contain her shock. "Why didn't you say so?" she demanded.

"Because I deserved it," Pick replied casually. "And the way you get indignant like that is fascinating to watch. Truly mesmerizing."

Elisan stared at him. "I am not here for your entertainment, and my emotions are not your plaything," she snapped.

Pick laughed and turned, grabbing the last crate, and he and Elisan began handing out the vegetables side by side to the waiting inmates. "Yup, every bit as spunky as I remember," he chortled.

"You have no more access to me, Mr. Thomas," Elisan informed him evenly.

"It's Sergeant Thomas now, actually."

Elisan rolled her eyes at him. "I'm not going to call someone a sergeant who is so in the army of an illegitimate country."

Pick seemed to be more amused than offended and good humoredly worked beside her. A moment later, he brightened up and looked at her. "Hey, how's old Jack doing? Do you know where he ended up?"

"Yes, he's here in Chicago with his family. I'll let him know you're here and see if he'll want to come visit. He's been getting an education, and I think he's doing all right."

"Would you? It sure would be good to see him. I'm glad he got out when he did, he was too young for all of that mess."

Elisan fell silent and finished her work without further conversation, leaving for the reading room when all the empty crates had been stacked back into the wagon. She found a handful of men waiting for her there, and was kept busy writing the letters they dictated until her father was ready to go almost two hours later. He came out of the chapel with Pick and two other prisoners and waited as she gathered her stack of letters to drop at the post office on the way home.

"It was nice seeing you again, Miss Elisan," Pick said with a tip of his hat. "I'm sorry for teasing you, and I promise I'll be more polite next time."

"You really think there's going to be a next time?" Elisan asked him, astonished at his presumption.

"I can only hope so," he said, offering his hand. She ignored it, and taking her father's, swung up into the wagon.

"You and Sergeant Thomas had trouble speaking to each other in normal tones today," Reverend Dinsmore said after they rolled out of the camp. "I take it you met before?"

"Yes," Elisan said shortly. "He's in Jack's company and was horribly rude to me when I was there."

The reverend's eyebrows rose. "I didn't realize that. I suppose I don't usually ask what regiment everyone is in. Well, Sergeant Thomas has been invaluable to me. He leads Bible studies in the camp every week and has such a mature understanding of Christian theology for being a fairly young believer. It comes from being so devoted to the Word and the amount of time he spends in it."

"I'm dumbfounded, to say the least," Elisan answered, a little annoyed at her father for calling him sergeant. "I believe I've been exposed to a completely different side of Pick than you have."

"Perhaps so. After all, I'm not a pretty young lady."

"Oh, you don't actually think that's why, do you?" Elisan exclaimed, aghast. "I would have thought gentlemen would use better manners with ladies, not worse."

"I'm afraid it's possible, my dear, as men have all sorts of reactions to young ladies. I wouldn't let Sergeant Thomas get to you, though. Despite what he wants to make you believe, he's a good man."

Elisan didn't reply and was quiet the rest of the way home, convinced that her father was mistaken and most likely manipulated by Pick.

-19-

February 7, 1864

Over the course of the months since he'd spoken to Justin, Luke took subtle opportunities to spend time with Kellie and make himself available to her. He was never overt in his gestures, but every couple of weeks he tried to make a conversation happen between them, whether walking together when the group went out or seating himself next to her at dinner.

As a result of the distance Justin created in all of his relationships as he fell into a deeper depression, Kellie became more and more open with Luke. She became his main source of information on how things were going at the Youngs', and he earned her trust little by little by listening well and not trying to fix the troubles she shared.

He came calling on her for the first time on a cold snowless Sunday afternoon in early February, inviting her on a carriage ride with just him. Justin realized that this was Luke's moment as the door closed behind them and Luke escorted her down the stairs. Luke helped her into the carriage and tucked the lap blanket around her, then hoisted himself up next to her and picked up the reins.

"Where are we going?" she asked.

"Nowhere in particular. I just wanted a chance to talk to you," Luke said with a grin as the horse pulled the carriage forward. He was in no hurry and allowed the conversation to progress naturally as he listened to her tell about her week and they chatted about the books they were reading and even the morning's sermon.

An hour was almost up and they were nearing the apartment again before he revealed the reason for the outing.

"Kellie, I am interested in calling on you," he said, pulling the reins to stop the carriage and turning to face her. "I've been thinking about it for a little while, and I don't want you to answer today so you have time to think about it too. Unless you already have."

"No," Kellie admitted, "I haven't."

Luke nodded. "I don't think it's fair for men to have time to think things through and then expect women to be able to give an answer right away. So I would like for you to have that opportunity, and we can talk about it as much as you need to, before you give an answer. Would you do that?"

"Yes, I'll do that," Kellie said, thinking about Justin and wondering how he would feel about Luke calling on her.

Luke smiled at her then, and drove around the corner to drop her off at her door. Kellie didn't move right away, so Luke gave her a minute as the wheels turned in her head. She looked up at him with her sapphire blue eyes, opened her mouth, shut it, and opened it again with a little bob of her head.

"Why?"

"Because you're the prettiest girl I know," Luke said, his eyes dancing because he knew that she knew his character better than to think that was really why.

"Luke, be serious."

Luke inhaled and let it out. "Well, a lot of reasons, but the main reason I'd like to call on you is because I want to."

Kellie looked amused, and Luke continued. "I want to spend more time with you, talking with you, learning from you and being a blessing to you. I think we fit well together and I would like to learn to love you and see if you can learn to love me." He pursed his lips thoughtfully then looked up at her. "I'm not in a hurry, and I am comfortable with taking our time to work through our needs and our families' needs. But I believe you are just the woman I've been waiting for, and I want to make myself available to you."

Deep in thought, Kellie looked past him as she considered his words. After a few minutes, she blinked and looked back at him.

"Those are good reasons," she said softly.

Kellie found Justin on the couch awaiting her arrival when she quietly entered the flat a few minutes later.

"How was your ride?"

"Very pleasant, thank you," Kellie said, taken aback by his initiating the conversation. She put her hat and gloves in her room with her cloak before joining Justin on the couch.

"Luke asked if he could start calling on me," she told him without wasting any time, and could tell by the look on Justin's face that he was already privy to the information.

"What did you tell him when he talked to you?" she asked once she realized that Luke had done so.

"I told him that if it was what both you and he wanted, that I would be happy for you."

"Oh. Thank you."

"What did you tell him?" Justin asked her back.

"He didn't want me to answer today, and told me to take some time to think about it." Kellie leaned her elbow on the back of the couch as she sat turned sideways, facing her brother. "What would you do if I got married again?"

"Oh, I haven't thought about that," Justin said dismissively. "Don't let us hold you back; we'll figure something out. At least we would still be in Chicago together, so I wouldn't really be losing you."

Kellie shook her head. "No, I wouldn't leave you now. I never even thought about marrying again before today. I would never have considered it if it was anyone but Luke, and I appreciate how respectful he is being about the idea."

Justin tenderly placed his hand on hers. "I want you to be happy and I'll trust your decision, whatever you decide."

His words meant a lot to her, and she thanked him. He had barely talked to her for months, and she was grateful for him now and his reassurance when she needed it. She leaned to rest her head on his shoulder, and they fell into their separate thoughts as Kellie began to work through in her mind everything that courting, and marrying, Luke would mean to her, to him, and to everyone else around them.

The following Sunday, the sun was out and the temperature rose several degrees, so at church, Kellie asked Luke if he would be available to take a stroll with her that afternoon and he quickly agreed. After Sunday dinner, he walked to the apartment and they started out together.

"Luke, there are some things I need to talk to you about before we make a decision about courting," Kellie began. She glanced up at him briefly, then back to the street. "I think there are some important things to consider. I've never talked to anyone about this, and I would never have thought that I would be talking to you about it, but I think I need to."

She took a deep breath and pursed her lips as he listened intently.

"Nathan and I were married for a year before he left," she said. "When he died, he left only me behind. I . . . I don't know why. And it's possible that it would be the same if I married you."

Luke stopped walking as he understood what she was telling him. "You mean . . . "

"I mean that a year is a long time to not have a family," Kellie said softly, hugging her arms across her chest. "I never thought I would get married again, so I didn't think it would come up. I don't want you to give me an answer today, because I've had time to think about it, and I want you to have time to think it through too. It's not a small matter."

Luke appreciated that she was returning to him the respect that he had granted her, and agreed to think about it, smiling reassuringly at her.

"It could be that God spared you so that you wouldn't be left alone with a small child," he suggested.

"I've thought about that, and you could be right. But I don't want you going further in a relationship with me without coming to terms with all of the implications that could affect your life."

Luke looked down at her curly black head compassionately.

"What about you? Have you come to terms with it?"

Kellie swallowed hard and was silent as Luke gave her space to form a response.

"I've lost a lot of things. In some ways, it was just one more thing that was taken from me, just one more thing that I had to let go of. But it's a different kind of loss, and in some ways, that made it harder. I can't talk about these things that I've been through without talking about the goodness of God, because He was always abundantly gracious to me and I never walked alone."

She glanced up at him. "You have to understand, Luke. I never even talked to Nathan about it, let alone Justin. But I want you to be able to make an informed decision."

"Thank you, Kellie."

In that moment, Luke realized that he would never be able to take away her pain and be her hero. He would not be a knight in shining armor rescuing Kellie from the wounds of her past, and he embraced the realization that that was not his job or his calling. Jesus alone was her rescuer, and Luke knew that his role was to love her, to be joined to her and walk beside her in her pain and not to try to erase it. So before the conversation was over, he had made his decision, but he honored her request to not make an answer right away. In doing so, he was acknowledging the gravity of the cross he was choosing to bear with her.

"Is your answer to me dependent on my answer to you? Or is there more that you're considering?"

Kellie tilted her head for a moment before answering. "No, I think that's all. If we are able to work through this, I don't have anything else that would prevent me from accepting. I'm obviously concerned about what my brothers will do without me, but I assume you've already thought that through."

"I have, but ultimately that is up to them and to you. I'm not in a hurry to change everything overnight, so we'll just have to give it time and see how things play out."

"Something's going to happen sometime," Kellie stated. "It's not going to stay the way things are right now. It can't. I don't know what the repercussions will be, though."

"We'll take it one step at a time," Luke said as they reached the bakery. "We can't know what your brothers will choose to do or how God will answer our prayers." He stuffed his hands in his pockets and tipped his head to look into her eyes. "Thank you for the things you talked to me about. It means a lot to me that you did."

Kellie nodded but her eyes were sad as she headed up the stairs to the apartment, and Luke knew how much it had taken out of her to have to face her wounds again. He lingered for a minute, thinking, then sighed and turned toward home.

Justin caught Luke alone in the hall after dinner that Friday night.

"What happened the other afternoon? Kellie came home crying, and she went straight to her room."

Luke stopped to look at Justin, biting back a sarcastic response.

"She wouldn't mind if you asked her things yourself, you know. She probably would have talked to you about it."

Justin was silenced, and hung his head. "I'm sorry."

"It wasn't me," Luke told him anyway. "She was working through things from her first marriage."

"Has she given you an answer yet?"

"Not yet; we're still figuring out all the implications of a courtship before we make a final decision," Luke said, leaning against the wall.

Justin nodded. "What do you think? Does it look like you'll be able to work it out?"

"Yes, it does. I was hoping to catch her tonight for a minute, actually."

"I can get her for you," Justin said, opening the drawing room door, and shortly, Kellie came out to where Luke waited.

"Hi. I didn't want to take you away from everyone tonight," he said. "I just wanted to give you this." He pulled a thin letter from his pocket and handed it to her, and after glancing at it, she looked at his face.

"Is this your answer?"

"It is."

"So you're going to make me wait for it, then?"

Luke grinned and shrugged. "You can read it now if you like. I was afraid that if I tried to say it to you, everything would come out different from how I intended it. By writing it, I was able to take my time."

"You are not known to be a person who misspeaks," Kellie said, smiling at him as she put it in her pocket. "I'll read it tonight, and we can go spend time with the family now."

Luke reached over and opened the door before following her into the drawing room.

Before the Youngs left that night, Reverend Dinsmore pulled Justin aside.

"My office door is always open for you, Justin," he said sincerely, pausing to let the invitation sink in. "If you need prayer or to talk, please come. I know you're hurting, and if you're willing, I'd like to meet with you."

Justin saw his concern, and he felt comforted. He'd known all along that he could have gone to the reverend at any time and he could not in the least articulate why he had held back. He nodded acceptance, inwardly vowing to make himself take up the offer.

That night in her room, Kellie sat on her bed in her nightgown as a candle flickered on her bedside table. She pulled her knees to her chest, and carefully opened Luke's letter.

Dearest Kellie, she read, and smiled to hear his voice in her head calling her that.

Your honesty and vulnerability to me is not something that I take lightly, and I treasure your confidence as I would a sacred gift that I protect and respect. I realize that for you to consider my offer meant reopening scars that for you had been lain aside and buried—and that now they are reawakened and are requiring you to reface them.

I have not known a fraction of the loss that you have, and to that degree, I believe I make a poor friend, companion, and lover for you. The depths of my understanding of what you have endured and how God has met you in it is limited, and it is not something I can recreate of my own willpower. However, my respect for you and appreciation for the way that God has carried you through each trial is deep. You are an extraordinary woman who serves an extraordinary God, and although my qualifications are meager, I present myself to you desiring to be your humble companion. The loss you have borne was not your choice, but it is mine. I choose you, and to walk beside you and to sit with you in the pain, because I can do nothing else.

I am
Your humble servant,
Luke

Kellie put the letter down, pressed her eyes against her knees, and cried.

February 17, 1864

A month after her visit to Camp Douglas, Elisan apprehensively accepted another request from her father to return to the camp to assist him. She didn't mind the work, and actually enjoyed the letter writing, but she was reticent to see Pick again and hoped to do a better job of avoiding him this time. Her hopes were dashed, however, when Reverend Dinsmore pleasantly asked Pick to help her again and he readily obliged. She worked quietly next to him and he kept his promise to be more polite, but she still found it awkward to be serving next to a slave owner who had said such terrible things about her.

"It looks cleaner here now than the last time I came," she said after several minutes of silence.

Pick glanced over, obviously pleased to hear her start a conversation.

"We finished putting the new floorboards in, and it raised everyone up out of the mud," he said. "We all keep each other accountable about personal cleanliness too, because we're trying to keep disease from spreading."

"You all have to work here?"

"If we want to. The powers that be pay us in tobacco and clothes for doing maintenance and building more buildings. So we don't have to work if we don't want to, but it gives us something to do. We have Bible studies on Tuesdays and Thursdays, and go to chapel on Sunday." Pick began stacking empty crates back into the wagon behind her. "It's not a fun place to be, but it's exciting to see God working. I've seen several men get saved and we all dig into God's Word together, and that keeps us going."

"So you really have changed," Elisan said meekly, and Pick couldn't hide his smile.

"Thankfully, yes."

"Tell me about that. Did you get saved in Virginia?"

"I sure did. I was hanging around with all those church boys, Tom and Charlie and the others, and they kept bringing me to chapel every Sunday, and I guess it all finally got through my thick skull."

"What did your parents think about your conversion?" Elisan asked. "Did they take you to church growing up?"

Pick took a crate from her and stacked it in the wagon. "Well, you know, they always went to the Episcopalian Church since my mother's English, but it seemed mostly to be for appearances. I'm actually not sure how close to God they really are, but they seemed to like that I turned my life around."

"If your father is North Carolinian, how did he meet your mother? I didn't know she's not a southerner until you told me about your name."

"He is. He met my mother when he was at Cambridge. My family has owned land and businesses in Carolina for centuries, so of course he returned to work with my grandfather and brought her back. I was going to carry on the family business too, but I'm not sure how things are looking now with the war. Confederate money isn't doing well, you know."

"Are you close with your parents?"

Pick cocked his head and nodded. "Tolerably well, I'd say. I'm the only one left, so we're closer now."

"You don't have any siblings?" Elisan asked with surprise.

"I did, but my sister Evangeline died when she was sixteen."

Pick had finished the crates, and Elisan knew that he was supposed to go to the chapel, but he still stood by the wagon, running his finger along the backboard, happy to answer all of her questions.

"I'm so sorry. Was that hard on you?"

Pick glanced at her and back at the backboard. "Pretty hard."

"I'm sorry," Elisan said again.

"You have siblings?" he asked her in return.

"Yes, four of them, but they aren't 'fiery,' just me. They're good people."

Pick looked amused. "So they're boring then."

"They aren't boring, but I do know this, if they knew the things you've said to me, they would not understand why I'm standing here talking to you."

"Why are you standing here talking to me?"

Elisan stopped short, trying to think of an answer, and realized that she didn't know. "I really shouldn't. You've never even apologized to me. I need to go write letters anyway."

"If I apologize, will you stay?"

"No. But I don't know how you sleep at night without clearing your conscience like that," Elisan said.

Pick stopped rubbing the wagon. "I didn't know you were interested in my sleeping habits," he teased, and feeling annoyed, Elisan turned to go.

"Wait," Pick called, and reached out a hand to her shoulder to stop her. She looked at his hand touching her, and wriggled away with a look of horror on her face as if she'd had a scorpion on her.

"Elisan. I'm sorry," he said, and she could see he truly meant it. "I behaved abysmally, so much so that I won't even ask you to forgive me. But the way I treated you was disgusting, and I embarrassed you and Tom in front of everyone, and it was abominable of me to speak of you and to you the way I did. And you're right, if it weren't for the grace of God, I wouldn't sleep at night, because I don't deserve it."

"I forgive you," Elisan said.

"I wasn't done yet!"

"I think that was enough. It convinced me to forgive you, and I need to go."

Pick shrugged. "Okay then, thank you. I'll see you later."

Elisan left him and headed to the reading room, where she found a few of the same men from last time gathered. She smiled at them and took a seat, pulling sheets of writing paper out of her sack.

"I'm sorry I'm late, but let's get started," she said.

She enjoyed hearing their dictation, because it gave her a far more intimate peek into the men themselves than she would ever get if they were talking to her. Her favorites were the married men writing to their wives, because even though their letters sometimes made her blush, the maturity of their love was far more romantic than the fluff that the unmarried men wanted to send to their lovers. The way that they tried to downplay their suffering was sweet and amusing, but once in a while there was a complainer who didn't mind laying out the truth of his situation, and Elisan learned a lot from those letters as well.

When her father helped her into the wagon later, Elisan turned to Pick.

"I'll see you next week," she said, and Reverend Dinsmore and Pick both turned to hide their smiles.

She began accompanying her father every week after that; some weeks she barely saw Pick when he spent most of the morning in the chapel, and didn't really mind since he was so much of a distraction to her purpose for being there. He was annoying, always smiling at her and expecting her to act like they were friends although he never really stopped teasing her. But she kept coming back for the letters, and because her heart ached for the men's living conditions and she wanted to do what she could to help.

Inwardly, she was fascinated by the juxtaposition of how she could find southerners so sweet and endearing—Pick excluded—and yet be so wrong in their beliefs on the equality of human beings. She couldn't figure it out, but she couldn't stop coming once she had seen their suffering, unable to turn away from it just like her father.

As a result, her bond with him grew stronger as they served together every week and shared the burden of the ministry. Traveling to and from the camp every week, they chatted about the men they both knew and the Bible studies, and discussed the news of the camp as commanders, rules, and living conditions changed and then changed again.

Reverend Dinsmore was proud of her, for her resilience and work ethic, and he could not be more pleased to have the company of his youngest daughter every Wednesday. For all the horror of the place, their Wednesday treks to Camp Douglas became something they all looked forward to every week; for Reverend Dinsmore, Elisan, and certainly for Pick.

-20-

Just as he had hoped, Luke's new relationship with Kellie allowed him to begin spending a significant amount of time with the Youngs and gave him access in their home that he hadn't had since before Justin's siblings came. Everyone appreciated his presence, as he brought with him a tranquility that they each desperately needed, and the evenings that he was around, their home was peaceful and free from conflict. He had a way about him that made each of his friends feel valued, and the joy that his attention brought to Kellie was healing for her and appreciated by her brothers. Although Justin and Jack's conflicts didn't cease, they became fewer the more that Luke was around and the less that Justin cared enough to engage.

It was difficult for Luke and Kellie to talk openly in the tiny flat when the objects of their concern were always around, and it was still too cold for regular walks. Kellie began spending Sunday afternoons with Luke in the reverend's library, where she could be free to unload her heart without fear of being overheard.

"I don't know what I would do without you these days," she told Luke. "I think better when I can talk through things, and I don't have anyone at home who will engage."

Luke sat opposite her with his coffee in his hands, fingering the handle of the cup. "I don't know what to make of it. I've never seen Justin this depressed before. He's obviously struggling, but you can't make someone open up, and if he isn't willing to talk about it and let us help him, there's not much we can do."

"Sometimes I think I'm not doing enough," Kellie admitted softly. "Maybe I need to try harder, or maybe I did something to make him stop trusting me."

Immediately Luke sat up and leaned forward, looking her in the eye.

"Stop," he said, gently but firmly. "You cannot blame yourself for his choices, and you have to remember he still adores you. You're doing enough, and you can't put the weight of his struggles on yourself." It wasn't the first time that Luke had to remind her that she wasn't at fault, and he would be there the next time she forgot, to tell her again.

"He's so uptight and tense these days," Kellie said, letting out a deep sigh. "Sometimes he goes straight to bed, and other times he just sits with his Bible all evening, but he never wants to do anything and is always peevish at Jack and closed with me."

She remembered Christmas, and how Justin's words had been so meaningful and full of hope to her, and she vowed to herself to keep loving him through whatever it was he was struggling with, choosing to believe that one day God would bring restoration to their home.

"I know that Justin really believes that our only hope for healing is in Jesus," she murmured. "I'm sure that he probably needs us to keep reminding him of that, keep giving him hope, when he has trouble seeing for himself."

"The sermon today did that too," Luke said, relaxing back into his chair and taking a minute to think through what they had heard that morning.

Across from him, Kellie brightened. "I'm so glad you brought that up, because I wanted to talk about that too. The story of Hagar is my favorite story in the Bible, and I love hearing it again. How the slave woman and her son were sent away into the wilderness and how God met her there, and she knew that in her rejection and abandonment, she was seen. I always related to Ishmael growing up. Whether or not my aunt intended it, I was often made to feel that I was like the illegitimate older child and that since I wasn't the promised child, I didn't belong. To be told that God sees me, a little orphan nobody, and comes and meets with me where I am, in my wilderness—it always resonated deeply with me."

Luke listened enraptured, and he wanted to capture the joy on Kellie's face in a bottle. He could see that God *had* met with Kellie through that passage in the Bible, and her spirit glowed from even the memories.

"I used to read the story every time I was down," Kellie finished. "It is so humbling, and powerful." She paused, then looked up at Luke, who was listening in reverence. "You're right; it's a message of hope that everyone can rest in, and I think Justin is in the depths of deep rejection right now."

"God showed His great mercy too, not just His grace. Hagar may have been a slave and thrown out, but she had a part in getting to that place herself. She wasn't innocent, but God came to her in gentleness, not condemnation, even blessing her and her son," Luke added thoughtfully.

"We were never innocent." Kellie's voice dropped. "We are all children of the slave woman, born in sin, but we look to the Child of promise, Jesus, the Son of the free woman and He makes us free. 'He who the Son sets free is free indeed.'"

Luke loved listening to Kellie talk about the Bible since she read it not just as an educational tool but had encountered God Himself in its pages, and he found that she constantly challenged him. Standing up, he retrieved a Bible from the shelf and returned to his seat to settle in for his favorite part of the week: growing deeper in love with the Word of God, and growing deeper in love with Kellie.

As winter finally came to an end, Luke was quick to revive the evening walks with his sisters, oblivious to how complicated the simple exercise had become for them. Since he was always paired with Kellie now, Rebecca was stuck walking alone with Justin if she came. That would never do, and Rebecca's interest in going waned as a result, compelling Elisan to make more of an effort to join whenever possible, for her sake. But Justin hardly had the energy to join in anymore either, so then it seemed needless for Rebecca and Elisan to both come merely as chaperones for Luke. He encouraged them to come for the exercise since he preferred the feeling of it being a group outing, but he was clueless to the difficulties he was creating, and they did their best to keep it that way.

"It feels wonderful to get some fresh air," Kellie gushed to Luke as they headed down the stairs one Wednesday when both of her brothers and both of his sisters had decided to join. "It's lovely when the sun is still out at dinnertime again. Winters are terribly long here."

"That they are," Luke said as he reached the bottom step and offered her his elbow. "How was your day?"

"I had a letter from Jed, so it was a good day. I was sharing it with Justin and Jack a minute ago while they ate."

"Is it only the second one you've had from him?" Luke wasn't sure if he had missed hearing about any others in the six months since Jed left.

"Yes, and he didn't say much, but he said he loves me and thinks of me often, so that meant a lot."

"I'm sure it did. Did he at least say if he's well?"

"He said he was, and that he's been busy. I suppose he can't tell me much about where he's been or what he's doing since he's sending it across lines, but I'm overjoyed to hear from him anyway."

"I'm happy for you." Luke smiled down at her, admiring how pretty she looked in her steel blue and navy striped dress. She had piped it with navy cording at the seams and yoke and made braided navy buttons for the front, and it was becoming on her, even with her everyday gray cloak over it.

"I wanted to ask you, there's a benefit for the Christian Commission next Saturday, and I was wondering if you would go with me."

"Oh, how fun!" Kellie's eyes brightened at the first proper date Luke ever asked her on. "Is it a dance?"

"It is."

"I've never danced with you before," she said, as she quickly began reviewing what she had to wear and realized that she had nothing suitable. She had brought only black crepe with her from Maryland, and since she had come out of mourning, she had made herself two day dresses but no evening dresses.

"You haven't missed much, but it will be fun. I'm sure I could use the practice."

Kellie's mind drifted off as she figured how much money and time she had to make a dress with and which new styles she was most anxious to try now that she had the chance. She was out of mourning, sure, but she was also not a young debutante anymore, and her clothing would need to reflect the stage of life she was in. Still, she looked with anticipation to beginning her project first thing in the morning.

March 26, 1864

On Saturday next, Justin volunteered to cook dinner for himself and Jack so that Kellie could prepare for Luke's arrival. He was frying salt pork when Kellie came out of her room. He heard the rustle of her skirts behind him as she fluffed her skirt over her hoop so that the folds all fell just the right way. She straightened up again as Justin turned around, and he almost didn't recognize his sister.

She wore a deep burgundy taffeta evening dress that fell off her shoulders with a bodice tailored perfectly to her tiny waist. The skirt was gathered up around the bottom to rosettes made of the taffeta fabric, revealing a black lace underskirt that was repeated with the same black lace at the bosom. Her black curls were loosely arranged in a chignon, with a few falling free to frame her face, and she wore jadeite drop earrings. The work she had done on the dress was exquisite, and he was impressed by her skill and by the speed with which she had accomplished such a project, since he had seen her working on rosettes and carefully darting the bodice over the previous several evenings, finishing the hem only that morning.

Kellie glanced up to see Justin watching her as she reached for her black gloves.

"How do I look?" she asked with a smile.

"Stunning. I can't wait to see Luke's face when he sees you."

Kellie pulled her gloves on. "You should have come too. I'd like to see you dress up."

"Trust me, I can't compete with that. You're beautiful."

"Thank you."

Jack came out of the bedroom to see her, and leaned over the stove.

"Don't burn dinner," he said to Justin when he saw the crackling pork, sitting down at the table as Justin quickly turned back to the blackening meat.

"I like your dress, Kellie. I wish I was taking you."

"Oh, you're sweet. I would have been glad to go with you," Kellie said.

Luke's knock came at the door, and she moved to it.

The door opened to reveal Luke in the doorway in his best suit, a gray double-breasted silk vest that he never had reason to wear, and a red and silver striped cravat that Elisan had brought him from Paris. His hair was oiled, his face clean-shaven, and he held his black topper hat in one hand and a colorful nosegay of roses and wildflowers in the other.

Luke took one look at Kellie and his mouth came unhinged. "I think I asked the right girl after all. You look incredible."

Luke greeted Kellie's brothers and handed her the flowers. "These are for you. I wasn't expecting you to be ready already."

Kellie thanked him and set to work pinning the flowers into her sterling silver tussie-mussie, the flower holder that hung at her waist, carefully noting what each of them meant: loyalty, trust, friendship. In the center of the nosegay was one pink rose surrounded by three yellow ones, and Kellie stopped short. Yellow roses stood for friendship, but pink ones meant love, and just last month he had given her a nosegay with four roses, all yellow.

"I suppose I was just excited and got ready early," she said calmly. "Let me get my cloak and we can go."

Justin set a plate in front of Jack and forked some meat on to it.

"That smells good," Luke said, but Jack didn't seem as impressed.

"It's burned."

"Then you should have cooked," Justin said, glancing up at Luke. "Take good care of her, have her home by nine, and behave yourself with her," he instructed in mock seriousness, and Luke laughed as Kellie rejoined him.

"I think I can manage the first one, sir, but don't get your expectations up about the other two."

"Oh, honestly," Kellie said with a snort. "We'll be good, Papa," she promised, kissing Justin's cheek and leaving with Luke.

"I hope she marries him," Jack said, looking forlornly at his burned meat without touching it. "He makes her so happy."

"Yeah." Justin sighed softly. "It's nice to see her like this."

"Making herself new dresses and going to parties. She deserves it." Jack stood up and picked up his boots.

"Aren't you going to eat that?" Justin demanded, eying his brother's plate.

"Naw, I'm gonna take my chances at the saloon tonight," Jack said, and yanked his boot on.

Justin was still up and alone when Kellie returned late that night, pink-cheeked and smiling.

"Hi," he said, looking up from the ledger he was studying at the table. "Did you have a good time?"

"I did." Kellie untied her cloak and pulled her gloves off. "It's been a long time since I've been to something like that, and it was nice to get out again. And Luke really isn't as bad of a dancer as he made it sound."

"Did he kiss you?"

"Justin!" Kellie exclaimed.

"You wouldn't want to tell me?"

"Well, I don't know. It seems personal. But he didn't."

"Mmm." Justin stood up and got a drink of water from the dipper on the water pail. "I would have if I were him. You look amazing. And you don't need to tell me, I was only wondering when things were getting serious between you."

"Oh. I suppose it's always been serious, since Luke doesn't seem like he's just looking for a good time. He isn't that type of person, but he's said all along that he doesn't want to rush with me."

"For your sake, or his?"

"For everyone's," Kellie said pointedly, and headed for her bedroom.

"How are you, Elisan?" Pick drawled in his slow way as he approached her the following Wednesday.

She was just finishing loading the empty crates into the wagon and hadn't seen him yet that morning, but passing out vegetables had gone well without his help.

"I'm well, thank you. Have you been working on the new hospital? Some of the others were telling me about it, and it sounds like they're pretty proud of it."

"Yep, should be finished in a week or two. Helps to pass the time," Pick said, pushing his hat up on his forehead. "They've been making everyone do some work these days, moving the buildings, building fences and stuff. I don't mind, 'cause I was working anyway, but this new regiment is a lot stricter and no one likes that. They finally let Jack in to see me last week. He said they denied his visitor passes twice before, but it was good to see him and catch up with an old buddy. Anyway, look, I was wondering if you could post some letters for me."

"Yes, of course," Elisan said.

Pick reached into his pocket and pulled out a stack of letters.

"Are these for all your sweethearts back home?" she teasingly asked as her eyes widened.

"Oh, no. A couple of them are my buddy's." Pick leafed through the envelopes, reviewing the names of the addressees.

"For my mother, my aunt, my Nanny."

"Your nanny? She can read?"

"No, but my mother will read it to her."

"So she raised you?"

Pick didn't know what to think of Elisan's questions. "She took care of me my whole life, but my parents and tutors raised me too. But there's no one like her, and she really misses me."

Pick could see the look in Elisan's eyes, and he raised his hand as if to stop her train of thought in its track. "We really love each other, Elisan, and she's always been happy. Nanny is lucky to have the job she has."

Elisan's expression grew dangerously close to rolling her eyes. "Did she have her own children?"

"Yes, but they weren't around the house much," Pick said, and began looking for ways to end the conversation.

"Don't you think she would truly rather have been freed and taking care of her own children?"

"No, I don't," Pick said firmly. "Because then she would have been struggling to feed them and keep them clothed, and at our house they had everything they needed. And you," he added quickly as she inhaled to cut in, "don't have a reason to judge me when you've never even loved a Negro like I have."

"You love her because of all the things she did for you. Would you still love her if she just lived next door to you and never served you?"

Pick stuck his letters back into his pocket. "You have no idea what you're talking about," he told her tersely. "I'll give these to someone else to send."

He almost turned on his heel to walk away but paused once more. "I've never met anyone who is as quick to judge others as you are. You read Uncle Tom's Cabin and other propaganda, and suddenly think that you know what's best for the Negro, but you sit up here having no idea. You've never met my family or seen my property or met my slaves, yet you've made yourself my judge and jury."

"I'm sorry," Elisan said quickly before he left for good. "For offending you. I would love to meet them. But regardless, I don't believe that those who own other people should be the ones deciding what is best for those people, either. They should be the ones to decide for themselves what they need and what would help them."

Pick looked at Elisan dubiously and slowly said, "Nothing's as simple as you Yankees like to think, and marching your armies down south to force your way of thinking on a people and culture you don't understand isn't going to solve anything. If y'all win this war, you're going to find bigger problems on your hands that you aren't prepared to deal with."

He let Elisan think on that before adding, "You are welcome to come anytime, as long as you come with respect, treating my Nanny and my mother and neighbors as the intelligent people they are, to listen to them and learn and look for a feasible solution, not as stereotyped cartoons for you to force your agenda on."

Elisan paused thoughtfully, then nodded. "Thank you. When the war is over, I would be glad to come," and Pick knew she really would.

"There's a lot of southerners fighting in the war who would love to see slavery end, Elisan. If northerners were actually willing to help and not just spout propaganda at the cost of people's lives and the southern economy, it would go a long way."

"I appreciate the sentiment, truly. You've given me a lot to think about, but I can't help but think that you seek a solution on the terms that are beneficial to your time table and your economy, without regard to what has been done to the economies of the African countries that these slaves were kidnapped from," Elisan said, and Pick was astounded at the tenacity of the woman.

"The slave trade, you mean, that the United States government had several opportunities to oppose before they actually had the courage to do so? Do you realize that the international slave trade is illegal under the Confederate Constitution, but it was legal under the United States Constitution for many years? They don't talk about these things in the abolitionist newspapers, do they?"

"No." Elisan shook her head. "They don't. Where did you go to school?"

"William and Mary College, in Virginia." Elisan didn't say anything, so Pick chatted on. "If domestic relations had been friendlier, I think my parents would have made me go to Yale or Princeton, but they supported me when I asked to stay in the south and closer to home."

Pick knew that her friends were waiting for her to write their letters, but she was apparently having trouble pulling away.

"When did you finish?"

"In 1860, when I was eighteen. Spent a year working with my father before the war started. Where did you go to school?"

"I didn't get to go to college," Elisan said, her eyes dropping. "When you're the third daughter of a minister, there isn't room for it in the budget. I did go to the private school that Titan goes to until I was thirteen, but since then I've just done a lot of reading on my own and with my book society."

"Reading is good, as long as you're reading a variety of perspectives and supplementing your reading with interactions in the real world, like volunteering every week at a Confederate prison camp," Pick said, ending with a wink.

Elisan reached out her hand. "I'll post those letters for you," she said humbly, and he handed them over, watching her fondly as she took them and walked away.

-21-

April 1, 1864

"I want to talk to you about Jack's birthday," Kellie told Justin one spring evening when they were alone at home.

"Sure." Justin stood up from the couch and put his ledger away on the shelf before turning back to her. "What do you have in mind?"

"Well, I don't know if it's too much, but they're putting on *Hamlet* at the theater this month, and we could take him the night before his birthday. I think he would love it." Kellie turned the sock she was darning over in her hands, and satisfied with how it looked, tied off the end of her string.

Justin thought for a moment, and nodded. "He would love that. Will we still have cake or do anything else?"

"I thought maybe we could make him something nice for dinner and have cake on his actual birthday, but it can just be us. The show is a little expensive, so it's a big enough gift on its own."

"I think it's a good idea." Justin sat back down with his Bible in hand. "Why don't you take Jack to the show yourself, and spare the cost of my ticket. Then you can get him a nice piece of meat or something for dinner the next day."

Kellie frowned at him. "Are you sure? It would be nice to all go together."

"I'm sure. Shakespeare is lost on me anyway," Justin said, opening his Bible and ending the conversation.

The night of the show, Kellie wore her new evening dress, Jack dressed up sharply in his nicest church clothes, and they made a stunning pair at the theater. It was Jack's first time to ever go to one, and Kellie hadn't been in years, so they both hung on every word, enchanted by the production.

Jack gushed about it in the rented buggy the whole way home, and Kellie drank in the way his face lit up, the happiest he had been since Jed left. As they walked down the street from the livery, she gently hung onto Jack's offered elbow.

"Thank you for taking me tonight. It was special to do it with you," Jack said, turning his bright blue eyes down on her.

"I'm glad you liked it. Happy seventeenth birthday, little brother. We'll have cake tomorrow."

"Thanks," he repeated, but the next night, things were a different story.

"I'd like to have cake a little later," he told Kellie as they neared the end of dinner. "I could use a drink right now, but I'll be back after a while."

"Oh. Okay, we'll be here," Kellie said, visibly disappointed. Justin glared at him as he pulled his boots on and left.

"I can't believe him," Justin grumbled, standing up from the table. "He has so much nerve, leaving on his birthday like that."

Kellie gave a little sigh. "It will be fine, Justin, we can just have cake when he gets back."

But Jack didn't come back, even though Kellie fell asleep on the couch waiting for him. He hadn't returned in the middle of the night when she woke up and moved to her bed, and he didn't show up until the next morning when Justin was getting ready for work. By the time they heard Jack's boots treading heavily up the stairs, Justin was livid.

"Don't you dare say anything to him," Kellie warned as they waited for the door to open. "You are not calm enough to do this right now. Go to work, let him get some sleep, and we can talk about it tonight."

Justin didn't look happy about it, but he kept his mouth clenched tight as the door opened and Jack came in. His hair was disheveled and he was walking with effort.

"Come on, Jack. Let's get you to bed," Kellie said quietly, and she followed him to the room, shooing Justin toward the door as she went. She heard the door click behind her as Jack fell onto his bed and she began untying his boots.

"Are you mad at me?" he asked tiredly as his heavy eyes closed and he rubbed his forehead with his fingers.

"Yes." Kellie yanked his boots off, dropping them with a thud on the floor, then sat down beside him and swept his sweaty hair off of his forehead. "Justin and I are both pretty angry right now."

"I didn't mean to, Kellie."

He sounded remorseful, and her heart softened a touch. "We'll talk about it later. Get some sleep now."

She stood up and left the room, and didn't hear a sound out of Jack for several hours. When he finally came out later in the afternoon, he and his sister remained quiet towards each other, even after Justin came home and through dinner.

A friendly knock came on the door as Kellie finished eating, interrupting the silence. She got up from the table and opened it to find Luke on the other side.

"Are you free for a walk this evening?" he asked, removing his hat.

"That would be lovely," Kellie said with a grateful sigh, and retrieved her shawl before joining him. "I'll be back in a while," she told her brothers, who mutely nodded acceptance.

"It seems quiet at your house tonight," Luke said as they headed down the stairs. "Is everything okay?"

"I honestly don't want to talk about it," Kellie said wearily, thankful that she was going to miss whatever was going to go down between Justin and Jack in her absence.

Back in the apartment, Justin stood up and began clearing dinner away as he lit into Jack, true to Kellie's prediction.

"Do you mind telling me what happened last night?"

Jack toyed with the fork in his hand even though his plate was empty, his face set like a stone.

"It was my birthday, and I needed a drink. So I went and got a drink," he muttered.

"And it took until seven o'clock this morning? So when you told your sister you would be back later for cake, you meant twelve hours later?"

"No."

"Well, then?" Justin had little patience to deal with Jack's belligerence.

"I had a drink and then time got away from me and I ended up having a couple of more, and things just happened." Jack pushed back from the table.

"'Things,'" Justin repeated sarcastically. "'Things' happened."

"Guess so." Jack stood up and was about to leave the room and the conversation, but Justin waved his finger in his face.

"Sit right back down. I am not done with you," he demanded.

Jack stood staring dully at him, but he didn't leave. "Look, it was my birthday, and I wanted a drink. I don't see what the big deal is."

"The big deal is that your sister put in a lot of effort to give you a nice birthday, and you blew her off. And you promised to come back, but you didn't. These things don't happen to you, Jack. You made a choice to have another drink, and another, and not come back all night, while Kellie was on the couch waiting up for you and you told her that you would be back for cake."

"No one said she had to do that," Jack said, clenching his jaw.

"But she did, because she thinks about others, but you only ever think about yourself. How could you treat her like that?" Justin's voice rose with fury as Jack blinked emotionlessly back at him. "How could you lie to her and show such little concern for everything she did for you? What the hell was more important to you than her?"

"I didn't say anything was more important, and I didn't tell her to make me a cake. Nobody asked me what I wanted to do for my birthday."

Justin's jaw came unhinged and he couldn't believe what he was hearing. Without stopping to think, he lifted his hand and slapped Jack hard across the face.

"Go to hell, Jack!" he shouted. He turned and stomped out the front door, slamming it behind him and thundering down the stairs.

When Kellie returned several minutes later, she found half of the dishes still on the table and Jack sitting alone on the couch with a red and purple face. As soon as her eyes landed on him, she stopped still in horror at the sight, and panic rose inside her.

"What happened to you?"

"What do you think happened?" Jack replied sullenly.

"Oh dear God, where is he?"

"I don't know. He's a coward and left."

"Oh, Jack."

The longer Kellie stood looking at the bruise on his face, the more incensed she became, and she began to tremble with anger. Throwing her shawl over the back of a chair, she yanked the icebox open and chopping off a piece of ice with the pick, grabbed it with a dish towel and brought it to the couch. Kellie sat down next to Jack and pressed the towel against his face.

"I am so sorry." Kellie's body shook as she reached an arm around him. "He had no right to do this to you."

"Don't worry about it. I'm going to go to bed," Jack said, standing up with the block of ice. "Thanks."

Kellie took a deep, quavering breath as she watched him walk away and close the bedroom door.

She was waiting by the front door when Justin returned a half hour later, entering the apartment with his lips pressed into a thin line.

"Who do you think you are?"

Kellie was clearly furious, although she spoke in an even, low voice, but Justin saw the look on her face and pushed wordlessly past her. He strode to the bedroom, where he found Jack lying on his bed, staring at the ceiling. Justin sat heavily on the edge of his own bed with his hands on his knees.

"I'm sorry for hitting you. I lost my temper, and I was wrong."

Jack didn't reply, so after waiting through a few minutes of silence, Justin rose and left the room. Kellie stood in the center of the living room with her hands on her hips, ready for battle.

"How could you?"

"He deserved it," Justin replied tersely. "He's a narcissist and a jerk."

"No!" Kellie's eyes filled with angry, hot tears, and her whole being shook as her voice rose. "No, Justin. We do not hit him!"

Justin stood still, facing her and taking deep breaths.

"Okay," he finally said. "I apologized to him."

"No, look at me, I mean it! We do not hit him, Justin! Listen to me!" Kellie screamed, trembling angrily. "That is not okay! How could you?"

Justin held his hands up, more defensive than apologetic, not knowing what else to say. "I'm sorry. I lost my temper."

"Justin. That is never going to happen again. Do you understand me?" Kellie swiped at her red, wet face with her fingers.

"Yes. It won't happen again."

Another sob shook Kellie and she turned on her heel and went to her room without another word.

Elisan arrived at the camp later that month to find everyone quieter than usual. The new hospital and sutlery had opened two weeks earlier, but morale had been low lately due to increased security and restrictions on the inmates under the new administration. Still, something more seemed off, so she was glad when Pick showed up to help her so she could ask why everyone was so glum.

"You didn't hear?" he asked, raising an eyebrow. "General Grant is cancelling all prisoner exchanges."

"Really? So you're all stuck here?" For the first time, Elisan's opinion of the Yankee hero sunk.

"Yeah. I've been here since October, a whole bunch of us, and we were thinking that it was about our turn to get exchanged, but now our hope is gone. He won't exchange prisoners if the South won't include the Negro soldiers in the exchanges, so now nobody's going anywhere."

Elisan quickly changed her mind back about General Grant, and was proud of him for sticking to his morals, even if it was at the expense of her friends. "I'm sorry for your sake," she said, however, and meant it.

Pick tried to make it a point not to complain to Elisan when things were difficult, so he fell silent in an attempt to avoid letting her know how deeply the news affected him.

"Do you have any letters for me to send today?" she asked softly before starting on the crates, and he reached into his pocket. Elisan looked at the top envelope, addressed to Pick's mother, Margaret Thomas.

"What do you say to your mother every week?" she asked, sticking the letters in her satchel and grabbing the top crate in the wagon.

"I just tell her about anything interesting that happened and that I'm well. She likes to hear about my friends and sometimes I write about things I remember from growing up so she can think about happier times," Pick said. He took the crate from Elisan and carried it a few feet away to the line where they would begin distribution.

"So you don't tell her how hard things are?"

"Not really."

Elisan thought for a couple of moments as she worked. "What's she like?"

Pick gave her a half smile. "You've been making assumptions about her since the first time I met you, but this is the first time you've asked me about her."

"I don't ask every person I run into about their mothers, but if we are going to be friends after all, I'm interested in knowing about her," Elisan said innocently, and Pick turned around with his crate so she couldn't see him grinning to himself.

When he could manage a straight face again, he set it down and turned back around.

"Well, if we are going to be friends, perhaps you should," he said. "She's very youthful and fashionable. She spends a lot of effort taking care of herself, and it shows, because she's beautiful and everyone is surprised that she's old enough to have me. I think anyone who is that wealthy cares about appearances anyway, and since she's English, she's like a goddess in our circles. She used to go home every year and come back with the latest fashions and everyone in North Carolina tried to copy her," Pick said with a laugh, and Elisan smiled.

"My father worships the ground she walks on, so she's always kind of been the one in power in our house. I don't think me ending up here is what she had planned for my life. She liked me wearing a spiffy uniform, but once I actually went to battle, I think she stopped thinking this was a good idea."

"Is she loving, though?" Elisan asked, wondering if Mrs. Thomas was as shallow as she seemed.

"She is to us, at least. I think when my sister died it changed her some and she was reminded of what's important in life. She was always gentle, but we got closer and started writing more after that."

"You were at school when she died?"

Pick looked up at Elisan with surprise. "No, Evangeline's four years younger than me. It was when I was in the army, about a month before you came. When I met you, I'd only just returned from her funeral a few days before."

"Oh, I didn't realize."

Elisan tried to picture the Pick she had met in 1862 as a grieving older brother. "So . . . were you always like that growing up? Like when I met you?"

Pick looked sideways at her, regretful that he was going to have to hear about that episode as long as he lived.

"I was a bit of a loudmouth, sure. Spent my life being a clown and the center of attention, trying to have a bit of fun. And never knowing when it went too far," he added, meaning her. "It had nothing to do with my parents, and you were right that my mother would have been embarrassed to hear the things I said and the way I treated ladies in general back then. Were you always that uptight?"

Elisan gave a little gasp. "I never," she said indignantly, then stopped and cracked a smile. "I mean, I was the one getting my mouth into trouble too, but I'd never been in a situation like that one before or since."

"So we have something in common then," Pick declared, but Elisan shook her head vigorously.

"I have nothing in common with the person you used to be," she said vehemently.

"I still like to crack jokes and have a good time," Pick said, heaving a crate towards the line. "Cleaned it up a bit lately, though. It never got me much respect before."

"I think humor is a gift, as long as it's good humor," Elisan said. "I've always enjoyed a good laugh, and I feel sorry for people who don't appreciate the funny things in life. Like how my father is discipling the slave owner who called me a whore to my face."

The crates were unloaded, and Elisan and Pick began to distribute the vegetables together to the men in line.

"You're never going to let me live down the way we met, are you?" Pick challenged. "You know, if you were any other Yankee girl here today, we'd be getting along famously, but with you, I always have a deficit I have to make up."

"Look around, Pick," Elisan replied dryly. "If I was any other Yankee girl, I wouldn't be here today. They aren't coming out in droves to Confederate prison camps. Their mothers wouldn't let them near the place, even if they cared to come."

"No. I never imagined I would see you again, either. What are the chances that our paths would cross again, a thousand miles away?"

"Just goes to show," Elisan said, smiling at the man she was handing carrots to, "you should always be kind to everyone you meet, because you never know."

"What does your mother think of you coming here? Were you always close with yours?"

"Not at all." Elisan's countenance changed. "My mother doesn't . . . feel . . . very strongly. She's always been rather distant. She's a good woman, but she's not the type of person that someone gets close to, and I don't think she's worried about me a day in my life."

"That must be challenging," Pick deduced, watching closely as Elisan's mouth turned into a thin line and her eyes dropped.

"It's . . . not how I'd want it to be. We never talk about it, but it's been more difficult than I'd like to admit."

"I have to say, I'm surprised that your father married someone so different from himself," Pick said.

Elisan looked at him knowingly. "We've always been confused by that too."

She turned back to set her empty crate aside as Pick asked, "Your siblings?" and she nodded.

"At least we have him, though. He's worth ten attentive mothers."

Pick paused, turning toward her. "Your father is a wonderful man, Elisan. I can't imagine getting to live with him and all that wisdom. I've learned so much from him."

Elisan was silent, thinking how right Pick was and how good it felt to hear someone else speak of her father that way.

"I don't take him for granted."

"Maybe one day you'll start learning from him, too," Pick couldn't resist adding, and Elisan jerked upright in indignation and whacked him in the arm with the carrot she was holding.

"You just won't quit, will you?"

"That makes two of us, doesn't it?" Pick said with a laugh. "I was just testing you; it actually looks like maybe I can still rile you up, after you said I can't get to you anymore."

He continued to pass out potatoes with a cheerful smile, and Elisan shook her head and sighed, realizing that he was right. She quietly resumed her work and wondered how she got to the point where she actually didn't hate working next to Pick, teasing and all.

-22-

July 21, 1864

It was a rare quiet evening at the apartment; Justin was reading his Bible on the couch, and Jack lounged in an armchair whittling when Luke knocked on the door and Justin called for him to come in.

"Good evening," Luke said cheerily as he let himself in and looked around the sweltering hot room. "It's just me today, since Rebecca's away."

"She is?" Justin hadn't noticed. "Where did she go?"

Luke squinted unbelievingly at his friend. "She's been gone since last week. She went to Christina's for a couple of months to help with George and the new baby."

Justin vaguely remembered hearing that the Dinsmores had a new baby niece, and the look on Luke's face told him that he should have paid more attention. "It's a girl, right? How old is George these days?"

"He's two now, and she just had Annette, so Rebecca is getting her fill of baby snuggles and I'm sure she's loving it. Is Kellie here?"

"Yes, she is," Justin said. "She said to tell you she can't take visitors tonight."

"Oh." Luke plopped down in the other armchair to process the strange information. "Did she say why?"

"No, she just went to her room after dinner and said that she needed to be alone tonight and she wasn't going to see anyone. She didn't seem herself, but I don't know what's wrong."

"Is she not feeling well?"

Justin looked at Jack then at Luke again and shrugged. "No, I think she feels fine. She did all of her normal things today, and when she's under the weather, she stays in her room most of the day. She was quiet through supper and started crying when she was washing the dishes. What was she like today, Jack? Did she say anything to you?"

Jack shook his head and wiped at the sweat on his forehead. "She didn't say anything, but she was like that all day. Cried a couple times."

Luke stood up and looked at Kellie's door as if he was contemplating going over to it. "I wonder what's wrong that she doesn't want to talk to me about," he said pensively.

"You're an idiot," Jack stated, carefully making tiny slits on the little block of wood he was carving. He turned it over in his hand and wiped sawdust off with his thumb before glancing up and realizing that Luke and Justin were both staring at him. "It's the anniversary of Manassas today," Jack explained patiently.

"Oh, blasted," Luke said, and then stopped short and looked guilty as if he hadn't meant for it to come out. "I am an idiot." He wiped his nose, ran his fingers through his hair, and then slumped back into his chair. Everyone was silent for a few minutes. Jack kept whittling, and Justin sat motionlessly watching his brother's fingers move, feeling guilty for not realizing what was wrong with Kellie.

"She probably doesn't want to see me because she doesn't think she should feel as sad as she does," Luke said slowly, thinking aloud. "Poor lady."

Finally, he had an idea and straightened up. "Do you have a sheet of paper I can have?" he asked.

Justin nodded and stood up to retrieve one. Luke took it and went to sit at the table, where he sat for the space of several minutes scratching out words with a pencil. When he finished, he folded his letter and stood up, sticking his pencil back into his pocket. He went over to Kellie's door and knocked softly.

"Kellie, you don't have to talk to me," he called through the door before she had a chance to answer. "I'm going to go now, I just wanted to let you know that I came and I love you."

There was silence for a moment, then Kellie steadily replied, "Thank you, Luke."

He bent down and slipped the letter under the door, and after straightening up stopped for a minute, but he couldn't think of anything else to say. He turned around and walked towards the front door.

"Thanks, Jack," he said. "Good night."

"Good night," Justin said and watched him go.

Justin's birthday was on Friday that year, and despite his insistence that he didn't want any fuss, there was cake after dinner at the Dinsmores'. As Elisan cut it into slices for everyone to take to the drawing room, Justin looked around at the people that meant the most to him in the world.

"I'm grateful for all of you," he said sincerely, his eyes landing on Jack. "You all make my life rich."

He had just been arguing with his brother on the way over earlier in the evening, and now he realized that he needed to apologize later for being too harsh. Kellie leaned over, kissed his cheek, and handed him a piece of cake. She took the initiative to pass the pieces out to each individual as they left for the drawing room so that she would have a reason to be one of the last to leave, giving her a moment with Luke as Elisan cleaned the cake up.

"I appreciated your letter last night," she said, looking tenderly up at him. "It meant a great deal to me to know that you respect my grief, and that you gave me time to think through what it means to me at this point in my life. Every year it gets a little easier, but it took me by surprise yesterday, so I was rather unprepared for it."

Kellie gave a little sigh and looked like she was searching for words, so Luke waited, watching her compassionately.

"I think I thought that it would be different this year, and I didn't have the strength to try to explain why it wasn't to anyone."

"Dear Kellie," Luke said softly. "You must never feel that you have to explain it or make apology, and your grief concerns me to the extent that if you didn't mourn the loss of your husband, I would think something was amiss."

"Thank you for understanding," she whispered, dropping her voice to match his.

"I'm sorry yesterday was hard, and that I forgot what day it was."

Behind them, Elisan finished her work and quietly left the room, causing Luke to look up and remember himself.

"We should join the others," he said, turning to pick up the last two pieces of cake. As he paused to give space for Kellie to precede him into the hallway, he added, "That was sweet, what Justin said this evening. You could tell he meant it."

"It was," Kellie said. "I hope he feels loved tonight."

"I have something for you," Luke said abruptly, stopping in the hall and setting the plates of cake on the side table there. He plucked a prepared nosegay from a vase on the table and handed it to Kellie before picking up the cake again. When Kellie got into the light of the drawing room, she looked at the flowers in her hand and saw in the center of the bouquet one yellow rose, and three pink ones.

Elisan found summer at Camp Douglas to be a far more enjoyable time to visit, when her fingers weren't frozen stiff and she had a greater variety of fruits and vegetables available. In the winter, she was restricted to potatoes, carrots, and apples every week. There was never enough for everyone, but the camp was so overcrowded that it would be impossible for one church to provide that much, and her father was able to fulfill his primary reason for going with his weekly meetings. After seven months of consistently volunteering, Elisan had made friends especially with the men she wrote for, and often had to cut short her conversations with them so that she'd have time to get to their letters.

One Wednesday in the beginning of August, she was told upon her arrival that Pick was sick in the hospital, and she and her father weren't allowed to visit that part of the camp out of fear of infection. She worried about him all week, but the next Wednesday he was back again, as healthy and chipper as ever.

"It turned out to just be food poisoning," he told her when she asked, and she was surprised by how relieved she felt to see him well again.

Everything ran more smoothly when Pick was there helping with crates, and his conversation helped to make the task go quicker as the rhythm in their work became habit.

"What were you studying with my father this week?" she asked to make conversation one day on the distribution line.

Pick flipped the corn cob he was holding around in his hand and handed it to the man in front of him.

"The Sermon on the Mount, where Jesus was teaching to turn the other cheek. You know, that seems like the person your pa really is. He doesn't take offense and is one of the most forgiving people I know, but you . . . you seem to be more interested in justice than forgiveness."

"God is a God of justice, too," Elisan reminded him. "But I'm familiar with how you Confederates like to pick and choose which parts of the Bible you read."

Pick almost laughed, but then he stopped and looked at her. "You aren't joking, are you?"

It was more a statement than a question, and Elisan knew that he was right. "I guess not," she admitted, handing vegetables to the man in front of her from her crate as well as Pick's.

Pick turned to the line of soldiers waiting and called, "Help yourselves." Taking Elisan by the elbow, he steered her in the direction of the wagon.

"What are you doing?" she hissed when he had gotten her several feet away from the others.

"When do you want to talk about this?" Pick asked calmly, dropping her arm.

"Are you mad at me?"

Pick blinked at her. "Of course not. I just don't want to do this in front of seven thousand men who are suffering for a cause that they believe in. We're going to do this respectfully, for both of us."

"Do what? Talk about the Confederacy?"

"That, and slavery, which is what it's really about."

"We have talked about it."

Pick shook his head. "No, we talked about it for five minutes, and if they're fighting a war over it, it's obviously more than a five minute conversation."

Elisan pursed her lips, looking at him warily. "Why do you want to talk to me about it?"

"Because it's important to you."

Elisan pondered this. "Why do you care about what's important to me?"

"Because we're friends, Elisan," Pick said patiently.

"Are you doing this just to get me to stop bringing it up?"

Pick stared at her, befuddled. "Why would I want to silence you? And why would I do it by asking to talk to you? Do people do that?"

"I suppose only rude ones," Elisan said, her voice dropping with the realization of how unfair she was being to him. "How about now?"

"No, not now. Everyone is looking at us. Next week?"

"Okay, then." Elisan looked over at the crates, knowing that she should get back to her job. "I'll look forward to it."

"Me too."

On the way home later, Elisan bounced along on the seat next to her father. "Papa, Pick and I need to talk next week, and he doesn't want to do it in front of everyone. When would be a good time for us to do it?"

Reverend Dinsmore's eyes were questioning as he looked sideways at her. "Is there . . . something I should know about?"

"Oh seriously, Papa! We're going to talk about slavery and he doesn't want to make a scene, that's all."

"I see, very well." He thought for a moment. "Why don't you let me write the letters next week then, and you can have your meeting after you finish with the vegetables."

"Thank you; that's kind of you to do that for us," Elisan said, and began plotting in her head everything she was going to say to Pick.

September 14, 1864

Elisan and Pick had the chapel to themselves the next Wednesday as they took seats on benches across the aisle from each other.

"Is this a trap?" Elisan asked, looking around nervously, still unsure of why Pick was willing to have this conversation with her.

Pick took his hat off and jutted his jaw to the side, looking at her with displeasure. "We need to talk about that too. Actually, there are a lot of things I want to talk about with you, but let's start with why you don't trust me. Do you have a history of people showing themselves untrustworthy to you?"

Elisan scowled slightly. "No."

"Have I done something to lose your trust? Or is it because I'm a man? Or a Confederate?" Pick continued. "Or is it because you haven't actually forgiven me for the way we met yet?"

Elisan was silent. She hadn't noticed before that she had been overtly distrustful of him, but whatever the cause was, she was surprised that it mattered enough to him to bring it up.

"I'm sorry, Pick. I didn't realize I had made a habit of treating you like that, but I'll try to be more mindful of it. Right now I don't understand why you want to talk to me about slavery when you own . . . how many slaves do you own?"

"It was over six hundred, but several have left now," Pick answered, his brown eyes looking at her with honesty. "I want to talk through it because as I study the Bible, I'm seeing how God desires his followers to have unity, and that Jesus unites us in Him. You and I serve together every week, but there's this huge divide between us, and I think that to be faithful to the gospel that we're proclaiming through our service, we should actively seek to be at peace with one another."

Elisan was impressed by his heart and the leadership he was taking, and she had to admit that she was anxious to clear the air with him as well.

"What do you think unity means, though?" she challenged, ready to jump in. "Does it mean that all Christians need to have the same opinions as each other?"

"No, I don't think so, but I would expect it means that they're not fighting an actual war over something. Here we are supposed to be a Christian nation, but we have followers of God on two different sides literally meeting each other on a battlefield to end each other's lives. I don't think that this is how the problems should be handled. I can't walk down to Virginia to get everyone to sit down and talk it out, but I can sit down with the person that I serve with every week and talk it out with you so that we can at least seek peace together."

"I can respect that. Where do you want to start?" Elisan asked, significantly mellowed.

"Well, I want to hear your history with the topic of slavery, how your opinions were formed and what you think, but first let's talk about what you said last week about Confederates not reading the whole Bible." Pick pulled his foot over his knee. "The book of Ephesians instructs slaves to obey their masters, so I don't think it condemns slavery across the board."

"You're right, it does say that," Elisan said, settling in and beginning with all of her favorite arguments. "The slaves in those days either owed a debt to their masters or were spoils of war, not kidnapped from their homeland for no reason. The biggest difference though, is that the children born to slaves were free, not considered property of their parents' owner. The institution of slavery in America is systematically unjust and it is based on the belief that certain people groups are not as fully human as others. That's a belief that I don't find anywhere in the Bible and turns my stomach. When people are believed to be and treated as less than human, less than made in the image of God, I believe that we are being tremendously dishonoring to God's name."

Two hours later, Reverend Dinsmore stuck his head in the chapel and found Elisan and Pick still engaged in conversation.

"I'm sorry, Papa, can you give us a few more minutes?" she asked when she saw him, and the reverend smiled.

"Take your time. I can certainly find ways to keep myself occupied out here," he said. Every week dozens of men came to him for prayer, and he could easily fill his time.

"Less than a quarter of white southerners own any slaves at all." Pick continued what he was saying, turning back to Elisan. "Very few own as many as I do, and even then, when I was on the battlefield staring down a dozen howitzers on a hill, I wasn't thinking that I was there so that next year's tobacco crop could get harvested with slave labor. We were all on that battlefield thinking of our mothers and our homes and our country and how we need to defend it against invasion. We're protecting our culture and history. We're keeping a big federal government from taking away our individual rights and controlling us from Washington with a president and Congress that don't understand our needs and way of life, and hit us with tariffs that are unfair and our economy can't maintain. No one is standing there willing to give their lives so that they don't have to carry their own firewood."

"I've been wondering why you joined up, when you're as rich as you are. The wealthy families here have been paying for replacements so their sons don't have to serve," Elisan said, but Pick squinted at her.

"I wasn't drafted, Elisan. And in the south . . . the war is in our homeland, and it's different down there. I couldn't show my face in public if I'd paid for a replacement, not that I would have dreamed of doing such a thing."

Reverend Dinsmore came back again a while later, but Elisan just smiled sheepishly at him. "How much time has passed?" she asked.

"I came by an hour ago," he replied without condemnation.

"I'm sorry. It went so quickly, I didn't realize. We'll be done soon."

"That's fine. I'll be out front, so just come out when you're finished," he said and left again.

Elisan and Pick's discussion moved from the causes of the war to their own formative experiences and relationships, and neither of them seemed able to pull away from the conversation as layers peeled back on their hearts and minds and they opened up to each other more than they ever had.

Eventually, the reverend came back and informed them that they really did need to end the conversation. "You've been in here for four hours, and we've missed lunch. I'm afraid you'll have to call it quits for now. Have you solved all the world's problems yet?"

"Most of them," Elisan said with a grin, and Pick stood up and stretched.

"She's got a good mind, and it's been a pleasure. Thank you kindly for doing this for me."

"For you? I appreciated it so much myself. Thank you too, Pick."

As Elisan told her father about the conversation on the drive home, she couldn't help but admit to herself that she had miscalculated Pick, and it threw her off guard. She was surprised to learn Pick had studied the issue of slavery himself, and that he would ask her, a white northerner, to respect his nanny. She told herself that she would never agree with his opinions, but then she never expected that she would start listening to him, either.

Elisan spent hours that week nibbling on the end of her pencil as she stared at her journal, which had received a full report on her discussion with Pick. Something had changed in her that day, and she spent several days doing her best to deny it. For months now, she and Pick had been faithfully serving together, and she had seen him go from being an enemy to a friend, but she had never seen whatever it was that made her father think so highly of him. But that Wednesday, they had gone beyond the banter and teasing that characterized their friendship, and what she saw in him captured her. She didn't say anything about it, even to her father, but she knew a corner had been turned, and didn't know what to do with that knowledge.

From then on, the banter and teasing were still there on Wednesdays, but there was more. There was mutual respect; there were gazes met; there was understanding, and appreciation. Elisan could feel it, Pick could feel it, and listening to Elisan's reports on the way home every week, Reverend Dinsmore could feel it too. The autumn brought winds from a new direction, but they were soft and light, and felt strangely more like spring.

-23-

October 27, 1864

Justin rounded the corner of the bakery on his way home from work and came upon the postman standing outside the stairwell door. He still wasn't used to the idea of home mail delivery since it had begun the previous year, especially since his family almost never received mail. But there was the postman with a letter in hand, so after a short greeting, Justin took it and headed up the stairs. Since he owed letters to all of his friends in Kentucky, he assumed that it was from one of Kellie's friends and set it by her place at the table before putting down his lunch pail and washing his hands.

"Welcome home," Kellie called without turning around from the stove.

"Thanks." He glanced over to the couch where Jack was whittling another piece to his chess set, the shavings falling over the couch and floor again. "You'd better clean that up," he said.

Jack looked up but didn't answer, continuing to chip away at his piece.

"Is dinner almost ready?" Jack asked instead, ignoring Justin.

Justin was tempted to push the issue, but he was tired and didn't feel like dealing with Jack's disrespect, so he turned back to the wash basin.

"Yes, it is," Kellie said, dishing steaming potatoes and cabbage onto three plates and setting them on the table. She handed Justin a basket of biscuits, which he brought with him to the table and pulled out Kellie's chair for her. They settled into their seats, but before Justin could say the blessing, Kellie spied the envelope.

"What's this?" she asked, picking it up and examining the address.

"Oh, I didn't really look at it. I assumed it's for you," Justin said.

"It's addressed to all of us." Kellie carefully broke the seal and pulled out a single piece of paper. She began to read silently, then her hand flew to her mouth. "Oh!"

Jack began to eat alone, but Justin was watching Kellie with concern.

"What is it?" he asked, coming over to look over her shoulder.

"Dear sirs and ma'am," he read out loud. "*I am writing to you regarding your brother Jed, who serves with us in the 43rd Battalion Virginia Cavalry.*"

Justin stopped and looked at Jack. "Did you know he was in Mosby's Rangers?" He sounded more demanding than he meant to, but Jack just reached for a biscuit and took a bite without indicating that he had heard. Justin continued reading out loud.

"Last Thursday, we encountered a little skirmish up in West Virginia, and although our band fought gloriously, I regret to inform you that we have not seen or heard from Jed Young since that ruckus. We believe one of our band witnessed him being shot, but we were not able to return to retrieve our casualties. The next day, his horse came back and found us without its rider. We are unable to confirm whether he was wounded and captured, but at this time, he is presumed dead. I promise I will write again if we receive any new

information or if we hear from him. Due to the amount of time that has passed, I think it is best to not get your hopes up. Please accept my deepest regrets for your loss.

Sincerely,

Colonel William H. Chapman"

Jack stopped chewing, looking blankly at the wall across the room as Justin stared at the letter in shock. Kellie laid the paper on the table and hugged herself tightly, big tears rolling down her face. She became unable to steady her emotions and excused herself from the table, sinking into the couch and covering her face with her hands. Justin quickly moved to her side and wrapped his arms around her so that she could cry into his chest. No one spoke. Minutes ticked by as Jack sat at the table alone and Justin held his sobbing sister.

Kellie cried until her tears were spent, but she couldn't help but wonder if Justin even cared about Jed at all, or if he was just holding her because he didn't like to see her sad. She felt angry that she even had to wonder—why couldn't she have confidence that Justin even loved his brothers? What was the real problem that was underlying everything, where had they gone wrong, and why couldn't they figure each other out?

She was exhausted from the tension and confusion and hurt and trying to understand. And now . . . now to have lost Jed. After years of waiting, she had gotten him back for just one year and he had made such a deep impression on her heart, but he had left alone and died alone. He was the one who'd made her feel understood, but he didn't know her God and as far as she knew, he had died estranged from his creator.

She felt walls crumbling around her, her heart ripped from her chest, and all her strength drained out. Jed, Jed, Jed! Why did he have to go and get himself killed? She felt weak and lightheaded from crying and wanted to be alone.

She wished she had the strength to reach out to Jack, quiet at the table. How must he be feeling? But she couldn't, she couldn't. All she could manage now was to somehow make it to her room. She would speak to him tomorrow, she would tell him out loud how much she loved him and how sorry she was for how things had turned out, but right now she had to lie down before she passed out.

As soon as Kellie closed her door, Jack came alive.

"This is all your fault," he erupted at Justin, fire blazing from his eyes. "You drove Jed away and now he's dead. If he were here, he would still be alive, and he's dead because of you."

"Shut up, Jack," Justin said tersely from the couch.

Jack stood up, pushing his chair back. "Yeah, you only want to listen to people who praise you and shut up anyone who doesn't worship the ground you walk on. Well, I'm not the Dinsmores, Justin, and maybe it would be good for you to accept responsibility for this wreckage you've made."

"That I've made? For the love of God, Jack, get ahold of yourself. This is not a good time for this."

"Okay then, tell me when is a good time for you to face the truth. Because you've been running and hiding from it for months, and I sure as hell am sick of it and how you act all high society for the proper folks and are a coward and a jerk to your own family."

Jack came around the table to face the couch, anger seething from his being. "The truth is that Jed couldn't stand another day of you being embarrassed of him, and he left because you couldn't accept him for who he was. He's not as stupid as you like to think; at least he was smart enough to know he would never fit into your shining image and if he continued to try, he'd just be miserable for the rest of his life." Jack gritted his teeth. "I'm still not sure why I didn't leave with him, why I was stupid enough to try to stick it out. Maybe it has something to do with the fact that I'm used to being miserable, so I can handle that better than being dead."

"You're a pompous bastard, Jack. Kellie and I have broken our backs to give you everything we possibly could, and your rage is all the thanks we have ever gotten. All you do is complain about how miserable you are; well, tell me, high and mighty one, what have you done for anyone else? Or what have you even done for your own self besides run around town making yourself even more miserable blowing my money on things that make you feel like a carcass in the morning?"

Justin was really beginning to feel angry. Kellie was in the other room heartbroken, and as usual, Jack had to make things worse. It infuriated him.

"I don't know very many prisoners who are grateful to the prison guards for keeping them safe, but if you want to keep patting yourself on the back for all you've done for me, go ahead," Jack snarled. "I thought I was coming to join a family, not become a prisoner with no freedom or rights. If you had let me work, I could have had my own money to make myself a carcass out of."

Justin felt the heat coming up the back of his neck. He stood up so that he was face to face with Jack, keeping his promise to Kellie not to touch him.

"Do you know what, maybe I didn't do everything perfectly because I haven't ever done this before, either. But at least I tried. And Kellie tried. The only one of us here who didn't even try is you. If you decided you were a prisoner and not a member of the family, that was all in your own head and you made yourself into that, because you put zero effort into being anything different. Of course I wouldn't think that a deadbeat who wouldn't carry a pail of water up the stairs for his sister, would be able to work a job!"

Justin clenched his fists and leaned forward so his face was inches from Jack's, his words becoming louder and more enunciated the more he went on. "If you knew what's good for you, you would have taken seriously the image I tried to help you achieve, because I knew you were capable of being more than a deadbeat, but over and over again, you proved me wrong. You're only a good-for-nothing because that's what you chose to be!"

"You always thought that Jed and I were second class citizens, so I gave you what you wanted," Jack shouted. "You never saw us as equals. You always saw us as peons to improve upon and children you could control. You wanted me to be your child and a deadbeat, so that's what you got! In the south, we don't talk the same way and we don't act the same way, but that doesn't mean that we're inferior to you. If you went to Carolina, you sure as heck would stand out, but maybe then you would see that southerners aren't low grade people; they just see things differently. But you always thought Jed and I weren't good enough and you had to fix us, when you're a bloody hypocrite! You can't control me, you're not better than me, and you aren't my father!" Jack shoved at Justin, and Justin stumbled back but didn't retaliate.

"I never once tried to be your father, Jack," he said evenly. "Your father was Henry Young, and he was ten times the man you are. I'm glad he can't see you now. You came into this family with your own issues that keep you from seeing things straight, probably because you never had the privilege of knowing him. You're making lies up because you have no clue what you're talking about."

Jack stomped toward his room and grabbed his knapsack. "Then you'll be happy to know that I'm taking my issues back with me, and Kellie and you can live happily ever after in your proper high society."

He picked Justin's wallet up off of the nightstand and took out some cash, stuffing it in the bag along with his clothes. He reached under his mattress for his pistol, which he stuck in the back of his belt, and on the way out of the bedroom, he grabbed his black slouch hat.

"You can tell Kellie I said goodbye and explain to her how half your family can't even stand to live with you," Jack said, heading for the door.

Justin felt like he had to do something, but he had no words and anger clouded his thoughts.

"Jack!" he called, the only thing he could manage to verbalize, but Jack didn't stop.

"I hate you, and I hate Chicago and all the damn Yankee arrogance!" Jack yelled behind him as the door slammed and he thundered down the steps.

Justin stood in the silent room staring at the closed door, panting as the rage dissipated, leaving a gaping hole inside of him. He heard a noise behind him and slowly turned around, as if in a trance. Kellie stood supported by her doorway, her ashen face ethereal and her hand at her throat.

"I never blamed you for Jed leaving," she rasped, her voice strained and odd, shaking with emotion. "But if Jack does not come back, I will *always* blame you for his leaving."

Justin opened his mouth, but nothing came out.

"His brother is dead and he needed you," Kellie went on. "You had a chance to be there for him and instead, you drove him away."

Justin turned away, unable to face the pain emanating from his sister.

"He attacked me," he said hoarsely.

"He opened up to you!" Kellie exclaimed. "You shut him down; you always shut everyone down, including yourself. Because you don't know what to do with the reality of pain, so you always shut everything down."

Justin visibly winced, and the look on his face told Kellie that after months of speculation, she had landed on the truth.

"I don't know what everyone expects from me. If I don't keep it away, I can't get up in the morning, go to work, I can't take care of everyone. I can't do everything, Kellie." He refused to look at her. "You can't afford for me to face the pain."

"That's not fair. I can handle a lot more than you seem to remember."

Justin went to the door and put his hand on the knob. "I did everything I thought I was supposed to do. You think I can simply go to work and come home and have cheerful dinner conversations with my family and we will all be happy, but you have no idea the battles I face every day to just keep one foot in front of the other."

"No! I don't!" Kellie cried as Justin opened the door. "Because you won't talk to me and give me any idea. You haven't even given me a chance. You just push us all away! You have to work through the hard things. You can't run from them forever, Justin!"

Justin closed the door behind him and hurried down the stairs into the cool night air. The only thing he knew was that he needed to find Jack before he left the city, but he had no idea which way he would have gone. South? Or to the train station? If so, which one?

He walked briskly through the streets, suffocating under the guilt of Kellie's words, trying to push her face out of his mind. Work through the hard things, she'd said. When? When was he supposed to find the space to do that when his family was always on top of him the moment he came home from work, and he had no time to himself to think?

His mind swirled back to the letter and all the horrifying truths it contained. Jed was worse than an ordinary rebel; he was a no-good guerilla, and now he had gone and gotten himself killed and broken Kellie's heart. Justin couldn't believe his brother would have joined up with such a despicable, vile band that wasn't even a proper military unit. Mosby's Rangers were hated by northerners for their unconventional warfare, and that was, of course, the unit that Jed joined. Furthermore, Kellie would have known it all this time, and she'd never mentioned it to him.

Without knocking, Justin burst into the Dinsmore drawing room. The family was gathered around for the evening reading; Rebecca's hands were occupied with crocheting and Mrs. Dinsmore mended while the reverend read from the family Bible.

When the door opened, the reading stopped, and all eyes turned to the wretched figure standing before them. Justin was out of breath and wild-eyed as he entered and sat down in an empty seat. The entire family stared at him, waiting for an explanation, so he blurted out, "Jack's gone. He left."

Elisan clasped her hand to her mouth as everyone gasped.

"I came to see if Luke could come with me to look for him."

Without hesitation, Luke jumped to his feet. "Yes, of course," he said, concern covering his features, as Rebecca, recovering from the initial shock, reached out a hand to stop him.

"What happened?" she asked, and Justin noticed for the first time that she had returned from Christina's.

He stared vacantly across the room. "We received word that Jed is missing and is possibly dead." He breathed heavily before adding, "We all handled it very badly. Jack took some things and left."

He shuddered involuntarily, dropped his head, and rubbed the back of his neck roughly. Luke stood frozen in the middle of the room.

"I'm so sorry," Rebecca whispered, swallowing hard.

In the stunned silence, Reverend Dinsmore directed Titan to retrieve lanterns for Justin and Luke to take with them, and he left quietly. Justin didn't look up, and nobody moved. Here was the family, gathered to read the Bible, so peaceful and normal. He had done everything he could to model Reverend Dinsmore's leading of his family, but nothing he had done to care for and lead his own family had been successful.

How could Jack not see that he never wanted to lord over him, just to take care of them? He had done the evening readings and his own family had resented him for it. He was rejected and disrespected at every turn, and everyone blamed him for the constant conflict. But why wouldn't they? He had failed at everything, he knew better than anyone.

When Titan returned a few minutes later with lanterns trimmed and ready, Justin rose, and Luke prepared to leave with him.

"Is there anything else we can do?" Reverend Dinsmore asked, coming to his feet.

Justin didn't answer, only looking at the older man with tears, wishing he had accepted his invitation to talk a long time ago.

"Yes," Luke quickly replied. "Can you pray before we go?"

Everyone exhaled their collectively held breath, and the reverend prayed with his hands on Justin and Luke's shoulders.

"Our Father, You have been waiting at the door for Your prodigal son to return to You far longer than we have. Please allow him to be found and bring his heart home to Yourself and bring him home to us."

When he finished, he pulled Justin to himself in a comforting embrace. Had time not been of the essence, Justin would have stayed and wept, but he just closed his eyes and allowed the fatherly hug to renew his energy. Luke took the lanterns and quickly left the room, Justin at his heels.

The moment they were gone, Rebecca burst into tears, burying her face in her hands. Elisan quietly rose and went to her sister with a handkerchief, tenderly wrapping her in her arms.

"Honestly, Rebecca," her mother said tightly.

"I hate seeing him so devastated too." Elisan held Rebecca compassionately as she sobbed in her arms.

"I'm sorry." Rebecca tried to regain her composure. "It's just getting harder." She pressed the handkerchief to her eyes.

"It hasn't been an easy road," her father said mildly.

"Poor Jed," Elisan added. "They all must be so crushed."

Rebecca cried harder again, grieving for her friends and their loss. She briefly thought of Kellie home alone, and determined to call on her first thing in the morning, whether the boys found Jack or not. She kept thinking of Justin's wild, desperate face and wished she could comfort his aching soul. Her own heart ached so deeply whenever his did. For now, though, unable to calm herself sufficiently, the best thing to do would be to spare her mother.

"I'm sorry, Papa, but may I retire?"

Her father excused her, and after she left the room, he picked the Bible back up and quietly resumed reading.

Once outside, Justin didn't stop. "I'd like to check the stations first," he said as they hurried along. "The train seems the most likely way to head south, and maybe he'll just wait there overnight for the first train in the morning. Unless he decided to take a horse."

"What if he's not there?" Luke asked. "Where else do you think he'd be?"

"It's Jack," Justin replied drolly. "He's probably getting drunk somewhere."

Jack wasn't at either train station, so Justin and Luke began working their way back towards the south of the city, checking all the saloons they knew of as they went. At each one, they inquired of the bartender if he had seen a fellow that looked like Justin, "only a little taller and better looking." Most of the bartenders had no interest in being helpful and didn't seem to even consider the question before responding negatively, but near midnight, they finally heard differently.

"Oh, the Rebel?" the portly bartender said through the cigar hanging out of the corner of his mouth. "Yeah, he sure was here earlier. I threw him out when he started a big fistfight. You can't walk around this city with an accent like that and not get noticed."

He waved his towel toward the door. "Fella had a few too many; he was pretty drunk. I guess that was a couple hours ago."

Justin thanked him and apologized and left, not sure if he should feel thankful at the piece of news or not.

"He's still in the city," Luke said definitively. "If he was that drunk, he isn't leaving tonight." The thought made them hopeful, although Justin still felt humiliated by his brother's activity.

They wandered along the dark streets as their lanterns flickered and sputtered, through parts of town that neither of them had ever dared to visit before. Justin had a desperation about him and didn't seem to want to talk or call off the search, and Luke followed faithfully as they covered several miles deep into the night.

Finally, Justin stopped in the middle of the street. "I think we should check here," he stated, glancing at Luke.

Luke looked up at the sign for the brothel in front of them, and his skin went prickly. "I don't know, Justin," he said with hesitation. "If I went in there, the whole church would know by morning."

"I can't go in there by myself," Justin said stubbornly. "No one from church should be on this side of town. And remember, we don't pay attention to what the gossips say, anyway."

Luke was torn. He had never been unwilling to do anything that Justin needed, but the thought of going into a place like that made his skin crawl.

Justin eyes were pleading. "I have to find Jack," he said. "He might be in there. Come on, it would be worse if I had to go in alone."

Luke stood in the street, looking at the sign and taking deep breaths.

"What happened tonight?" he asked flatly.

Justin threw his arms in the air and turned around. "It was . . . I don't know. Everyone was upset. About Jed."

He put his hands on his hips as the exhaustion from the night started to catch up with him and moved about, not looking Luke in the eye. "We've just been out of sorts at home lately," he finished lamely.

"So finding Jack will make you feel less guilty?" Luke asked pointedly, but Justin refused to engage. He started walking toward the building.

"Something like that. Now come on."

With trepidation, Luke followed him through the door and they found themselves in a dimly lit front saloon. A trim woman in her forties in a neat navy blue taffeta dress was wiping down empty tables, and came over when she saw them enter. A couple of lone men finishing up their drinks glanced over at them from the bar.

"You boys looking for a room?" the matron asked.

"No, no," Justin quickly replied. "I'm looking for my brother. He looks like me but he's a little taller and better looking, and he has an accent."

Immediately, the woman started shaking her head. "No honey, we don't reveal our patrons. We are a discreet establishment," she said, shooing them toward the door.

Justin was about to open his mouth to argue when a girl with long curly blond hair swept loosely to the side came around the corner from the hallway. Her bright pink dress was cut way too low in the front and much too high at the hemline, and even her bare shoulders peeked through beneath fluttery tulle. Luke quickly looked away and pulled on Justin's shoulder.

"Oh, aren't you staying?" the girl squeaked in an unnaturally high voice as she approached them.

"I'm looking for my brother," Justin said, at the same time that Luke replied, "No, we're leaving."

"Oh, don't be in such a hurry." She smelled of roses, perhaps a bit too much so. "You're cute," she said to Luke, looking him in the eye suggestively.

Luke felt the condemnation of hellfire and felt like he was going to throw up. Thankfully, Justin moved with him towards the door.

"You are quite welcome to have a drink and make yourselves comfortable," the matron called after them, "but I am unable to disclose any information about our patrons."

"Thank you," Justin called over his shoulder, not looking back as they burst back out into the dark night. Luke was hyperventilating, and it took them a minute to calm down and start breathing regularly again.

"Just one more saloon," Justin begged tiredly, indicating the joint across the street. Luke followed him once more, and once more they received a negative reply at the bar.

Finally giving up hope, Justin sat down on the curb and hung his head between his knees, his hands clasped behind his neck. Luke sank down beside him, feeling the exhaustion and defeat. He had wanted so badly for Jack to be found, for his friend's pain and guilt to be eased, for the long search to have a happy ending.

"Do me one more favor, Luke," Justin said from under his arms. "Marry Kellie for me. You'll make her so much happier than I do."

Luke exhaled quickly. "I would love to, but that's not true. She loves you twice as much as she loves me."

Justin dropped his arms and stared at his friend. "Why on earth would you say that?" Luke never lied to make people feel better, and Justin didn't appreciate him starting now.

"She's been married before. She doesn't have the same anticipation for marriage that I have. She loves me, but she doesn't have that need for it. But you? You share her blood. And she waited fourteen years to have you in her life again. The ties she feels for you are stronger than anything I could ever hope for."

"Maybe it was that way before, but I don't think it is now."

Luke shook his head slowly, not believing his ears. "You're an idiot. Why are you arguing with me? I'm telling you solid facts, not some theories I made up."

Justin kept replaying Kellie's voice in his head, strange and pain-filled. *"If Jack doesn't come back, I will always blame you. He needed you . . . "* Knots turned around and around in his stomach and the guilt washed over and over his head.

"She loves you because you're her brother, not because of the things you do. She loves you unconditionally, man. The way God and I do too." Luke kicked at the dirt in front of him and stopped when he realized it wasn't dirt. "What's keeping you from accepting it?"

Justin was silent for a long time. "I really blew it tonight. I don't think I can pick up the pieces from this." His breath was shaky and heavy. He covered his eyes and tried to clear the memories away.

Luke reached over and put his hand on his friend's back. "I'm sorry." He sat with him in the silence and then added, "Do you want to talk about it?"

Justin ran his fingers through his curls. "I should, but I should probably sleep on it first. And I need to get back to Kellie."

The thought crossed his mind that Kellie might not be there either when he returned, but a quick review of her personality and situation told him that she didn't go anywhere. He didn't know if she had stayed up waiting for him, but he knew that even if she was asleep when he got home, that he was going to have to wake her up. His guilt was suffocating him, and she needed to hear him apologize.

"I'd like to come by tomorrow evening to see her, if it's okay," Luke said as he stood and stretched his back. "She's probably devastated about Jed."

Justin came to his feet and looked at Luke as if the thought had not crossed his mind. "Yes, of course," he replied, embarrassed. He could see that once again he had been a jerk without realizing it, and it reinforced in his mind that living with Luke would be a much better arrangement for his sister than with him. "I know she'd appreciate that."

As they wandered slowly back to the seventh ward through quiet streets, Justin suddenly snickered. "The way that girl looked at you," he said abruptly and then laughed outright when Luke glanced at him.

"That is not remotely funny," Luke muttered, but he had to let out a little chuckle. "Don't you dare tell Kellie about that."

"There is no way on earth that I'm going to let Kellie know we went in there," Justin said, and laughed again. "Maybe she should know how 'cute' you are."

Luke rolled his eyes and shoved his hand in his pocket. "Thanks, but for the first time tonight I wished I was ugly."

They came to the familiar corner where they parted ways.

"Thank you," Justin said simply, and Luke waved his hand.

"I wish we could have found him. Get some rest. I'll be praying. I'll let you know if I see him at the station tomorrow."

He turned and swung down the street, and Justin headed to the bakery. His feet were heavy treading up the stairs to the apartment, and when he opened the door, he found the room dark and quiet. Holding his lantern up, he saw that dinner had been cleared away—the dinner that no one had eaten—and he suddenly realized how hungry he was.

Kellie's door was cracked, but when he softly knocked, there was no answer. Justin pushed the door open. The candle on Kellie's nightstand was still lit, but it had begun to flicker and wane. By the dim light, he could see Kellie's face on the pillow and immediately knew that everything was not right. Her eyes were closed, but her face was shiny with perspiration, damp black curls plastered on her forehead. She was still fully dressed, and she tossed around briefly before becoming still again.

"Kellie!" Justin shouted, setting his lantern down and dropping to his knees by her bed. "Kellie, are you okay?"

She was obviously gravely ill, and did not answer. Panic rose in his throat and he dashed to the kitchen for a pail. There was no water, so he had to run down the stairs and outside, pump some water, and carry it back up. He gathered more candles and rags and hurried back to her room, quickly immersing a rag in the pail and pressing it to her forehead and neck. He stoked the fire and came back to her side to change the rags out for fresh ones.

"Kellie!" he continued to call, working busily over her feverish body. He loosened her outer skirt, tugged it off, and unbuttoned her blouse. After contemplating for a minute, he gently pulled that and her corset off as well, leaving her limp in his arms in her chemise, petticoats, and stockings. Without the restrictive outer clothes in the way, he could now focus on trying to lower her fever. He patted her skin with the cool rags, changing them out every few minutes.

Once he had seated himself by her and settled into a routine, the weight of the entire evening's events rolled over him. Huge sobs shook his body as he clutched Kellie's limp hand to his face and words began to tumble out through his tears.

"I'm sorry, Kellie. I'm so, so sorry. I love you so much and I'm so sorry for all the times I've hurt you. I've let you down again and again, and failed you as your protector and brother and friend. I love you, Kellie, and I'm so sorry."

He wept and worked and talked to his lifeless sister as hours passed and the fever ravaged her body. She tossed and turned, twice calling out in delirium for Nathan and once for Justin. He tried to calm her and let her know he was there, frustrated that he couldn't even send for the doctor and her care was dependent on him alone. Never in his life had he cared for a sick person, and he hoped he was doing everything he should be, but he didn't even know.

"I know I've failed you, and I don't know if you'll want anything to do with me again," he said. "You're all I have left, and I don't deserve to have you. I . . . nothing went as I thought it would. I didn't manage living with my family how I always pictured that I would. I fell on my face, and I'm ashamed of myself and my shortcomings and the many times that you wanted more from me and I closed you off. I . . . I failed, Kellie. I failed from the beginning, and I've been too ashamed to face it."

He fell to the floor beside her, wrapping his arms around her and crying out, to her for forgiveness, to God to heal her, at his own self in anger and shame as the long night stretched on and on and candles flickered in the tiny room.

It wasn't until it was almost dawn that the fever slowly lessened and she began to sleep more calmly. Without leaving her side, Justin lay his head next to hers and finally fell asleep as the first rays of morning peeked through the kitchen window.

-24-

When Rebecca came down the stairs the following morning, a bleary-eyed Luke was already at the table eating a bowl of oatmeal before heading to work.

"How did it go last night?" she asked, grabbing an apple from the basket and sitting down beside him.

Luke looked up briefly and shook his head as he turned back to his oatmeal. "We didn't find him," he said quietly.

"You didn't?" Rebecca stopped still as her heart fell. "How is Justin?"

Luke finished his bite and his shoulders dropped. "I've never seen him this low. He's really upset."

"What time did you get home?"

"I don't know. Maybe one? I tried to talk to him, but he didn't seem ready. He has a lot he's going to need to figure out."

Rebecca sat quietly for a minute then stood up, taking her apple with her. She went to her room to retrieve her cloak, and ran into Elisan.

"I'm going to go try to see Justin on his way to work," she said. "And hopefully check on how Kellie is doing."

She headed out into the crisp morning and walked in the direction of the apartment.

Justin was up when she arrived, and relief washed over his tired gray face when he saw her.

"I'm so thankful you're here," he said, swinging the door open.

She stepped into the room, taken aback by his greeting. He didn't stop, but moved about as he talked.

"Kellie is quite ill. Can you stay with her? I was up with her all night, and her fever broke about five. She's sleeping now. I'm going to swing by Dr. Ricketts' on the way to work. You'll stay, won't you?" He picked up a biscuit from last night's dinner and took a bite, turning questioningly toward Rebecca.

"I . . . yes, of course, Justin." The plans Rebecca had for talking to Justin as she walked him to work were altered, but she would have done anything to help him or care for Kellie without a second thought.

Justin exhaled with relief. "Thank you so much."

"Did you get any sleep?"

"I got about an hour."

"Are you okay? Is everything okay?"

Justin swallowed hard. He turned his back to her to drink from the water dipper, then turned back around.

"No," he said, looking her in the eye. "Nothing is okay." He took another bite and chewed it.

Rebecca's heart broke for him and she didn't know what to say. The only thing she could think of was to tell him how much she loved him, and suddenly that didn't seem to be the right thing to say in the moment.

"Luke said you didn't find Jack," she finally said, knowing that wasn't helpful, either.

Justin just shook his head. He picked up another biscuit for his lunch and stuffed it in his pocket. Grabbing his canteen and cap, he turned toward the door.

"Is there anything else I can do for you?" Rebecca asked before he left.

Justin turned towards her, and for several long moments, his eyes held hers.

"Just be here when I get home tonight," he said softly.

"Anything, Justin," she said. "I'll be here."

He paused, showing his appreciation on his face, and then left for work. Rebecca stood in the quiet kitchen, wondering what had just happened and reconciling the changes to her morning's agenda. She checked on Kellie, who was still sleeping peacefully, and settled into the chair by the bed. Picking up Kellie's Bible from the nightstand, she began reading to pass her day.

Jack felt the emptiness before he even opened his eyes that morning. He groaned and rolled over, the satin sheets cool to his touch. The other side of the bed was empty, unlike when he had fallen asleep the night before. He always hated to be alone and tried to have someone, anyone, to be with, even if for one night. In the army, he had all the other men constantly around, and it had helped. But having people around was different from being known, and never had he had anyone try to get close to him the way his siblings did. And nothing had been so terrifying.

Now that they were gone, waking up alone once more, the void was overwhelming. A carcass. Well, that was a correct description of how he felt this morning. Run over and left for dead. His head was pounding from the night before, as usual, but now, now the vacuum inside his heart was paralyzing. He had always been scrappy, a fighter who did anything to survive; but for the first time, he woke up in the morning not caring if he survived anymore at all, and that was the most frightening part.

The bed wasn't welcoming—he detested the entire charade it had afforded him—but he had nowhere to go. He had nothing to go back to the south for, and even Jed was dead. So there was no point in leaving, really. Everywhere he went, he would be alone except for the charades here and there filling his nights, and he knew that wouldn't be enough anymore. There was no hope that his life would be any different anywhere. The only place his life had ever had hope was in the apartment, but the exposure and shame that had accompanied it was too crushing to handle. To go back would require facing that, and facing it meant only one thing. He knew it, and he had always known it. In the end, there really wasn't a choice to make. There was only one thing to do and only one place to go, and it was time.

Reverend Dinsmore looked up from his notes at the knock on his study door. It was ajar, so he stayed seated and called, "Come in." His years in the ministry had taught him to expect the unexpected, so it seemed the most normal thing in the world when Jack Young stepped into the room.

"Jack," he said, coming to his feet as he breathed a prayer of gratitude for the answer to his petitions. "Come in. What can I do for you?"

Jack stood uncertainly inside the door and then reached back and closed it behind him, as if he didn't want to risk anyone seeing him in there.

"I need you to help me become a Christian."

Reverend Dinsmore paused, then nodded toward the leather chair opposite his desk and Jack took a seat.

"What brings you to want that?" he asked.

He was perceptive enough to have a pretty good idea of everything the Young family had tried to keep in the privacy of their own home and had accurately deduced most of the motives each family member had been working from. Still, before proceeding, he needed to know whether it was conviction of the Spirit or the desire to please people that brought Jack in and where the boy's faith stood this morning.

Jack held his palms out. "I'm done," he said. "I have nothing left. All I know is that I need to get saved, and I'm here because I quit fighting." He straightened up. "So how does this work? Do I tell you all my sins? It's a lot, but I think you said Jesus will forgive all of them. He knows it's a lot, right?"

Explaining the gospel was Reverend Dinsmore's favorite part of his job. Once again, he would get a chance to talk about the grace and mercy of his Savior, and it never got old. Once again, he would be reminded of the precious, precious blood of Jesus and the extent that God values each human life.

"Whether you tell me is up to you," he said, "since I'm not the one who saves you. Some people find it helpful because in speaking their sin out loud, it helps to loosen the grip the hidden things have on them by exposing them and laying them down. But I don't need to know, and Jesus already does. If it would help you, though, I can walk through it with you."

Jack nodded decisively. "It would," he said. "No one knows these things, Reverend. I've been too scared of Justin and Kellie knowing the truth about me and not wanting to have anything to do with me. But now I have nothing to lose, and I just want to get rid of this stuff. I hate it, and I don't want to carry it around anymore. I just have to get it out."

His chin quivered. He pursed his lips, took a deep breath, and for the first time in his life, began to tell his story.

When Justin walked in the door that night, Kellie was asleep again, and Rebecca had dinner on the table. The smells that greeted him were inviting as he sank tiredly into the first armchair he came to.

"It smells delicious in here," he said gratefully.

Rebecca brought him a plate of food and sat down next to him as he began to eat. She reported on Kellie, who had been resting for most of the day and seemed to be improving, and the doctor's visit.

"He didn't find anything wrong with her except that she's still weak from last night's fever, and said to make sure she gets enough liquids and rest. How are you?"

Justin shook his head as Rebecca watched him closely. "I'm not sure if I'm more tired or hungry," he admitted. "Mostly I'm torn up."

She hoped that he would continue and open up more to her, but he changed the subject. "You must be tired. Let me walk you home and I can finish eating later."

Despite her disappointment, she knew it was best for everyone, because she really was tired and it would be getting dark and cold soon. She got up to check on Kellie once more and gather her cloak. When she returned, Justin was asleep, the plate of food on his lap barely eaten. Maybe if she stayed and ate a little herself and let him rest, he would be able to wake up and walk her home after a while, she thought, if Luke didn't come for her before then. She took her dinner in to eat by Kellie's bed so Justin could sleep and she could keep an eye on her friend.

Shortly after settling in with her plate, she heard a noise in the living room and came out again. To her astonishment, Jack was sitting next to Justin, who was still asleep, holding his brother's half-eaten plate of food and cleaning it off.

"Jack!" she whispered in surprise.

He looked up guiltily and put the plate down on the table next to him.

"What's going on?" he whispered back, just as surprised to see her instead of Kellie.

Rebecca almost replied, then stopped and looked at the sleeping Justin. "Can you walk me home? I can tell you then."

He agreed, and a minute later they were walking down the sidewalk together. Rebecca pulled her cloak close at her neck and caught him up on things at his home.

"Justin will be overjoyed to see you," she said. "He and Luke searched for you for hours last night. Where were you?"

Jack had been walking along, looking down at the sidewalk in front of him, but now he turned to Rebecca.

"I got saved today," he announced suddenly. "I guess you'll be the first to know."

"What?" Rebecca stopped and gaped at him. "Really? Jack, that's fantastic!" She reached out, gave him a quick hug, and stepped back. "I'm so happy for you. It makes all the difference. At least, it has in my life."

Jack smiled and started walking again. "It has already. I feel a hundred times lighter. All the things I used to carry and worry about . . . Now I don't have to think about them anymore. I feel like I've been set free."

"You have been."

She thought of Justin and Kellie and wished she could be there when they found out, her heart soaring to think of the joy the news would bring them. They talked the rest of the way until arriving at the corner of the church.

"You can head back, I'm fine from here," Rebecca said, guessing that he probably didn't want to make a scene at her house before he had a chance to talk to his own siblings. She was right, but Jack waited for her to reach her door before turning back toward home.

This time, the door clicking awakened Justin. He hadn't meant to fall asleep, and he awoke in a small panic, wondering how much time had passed. He looked up and seeing Jack, blinked twice.

"Jack!" he shouted, jumping to his feet. He half reached out his arms, but stopped suddenly.

"I'm so sorry, Jack. For everything. You were right. I . . . "

Jack held up a hand and stopped him. He looked like he was going to say something, but instead looked towards Kellie's room.

"Is Kellie awake? Then I can talk to you together."

"I'm not sure, but Rebecca is here."

Jack shook his head as he headed toward Kellie's room. "Not anymore. I walked her home."

Justin blinked again, wondering how long he'd been asleep. He turned back to pick up his dinner plate, realized with confusion it was empty, and set it on the kitchen table before joining Jack. Kellie was awake and already had tears running down her cheeks, clasping Jack's hand in hers as he bent over her bed.

Quickly, before anyone else could speak, Jack straightened up and looked between them. "I met Jesus today," he said. "I spent most of the day at the church talking to the reverend, and I prayed with him to confess my sins."

"Jack!" Justin exclaimed. He grabbed Jack by the shoulders, laughing in elation through his tears. Justin squeezed him into an embrace, fear and worry replaced by sheer joy. He had given up hope for his family, but God in His great mercy had brought Jack back again, more whole than when he left.

"I'm so glad!" Kellie gasped, her face flushed. "Oh Jack, this is the best news." Her voice trailed off weakly, but she scooted over and patted the bed next to her. "Come sit and tell us about it."

Jack sat halfway down her bed where he could see her face, still holding her hand. Justin took a seat in the chair by the head of the bed.

"Well," Jack said, thinking for a moment. "I realized I have nowhere else to go but here because what I was running from was God and that wouldn't change wherever I went. And I just didn't have anything left in me that wanted to keep running."

He drew a deep sigh. "There are a lot of things . . . things I've done, things that I thought kept me from being able to come to Him. I guess I thought I was too big of a mess. But I got to the point where I had nothing else. Nothing to lose. I figured I might as well come to Him and try, and see if I could believe that He had enough forgiveness for me too. So I went to the church this morning."

Justin arched his eyebrows. His entire miserable day at work, sick with anxiety over his brother, Jack had been at the church with the reverend. He couldn't wrap his mind around it.

"Reverend Dinsmore took all day to explain everything to me, answered all my questions, and helped me understand, and I finally realized that the whole point of my life is to know God and worship Him. And he talked through all my problems and sins with me, and for the first time I . . . I gave them up, you know? I don't need them anymore and I was finally able to think of myself differently," Jack finished proudly. "Now I can think of myself as a child of God, and I'm saved now."

Justin and Kellie sat flabbergasted by everything they had just heard. The Jack that sat in front of them was in every way different from the Jack that had slammed the door and left the night before. The change in him was drastic in a way they had never before seen, and he sat in front of them a literal miracle.

"You've put up with a lot from me," Jack added. "I know that. And I want to say once and for all that I'm sorry. I'm sorry for all of the anger and disrespect and fighting I've thrown your way. Both of you. I don't deserve you two."

Kellie rubbed his arm. "Never mind, Jack. None of that matters."

"Besides, it wasn't all you," Justin said. "I know that I've not treated you well and I made things worse. God convicted me too, because the way I've handled it all has been terrible. I wanted to let you know how sorry I am and I was afraid I would never get the chance." He was still for a second before looking up. "I'm grateful that God brought you back to us and gave us a second chance."

"Third chance, really," Kellie said. "If you count losing you as a baby."

"Yes, third chance," Justin said. "Anyway, things will be different now. Even before I knew you got saved, I knew that I need to treat you with more respect. And let you know that we're here for you, wherever your faith is. You'll always be our brother and that will never change, and I should have done a better job of making sure you knew that you will always be welcome here, whether or not you help or want to go to church with us."

Jack looked back and forth between them. "There's a lot more that I need to talk to you about. It's late now, though, and I don't want to keep you two up. I know you're not well and need to rest," he said, glancing at Kellie.

"I took a nap, so I'm good for a while more," Justin said. "It's up to Kellie. Tomorrow's Saturday, so we can talk then too."

Kellie scooted up a little higher on her pillows, her rumpled curls cascading around her shoulders. "I'm mostly hungry. I've slept all day, so if we ate, I could stay up a little longer. Besides, I don't think I could even fall asleep now."

"Rebecca cooked dinner, and it's out on the table. Why don't we each have a plate and talk now," Justin suggested.

While Jack filled plates of food, Justin helped Kellie to the couch, arranging a blanket over her lap.

"Are you okay?" he asked her, fussing over her while Jack put the kettle on to boil for tea.

Kellie put her hand on his arm. "Thank you for taking care of me," she said, meeting his eyes. "I don't know what happened; the fever came out of nowhere. But you were there last night, weren't you?"

Justin nodded slightly. "I was there. You scared me."

"Don't worry about me. I'll be fine."

"Do you remember any of it? Last night?" He sat beside her and picked up his second plate of dinner.

"Some of it," Kellie said in a soft voice.

Jack came over then with steaming mugs of tea, and after placing them on the coffee table, settled into the armchair opposite the couch.

"It's good to be home," he said, then paused. "It's good to have a home. And to not be afraid of it anymore."

"Afraid of here?" Kellie's fork stopped midair.

"Not here. I think I was afraid of having a home, because I'd never had one before." Jack grinned broadly. "Now, with God, I have a home everywhere."

This really is unbelievable, Justin thought. Would he ever get used to hearing his brother talk this way? Jack, who sat around dark and brooding all the time? He shook his head incredulously.

"Today in my conversation with Reverend Dinsmore, I told him a lot of my background because it helped me sort out a lot of things. He thought it would help our family if I told you about my past too."

Jack suddenly became somber and picked up a cup of tea so he would have something to occupy his hands. "It's not that I enjoy talking about it. Actually, I've really been scared for you to know. It just seemed a better idea to get you to dislike me other ways. As if that would be less painful or something. But to start my new life, the reverend said I need to start being honest with you, and I know he's right."

Jack looked up uncertainly. "That is, if you're interested, anyway." He took a sip of tea and waited.

"Your past doesn't change how we feel about you," Justin said. "We would love to know about you though, because you're our brother."

Kellie nodded in agreement, and Jack sipped his tea again.

"Well then," he said. "We'll see how this goes. It's not much. And it's sure not pretty." He sat for a minute, watching the steam curl up from his mug. Finally, he began.

"I don't know too much about the beginning because I was a little chap, but the first I remember, I lived with Uncle Richard and Aunt Meg. I think she took care of me fine, but I don't recall much in the way of love or warmth. The vague memories I have were that she was nice enough and I always had food and baths and stuff. Well, she died sometime. I don't know much about it and I don't know how old I was, because no one ever told me. So then it was just me and Uncle Richard, but mostly just me because he never did anything for me. He wanted me to stay quiet and not make any trouble and not eat too much, so that was kind of difficult as a kid, and he wasn't very nice. One day when I came home from being out, the door was locked and that was that. I was on my own ever since."

"Do you have any idea how old you were?" Kellie was shocked.

Jack shook his head. "Not really. I'm guessing seven or eight. I took care of my own self, and once in a while I'd make a friend who'd help me out for a little while. The livery man used to let me sleep in the straw, and for a while the bakery left loaf ends for me. I didn't have much morals though, cause no one had ever taught me any, so that would usually mess things up for me. So I kept on this way for the rest of my childhood.

"Then I started making friends with this girl who lived in town, and I'd see her when she went shopping with her mother. I couldn't talk to her; at first we'd just smile at each other, you know. Well, time went on and I started sneaking over to the yard to talk to her and then it was almost winter. So she started letting me climb in the window at night and sleep on the rug by the hearth, and I'd leave in the morning before it was light. That went on for a while. Then it was warmer to sleep in the bed."

Jack shifted uncomfortably, and his sudden lack of eye contact filled in the rest of the story for his siblings. "Her father caught me one night, and he beat me up. I mean, I was left for dead. I had a bunch of broken bones and I was in a bad way. It took me a real long time to recover since I didn't really have a doctor, but for some reason I made it through just with the help of my buddies. The pain was real bad, and I started drinking then to help numb the pain. That and a little food is about all they could really scrounge up for me, anyway. So that's how, by the time I was about thirteen, I was a drunk and a . . . a . . . " Jack licked his lips and didn't look at anyone. "And I guess you could say, a prostitute," he finished.

The room was silent and the three sat motionless. Jack looked up finally and explained, "The one funded the other, you see. And it got to the point where I couldn't go very long without either one."

"I didn't even know something like that existed," Kellie admitted sheepishly.

"It's a pretty discreet occupation," Jack said, dropping his eyes and picking at his fingers.

Justin couldn't fathom how a thirteen-year-old could generate income from such a thing. "At a brothel?"

"No, I didn't work for anyone else. I'd meet them at parties in the big houses, you know, where there's all these empty rooms upstairs and girls can make excuses to go freshen up."

"You were awfully young," Kellie exclaimed in disbelief.

Jack shrugged. "Yeah, that's the thing. I'd been on my own for so long, I never thought of myself as a kid. Now I look back and it's crazy to think about, but at the time, I thought I was pretty grown and tough."

He took a breath and bit his lip. "I got intoxicated on the way they craved my freedom. I think they wanted me because I *was* an orphan, and they'd feel like they were helping me, sneaking me food and wine, and I'd give them what they wanted and then I'd leave with a pocket full of cash. Most of them didn't want everything, you know. I think they just wanted to feel wild and free and I'm a pretty good—" Jack stopped suddenly, realizing that he was going maybe too far in his information.

"Well, you know how Jed would get that euphoria when he won a big night, and it was mostly the feeling that he screwed everyone over and didn't get caught? That's what it was for me, but a hundred times that, because I knew that their suitors were going to the brothels and I was giving their partners what they couldn't."

Everyone was quiet for a minute, then he continued, "That's how the next couple of years were. 'Til the war started, and I was able to escape. The army gave me a home, food, and friends for the first time in my life. And then, a family. But the mess I got into before the war . . . it has a way of following me everywhere. I've never been able to break free, so I hope Jesus can help me with that. I tried, at the beginning, in Baltimore and then when we came here. I wanted to make you all happy so you'd keep me, but I'm in too deep. I've never been able to go long without a drink and I broke every rule you made."

Jack looked up at his brother and sister. "The reverend said that no one can make themselves pure, though, and that we can change only when Jesus works in our hearts." The hope in his eyes lit them up in a way that Justin had never seen before.

"I haven't had an addiction like that, but He certainly changed my heart and cleaned up some things I was struggling with when I trusted Him, too," Justin said. "Sometimes God changes us more slowly than we would wish, so if it takes some time, don't be afraid that you're doing something wrong. God is slow to anger and is so patient with us. He's begun a huge change in you already, Jack. It's as plain as day. And He promises that He will finish what He started."

He glanced between Jack and Kellie ruefully. "There's still a great deal He needs to finish in me, and I've known Him a lot longer than you have. I can't judge you for what you've been through or for the things you've done, Jack. And to be honest, I wish I would have known sooner so we could have done more to help you instead of being so hard on you."

Kellie nodded, tears in her eyes. "We don't think of you any differently," she whispered. "None of us have been very good at supporting each other. I think . . . I think it starts with being more honest with each other. You took the first step, and that was so brave, Jack. It's not easy to do that. We need to start talking more, and not hiding what we're struggling with, so we can help each other."

Justin knew that was directed at him, but he had no reply. He felt inadequate to meet Kellie's expectations of him, and didn't know how to communicate that to her. Even now, in the midst of their reconciliation, he felt cornered and uncomfortable.

Jack jumped in, however, and the conversation continued for another half hour before Justin called it a night for Kellie's sake.

"We have all day tomorrow," he promised as he cleared the dishes and prepared to help Kellie back to bed.

She stood up and hugged Jack around his neck for a long time. "I love you," she said. "I can't thank God enough for today."

"Me either. And I love you, too," he said, hugging her back.

She finally kissed him and let go, and allowed Justin to help her to her room. He set her candle on the table and she sat on the bed.

"Can you believe it?" she asked in awe, nodding her head toward the living room.

Justin cracked a half smile. "It's amazing, isn't it?" he said, making no movement to go. Looking up after a moment, he said, "I told you a lot of things last night, and I want to make sure you heard. Everything that God has done with Jack doesn't excuse the way I've handled everything or make it okay. I'm sorry, Kellie. And I'm going to try to do better for you."

Kellie blinked sleepily at him. "I adore you, Justin. I don't hold anything against you. I . . . mostly wish you trusted me enough to be more honest with me. I think . . . that it would help a lot of things."

Justin's chest tightened and he nodded, swallowing hard. "I know. I'll . . . I'll work on that," he said, wishing it was as easy as she seemed to think it was. He turned to go, but stopped again as Kellie lay down. Justin pulled her covers up and blew out her candle.

"Goodnight. Get well."

Once in his room, he was asleep within minutes, exhausted from the long night and day, and resting in the new peace that God had brought to their home.

-25-

The sun was high in the sky the next morning when Kellie finally padded out of her room, her robe tied around her trim waist.

"I smell coffee," she announced when she saw Justin, alone in an armchair with his Bible on his lap.

"Yes, it's ready. I left you some in the pot." As she moved to the kitchen, Justin asked how she was feeling.

"Much better. I slept so well," she said cheerily. "Has Jack been up yet?"

Justin gave a little laugh. "Sure has. I got up early to spend some time praying since I have so much I wanted to thank God for. But he got up too, and spent over an hour asking me questions about the Bible. I didn't get much praying done, but he was like a starved man. It was something else."

"Really?" Kellie came to join him, carrying her mug of hot coffee. "Where is he now?"

"He went downstairs to tell Mrs. Katz the news. I'm sorry I haven't made breakfast yet. I've been tied up."

"It's okay, I can whip something up. It sounds like you were doing better work anyway."

"Oh, I forgot to tell you. Luke wanted come by to see you, but that was before you were ill. I'm sure he found out and that's why he didn't come last night, but he'll probably want to come by as soon as you're well."

"I would like that, thank you."

Justin started to say something, stopped, and started again. "Are you in love with him?"

Kellie didn't hesitate or even blush. "Yes, I am."

Justin nodded and thought for a moment. "Do you think you'll marry him?"

"I'd like to, but I'm not sure when the time would be right for our family. I don't suppose we'll live together forever, but I don't want to leave before we're ready."

"You know you stole him from me," Justin accused playfully. "He used to come over to spend time with me. Nowadays, I can hardly get a moment alone with him."

Kellie pursed her lips, a twinkle in her eye. "I feel a little bit sorry for you, but not enough to stop. Besides, I know that you're the mastermind behind all of it. You wanted to make him your brother officially, so you set us up together."

"I did," Justin said with a chuckle. "That's why I brought you to Chicago in the first place. It was my plan all along."

Kellie laughed, but then she arched her eyebrows at him. "I suppose you'll want to meet someone and get married sometime too."

Justin shrugged. "Yes, I probably will eventually."

"Have you ever had anyone? Or thought of pursuing any of the girls at church?" Kellie realized she didn't even know.

"I did have someone once. I just haven't thought about it for a while. But if you want to marry Luke, you don't have to wait on account of us. Do whatever you two decide is best for you, okay?"

"If he asks me, I'll be sure to let you know," she said merrily, standing up. "I should get dressed and get some breakfast made before Jack gets back."

"I wouldn't worry about him. I'm sure Mrs. Katz has fed him by now. He's been gone a long time."

"I can't wait to all go to church together tomorrow," Kellie said as she sailed into her bedroom. "It's going to be the best feeling."

The door closed behind her and Justin finally turned back to his Bible in peace.

After Jack returned from Mrs. Katz's, the Youngs stayed home together the rest of the day. The conversation ebbed and flowed; sometimes on difficult topics where tears fell, and sometimes laughing together over funny stories. The camaraderie and joy in their home was at its peak, higher even than when they had first all arrived in Chicago together. For the first time there was true unity in their spirits.

"Honestly, there is one thing from your story yesterday that I can't wrap my mind around," Justin told Jack. "You said that Jed would get euphoric when he won at gambling, and I just cannot picture Jed showing that kind of excitement."

"Me neither," Kellie said. "I wondered about that too. I barely saw him as much as crack a smile the whole year he lived here."

Jack laughed. "No, he didn't express it like I do, and you were never there to see it. But when he won big, he would sit there picking up his pile of money and he'd have this look on his face where his lips would turn up at the corners, and I knew just how he was feeling. Money never motivated me the way it motivated him," he continued. "For me it was all about the liquor and the ladies, but I understood the powerful feeling he got when he'd just hustled a bunch of people."

He stopped suddenly, dropping his eyes, and everyone thought about Thursday's letter as the air in the room grew somber.

Kellie finally cleared her throat and cocked her head at Jack. "So your scars . . . are they all from that father?"

"Most of them," Jack said, and grinned impishly. "Some of them are from stupid things I did where I hurt myself, and then I got a bit of shrapnel in the war. This one and this one," he said, pointing to his chest, "Are from where he broke my ribs. The girls always like to see those."

"I'm glad he didn't kill you," Kellie murmured. "It sounds awful."

"I thought he was going to. I have more nightmares about that than I have from the war," Jack admitted, and Justin wished again that he had been more compassionate towards his baby brother.

The following day, they were all smiles at church, Kellie hanging on Jack's arm like she wanted to not miss a single moment where he rediscovered each of the different elements of worship as a believer. Jack was baptized after the service, a decision that had been made during his conversation with the reverend on Friday, and celebrated with dinner afterwards at the manse.

With all the excitement, Kellie arranged to meet Luke for lunch on Monday so that they could get quiet conversation alone for the first time since everything happened. They sat on a bench in a green space a couple of blocks from Great Central Station. The day was breezy and it was nippy in the shade, so they were thankful to find a seat in the sunshine.

Luke had his own lunch that his mother packed for him, so Kellie brought a pear, bread, and cheese for just herself. Before he opened his pail, Luke looked at Kellie, his eyebrows scrunched together.

"I'm so sorry about Jed. I've hurt so much for you since I found out," he said. If he was honest, he would have had to admit that seeing her in black crepe again broke his heart, when he had only ever seen her wear colors barely a year. Kellie nodded silently, but she was appreciative of his concern, and it showed on her face.

"Do you think there is much chance that he's still alive?"

Kellie sighed. "I have no idea. If he is, he was probably taken prisoner somewhere. If he's wounded, it may be quite a while before he's able to write, and even then, letters across the lines have had a pretty low chance of making it here. I don't know if I would even hear. So I don't know. His colonel seemed to think that there wasn't much hope, though."

"I am sorry," Luke said again. "I brought you a little something," he added. Reaching into his lunch pail, he produced a small nosegay with four miniature pink roses in the center, surrounded by balm and baby's breath.

"Oh, Luke. They're beautiful." Kellie lifted the flowers to her nose and closed her eyes, taking a moment to internalize what it meant to him. "Thank you."

"Tell me about the last couple of days. Much has happened."

Kellie told him about the highs and lows, her sudden illness, and the conversations with her brothers, while Luke ate his lunch and listened.

"Here," he said, holding out a forkful of meat. "Try this. It's so good."

Kellie leaned forward and took a bite of the pot roast and her eyes widened. "Did Rebecca make that?"

"Yes, she did."

"I should have her teach me. She's amazing. You should hear this," she said, her face brightening. "Jack has decided that he wants her to teach him piano. He said he can get a paper route or something to pay for it. He's really serious, since he didn't grow up with any way to learn about music. He hasn't stopped surprising me the past few days."

Luke blinked. "That's great. You know she isn't going to take a cent from him, though."

"She really should let him pay. I'm glad that he's looking for productive ways to fill his time now. I'm afraid the reality is going to be a little rough for him as he adjusts to living without the things he's been addicted to, but learning to play the piano could be a good distraction."

A few minutes further in the conversation, Kellie wiped her mouth. "Justin said he once had a girl he was interested in. What do you know about that?" She bit into her pear.

Luke looked at her suspiciously. "The first time you and I really talked, you were apprehensive of gossiping about him with me."

Kellie hid her smile behind the pear. "That was before. I trust you now, and he still doesn't talk about himself enough."

"Is that all he told you?"

Kellie nodded. "Do you know the girl? Or what happened?"

"I do know the girl. She's my sister." Luke tapped his finger thoughtfully against his fork, and Kellie almost dropped her pear.

"Rebecca?"

"Mm-hmm."

Kellie stared at him, flabbergasted. "I've lived here for two years. How did I not know this?"

"Well, she tries to hide it, and I don't know what happened. I brought it up once, and she didn't want to talk about it. She's obviously still in love with him, though."

"She is?"

"Definitely. She's always sad around him. And I can tell by the way she looks at him. It can only mean one thing."

Kellie felt idiotic for not noticing. "I suppose I thought she had a melancholy personality. I don't see her very often when he's not with me. I never thought anything of it, and I've lived here for over two years." She let out her breath. "Justin and Rebecca. I can't believe I didn't know."

Luke shook his head. "She's not a sad person. It's definitely him. And don't feel bad, you had a lot you were taking in and learning about your family and everyone else. I noticed though, because I know her better than anyone."

"I wonder what happened," Kellie said softly. "And why he never told me. So you never talked to him about it."

"No. It seems like he's over it and has moved on."

Kellie took another bite of her pear and swallowed. "Well, I think it's sad. They would make a nice couple. I doubt I could get him to tell me any more about it, though."

They finished off their lunch, and Kellie walked Luke back to the station before heading home. She needed to start thinking about supper, and she found herself looking forward to being back in the apartment with her brothers and seeing what Jack wanted to talk about next.

He was reading her Bible again when she got home, and read a passage aloud to her as she swept and began dinner preparations. All of her reading lessons were suddenly paying off in a big way, and it made her heart leap to see the fruit of all the tiny seeds she had planted day after day over the past few years.

Justin came home from work the next Monday with an announcement as the family sat around the table finishing dinner. He set his fork on his plate and turned to Jack. "If you're interested, they have a place for you down at the docks. I talked to the foreman today, and he said he'd give you a job. I know it's not what you've been studying all this time for, but it's decent wages and you can start tomorrow."

Jack took a moment to let the news sink in, expressing his gratitude before replying. "I was looking forward to learning how to play the piano," he admitted. "I wonder if Rebecca would do evening lessons with me."

"You can ask. It's up to you," Justin said.

"They must think highly of you to offer me a job when they haven't even met me."

Justin leaned back and pushed his plate away. "I work hard, and I've been there a long time. I told them that they'd like you." If those things weren't enough to get him a promotion, at least it was enough to get his brother a job, he thought.

"Well, thank you. I'll take it then, and hope that I can live up to the reputation."

November 11, 1864

"How has Jack been doing at work?" Kellie asked Justin on Friday morning as she poured herself coffee.

"I think he's getting on fine, to be honest." Justin slid fried eggs from a pan onto plates on the table. "For not being used to physical exertion, he seems to be adjusting pretty well."

He looked up to see Jack coming out of the bedroom just then, running a comb through his hair.

"I'm hungrier these days, though," Jack said, eyeing the eggs on his plate. "Can I have a couple more?"

"If you pay for them!" Kellie said with a laugh. "You've eaten so much this week, that's about all the food left in the house, so it's a good thing we're going to the Dinsmores' for supper. I'll need your pay tonight so I can go to the grocer in the morning."

"And you shall have it," Jack promised as she headed into her room to get dressed and he sat down.

They were just finishing up their eggs and a hearty theological discussion when footsteps thundered up the stairs and there was loud, desperate banging on the door. Justin jumped up and yanked the door open to find Titan, breathless and panicked.

"There was an accident," he panted as Kellie hurried out of her room, still hooking her cuffs. "It's Luke. He was run over on his way to work this morning."

Jack made it to Kellie's side in time to catch her before she hit the ground, knocking his chair over with a bang on the way.

Justin grabbed Titan's arm. "What happened? Is he alive?"

"I don't know." Titan breathed heavily. "He was, but it's really bad. Really, really bad. I think there was a runaway wagon. Are you coming?"

Justin looked at Jack holding Kellie on his knees and saw that Kellie was completely unconscious.

"Grab me her smelling salts and go," Jack said, waving his free arm.

"Are you sure?" Justin ran to Kellie's room and brought Jack the satchel.

"Yes, I have her. She'll be okay. Go."

Justin hesitated. "As soon as you get a chance, send a message to Mr. Brewster, okay?"

"I will," Jack said, continuing to shoo Justin toward the door.

Justin turned and ran out of the room with Titan to the carriage waiting downstairs.

"Where is he?"

Titan picked up the reins and shouted "Giddyap!"

As the carriage took off, he said, "They're at the hospital. Everyone is at the hospital. It's not good, Justin. I don't know if he's going to make it."

They didn't speak the rest of the way to the hospital as Justin's chest tightened with fear. He gripped the side of the carriage, thankful that Titan was in a hurry as they rattled across the cobblestone streets. The carriage stopped in front of the hospital, and Justin ran ahead as Titan tied the horses up.

Inside, he found the reverend and his daughters huddled on a bench in the hall outside of the surgery. He pointed questioningly to the closed door beside them, and Reverend Dinsmore nodded, so he turned the knob and entered. Only Mrs. Dinsmore was in the room, and she met him at the door, her face red and swollen. Justin stopped and pulled her into his arms, holding her tightly as he looked over her to the bed.

The body on the bed was unrecognizable, and it looked like a massacre. Blood-soaked bandages covered body parts that were still waiting to be stitched up as doctors and nurses came and went from the room, preparing for the extensive surgeries. What had formerly been Luke's face was purple, swollen, and covered with cuts and dirt, and none of his hair was visible under a thick white bandage.

Justin let go of Mrs. Dinsmore and made his way to the bedside. He touched Luke's hand gingerly, and softly said his name. Luke didn't move, but Justin saw the sheet covering his chest faintly rise and fall.

At that moment, the nurses came over, ready to begin cleaning him up, and gestured that he should leave. Justin numbly stepped back, and looking down at his hand that had been on Luke's, saw that it was covered with blood. Luke's blood. His best friend's blood, and this could be the last time that he would see him alive.

Trembling, unaware even of his own movements, he made his way out of the room to the bench outside, where Titan had joined the others. Elisan was on the floor at her father's knee, and Titan was on the end of the bench next to her. Their eyes were closed, faces teary, and their lips moved in joint prayer. To Reverend Dinsmore's right sat Rebecca, clutching his arm with her head on his shoulder. Justin sat down next to her and leaned forward, resting his forehead on his free hand. He sat staring at his blood covered right hand, too stunned to move.

Minutes ticked by, and no one moved. Reverend Dinsmore rested his left hand on Elisan's shoulder, cocking his head over to hear his children's prayers, while Rebecca and Justin sat together on the other end of the bench in silent shock. Everyone wanted to try to comfort each other, but no one had any words, their hearts shattered to pieces.

Justin knew he couldn't stay. He knew he needed to get back to Kellie, and that he really needed to be caring for her. Mr. Brewster would even be expecting him in to work, and he tried to weigh the ramifications of not showing up at all. Still, it was a long time before he could manage to stand up. He turned to the family, but his head drooped. He pulled out a handkerchief and wiped his hand as he opened his mouth twice to say something with no success. Finally, he gave up and started for the door. He had almost reached it when he stopped once more.

"We'll be over for dinner tonight. There's nothing to eat at our house. But we'll come over early to cook for everyone."

No one replied, but Reverend Dinsmore nodded acceptance. Justin turned once more and walked out the door as if in a trance. When the door closed, Rebecca covered her eyes with her hands, trembling to her core. Her father softly patted her knee.

"Go," he whispered.

It was his permission. Permission to acknowledge and not deny, permission to reach out instead of hide, permission to finally be honest and face the consequences, whatever they would be. She jumped up and hurried for the door.

"Justin!" Rebecca called as she ran out into the sun and the door swung shut behind her. He had not been walking fast and had just reached the corner when he heard her call. Stopping, he turned toward her, his hands in his pockets. His face was expressionless although the streaks from the earlier emotion remained, and his shoulders slumped.

Rebecca took a few steps towards him and stopped. "I couldn't let you leave like that."

Taking a deep breath, she remembered the speeches she had rehearsed in her head a million times, everything she had wanted to say to him over the past two years. If anyone was well prepared for the moment, it was her for this one. It was the dying brother part that she had failed to take into account in advance.

"I know that this is a bad time. But I need to talk to you."

Justin squinted and nodded silently, looking at her hazel eyes as blankly as he had for months.

"I know you told me not to love you and not to wait for you. You have responsibilities and I understand that and with Luke . . . well, I don't know what's going to happen now."

She searched his face, took another breath, and started again. "I've watched you go through so many struggles and trials this year and I've watched you close yourself off more and more, to me, to everyone."

She had started to cry now, but didn't slow down. "It's so painful to watch you do that to yourself. Life hasn't been easy for you, and I just wish you knew that it's okay to choose some happiness for yourself. It's okay for you to have something in your life that gives you hope and helps carry you through the hard times. It's okay for you to allow yourself to love someone and have someone to walk through things with you."

She pulled her handkerchief from the pocket of her mint green day dress, and sobbing now, continued as she began to wave it around.

"You told me not to wait for you, but you never asked me what I wanted. I want your face to light up when I walk in the room, the way it used to. I want you to know that there is someone who has your back and that I am always on your side. I want you to have someone that you'll let in and help bear your burdens so you don't end up isolating yourself. I want you to know, Justin, that I love you, and that I'll wait a hundred years for you if I have to."

Tears started rolling down his face and they stood apart, facing each other and both crying. "I don't know what will happen now with Luke and with Kellie, and this is a terrible time," Rebecca repeated. "But please. Please let me love you."

She took one step forward, unintentionally. "Please let me in again."

Justin still said nothing. He stood on the sidewalk, tears falling, wavering within himself. More than once, he very nearly turned around and walked away. He couldn't do this now, not while his best friend and brother was dying and his family needed him. How could he even think of himself and Rebecca together again?

But the chance to rethink his feelings towards her weakened him considerably. As selfish as it seemed, maybe she was right—maybe he was allowed to have some hope and happiness in the midst of the storm clouds that had been chasing him mercilessly. Maybe loving her, and letting her love him, wasn't really selfish at all. Looking at her standing before him with tears streaming down her face, he realized acutely for the first time how much he'd hurt her, and in allowing himself to feel towards her again, he became cognizant of how deeply the divide had hurt him too.

Suddenly he moved, reaching out and pulling himself to her. Grasping her face with both hands, he bent down and kissed her as his tears fell to her face and slid down her cheeks.

Breathless, Rebecca threw her hands around his neck and held on for dear life, kissing him back for all she was worth, and that's when Justin knew there would be no going back. He wrapped his arms around her and held her tight as he continued to kiss her and cry, his heart pounding, a million thoughts fighting for his attention, a million intense emotions exploding in his chest: pain and passion, fear and wonder, regret and healing, anguish and love, as he shakily accepted her love for him, tender and fervent.

When he finally stopped for breath, he lifted a hand to the back of her neck, his forehead still pressed to hers.

"I need to go," he said, panting heavily. "I need to go to Kellie."

Rebecca clung to him desperately. "I know."

"But I will talk to you. Maybe tonight, or tomorrow. I don't know when but I will, okay?"

"Okay."

Before he could waver again, Justin let go, swinging around and walking away without looking back.

Rebecca stood sobbing, watching him go, her head spinning. He had kissed her like he meant it, but there was no explanation to accompany it. He could still say anything tomorrow; he hadn't told her he loved her or offered any commitment. The kiss, however, only said one thing. He cared, and he cared a lot. She didn't see a way that it could be interpreted as anything else. Gaining confidence, she stayed a long time out in the warm sun, remembering the feeling of Justin's lips on hers and his curly hair in her fingers, and she never once realized that the whole scene had been on a public street corner and at least thirty other people had witnessed it too.

In the end, Jack was the only one who made it to the docks that day, since Justin decided to stay with Kellie and head over to the Dinsmores' early to cook for the family. Neither he nor Kellie were particularly stable emotionally, and it was a difficult day as they waited on edge for any news. Reverend Dinsmore and his wife stayed at the hospital up until dinnertime, but the girls and Titan came home early in the afternoon and were there when Justin and Kellie arrived.

Rebecca had a headache and went to lie down, but Elisan sat in the kitchen, catching her friends up on the news and telling them where to find things. Luke, she told them, was out of surgery; everything was cleaned and stitched up, but he remained unconscious. His head injury was the most worrisome, and the only thing they could do now was wait to see if he woke up. In addition to the head injury, his broken bones, cuts, and bruises were numerous. Should he wake up as soon as the following day, his recovery would still be excruciatingly long, painful, and uncertain.

Kellie bore the news quietly as she chopped potatoes. Justin kept glancing over to see how she was holding up, but she worked steadily on. Reverend and Mrs. Dinsmore arrived and were taking a few minutes to freshen up before dinner when Titan came into the kitchen to get Justin.

"Jack's here," he said in a low tone. "He needs to see you."

Justin followed Titan without asking questions, and was surprised when he was led out the front door. Jack sat on the front steps, tears in his eyes. Immediately Justin smelled the alcohol, and his heart sank.

Titan left them, and Justin sat down next to his brother. He wanted to feel angry, he wanted to shout "*How could you? How could you do this to Kellie, or yourself? How could you show up here like this?*" but he didn't. He wrapped his arms around Jack, and Jack leaned into his shoulder and they cried together.

Kellie came out a few minutes later to look for them, and Jack came to his feet when he saw her.

"I'm so sorry, Kellie," he sobbed.

Her eyes were compassionate, not hurt, when she took his hand. "Do we need to take you home?" she asked softly, looking into his eyes.

Jack shook his head. "Unless you think you need to. I only had a half a bottle, I'm not drunk. I just feel terrible."

Kellie turned to Justin, who had dried his face. "Why don't you head in and tell them to start dinner. Jack and I will be in in a minute."

As Justin stepped through the door, he heard Jack apologizing again to Kellie. His heart broke; the last couple of weeks sober had not been easy for Jack, and on a day as hard as this one, he'd been left with the other men at the docks on a Friday night. Justin knew he should have done something to help protect his brother from the obvious stumbling block he had run into. Although he knew Kellie would explain God's gracious forgiveness once more, he wished he would have warned the poor guilt-ridden boy ahead of time of the temptations at the docks, and he felt responsible.

When Kellie and a subdued Jack came to take their seats, they found the dinner table silent and the food barely picked at. Justin was seated across from Rebecca, the first time he had seen her since leaving her outside the hospital, really seeing her for the first time in ages.

Reverend Dinsmore softly announced that he and Mrs. Dinsmore would be staying the night at the hospital. Until something changed with Luke, they thought that everyone could take shifts so that someone from the two families was always by his side.

Kellie was quick to speak up. "Could I take the morning shift tomorrow?"

Rebecca added, "I can come by for the afternoon," so it was settled.

The room fell silent again, with the exception of silverware clinking. Suddenly, Mrs. Dinsmore dropped her fork with a loud clatter, pushed back her chair, and bolted from the room, leaving the rest of the family frozen around the table. Reverend Dinsmore quietly stood, gave a silent nod to excuse himself, and followed his wife to her bedroom.

For a minute, no one moved or spoke, and then Rebecca stood up. She grabbed a serving dish off of the table and hurried to the kitchen, so Justin picked up the rolls and went after her. He found her leaning with her hands on the counter, sobbing. He stood awkwardly holding the rolls, not sure what he should do and wondering why he had come.

"I'd never seen your mother cry before this morning," he eventually ventured.

Rebecca nodded and wiped her face. "Just twice before," she said with a sniffle. "Only over Luke. That time we lost him when we went to hear Mr. Lincoln, and when you both left for the war."

Justin had heard the story, of the family going to hear Abraham Lincoln speak during one of his visits to Chicago as a senator. Luke was about ten at the time and had gotten separated from the family. They didn't find him for over an hour; when they did, he was quietly in a corner teaching a younger boy how to yo-yo, but the episode had frightened Mrs. Dinsmore severely. Rebecca sniffled again, and Justin wished his handkerchief wasn't completely used up, or he would have offered it to her.

"You know he was going to ask Kellie to marry him this week? He showed me the ring the other day. It was in his pocket today," she whispered.

Justin's eyebrows shot up. "He was?"

Rebecca looked confused. "I thought he would have asked you."

"I told him that I'm not Kellie's guardian so he didn't need my permission." Justin thought for a minute. "I did know that it was coming sometime. Actually, I kind of told him to do it."

"You did?"

This wasn't really the time to get into his conversation with Luke in the gutter outside of the brothel, so Justin just nodded.

"He gave her pink roses last week, too," Rebecca continued, "so I figured it was going to be soon anyway."

"Pink roses?" Now Justin was confused.

"You know," Rebecca said, and stopped when the look on Justin's face told her that he did not, in fact, know. "Pink roses signify love."

"Oh."

At that moment, Jack came into the kitchen and found them.

"We need to pray," he said. "Come on."

Justin and Rebecca gave each other a wide-eyed glance and followed him to the drawing room, where he had gathered his siblings and friends. Jack knelt in the middle of the floor, so the others followed suit, kneeling in a circle on the rug.

He looked around at each one. "Okay, then. We can start with confession and then begin petitions. Luke needs our prayers, and you know he would do the same if it was one of us."

They all nodded, and Jack took a deep breath. "I'll start," he said and closed his eyes. But when he began to earnestly confess his sins aloud, he began to weep, and then everyone else began to weep as well. When Reverend Dinsmore came out of the bedroom to let them know that he and Mrs. Dinsmore were leaving for the hospital, he found Jack prostrate on the ground with the others gathered around him, crying and praying aloud, and he had never seen a scene so beautiful in his entire life.

-26-

It was late and everyone was emotionally spent when the Youngs reached home that night. Jack informed Justin that Mr. Brewster had been forgiving of him not showing up for work, but requested that he come to work the following day, Saturday. He gave Kellie his wages and reported that Mr. Brewster had promised to pay Justin the next day.

Kellie was anxious to get some sleep so that she could head to the hospital first thing in the morning, so they all went straight to bed, but sleep was elusive and fitful for them all.

Justin finally got up to get a drink from the kitchen in the dark hours of the night, and when he did, he heard a noise coming from Kellie's room. He gently pushed her door open and found her lying in bed, crying. He padded over to her bed and sat down on it, lifting her by the shoulders so that she leaned on his lap. He sat stroking her hair as she cried, until eventually she calmed down and then slept again. Not wanting to disturb her, he leaned back against the wall and sat awake until morning.

Rebecca was alone in a chair next to Luke's bed watching his chest rise and fall, a neglected book slipping down her lap when Justin arrived straight from work the next day. She had rarely ever seen him in his work clothes and smiled to see his disheveled black mop framing his smoky grey eyes. He had tried to wash his hands and face, but he was dirty and smelled like sweat and sawdust and he carried his cap and lunch pail. She came to her feet as he approached.

Justin came to a stop when he reached the other side of Luke's bed and dropped his eyes to his best friend's still frame.

"How is he? Any changes?" he asked just above a whisper.

"No. He's barely breathing, but he hasn't stirred or shown any other signs of life."

Luke's wounds had all been neatly covered since Justin had seen him the previous day, his head and arms bound in clean white bandages, and a white sheet was pulled up to his chest. The blood and dirt had all been cleared away, and the swelling in his face had receded moderately.

"Did you see Kellie?" Justin continued in a low voice.

"Yes, she was here when I came after lunch and she stayed and visited with me for a little while before she left."

"How was she?" Justin's eyes moved from Luke's face to Rebecca's.

"She was tired. You know Kellie. She doesn't complain, but she's crushed. She's a rock, though."

Justin nodded and looked back at Luke. "I know." He took a deep breath. "I hate that she has to go through this now too."

Rebecca didn't respond as she brushed Luke's bandaged hand with her own.

After a minute, Justin whispered, "I never wanted to hurt you, Rebecca."

Her heart raced as her eyes darted to his face and saw his distress.

"I know that, Justin."

"When I was in the army, I had every intention of marrying you when I got home," Justin continued whispering. "I wanted to be with you. But when my family came, everything changed. I couldn't bring them here and then divert my attention elsewhere."

"I understand that," Rebecca said again.

"How could I tell you not to wait for me and then send you a different message by my actions? I wanted you to be free to have other relationships if someone else came along, but you know me better than anyone. I couldn't let you in and then expect you to be free." Justin softly waved his cap around as he whispered.

Rebecca shook her head, trying not to be frustrated. "I wasn't free anyway. I was in love with you, and I've never been interested in seeing anyone else," she insisted, the volume of her whisper rising.

"That was your choice then, not a result of me sowing confusion by duplicitous actions."

Rebecca fell silent, glancing at Luke then back at Justin. He obviously didn't understand how many times she had wished she could escape from loving him, how much she'd wished she could stop the pain of caring so much for someone who had shut her out so completely.

Justin finally came around the bed to her. He motioned to the chair and she sat, and he seated himself on the floor, placing his things down beside him. Looking up at her, he rested his arms on his raised knees.

"I want you to know how sorry I am. I failed you and everyone else, and I haven't apologized to you yet."

There was the sense of defeat again, that had cloaked him for months, that had driven Rebecca to run after him the previous day, and she stared at him, bewildered.

"What are you talking about? Who have you failed?"

Justin's eyes grew large with surprise at her apparent ignorance.

"Everyone, Rebecca. I brought my family here, and I expected to lead them and provide for them and give them something to belong to, and I didn't do any of that. Luke, well I haven't been much of a friend for him lately, as much as he does for me. And you, I came home just to crush your dreams."

How could she not see what he was talking about? Hadn't everyone been talking about his shortcomings the past two years? What else was there to see?

"You haven't failed anyone, Justin," she hissed back. After all, her dreams were still alive and well, thank you very much. "Nobody thinks that. It seemed like you quit trying, and closed yourself off to the people who love you when your siblings turned out to be such a disappointment to you."

"My siblings?" Justin exclaimed in a horrified whisper. "The only person who has been a disappointment to me is my own self."

Rebecca stared at him and he stared back at her. "It appeared to me that bringing them here ended up being significantly more difficult for you than you expected. I thought you were resentful of them."

"Is that what everyone really thinks? Good God," Justin moaned, kneading his hands together.

"I don't truly know what everyone thinks. I haven't talked to anyone about you. I'm sure Kellie thought it though, because of how she acted around you."

"There's more to it," Justin blurted out, not stopping to ask what she meant about Kellie. "It's true that we weren't prepared for how difficult it would be, but I'm not resentful of them. I used to think our problem was that we all had unmet expectations and became disillusioned too, but it's not just that. There's much more to it."

Rebecca watched with surprise as he grew agitated and came to his feet. He began to pace at the foot of Luke's bed, wringing his cap in his hands.

"I don't know how to talk about it, Rebecca," he said helplessly, waving his cap at her. "I don't talk to Kellie or you or anyone because I don't know what to say. I don't hurt her on purpose; I really don't know how to talk to her."

He stopped suddenly and stood still as he carefully chose his words. "Do you know what it's like to have in your hands the one thing you've always wanted more than anything, and watch it slip away through your fingers? To find yourself simply unable to hold it, no matter how hard you try?"

"Yes," Rebecca said. "I do."

Justin stood motionless and blinked at her. "Yes. Right." He looked embarrassed. "I suppose we understand each other then."

He cleared his throat then gestured with his hands as he continued. "I knew how it felt to lose my family once. These past two years it's been as if I'm carrying a fragile gift, and if I drop it, they'll be gone and I'll be ripped down the middle again. I never would have thought having them back would be so terrifying. I never would have thought that I was so . . . ill-equipped for all of it."

Justin started pacing again, taking a deep breath. "I had every advantage that they didn't have. I was raised by people that cared for me and taught me about God. I came here and found a family that took me in and made me one of their own. I'm healthy and strong and should have been able to do better for them, but my inability to lead them through their pain, and mine, just caused a train wreck. Or at least, I couldn't stop the train wreck. I thought—you know, Rebecca, I thought love was supposed to be healing. But it's the most painful thing I've ever done."

He slumped back on the floor again, and she realized that he was just now processing not only the events of the past year, but his life. Despite their closeness before the war, he had never once mentioned being in pain to her before. The weight of her position in the moment descended on her, and she listened intently as he spoke haltingly.

"We all tried to act like we were normal. I tried to do the right things and they tried to go along with it. Until Jed's leaving publicized how much I'd failed all along. And then I never could seem to get myself back on the right track with either of the others."

Rebecca couldn't put her finger on what was behind Justin's agitation, and squinted, trying to understand. "But Justin, even Jack has taken his share of the blame now. Why does whose fault it is even matter anymore? Why are you still carrying around so much guilt? Since Jack got saved, haven't things improved between you?"

Justin furrowed his brow, stopping for a moment before taking a shaky breath. "I brought them here, don't you see? I was the one that promised them a home and a family. I was supposed to be the strong one, the leader, but Kellie's been the one holding us together this whole time."

Justin wiped at his mouth with the back of his hand, trying to find words that had been stuck inside him and force them out. "But Rebecca . . . I don't know how to say it. To be honest, I think . . . I suffer from what happened too. I was a child when my mother died and I wasn't even allowed to see her or say goodbye, and then Pa was killed, and Kellie was torn away from me, and I lost everyone that I loved. The boys were babies and they don't remember our parents, but I remember what it felt like. As much as I want to, I have never forgotten or recovered from it. I didn't come into this . . . experiment . . . just looking for love and support. I think . . . I don't know." He shook his head, speaking slowly. "I think I was hoping that uniting us again would undo the past, that what tore inside me when they were torn away would be mended."

The bandage was ripped off; Justin suddenly felt a sting from exposing the wound his heart had been trying for years to keep hidden from his head. It was the sting he'd felt when Kellie figured it out the night Jack left. The sting that told him that he wasn't okay, he wasn't strong, and something inside him was deeply broken.

Rebecca inhaled, finally beginning to understand what Justin still failed to see. "You thought you were giving the orphans a home by bringing them here." She spoke gently and ran her hand down his arm, leaning forward toward him.

Justin looked at her blankly. "Well yes, that was the idea."

"You forgot that you're an orphan, too," she whispered pointedly.

"What?"

"You keep saying that you were supposed to be the leader. You didn't think of yourself as an orphan like them. They were the ones who needed a home, not you. And you didn't realize they weren't the only ones who needed to be healed. You just told me that you're healthy and strong, but at the same time, you know you've just been denying that you suffer too."

Justin knew she was right. But what did it all mean? Had his perspective been off this whole time, and was every accusation of Jack's actually true? Had he been lording over his brothers without realizing it?

"See?" He ran his hands through his hair. "It all comes down to me. I was wrong, only everyone explains it in different terms. But I don't know if I could have done any of it better. If I had known how to do better, I would have."

Rebecca shook her head earnestly. "No, that's the point, don't you see? You were like a captain leading injured troops but they and you didn't realize—or didn't want to admit—that you were limping too. So you did what you could; I don't think anyone would say you didn't try. But you couldn't do what a healthy captain would have done, or be the strong leader you wish you could have been, and no one realized it."

She looked at him compassionately. "Justin, I teach orphaned children, and they all want to be the strong one. Regardless of the individual circumstances, it's always jarring for a child to lose their parents. Your brothers have the advantage of not remembering. I'm not privy to what their lives have been like, but whatever they've suffered through doesn't erase the fact that you lost your ma and pa too, and you can actually picture that day in your head and relive it over and over again."

Justin leaned back and looked at the floor, finding inside himself the courage to tell her the truth that he had never been able to vocalize to Kellie. "I miss my parents more than ever. I thought bringing my siblings here would be the climax of what I've always wanted. But having them here only accented what was missing from the picture even more . . . " His chin quivered, but he took a couple of breaths and kept going. "Having them here unmasked pain that I have spent my life trying to ignore, it revealed a lot about myself that I didn't want to see . . . and . . . it brought the terror of losing them again."

Shaking his head, he added, "It's been a difficult couple of years, but God has been working in all of us, I know it. We've all grown through it. I've been learning to trust Him more, and to look to Him, not my family, for healing. And then coming to terms with where I've failed." He paused. "For the first time, I really believed we were moving in the right direction, and we would be okay. And then this happened with Luke."

"There's value in appreciating the journey, regrets and all, that brings us closer to God and reconciliation with one another, even this one." Rebecca reached out a hand again and lightly laid it on his. "The trials of learning and growing together may be frustrating and disappointing, but they don't make anyone a failure. They lead us to God, and He alone is our peace as we look to Him."

She sounded like Luke now, and Justin automatically lifted his head toward the bed, but Luke remained motionless.

"I've missed you, Rebecca. And I've needed you. I know it's been hard for you, and I'm sorry."

This was all Rebecca needed to hear. Just to know he had missed her too was as much as she'd been hoping for the past two years when all she'd been given were stoic looks and had questioned if he still cared. The kiss yesterday had hinted at it, but it was beautiful to hear him say the words.

Justin glanced at Luke again and back to her. "I'm not going to ask you to wait a hundred years, but I am going to have to ask you to wait a little longer. Just until we know what's going to happen with Luke. One way or another." He swallowed. "I just can't do it to Kellie right now in the middle of all this." Her hand was still on his, and he picked it up and played with it. "It won't be forever this time, I promise."

Rebecca nodded as emotion surged through her, the devastation of Luke's unknown future and the promise of reborn love at the same time. She had dreamed of this moment for so long, she had to convince herself that she wasn't still dreaming, but her senses were all engaged. She could see him, hear him, feel him, smell him next to her, and her heart sat lodged in her throat at the way he had just opened up so completely to her. She looked at her hand, his skin tenderly touching hers, and she wanted to keep that moment, to keep him, forever.

"I love you," she whispered, barely loud enough to reach his ears, and his eyes moved up to meet hers. His gaze locked and held hers for the first time.

"Why me?" he whispered back.

How do you answer a question like that, Rebecca wondered, thinking that it would take days to list all of the reasons. Her eyes squinted the slightest degree.

"You . . . opened my heart, years ago. And you make me feel alive."

Justin swallowed and dropped his eyes, toying with her fingers on his knee, finally allowing his mind to wander and remember the love they had begun growing before the war. He had never imagined when he'd made the deliberate, painful decision to set her free and shut that part of himself off, that Rebecca, who could have had any man she wanted, would still be here two years later, devoted wholly to him. He wondered what, if anything, he would have done differently had he known.

They sat in the silence, and then Rebecca interrupted his thoughts.

"You said that Kellie's been holding your family together, and I think in many ways, Luke is the same for my family," she said softly. "He's such a keen listener and has earned everyone's deepest trust. He and Kellie are both peacemakers, and their relationship reflects a sweet serenity that I think the world needs more of."

"He's been good for Kellie, and for all of us. She's happy when he's with her, and you're right, peaceful. I wanted that for her."

The conversation was beginning to feel somber with the shadow of Luke's silent presence next to them, so Justin added, "You'd be surprised about her, though. She's one woman you just don't cross. For being a peacemaker, she sure can be a fireball about getting everyone back into order, and Jack still calls her 'Colonel' sometimes."

They shared a laugh, and it was a welcome relief.

"So you approved of them being together. It seemed as much, but I wasn't sure at the time how you were going to take the idea."

Justin shifted knees and resumed stroking her hand. "I wasn't sure at first either, because love can be such a finicky thing, and our friendship with Luke is so long and so deep. But of course, I would trust him with my life, so I knew there is no one I would trust my sister with more than him."

Rebecca turned her eyes to Luke. "He fell for her so hard and so deliberately. He came home out of the blue one day and said, 'I'm going to fall in love with her' and he did. I think he talked to you within the week."

Justin gave a small smile and exhaled, realizing suddenly that it had gotten late and he should get home to the others. He reluctantly stood up and gently touched Luke's shoulder.

"Rest well, brother, and heal up so you can wake up soon," he told him, then turned back to Rebecca as she handed him his things and stood up.

"Thank you," she whispered. "For this. It was good."

"Thank *you.* For not giving up on me."

Justin almost turned to walk away, but stopped and leaned back towards her. "I do want to be the strong one, Rebecca. They need me."

How many times have I heard that before, Rebecca thought. *All the children at the orphanage think they need to be strong for someone else*, but she didn't say it. Instead, she replied calmly, "I know. God is your strength though, not you. And when you're weak, sometimes it's better for everyone that you're honest than to pretend."

Once again, her words stopped him in his tracks, and he shifted his weight so that he now stood close to her.

"You are going to need to stop that, or you're going to get yourself kissed again," he warned in a whisper.

Rebecca dropped her head modestly, her face growing warm. Nonetheless, she felt Justin's fingers on her chin, nudging her face back up to his, and his soft lips found hers and kissed her deeply. Yesterday's kiss felt desperate and pain-filled in contrast to the intimate and warm way he kissed her now, lingering over her.

Suddenly, Justin straightened. "Well, I didn't plan for that to happen today. So that's honesty." For a moment he looked regretful. "I did mean it about waiting."

Rebecca gave him a reassuring half smile. "I'll be patient."

"You always have been."

Rebecca inhaled, lifting her hand and running her thumb across his cheekbone.

"Does it help?"

"Kissing you?"

Rebecca nodded.

"No. It hurts like the dickens."

"Why?"

"Because now I want you. And when I didn't think about you, I didn't have to face how much I hurt you."

"Let it go, Justin," Rebecca said, easing away from him. "You know that you need to set yourself free from all of this guilt, burdens that you don't need to be carrying."

Justin dropped his eyes and nodded, then glanced once more at Luke.

"Take care, and send someone right away if anything changes."

"Yes, of course."

With that, he gave her hand one more squeeze and headed home, his mind filled with her, thankful for the steadiness of the woman and her God-given wisdom. He didn't know how she'd managed to sit by her dying brother and still offer him so much encouragement and hope, but he knew without question that she was the one that he needed by his side in life, and that he couldn't make her wait much longer.

-27-

Justin was alone when he reached the bakery corner on his way home from work on Wednesday. He had stopped at the vendor down the street for a basket of vegetables for Kellie, but Jack had gone ahead on home without waiting for his errand. Justin suddenly remembered that he had forgotten to buy a paper from the paper boy, who usually stood further down the previous street. He stopped to turn around, and when he did, he heard the voices of church women talking to Mrs. Katz around the corner. Had he not heard Rebecca's name, he would have gone along, but now he stopped short and listened intently.

"It really is a shame she wouldn't have any of them," Mrs. Linzer was saying. "With her skills and personality, she shouldn't still be single at this age and be running around with that orphan."

Mrs. Jefferson seemed to agree a little too readily. "She could do so much better than him. He has no propriety, making a scene on the street corner like that."

"Honestly," Mrs. Linzer huffed.

"Now, now," Justin heard Mrs. Katz cut in. "I won't hear you talk of Justin like that. He has the highest character. And just think of all he has been through, bringing his siblings here and supporting them when the boys were such heathens and then losing the one. The poor child has suffered enough in his life. I think he deserves to be happy with Rebecca. And she's certainly happy with him."

"I declare, in my day, girls were expected to be more dignified and hide their infatuations," Mrs. Jefferson said with a sniff. "The men were supposed to be the ones doing the pursuing."

Justin had heard enough, so he headed back for his paper. This time when he returned, he rounded the corner without stopping, tipping his hat to the three women before hurrying up the stairs. He came into the apartment, banging the door a little too hard behind him, and Jack and Kellie both jumped, turning toward him.

"What's the matter with you?" Kellie asked from the table, where she was rolling out biscuit dough. Justin set the basket next to her.

"It's nothing. Just some idle gossips that got to me." He remembered how Mrs. Katz stuck up for him, and he was inwardly grateful, if not a little surprised, at her loyalty.

"Oh, were they talking about you kissing Rebecca again?" Jack called saucily from the couch, where he was spread out with a prayer book.

Justin stopped short and stared at him. "What are you talking about?" he demanded as panic began to creep over him.

"Well, at least three church members saw it," Kellie said in Jack's defense. "It really is hard to avoid hearing about it these days."

Mouth agape, Justin stood frozen, looking from Kellie to Jack and back again.

"Don't look so surprised. If you're going to kiss her on a street corner in broad daylight, do you not think anyone would notice?" Kellie chided gently.

Justin blinked. "I . . . " he tried, but he had nothing to say.

"I'm sorry I missed it," Jack teased. "It sounds like it was quite the event."

Justin pointed a finger at him. "That is none of your business. And I have no idea what you're talking about."

Jack snorted. "I heard it went on for ten minutes."

"It was never ten minutes."

Kellie and Jack both giggled, enjoying the fun at Justin's expense far too much. "Mr. Heath said it went on and on for goodness knows how long. He said he kept thinking it would end, and it just continued."

"I've had quite enough of this," Justin said. "Really unbelievable."

He snapped the newspaper out of the basket and sat down at the table, opening it up to signal the end of the conversation.

"It's really fine," Kellie began in a low voice. "If you and Rebecca . . . "

Justin looked up at her sharply. "Rebecca and I are not," he said firmly, holding to his decision to put off calling on her for the time being.

"It doesn't sound like it."

"Yeah," Jack piped up again. "A whole lot of nothing happened on that street corner."

"Does Rebecca know that?" Kellie asked, giving Jack a warning glance.

"Rebecca and I talked," Justin said shortly. "Don't be expecting a repeat performance."

"Shucks. I was gonna sell tickets."

"JACK!" Justin and Kellie shouted together.

Jack hid his impish face behind his prayer book, and the house fell silent again. Kellie continued to roll her dough, and Justin stared at his newspaper without reading it.

After a minute, Kellie whispered, "I think maybe you should reconsider it. Maybe you . . . "

Glaring at her, Justin stood up and stalked to his bedroom with his newspaper, closing the door behind him.

As the week passed, Luke's loved ones fell into a routine with their shifts at his bedside. Rebecca and Elisan began trading on and off for the overnight shifts and Jack and Justin for the evenings. Kellie, Reverend and Mrs. Dinsmore, and Titan filled in the daytime hours, but the motionless body they watched continued to breathe without waking up. Luke's cuts and swelling were slowly improving, and when his dressings were changed each day, the nurses did not bandage back up the ones that were healing.

Kellie decided to do the wash on Saturday that week since Justin and Jack were both home and she no longer had help during the week. She washed it in tubs in the living room, giving Jack the job of scrubbing the difficult stains, primarily the boys' work clothes. Since the day was nice, Justin was recruited to carry the heavy baskets of wet laundry down to the clotheslines crisscrossing the tiny backyard. The windows were open and the sun shone as they worked together.

On his second trip, the heavy load caused Justin to lose his balance on the stairs and he tripped. Clean wet laundry went flying down the stairs and he thudded along the now slippery steps, landing with a crash at the bottom of the stairs. Jack and Kellie dashed to the top of the stairs to see what happened, and found Justin lying at the bottom, holding his leg with agonizing pain all over his face.

It was humiliating for him to be taken with a broken leg to the hospital where Luke lay with his life hanging by a thread, but there was nothing to be done about it. Once his leg was splinted, the nurses were considerate enough to put him in the bed next to Luke's until he had the strength to head home the following day.

Justin was thankful that it was Elisan's turn to have the overnight shift and not Rebecca's, so at least he was spared the awkwardness of the family having to change their schedule on his account. He would have happily considered the overnight to be his shift since he had to be there anyway, but the whole point of the bedside company was to have someone there to send for the others if Luke woke up, and he was unable to get up. So Elisan came, and she fell asleep with her head resting on her brother's bed the way she always did.

Justin did manage to convince them to all go to church the next morning and leave him to watch Luke. Jack came after church to move him home while Kellie stayed at the hospital for her shift.

"It's so embarrassing," Justin complained under his breath as Jack arranged pillows to make him comfortable on the couch.

Jack couldn't help but laugh. "It's quite funny. Your timing is terrible."

Justin looked rueful and did not join the laughter. "It will be some time before I'll be able to get back to work," he said, hesitating.

Jack patted his shoulder on the way to go make coffee.

"I can cover the bills for a while since I'm gainfully employed now."

"I appreciate that. A lot. But that's not the main thing I'm concerned about," Justin admitted. Jack didn't seem to know what Justin was trying to get at, so he continued. "When I suggested the job to you, I didn't think about the difficulties that the atmosphere at the docks could cause you. Not just the alcohol; it's not a good situation for other things either down there."

Jack set the coffee pot on the stove to boil before glancing over at Justin. "It won't happen again. You don't have to worry about me."

Justin pursed his lips. "I think we can get into trouble when we think we're immune to it. Especially with something that's had a hold on a person for such a long time. You'll be out there alone for quite awhile, it looks like. And not every day will you feel as strong as you do today."

Jack came over and sank into the armchair. "What do you propose we do? I don't think God intends for everyone to stay home all the time to avoid falling into sin."

"No, but having someone to literally walk through things with helps. I wanted to talk to you about it because I don't think I prepared you for everything that you might run into before you started, not because I think you need to be chained up."

"It's everywhere, Justin, more than you'd think. I was chained up, and I still got into it, even here."

"You were not chained up," Justin murmured, annoyed. "What about Dawson? He's a teetotaler and a Christian. Maybe he'll walk out with you every night. I think you should think about it proactively, and just having someone with you could avoid problems."

Jack looked like he'd rather not, but he reminded himself that he needed to be more respectful of Justin, so he forced himself to pause.

"Okay," he finally said as he got up to get the bubbling coffee pot. "I will."

Inwardly, he was frustrated that these things that had always haunted him didn't suddenly disappear when he got saved, and miffed that Justin knew it. He inhaled and told himself to be grateful that his brother cared enough to say something, as awkward as it was.

He brought Justin a cup of coffee, and set his own on the table.

"Chess?"

"Alright, but if you win, it's because I'm an invalid."

Jack knew the chances of him beating his older brother were slim, but he wanted the opportunity to play and improve his strategies. He pulled the board out and began to set out the pieces he'd made.

"If I win, it would only be because you let me."

"Not for long. I think you'll start giving me a run for my money soon. Can you talk to Mr. Brewster tomorrow and explain why I won't be in?"

Jack nodded. "Of course."

Justin watched Jack set the game up, and his heart swelled as it had numerous times over the past few weeks. For the first time, he felt like having a brother was close to how he'd always pictured it, and he thought of Jed, and of Kellie at the hospital, and knew perfect was still a long way off. But he was grateful, and he silently told God as much as he reached out, making the first move, and the game began.

"I have the morning shift at the hospital today. Won't you come with me?" Kellie asked Justin at breakfast the next day. Jack was at work, and Justin was idle at home as his leg began its slow recovery.

"Do you really want me? I have nothing to do there," Justin said, embarrassed that he would have to have a nurserymaid too.

"You don't have anything to do here, either. I'd enjoy your company."

So he agreed, and Kellie brought her knitting and a book for him to read to her. But as they sat side by side watching Luke's still frame, Justin's bulky leg propped up on the foot of the bed, it became apparent that reading was not actually on Kellie's agenda.

"You've been quiet lately," she said, and that was when Justin first realized that he was cornered.

"I'm sorry. I haven't had much to talk about."

Kellie let her breath out. "You mean you haven't had much that you've been willing to talk about."

Justin shifted uneasily as he struggled to find words. He thought of his conversation with Rebecca, and his promise to Kellie to be more honest, and he knew he had to make the effort if it killed him. Talking to Rebecca had lifted a giant weight off his chest, and had done wonders in helping him to accept his limitations and face his faults, but opening up to Kellie still intimidated him nonetheless. Kellie had always had expectations of him that Rebecca never did, and her opinion still mattered more to him than anyone else's. Despite how far they had come together lately, he had to struggle against the old familiar heaviness that crept over him and threatened to choke his words.

"I'm not good at this, Kellie."

"You don't have to be good at it. You just . . . jump in and try. Peel back one layer at a time." Her jaw tensed in frustration. "You've lived with me for two years, Justin. You should be used to it by now."

"I know, but before you, I never had anyone who needed me to talk to them. I've gotten used to that part, but I don't know what to say. For example, people say 'how are you?' I don't know how I am. I don't even know how to answer that question or what they mean by it, and it just gets more complicated from there."

Kellie sat her knitting on her knee and looked at him, and Justin knew his excuses sounded poor even to himself. Finally, she asked, "What are you so afraid of?"

Justin started to shake his head, but she persisted. "No, I mean it. Why are you so scared to talk to me?"

Justin sat staring at his foot, his face set. "You're not going to understand, and you're going to minimize my answer."

"Okay. I promise I won't do that. Try me."

Justin took a deep breath, but he still felt nervous. "I'm scared of hurting you."

"That's it?"

"That's it."

"Oh. Really?"

Justin nodded mutely, and now it was Kellie's turn to sit and try to process the information. All along, the way he struggled to open up to her had made her think that he was protecting himself from being hurt in some way, but now he was telling her that really it was to protect her. In a way she was touched, but she wasn't quite sure what to make of it.

"Wha . . . " she began and stopped, and Justin knew that he needed to explain.

"Kellie, you mean more to me than anything in the world. I'm . . . in every way I'm insufficient. There's nothing that I want more than to be enough for you, but I'm not, and when I hurt you, it kills me."

Kellie said nothing, so Justin looked up at her. "What?"

She turned her palms up and lifted her eyebrows. "You were right. I don't understand, and I'm being tempted to minimize your answer."

Justin nodded and turned back to gaze at his leg and the two sat wordlessly together.

Finally, Kellie said, "You know it hurts me when you don't talk to me, though."

"I know."

Again, silence. After a few more minutes, she asked, "What changed? You used to be more open. At the beginning. What happened?"

Justin bit his lip and didn't look at her. "Well, when Jed left . . . " his voice trailed off.

Kellie sighed. "I know he said those things to you, but you didn't need to take it so personally. You know he was lost and confused, like Jack. He was nasty to you, but it doesn't mean he was right."

"He was a lot more right than you think."

Kellie shook her black head fiercely. "Justin, you always think so poorly of yourself. You don't need to protect me from yourself. Being hurt by people is a normal part of this fallen world. See, I was honest with you when I said I didn't understand and wanted to minimize you. It's not what you wanted to hear, but I decided it was better for you to know the truth. I want to understand, but I don't want you to think things that aren't true about yourself, either."

Frustrated, Justin fought the urge to retreat. "That's the problem, Kellie. You always thought I could do better."

Kellie looked at him and waited.

"I didn't do such a great job. I don't have the answers you think I have. I don't have the faith you think I have. I lost my temper a lot, I didn't talk to you when you wanted me to, I misread everyone's needs, and you always thought I was more than that."

She nodded expectantly.

"I'm not more than that."

"Justin, you—"

Justin hit his knees with his hands. "This is exactly why we are having this conversation. You refuse to believe me."

"You're right, I don't believe you."

Justin sat glaring at his foot on the bed. "Well, now you know why I don't talk to you."

A moment passed, and he heard Kellie sniffle. He turned to see her eyes filled with tears. "Kellie, I—" With a sigh, he lifted a hand to her shoulder. "I hurt you, didn't I?"

She shook her head and wiped at her eyes. "No, you didn't."

"Yes, I did." Justin reached into his pocket and gave her his handkerchief. "You've always had me on a pedestal, Kellie, and I can't live up to all that you think I am. You always wanted me to lead more and Jack always wanted me to lead less, and I can't be everything we all want me to be. And I'm afraid—no, terrified—of letting you know how miserable the pressure you put on me makes me."

Tears ran down her face. "I do?"

"Please, please don't feel bad because I'm a failure. It isn't your fault. I . . . I can't stop letting you down. Even this conversation, I've let you down. I hate it, Kellie. I just—it's just better when I don't try to talk to you."

"It isn't better." Her persistence was so dogged, Justin almost laughed. She wiped all her tears away and looked at him. "I'm sorry, Justin. You're right. I need to accept you for where you are, even though I know that God has made you with great potential."

Justin did laugh then, albeit a bit ruefully, and Kellie's face twitched.

"I can't change overnight either, you know. And I'll always think more of you than you do, because I can see things in you that you can't see. But I promise to not be so hard on you so that you can trust me again, and I can know you more deeply."

Justin rubbed the back of his neck. "There isn't very much there."

"There's your romance."

"I don't have a romance, and I don't want to talk about it."

"Why?"

Justin didn't say anything, and he wondered how much time was left before they could leave the hospital. Kellie had already torn down a few walls today, and the progress gave her courage to continue.

"Why didn't you tell me that you and Rebecca have a past?"

"Where did you hear that?"

"Luke."

So she'd known for at least a week then, before the kiss in front of the hospital. Justin inwardly cursed his leg that prevented him from getting up and walking away. "There isn't anything to tell."

"For the love of God, Justin!" Kellie exclaimed peevishly.

Justin stared at his sister, surprised by her strong language.

"What happened between you two?"

"We were never in an official relationship, Kellie. It wasn't the right time for us."

"Is it now?"

Justin started to shake his head, so Kellie continued, "Will it ever be?"

"I don't know."

"Do you love her?"

"I think so."

"Luke said she still loves you," Kellie said, wondering how Justin could kiss Rebecca like that and then sit in front of her and say such things.

"I know." Justin squirmed. "What else did Luke tell you?"

"Just that he didn't know what had happened, but that he could tell she still loves you by the way she looks at you. Oh, and that he thought you were over her, but now we know that isn't true." *Because everyone knows you kissed her.*

This was telling to Justin; if even Luke didn't know what had happened, then Rebecca had kept it closer to her chest than he thought, and the knowledge brought him new respect for her.

"I don't know why we have to have this conversation."

"Because, I have a really good friend who's in love with my brother, and a brother who thinks he has to protect people from himself," Kellie said pertly.

"It's not like that with Rebecca." Even saying her name out loud hurt, but Justin would rather die than let Kellie know why he had broken up with her.

Kellie put her hand on his knee. "What is it then?" she asked, leaning forward. For two years, she had lived with him without knowing there was something between him and Rebecca, and she'd be damned if she let him keep hiding from her. Her persistence infuriated him, and Justin had to breathe heavily to calm himself down and figure out how to communicate with her.

"I don't think I can say that I love her when I've been too distracted to notice her for the past three years, and I didn't even know how she felt. It seems hypocritical. And I badly underestimated her."

"It's understandable though, since you've had reason to be distracted and I didn't notice either," Kellie said sympathetically. "Is it just time that you need?"

"It might be. She's had three years to think about it, and I haven't thought about it at all until recently. I told her . . . to wait until we know what's going to happen with Luke, since I can't think about starting something in the middle of all of this."

"You did?"

"Yes."

"Why didn't you want to tell—"

Justin held up his hand. "Please don't," he begged wearily.

Kellie leaned back and picked up her knitting needles again. "Fair enough." A minute later she added, "I'm glad to hear you're considering it."

"I am, thank you. And please don't talk to anyone else about it."

"I won't," Kellie promised, but inwardly she was overjoyed at the news, and that she had just had a real conversation with Justin.

"Are you scared?" he asked, ready to get back to his favorite topic of conversation: her.

"About Luke?"

Justin nodded, and Kellie cocked her head for a moment. "I am, but not in the way you might think." She paused and stretched her yarn out. "I don't want him to die," she said, her tone softening. "It would be devastating, for me and for all the people I love. But I'm not scared for myself."

"Why not?"

"Built up resilience, I suppose. I've lost people I love before. In fact, I've lost everything before. And I've seen that God has always taken care of me, and I suppose I've learned to trust Him. He has always carried me, even when I had nothing else left." Kellie looked Justin in the eye. "Actually, this time, I have more support than I've ever had in my life. So I know that whatever happens, it may be tremendously painful, but I know I'll be okay."

Justin shook his head in amazement. "You're incredible."

"You are too."

"I really wish you wouldn't think that about me."

Kellie sighed, dissatisfied that she couldn't change his mind. "Fine then, you're ridiculous."

"Thanks, that's better," Justin teased triumphantly. Picking up the book, he began to read aloud.

-28-

"Mr. Brewster said to tell you to come in tomorrow," Jack announced from the wash basin as he cleaned up from work. He unbuttoned his shirt and pulled it off, then began to lather his bare arms with a bar of soap.

"Don't do that in here," Justin said from his seat at the table, where he was opening the newspaper Jack had brought.

"Why not?"

"People usually stay clothed in their kitchens when other people are around."

"Oh." Jack looked around. "Well, it's just you and Kellie," he said without stopping.

"You did tell him that my leg is broken, right?"

"Yes, he knows your leg is broken. He said he wants to talk to you, and he might have some things you can do." Jack scrubbed the back of his neck.

"Are you taking a complete bath?" Kellie asked, turning around from the stove with her nose wrinkled up.

"I feel disgusting. Just cleaning up for dinner."

Justin pondered Mr. Brewster's request. "I wonder what he has that I can do. The only things you can do sitting down at the warehouse are his job or the clerk's. I don't want to clerk."

"But it would be income, and only temporary," Kellie said. "It would give you something to do."

"Are you ready to get rid of me already?" Justin asked with a laugh. "Did you find out all you wanted to know about me today?"

"Oh goodness, I wish I'd been around for that," Jack said as he rubbed a towel over his chest. "Did you get anything good, Kellie?"

Kellie smiled back at Justin. "You'll have to find out for yourself, Jack. He's a tough nut to crack. And of course I'm not tired of you, but I think it's nice that Mr. Brewster is offering something to help out."

"It is. He's always been a good boss," Justin said. "Okay, I suppose we'll borrow a buggy from the livery in the morning. Can you get up early tomorrow to get it, Jack?"

"Yes, I guess so." Jack headed towards his room for a fresh shirt but stopped and turned back to Kellie. "Did he talk about Rebecca? That's what I want to know about."

"Good luck. You'll need it if you think you're going to get that out of him."

Jack rolled his eyes at Justin and grumbled under his breath on the way out of the room.

"I'm glad you made it," Mr. Brewster said the next morning as Justin sat on a bench by his desk with the crutches he hadn't yet mastered.

"Thank you. I'm sorry about all this." He gestured towards his leg. "I figured I would be looking for a new job when I finally got back on my feet, so I really appreciate it."

"I hope you won't need to do that." Mr. Brewster sat down in his chair behind the desk. "I actually wanted to talk to you anyway. I was wondering if you would be interested in having my job."

Justin sat stunned, not sure if he heard right. "Your job? You mean . . . manager of the warehouses?" His head spun and his pulse quickened.

Mr. Brewster nodded. "I'm going to be leaving the docks next week. This is getting to be a lot for someone my age to keep up with, and I was just offered a job at the bank that is a slower pace and closer to home. Mr. Danford asked if I knew anyone that I would consider to take my place, so of course I thought of you."

"Me? Why me?" Justin was flabbergasted.

"Well, you're young and strong and work hard, but also you're a natural with numbers. And most importantly, I know that if you had this job for thirty years, not a cent would go missing. I can't say that about eighty percent of the men out there." Mr. Brewster waved towards the window. "Also, the others respect you, and that will make a big difference in the quality of work they do." Justin knew Mr. Brewster was speaking from experience.

"Well, I . . . I never dreamed of being manager. I would be completely honored to have this job. You have big shoes to fill."

"I know you can do it, though," Mr. Brewster said with a confidence that Justin didn't feel. "If you come in the rest of the week, I'll be here to train you, but I know you'll pick it up quickly. Mr. Danford wants to meet you before it's official, even though he told me that the choice for the position is mine. He will be here later today and I told him that he could meet you then."

"Yes, of course." Justin had never spoken to the owner of the three adjacent warehouses on the Chicago River, but the men occasionally saw him arrive in his carriage wearing silk suits, shiny leather shoes and a spotless top hat when he came from his downtown office to check on the numbers with Mr. Brewster or discuss new contracts.

Mr. Brewster spent the rest of the morning showing Justin some of the main tenets of the position, and Mr. Danford arrived with his assistant shortly after lunch. If Justin hadn't been overwhelmed before, he became completely nervous when he saw them coming his way. His inability to even stand to greet them, coupled with being in his ordinary work clothes, heightened his discomfort. He nodded his head and extended his hand when Mr. Brewster introduced them, and after shaking his hand, the men took seats around the desk.

"Mr. Young, Mr. Brewster tells me that you are the most qualified candidate to manage my warehouses."

"I certainly hope so, sir. I am grateful for his confidence," Justin said. "And I do want to apologize for the broken leg; I'll be back to normal within a few months, but Mr. Brewster believes it does not affect my ability to handle the duties of the office."

"He tells me that you've worked here for eight years? How old were you when you started?"

Justin bobbed his head. "Well, I was fifteen when I started, sir, but minus the year that I left to fight in the war."

"Ah, a patriot and a loyal employee. Both things that we appreciate. Are you married, Mr. Young?"

"I am not."

Mr. Danford held a finger up. "I need a manager who is settled down, so I don't have to worry about him deciding to go panning for gold or leave for Texas to become a cowboy."

At this point, Mr. Brewster cut in. "Justin has his orphaned siblings in his care," he informed his boss quietly.

Justin would have thought that his siblings all being adults would have made that point moot. "I happen to have marriage in my sights recently, and I have no intention of leaving Chicago or the docks. The shipping industry, particularly here in Chicago, is at an exciting stage, positioned for even more explosive growth in the coming decade. With the transcontinental railroad underway, that will open up the shipment of the natural resources from the West to the East with greater speed and volume than we have ever seen before, and Chicago will have a big role to play with our location between the two and on the Great Lakes. I find it exciting, and there is nowhere else I would rather spend my career."

Clearly impressed with Justin's sincerity, Mr. Danford accepted his credentials and moved on.

"As you know, most of the position is keeping accurate logs of all shipments and managing the laborers and their wages. If anything goes awry in the numbers or with the men, my manager will be held responsible."

"Yes, sir."

Mr. Danford seemed to have covered everything that he wanted to, and he tapped his gold cane on the ground. "You'll be able to buy a fine house for the lady you have your sights on with this salary. I guarantee you won't have to convince her to jump at your proposal now."

Justin smiled at his wording. "Thank you, sir. She would have been happy to have me a long time ago with just the shirt on my back, but I'm thankful that I can offer her a bit more than that now."

"Mr. Brewster will be here to train you for the rest of the week. I look forward to growing the shipping industry with you, Mr. Young."

"Thank you, sir."

Justin still thought he was dreaming when Jack drove him home that night. "What did Mr. Brewster find for you to do?" Jack asked curiously.

Justin had been silent, but now he glanced over at his brother. "I think I should wait until I can tell you and Kellie together."

"No way." Jack shook his head. "I know you talked to her about Rebecca. I'm getting this news first. Are you sharpening his pencils?"

"I'm taking his job."

"Whoa!" The horse stopped, and Jack turned to face Justin. "You what?"

"Keep going!" Justin gestured towards the road. "I want to go home."

Jack picked up the reins and the horse trotted at a faster clip. "So you're gonna become Danford's manager? What's happening to Brewster?"

"He's taking a job at the bank, and he said he can train me for his job this week. I met Mr. Danford today, and it's all settled."

"Are you messing with me?" Jack asked warily.

"Nope."

"Man, you're going to have to get some new clothes," Jack said, pulling up to the bakery. Justin climbed down on his good leg and pulled his crutches out.

"I'll be making some good money, so I can afford it."

"Don't you dare tell Kellie anything until I get back from the livery. I want to see her face."

Justin turned around and waved a crutch in the air. "It will take me that long to get up the stairs," he called behind him.

Kellie was as shocked at the news as her brothers were. "All along, you've been hoping for a foreman job, and instead, God made you manager of the whole warehouse!" she exclaimed, leaning over to hug Justin in his chair.

"I know; I can't believe it. It's intimidating. I never even considered the idea that I could ever be a manager before, and it's going to be a great deal of responsibility. But Mr. Brewster picked me out of everyone, and it will be quite a larger salary."

Jack pulled out a chair and took a seat next to Justin at the table. "So, I wanted to talk to you about my promotion to foreman," he began, but Justin swatted at him.

"Not on your life! I worked for eight years before I got promoted, so you probably would've had a better chance under Mr. Brewster than under me!"

Jack sniffed and muttered under his breath, but Kellie just laughed.

Turning back to the stove, she said, "Everything's been happening so fast lately."

"Yes, it's been a lot this month," Justin said. He exhaled slowly. "Do you ever have things you want to talk to Luke about, but then you remember that you can't?"

Kellie gave him a knowing glance over her shoulder. "Every hour. I tell him anyway when I see him."

"I miss him," Justin said, and the room fell silent. After a minute he added, "Tomorrow after work I should stop by the tailor to get fitted, since I'll need some new suits by next week."

"Isn't it your evening to be at the hospital?"

"Oh, that's right. Can you do tomorrow, Jack, and I'll do Thursday?"

Jack looked up from the newspaper he had opened. "If you'll promote me," he replied, and Justin rolled his eyes.

"If you don't swap with me, I'll fire you."

"Oh stop it, you two." Kellie waved her towel at them playfully. "Dinner's ready, so can you set the table?" She handed Jack three plates, and he got up to oblige.

"We should celebrate your promotion," Kellie said. "I'm not ready tonight, but maybe I'll make a cake tomorrow."

"I'll invite Rebecca," Jack volunteered. "I know she'll want to celebrate."

Justin leaned his forehead down on his arm to hide his laughter, and straightened back up after a minute with a more serious look on his face.

"Honestly though, I am overwhelmed by God's kindness. Getting this job is bigger than my biggest dreams, and sitting here at dinner with you two, having a good tease . . . I have a lot to celebrate and be thankful for."

Jack handed him a fork and knife. "I think I've been the most surprised by God's grace since I got saved," he said. "It's one thing to be forgiven of sin and know His mercy, but I wasn't expecting all of His good gifts. Every day I'm blown away by it."

Kellie set the food on the table and took her seat.

"Then why don't you say the blessing, Jack," Justin said, bowing his head.

Pick was by the chapel waiting for Reverend Dinsmore when he arrived with Elisan on Wednesday. He moved to Elisan's side first and offered her his hand as soon as the wagon stopped.

"I missed you last week. Is everything okay?" he asked by way of greeting as she took his hand and climbed down.

"My brother's in the hospital and it's been a difficult week," Elisan said, looking up into his brown eyes.

"What happened? Which brother?" Pick's face reflected concern as he surveyed her tired, drawn face and slumped shoulders.

"Luke. He was run over by a wagon, and he's unconscious so we don't know yet if he'll recover. I've been staying with him overnight every other night, and last Tuesday was my night so I was too tired to come on Wednesday. I'll be there again tonight."

"Oh, Elisan, I'm so sorry to hear. I wish I could do something to help. I'm amazed you're even here today then."

"I wanted to see you, and it doesn't help him for us to pace around the house all day, so I might as well come." Elisan sighed sadly, and Pick realized that the reverend had begun to unload crates alone.

"I'm here if you want to talk about it," Pick told her before moving to help Reverend Dinsmore and offer condolences to him as well.

As he and Elisan passed out vegetables together, she told him everything that had happened in the two weeks since she had last seen him. She appreciated his concern, but she noticed that he seemed quieter than normal and was moving slower. Halfway through their task, the truth dawned on her, and she turned abruptly towards him.

"You're sick, aren't you?"

Pick glanced at her blankly and continued working. "I'm fine."

Elisan stood taking him in, horrified to realize what was happening. "It's scurvy, isn't it? Tell me the truth."

Pick didn't tell her the truth or say anything else.

"Pick, you have to take extra vegetables today. You can't get sick."

"I'm not taking more than my share," Pick said dully.

"Don't be stubborn. You have to, please."

"Elisan. I'm not taking more than my share," he repeated.

Elisan's voice rose with panic. "Pick! Stop it! I'm not going to let this happen to you just because you want to be difficult."

"You're making a scene, and you can't tell me what to do."

"Yes, when you're making reckless choices, I can! I'm the distributer and I can distribute how I want, and I want you to get enough vegetables to take care of yourself. And now I know how you turned out the way you did, because you never listen to anyone else."

Pick stared at her, dumbfounded that she still refused to listen to him.

"Elisan Dinsmore! What's your middle name?"

"I'm not going to tell you my middle name just so you can patronize me," Elisan replied haughtily.

"But I don't know your middle name yet. Mine's Rockwell. It's the name of my mother's estate in Liverpool."

"She named you after a house and a butler? Yours is the strangest family I've ever heard of. Mine is a real name, my mother's maiden name."

Pick's eyes widened. "They were a very good house and a very good butler, Elisan Corwith Dinsmore."

Elisan immediately regretted telling him the clue to her name, but she never would have dreamed that he'd know it. "What? How did you know my mother's maiden name?"

Pick shrugged, somehow managing not to grin triumphantly at her. "Your father told us a story about his father-in-law once in Bible study, and he called him Mr. Corwith. He was a minister too, wasn't he?"

"And you remembered? Good grief. Well, never mind, you're trying to distract me from the point. You're sick, and I'm going to make you keep enough vegetables, and there's nothing more to be said."

Apparently, Pick thought otherwise. "Elisan Corwith Dinsmore, you do not tell me what to do," he stated firmly, and his brown eyes didn't sparkle under his kepi.

"Pickens Rockwell Thomas, you do not have my permission to use my full name like that," Elisan returned, annoyed at him for being so stubborn, for refusing to listen to her, and for knowing her middle name.

Pick jutted his jaw out, and the two worked silently together until the vegetables were distributed and Pick set his one share aside. He turned to begin loading the empty crates into the wagon, his movements painful and slow.

"I'll load up, Pick. You go rest," Elisan said in a low voice, picking up the next crate.

"I'm fine."

Elisan slammed her crate down into the wagon, and the sound made him jump and turn his tired eyes to her.

"I do not appreciate you lying to me!" she exclaimed, and Pick scowled darkly at her.

"I don't appreciate you being so disrespectful to me, Miss Dinsmore, or making a scene in front of everyone like you did."

Elisan stood looking at him without moving, her eyes filling with tears as Pick faced her in a standoff, both realizing that her tears had far more to do with her brother than with him.

"I'm just worried about you," she finally admitted. "I'm sorry for embarrassing you. I need you to take care of yourself."

She expected him to reply, but he didn't immediately, so she swallowed hard and picked up another crate. "Can I bring you some food as a personal gift?" she asked as she stacked it in the wagon.

Pick shook his head. "They would probably take it away, and if they didn't, I'd share it. I can't eat it in front of everyone, Elisan," he said, his voice husky. "And I can't take food that would go to someone else."

She was fighting tears, so he reached out a hand and touched her upper arm gently. "I'm doing my best to take care of myself, okay? You can pray for me, because there's nothing else you can do. But please don't worry about me. I'll be fine."

"I need you to be," Elisan said as the tears escaped, running down her cheeks unbidden.

"I know." Pick sighed. "I know it's been a hard week for you, and you need rest, too, so please promise me that you won't worry about me."

"I can't do that. I promise I'll pray for you, but I can't promise I won't worry. I would like to finish the crates myself and for you to go into the chapel now so Papa can pray for you."

Pick took a deep breath and let it out with a nod. "Okay."

He squeezed her arm and his hand dropped, and she watched him slowly limp towards the chapel. Elisan took a shaky breath, swallowing back her tears, and turned towards the crates again.

-29-

November 27, 1864

It was the middle of the night on Saturday night two weeks after Luke's accident when loud pounding came on the apartment door. Justin struck a match and lit a candle in the cold dark, and as Jack made his way out into the living room, Kellie's door creaked open behind him.

"Luke woke up," Titan shouted breathlessly when the door swung open. "Come on!"

Justin, Kellie, and Jack quickly threw on clothes without asking questions, and Jack helped Justin down the stairs out into the darkness. It wasn't until they were on their way in the carriage that they paused to catch their breath and get the details from Titan.

Rebecca had the overnight shift that night, and when Luke came to, she immediately got a nurse and sent for the rest of the family. After dropping the rest of the Dinsmore family off at the hospital, Titan headed to the Youngs'. Titan didn't know much else, other than that Luke was in and out of consciousness since he had woken up.

Kellie's white face peeked from under her hood as she pulled her cloak tight around her against the frosty autumn night. Justin put his arm around her shoulders and pulled her close, kissing her forehead wordlessly as they jostled over the muddy roads, lanterns swinging from the front of the carriage. She felt the scratchiness of his beard, pressing against him for warmth.

They entered the ward together, where they found the Dinsmores gathered around Luke's bed. He was sleeping again, but even in the flicker of candlelight, the color of his face was different. Rebecca turned from her seat by Luke's head and reached out a hand to pull Kellie close.

"Luke was asking about you. He said to wake him up when you got here."

"Oh, please don't do that," Kellie begged, looking tenderly down at him. She pulled her hood back, revealing her thick black braid hanging down her back. Her heart caught in her throat to know that Luke was alive, awake, able to speak, and that beyond a shadow of a doubt, his memory of her was intact.

Justin and Kellie greeted Luke's parents and Elisan, and Jack and Titan left to find more chairs since Rebecca and Mrs. Dinsmore occupied the two on either side of Luke. Kellie was self-conscious about disturbing the other patients in the ward, so they spoke in low whispers to gain as much information from Rebecca as they could. She told them about Luke stirring and waking up, of the short conversation she had with him informing him of the accident he didn't remember, and then his falling back asleep when she sent for their parents. He had woken up once more when Reverend and Mrs. Dinsmore arrived, and visited with them for just a few minutes until he couldn't stay awake any longer.

As they whispered back and forth, Luke opened his eyes again, smiled at his mother, and looked around until his eyes landed on Kellie on the other side of him. His face lit up, and she leaned forward so that he could see her better.

"Kellie." She strained to hear him and picked up his hand. "I'm so glad to see you."

"I'm glad to see your eyes. I've missed them." Kellie said, rubbing her thumb over his hand.

"You're so beautiful."

Kellie blushed and changed the subject as Jack and Titan returned with three more chairs they had begged off of the nurses. "How are you feeling?"

"Ah. Sleepy, and sore all over. It hurts to breathe. And my head . . . is throbbing."

"I don't even know how many ribs you have broken," she said sympathetically. "With the crack in your skull, we weren't even sure if you would wake up or be able to speak again."

"I remember having lunch with you . . . and going to work that week . . . but I don't remember the day of the accident." Luke breathed heavily. "I knew you were here . . . but you were so far away, I couldn't tell what you were saying."

Kellie smiled. "Mostly I told you that I love you."

"Ah." Luke closed his eyes. "I love you too."

A minute later he opened them again and saw his best friend at the foot of the bed. "Hi Justin. The middle of the night doesn't look so good on you."

Justin grinned. "Getting run over by a wagon doesn't look so good on you either, Luke," he teased back.

"What happened to you, were you there too?"

"No, I did this to myself," Justin said with a laugh, leaning on his crutches.

"Mmm." Luke looked around carefully at all of the faces. "Everyone is looking at me like I need to give a speech. What time is it?"

"It's about four," Reverend Dinsmore replied. "We just want to see you, so don't mind us."

"You first woke up about two-thirty," Rebecca added.

Luke turned back to Kellie. "I'm so sleepy. Will you still be here later?"

"I'll be here."

Luke nodded, closed his eyes, and fell asleep again. For the next couple of hours, the families lounged around Luke's bedside and the bench in the hall, sometimes visiting quietly and sometimes resting. Reverend Dinsmore left to send a message to Deacon Hennessey, asking him to preach that day since it was now Sunday morning. Around six o'clock, Jack and Elisan left to get breakfast for everyone.

"Don't come back without coffee," Justin ordered. "Plenty of it."

The two drove back to the bakery, and Elisan went in to order raisin rolls and strudel while Jack headed up to the apartment to put the coffee pot on.

Luke next woke up when the sun peeked through the windows and the other patients in the ward had begun stirring.

"Where are my things?" Luke asked as soon as his eyes opened.

"Your things?" Mrs. Dinsmore asked.

"My clothes I was wearing, and my personal effects."

Rebecca stood up and came to his side. "Your clothes were ruined, but you mean this."

She pulled a tiny packet from her pocket and pressed it tightly into Luke's hand as relief washed over his face.

"Thank you," he mouthed to her. His fingers clutched the packet, and he paused, realizing that he could move his hands.

"I'm not paralyzed, am I?" he asked, and everyone turned to look at the covers as he wiggled his toes. The covers only moved on one side. "Am I paralyzed on the right side?"

"No, that leg was crushed," Rebecca told him with a laugh, and Luke bit his lip in acceptance.

With that, he turned to Kellie, who was just finishing up her coffee, and patted the bed next to him. Kellie handed Jack her mug and sat down on the edge of the bed to face him. Luke breathed with effort and looked like he might fall asleep again, but then his eyes popped open and he handed her the packet.

"I'm sorry, I can't open it. It's for you."

Kellie untied the little purse to find a small sapphire ring flanked by tiny diamonds on either side. She inhaled quickly and her eyes darted to his face.

"Will you marry me?" he asked, grinning at her.

"Luke Dinsmore, you know that I would happily marry you, even if you were paralyzed!" she exclaimed, sliding the ring on her finger. She leaned forward and kissed his forehead while everyone began speaking at once and offering congratulations.

After a minute, Luke looked around. "Where's Rebecca?"

Everyone stopped and realized with a glance that Justin was missing too, but the euphoria left them unconcerned and they soon returned to their breakfast and the excitement around Luke's bed.

Out in the hall, Justin leaned with his back against the wall for support as he balanced on his crutches and pulled Rebecca in close. She didn't offer resistance when his lips found hers and he kissed her at length, pausing only to breathe.

Eventually, he stopped and straightened up to look her in the eyes.

"I know I'm years overdue," he said and stopped when he got lost in her eyes. "Marry me? I don't have a ring yet or anything, but I love you desperately, and I need you. Please let me care for you and be yours for the rest of your life. I'm all yours."

Rebecca would have answered then, but Justin continued. "I'll get a ring, and a big house, and whatever else you want. Just please marry me. Please."

"Oh no," she interrupted. "You're not going to start throwing money at me, and besides, we haven't even had a real courtship yet. And right now, Justin? Here?"

Justin's eyebrows went up. "This doesn't begin to compete with how bad your timing was the day of the accident," he reminded her before becoming serious. "Do you want to take the time to have a courtship first, when we already know each other this well? I'll dote on you during the engagement just the same."

Rebecca cocked her head. "An engagement will do, but you need time to get to know me better than you think you do, since I don't need a ring, and I've always wanted to live in the little apartment. Please don't buy me a house, at least until we get to live above the bakery for at least a year together."

"The apartment is so small and hot in the summer," Justin said with a sigh, and stopped. "Okay. No house yet. And you can spend the whole engagement telling me everything I need to know about yourself."

Still, Rebecca shook her head at him. "You have to talk too. If I'm going to be the wife of the manager of three of the biggest lumber warehouses on the Chicago River, I'm going to need you to be open with me so I can make sure your head isn't getting too big."

"If my head gets to be too big, it will only be because I somehow managed to land the incredibly intelligent and talented Rebecca Dinsmore for my wife," Justin returned in all seriousness. "Besides, after a week of after-dinner chats by the fire about the transportation of lumber, and I promise that you'll realize how boring of a person I really am, Rebecca. You'll wish that you could be occupied picking out chaise lounges and rugs for the new house instead of listening to that every evening."

He stopped and looked at her expectantly. "So it's a yes?"

"Say please one more time?" Rebecca teased, and Justin's grin made his eyes crinkle.

"Please," he whispered, biting his lip.

"Yes," Rebecca said. "I'll marry you."

Justin leaned down and kissed her again before pulling back. "You know the whole city thinks that you can do better than me, don't you?"

Rebecca rolled her eyes. "They don't know you like I do, Justin, or they'd know how wrong they are. If I did what the whole city thinks is best for myself, I'd be miserable."

"I don't want to take the attention from Luke and Kellie. They deserve to have their excitement, and we can make an announcement later. Is that okay?"

"Of course. There's no hurry." She wrapped her arms around his neck and began to kiss him without stopping.

A few minutes later, Reverend Dinsmore peeked into the hallway looking for them, and spying his daughter in Justin's arms, quietly turned with a little smile on his face.

"Did you find Justin and Rebecca?" Elisan asked when he returned.

"Yes, they're . . . reconciling," her father replied casually.

Kellie was still seated next to Luke on the bed, admiring her ring and talking to her new fiancé about his beautiful choice. Her heart bubbled with joy when she heard Reverend Dinsmore, and she silently offered a prayer of thanks. She turned back to Luke and whispered, "Justin and Rebecca started talking again last week. Actually, the whole city has been gossiping about them, because he kissed her."

Luke's eyes grew wide. "Justin?"

Kellie nodded in reply, and Luke exhaled. "I wish it didn't take me breaking my ribs to get him to wake up to things."

"I know," Kellie said. "He could've done it much simpler, but he can be rather dense sometimes. He has more news, but I'll let him tell you about it. It's not as likely that he'd tell you about Rebecca himself, so I had to do that."

Luke patted her hand. "I know you'll make a fine helpmeet for me," he said sleepily.

The rest of the day was spent by the families around Luke's bed as he slept and woke up in short intervals. Various members left at different times to get rest for a few hours or bring food for everyone, but Kellie and Mrs. Dinsmore remained flanking him the entire day. Doctors and nurses came and went as they tried to ascertain his condition and make decisions regarding the next steps of his care. Now that he was out of a coma and more was known of the condition of his internal organs, they began to make plans to transfer him home for his recovery. The discomfort the move would cause, bumping over cobblestone streets in his condition, forced them to postpone it a few more days, so that he could grow stronger first and thus make it that much less traumatic.

It was suppertime when the Youngs headed home to get rest before Justin's first day in his new position. The siblings collapsed on the living room furniture with cups of tea and crackers before heading to bed, still in the clothes they had thrown on in the middle of the night. Kellie realized she hadn't brushed her hair all day and that she had actually gotten engaged in that condition, and the thought was perturbing. She sipped her tea and glanced over at Justin.

"Are things good between you and Rebecca?"

Justin smiled automatically. "Yes, they are."

"You two were out there talking for quite a while," Jack said. "It was a good sign."

Justin pursed his lips, thankful that Jack failed to realize that talking wasn't the only thing that had happened in the hall.

Kellie caught the twinkle in his eye and stopped short.

"Did you make her an offer?" she asked, leaning forward with wide eyes.

Justin's mouth came unhinged. "What? How did you know? We aren't going to announce it yet."

"You did?" Jack also wondered how Kellie knew and what he'd missed.

Kellie shrugged. "For all your thinking you're a hypocrite, I just didn't think you would wait once you got the chance. And the promotion seemed to give you more confidence than you had before, so it seemed to be a possibility."

Justin sat back, unnerved that she had read him so well, but then she grinned slyly at him.

"But really, the way Rebecca was glowing tonight made it obvious."

"You can't tell anyone though, and it isn't fair that you know before the Dinsmores do." He sighed at Kellie. "I wanted you to have your day and not be a distraction."

"Well, congratulations," Kellie said sincerely. "I'm happy to hear it anyway. When do you think you'll announce it?"

"I don't know; it depends on how Luke is doing and when he gets home. I'm not planning on delaying it really."

"Do you want to have a double wedding? We should have a double wedding so I don't have to be the center of attention. Will you ask Rebecca about it?"

"Sure, I'll ask. She and Luke might enjoy sharing their day with each other since they're so close."

"I would really be able to enjoy it better if we did," Kellie said, and sipped her tea. "I'm sure it won't be until the spring at least for us. Not until Luke is well."

"That's fine. I think Rebecca would prefer a long engagement."

"It will be the end of us," Jack said, draining his cup and putting his feet up on the coffee table. "All going our separate directions."

"We aren't going far though, and Rebecca wants to live here for whatever absurd reason. Still, this crazy arrangement we've had will be over."

Jack set his mug down and glanced from Justin to Kellie. "Since you aren't going to ask me what I'm going to do, I'll just tell you. I've decided to go to school."

Justin and Kellie stared at him in shock.

"School? Like college?" Kellie exclaimed.

"Eventually seminary, actually, although I'll need to go to college first."

"You what?!" Justin couldn't believe his ears.

Jack took great pleasure in the surprise his siblings were registering, and paused to fully enjoy the moment.

"There's a seminary north of the city in Lakeview, the Theological Seminary of the Northwest. I talked to Reverend Dinsmore more about it today, and I'm actually really excited about it." He beamed at his siblings, whose brains were occupied trying to imagine Jack in the ministry. "I'm planning to enroll at Northwestern University this fall for my college courses."

"That's amazing, Jack," Kellie declared when she could speak again. "I'm thrilled to see you figuring out what you want to do with your life and see God leading you. I hope you learn much there. At least you'll be close enough to come home for holidays and Sundays."

"That I will. So I'll be spending this year saving up for it and meeting with Reverend Dinsmore every week for Bible study."

"I'm happy for you," Justin said. "I think that's a wonderful plan."

"I'm happy for both of you, too, and that all you lovebirds are finally settling down. Uncle Jack will look forward to coming home and visiting all my nieces and nephews."

Jack stood up and stretched. "Big day tomorrow. I have a new boss I need to impress, so I should get some sleep—before I have to chauffer him to work, that is."

Justin laughed, reaching for his crutches. "Good night, Jack. Don't be late tomorrow."

"You're here."

Pick sounded surprised when he helped Elisan climb down from the wagon on Wednesday morning, and as soon as she hit the ground, her anxious eyes scanned his face for any sign of improvement. "I thought maybe you'd have another overnight shift last night."

"Luke woke up on Sunday. He's still recovering, but we aren't staying overnight anymore. They're going to try to transport him home tomorrow, but it's going to be difficult. How are you?"

Pick visibly sighed with relief. "I've been praying for you. I'm so thankful to hear."

He began unloading the crates, and Elisan could see at once that he was still unwell and had avoided her question on purpose.

"Pick," she said softly, and he glanced up at her. "Here."

Reaching into her pocket, Elisan produced a balled-up handkerchief and handed it to him. Pick unwrapped it to find a peeled and quartered orange inside, and immediately he looked up at her, his face clouded.

"Stick it in your pocket and you can eat them without anyone noticing," she insisted quietly.

Pick sighed and shook his head at her, but he obeyed, and when she saw him popping a slice subtly into his mouth, she was grateful and relieved.

"They resumed mail delivery for us," he informed her, swinging a crate down to the ground. "We actually aren't allowed to give letters to anyone else anymore, because they want to examine everything we send now."

Elisan groaned with frustration at the growing restrictions placed on the prisoners and wondering who in command had time to review all of the prisoners' letters.

"And you'd get punished if you were caught sneaking some to me anyway?" she asked, already knowing the answer.

"Yup. It's not worth disobeying the rules around here, believe me. Except . . . " Pick looked sideways at her as he reached up for another crate. "We aren't supposed to mingle with you or any Yankee visitors, you know."

Elisan squinted suspiciously. "Have you had any issues with them from talking to me? I had a four hour conversation with you one day."

"I haven't yet." Pick ate another orange slice. "The police don't usually go into the chapel since it belongs to the YMCA, and I don't think they knew we were the only ones in there. Out here, I think we're fine as long as we keep working while we talk."

Elisan quickly grabbed a crate and looking around to see if anyone was watching them, picked up her pace. A small smile tugged at Pick's mouth as he moved just as slowly as he had been all along.

"We haven't had a problem in the past ten months, so don't worry about it, okay? I'm the one responsible to keep the rules and if a problem comes up, I'll be the one to make adjustments."

"I wouldn't want them to stop issuing Papa's visitor passes, though."

Pick sighed, and shook his head at her. "You just need an excuse to worry, don't you? You never listen to me. Look, your father is best comrades with Reverend Tuttle, and Reverend Tuttle is untouchable. I don't see his passes getting revoked unless one of us just kissed you in the middle of camp or something. Keep on doing what you're doing, and don't let the administration get to you."

"If you say so," Elisan finally acquiesced. "The last thing I'd want to do is lose the right to come every week or hinder my father's ministry."

Pick registered mock offense. "So you don't really care if I get into trouble or not?"

"Oh no, of course not! You're responsible for yourself, and you told me not to worry about you," Elisan said with a laugh. "I wouldn't dream of not listening to you."

And that day, Pick realized that he'd never met another woman who could beat him at his own game the way Elisan could.

-30-

December 2, 1864

"I'm not sure if we're having dinner at the Dinsmores' tonight or not," Kellie told Justin on Friday morning as she adjusted his cravat for him before work. "I'm going to go over there this morning and see how Luke's move home went, so I'll let you know when you get home from work."

She stepped back and squinted at his cravat, and satisfied that it looked perfect, smiled at him. "You look nice. Are you working late again tonight?"

"Still getting used to having to dress up for work," he said with a grin as he reached for his crutches and stood up from the table. "I think we should be able to make it home in time for dinner."

"I hope so. You've worked late every night this week, and I'm starting to be concerned about how stressful this job is."

"It really isn't," Justin said honestly, looking her in the eye. "It's only because I'm getting used to it and am being extra careful about everything right now, but I'll get the hang of things and then it will ease up. You ready, Jack?"

"Ready," Jack said, coming out of the bedroom in his stocking feet, buttoning his shirt as he came. He picked up an apple from the basket on the table and stuck it in his mouth to sit down and pull his boots on.

"You're going to make me late." Justin sighed impatiently and put his hat on his head.

"I'm not. I'm ready." Jack stood up and grabbed his jacket and the lunch pails from Kellie. "See?"

"You didn't even shave."

"The ladies like it better like this," Jack retorted, reaching up to rub the stubble on his chin. He opened the door for Justin and turned around to Kellie.

"Have a good day. Love you."

"Love you too."

When Kellie knocked on the Dinsmores' door, Elisan answered, broom in hand, and ushered her into the foyer.

"How's Luke today? Did he get moved okay?" Kellie asked as she removed her hat, cloak, and mittens.

"Yes, he's here. We put him in Mother and Papa's room because it's on this level, so we can all keep an eye on him better."

Rebecca came out of the drawing room with an apron on and duster in hand, and saw Kellie.

"Oh, good morning. I'm sorry you caught us in the middle of chores, but you can go in there. Mother's with him now, and I'm not sure if he's awake."

"He's been pretty done in since the move," Elisan added. "He slept most of yesterday after we got him settled. I think it was all rather rough on him, but of course he'll want to see you."

Kellie smiled and followed Elisan to her parents' bedroom. Elisan softly pushed the door open and peeked inside, then opened it wider for Kellie to go through before returning to her chores. Kellie found Luke asleep in the center of the big bed, supported by several pillows and covered by a clean white coverlet. He still had a bandage around his head and his face was white and still, but his hands looked nearly new again lying at his sides.

Mrs. Dinsmore stood up when Kellie entered, and offered her the chair.

"Good morning. He's been asleep for a while, but you can keep him company if you like."

"Are you sure? I don't want to disturb you," Kellie said, but Mrs. Dinsmore shook her head.

"I really do need to attend to some things, but I'll poke my head in a bit later," she said, leaving Kellie alone with Luke.

Kellie had never been in the bedroom before, but she found it to be far more comfortable quarters for Luke and his attendants than the hospital had been, and she settled in to the armchair at his side with her lacework.

Luke didn't wake up until nearly lunchtime, and when he opened his eyes, he lay blinking at Kellie without moving. A minute passed before Kellie noticed that he was watching her and she straightened up, setting her work aside.

"Hello there."

Luke took a breath and spoke with effort. "Good morning, beautiful."

Kellie reached over for his hand and found it limp. "How are you today?"

Luke swallowed and licked his lips. "Tired."

Kellie picked up his cup from the bedside table and gave him a drink of water. Setting it back down, she sat on the bed so that she could reach him better, and stroked the stubble on his face. "What can I get for you?"

Luke shook his head without speaking, and Kellie ran her finger down his jaw.

"Can you eat something?"

"I'm not hungry."

"You won't regain your strength if you don't eat," she gently reminded him. "Are you in a lot of pain?"

Luke looked at her for a second, then nodded slightly.

"I'm sorry."

"I love you." He mouthed it more than vocalizing the words, but she got the message.

"I love you too. Do you need anything rearranged? Can I make you more comfortable?"

Luke shook his head again, and Kellie sighed with the realization that there really wasn't anything she could do for him.

"Can I read to you?"

Luke nodded, so Kellie picked up his Bible from beside the bed and opened it. She was about to begin when Luke's mother reentered the room with a bowl of warm broth on a tray. She stopped beside the bed, tenderly looking into the eyes of her beloved son, and he smiled reassuringly at her.

"I can give it to him if you like," Kellie told her. "I need to leave in a little while, though."

Mrs. Dinsmore seemed content to leave the bowl with her, and as she helped Kellie arrange his pillows to help him sit up more, she assured Luke that she would return when Kellie left. When they were alone again, Kellie turned to Luke with the spoon in hand, but he grunted with dissatisfaction.

"It's fine," Kellie insisted, the corners of her mouth turning up despite his embarrassment at being spoon-fed. "And it would make me really happy."

Luke sighed and rolled his eyes, but obediently opened his mouth without further protest.

Kellie was reading the book of Isaiah to Luke the following week while he half dozed and half listened, when he suddenly stopped listening and interrupted her.

"What day is it?"

"The fifth of December," Kellie replied softly, and Luke's face fell.

"Your birthday. It was going to be special."

She could see his disappointment, and squeezed his hand encouragingly.

"It is special, because you're alive and that's the only thing I care about. And all the rest of my birthdays will be yours to direct, so never mind about this one."

Luke would have pressed further, but he didn't have the energy to do so, so he simply nodded as Kellie lightly rubbed her thumb across his knuckles.

He still slept most of the time and was too weak to converse much, but she read to him and kept her hands busy with handiwork by his side as the month went on. The apartment was quiet these days since Jack was working, and she was grateful that Mrs. Dinsmore didn't seem to mind her coming over so often, but she wondered whether Luke would be strong enough for her to plan for a spring wedding. Rebecca had quickly agreed to a double wedding, but nothing more was said about plans as everyone anxiously watched Luke to see what his condition would allow. Truth be told, his recovery was turning out to be far slower than she'd hoped, and she was disappointed to return day after day to no noticeable improvement.

Two weeks before Christmas, things took a drastic turn. Elisan was preparing to leave for Camp Douglas with her father when Rebecca stepped out of Luke's room and shut the door, her face somber.

"We need to send for the doctor. Luke's running a fever."

"Should we stay?" the reverend asked, his coat in his hands. "We're about to leave now, but we could get the doctor on our way."

"I think that's fine, if you could swing by on your way to the camp. We'll work to lower the fever, but we need to find out what's causing it."

Rebecca stepped away to get water and rags, so Elisan and the reverend took their leave.

Once they had left the doctor's and were southbound in the wagon, Elisan spoke up. "I was wanting to do something for the men for Christmas," she said. "Do you have any ideas of what we could do? There's just so many of them, I don't know what we could manage. There's no way that I could bring eleven thousand oranges or bake eleven thousand cookies, but I'd like to do something."

Her father nodded thoughtfully, but his expression was pleased. "I don't see a way that we can do something for every inmate unless you enlist the help of others. Maybe we could do something nonmaterial for them, though."

"Like a Christmas Eve service?"

"Christmas Eve is on a Saturday, and I have the church service that evening, so I would only be available to do a service if we did it earlier in the day," the reverend said, thinking aloud. "Could you find others to give a hand with it and do music?"

"I can sing and the men can do music, if we just brought instruments. I know some of them play violin and guitar, and I could borrow those. And I'll talk to the Camp Douglas Relief Society and my book club. Maybe we can't come up with eleven thousand cookies, but if they all pitched in, we could have quite a few to hand out."

Reverend Dinsmore glanced at Elisan with his eyebrows arched. "Your book club friends would do that for the prisoners?" he asked, and Elisan shrugged.

"I'm pretty sure they would do it for me."

"In that case, why don't we begin making plans for it today, and I'll talk to the commander about it. I think it's a good idea." Her father smiled at her, and Elisan grew excited as she began plotting for the event.

Her spirits fell when she arrived at camp and saw Pick still limping slowly along, but he didn't complain.

"I'm not worse," he said brightly, gratefully accepting the handkerchief full of orange sections that she snuck him.

Elisan sighed. "I'm thankful for that at least. It sounded like Luke was worse this morning when I left, but I haven't seen him yet."

"I'm sorry, Elisan. I think your oranges are helping me, and I appreciate them."

Elisan was anxious to tell him about the Christmas Eve service, and she revealed what she had thought of so far.

"Do you play an instrument?" she asked, realizing that she didn't know.

"Yes, the piano," Pick replied, and Elisan twisted her mouth in dissatisfaction.

"I do too, but we can't get a piano here. It's okay. I know that Anderson and Martins both play the guitar, and Roger Johnson plays the violin. What do you want to do?"

"Go home."

Elisan snorted. "I know, but I meant for the Christmas Eve service."

Pick gave her a half grin and popped an orange slice into his mouth. "I can read scripture," he said, and chewed it up. "Let's go do the vegetables now, and we can see what the others want to do."

"I'm sorry you aren't feeling any better," she said, following him.

"You agreed not to worry about me, woman." Pick glanced impishly over his shoulder at her as he reached into the wagon for a crate.

When Elisan and her father returned home that afternoon, Rebecca and Mrs. Dinsmore grimly broke the news about Luke.

"He has an infection, and we aren't sure what's causing it. The doctor said to limit the number of people who are around him, so we're the only ones who can go in there until he improves."

Elisan's face fell as she took in the news. "Is he awake?"

"Not much," Rebecca said. "He's running a high fever and is moving about a lot but doesn't seem to be conscious much. Kellie came by earlier and we had to send her home, so that was difficult."

"Well then," Elisan said resolutely, "I'll handle the cooking until he's improved, since you will both be tied up with him." She wondered how she would manage both the cooking and the preparations for the Christmas program, but family had to come first.

The reverend had reported that the commander had given him permission to use the dining hall for the Christmas Eve service, since it was the largest building in the camp. If it was crowded to capacity with standing room only, maybe a couple of thousand men could fit, so Elisan figured that was how many she would make arrangements for.

A Christmas Eve service had to have candles, but everyone didn't need one; if she could procure a few hundred and every ten men had one, it would still light up the room enough to give the appropriate atmosphere. And she wanted to have enough cookies to have one for each individual in attendance. Christmas was a busy time for the bakery, but perhaps Mrs. Katz would let her use the bakery at night, after hours, and she and her friends could get them knocked out in a half a week's time. She had to borrow the instruments, and of course, find funding for the whole thing, but Elisan knew just the person for that. Her future brother-in-law had recently taken a job as a lumberyard manager, and he was making more money than he'd ever made in his life, *and* he had a Confederate living in his own house, so he was an obvious choice.

Elisan didn't get much sleep that month, but then no one else really did either, since Luke was fighting for his life with an infection and fever that raged uncontrollably for weeks on end. Keeping busy distracted her from the pallor that hung on everyone's faces, and she managed to accomplish everything just how she had planned. She arrived with Reverend Dinsmore at the prison camp after lunch on Christmas Eve with candles, cookies, musical instruments, and a crate of new Bibles to give away.

Gathered in the dining hall with two thousand smelly, sickly enemy soldiers and the relief society volunteers holding their flames up in the darkness as they sang Silent Night, a funny feeling rose up Elisan's throat. She swallowed hard with the realization that there was nowhere else that she would rather be spending Christmas Eve, and she wondered how it had come about that she had grown so fond of her friends in the camp. She sat on the front row while her father preached, sandwiched between Pick and Robertson, one of the other two men that the reverend met with on Wednesdays. He was a father with four small children in Mississippi, and she pictured their little faces spending Christmas away from their papa once again, hoping for their sake that it would be the last one. She watched Pick toy with his fingers the whole time and knew he wasn't feeling well. She would have been aghast to learn that he was really fidgeting to keep his hands busy so they wouldn't creep over and try to hold hers in the darkness.

When the service ended, he stood beside her by the door, passing her cookies out and wishing everyone a merry Christmas. They gave the Bibles to whomever wanted one, and the reverend stayed by the altar speaking to a line of men for over an hour after the service ended. Pick and Elisan finished their job and wandered outside to the wagon together while they waited for him.

"I have something for you," Elisan announced, reaching into the back of the wagon for one more crate and handing it to him. "I wanted to do something for everyone, but I can't, so you're going to have to share this yourself," she said as he peeked inside to discover a basketful of oranges and two cakes wrapped in brown paper. He was still staring at the gifts in amazement when Elisan set another parcel on top. "It's small, but these are for just you."

Pick glanced up at her face in surprise and set the crate down so that he could open the package. The paper fell off and Pick held in his hands pairs of thick fur-lined knitted mittens and socks. Before he could say anything, Elisan quickly told him, "If they take them away, I'll just make new ones."

"They're wonderful. But you know I couldn't get you anything."

Elisan grinned triumphantly. "Exactly! How does it feel to not be able to show me up, Mr. Money Bags?"

"It feels like you're enjoying watching me accept your charity far too much," Pick teased, but Elisan shook her head.

"It's not charity, it's a gift, and everything isn't about you. Merry Christmas, Pick. May this be your last subzero Christmas."

"Thank you, Elisan. I'm sincerely grateful for you." He turned and gestured towards her crate. "And thank you for the oranges and cakes as well. You know I'm going to have the worst time figuring out how to share these with all of our friends."

"I know, that's why I'm making you do it, not me."

Pick did reach down then and take her hand, and Elisan felt the cracks and cuts in his dry, bony skin. He pressed her soft white hand to his lips, and she stood frozen as her father came out of the dining hall just then. Pick dropped her hand and bowed to her before turning to Reverend Dinsmore.

"Lovely service today, sir. Thank you greatly for coming out today and doing this for us. It meant the world to us."

Reverend Dinsmore shook his hand heartily. "It was our pleasure. Merry Christmas, Pick. We need to get home so that we can make it to the church in time for the service, but we will see you Wednesday." He helped Elisan up into the wagon and climbed up beside her as Pick tipped his hat and waved.

"He seemed quite grateful," the reverend said to Elisan once they left the premises, and she knew he was referring to the way Pick kissed her hand.

"Yes," she murmured. "I think everyone is missing their families at Christmas, and we've kind of become their family here."

"You think that's all that it is?"

Elisan took a shaky breath and bit her lip, wondering what possessed Pick to do such a thing after the conversation they'd had not a month ago.

"It's all it could ever be," she said softly.

Justin closed the warehouse at four o'clock that day so that he and all of his workers would be able to make it home for dinner and to the church services on time. Kellie had a turkey and stuffing on the table when he and Jack walked in the door, but she stopped her brothers before they could sit down.

"I want you to open your gifts early," she said, handing them each a wrapped parcel.

"Now?" Justin asked in surprise, sitting at the table. He'd just recently stopped using his crutches, but it hurt to be on his foot for too long, and Kellie was glad to see him still taking it easy.

"Yes, now."

Her brothers carefully unwrapped the paper to find excellently crafted navy and gold brocade vests and crisp new dress shirts.

"These are amazing, Kellie," Justin said, admiring the quality of her handiwork. "They're for us to wear to church tonight?"

"They are. Now hurry and get them on, and we can eat dinner before we leave."

Jack leaned over and kissed her on the cheek. "Thank you. They're beautiful." He headed into the bedroom with his, but Justin lingered behind.

"Are you doing okay?"

Kellie sighed, wishing he hadn't asked, and shook her head, taking a seat at the table. "I don't want to go tonight, but I'm going to do it for Jack. It's his first real Christmas and he's so happy. I don't want to dampen it for him."

"I'm sorry, Kellie," Justin said softly, reaching over to squeeze her hand. "I'm sorry it's another difficult Christmas."

"I thought it would be different this year. I thought it would be a happy time finally, and that we would all be celebrating together." Kellie swallowed and pressed her fingers to her eyes.

Once she started talking it out, she couldn't stop, and Justin let her unload it on him. "I thought . . . that I'd done my time, and that this, my engagement, was going to be a time of joy. I thought I'd be planning my wedding. I thought beauty had come from the ashes. But it's just more ashes."

She couldn't keep the tears at bay, and they rolled down her face. "I'm done, Justin. I'm so weary, and I'm struggling to see the light, struggling to reach for hope, struggling to see God in all of this."

Jack came back out of the bedroom, dressed for church and running his fingers through his hair with oil so that his jet black waves fell shiny and perfect over his forehead. Kellie turned to see the clothes on him, and the sight almost took her breath away. He was tall, lean, and achingly handsome, and the new shirt and vest fitted him exactly.

"You look good, Jack," she said simply, noticing the happiness emanating from him. "Joy looks good on you."

"It feels good too. Are you okay?" He came up, his eyebrows knit together in concern at her red, teary face.

Kellie didn't reply right away, so Justin answered for her. "She's struggling right now, and she needs us." He got up from the table and limped to the bedroom to change, letting Jack have some time with his sister.

"I'm sorry." Jack took the empty seat next to her and wrapped his arms around her.

"No, I'm the one who's sorry, Jack. I'll be okay, I'm just having a hard time with Luke being ill, and I haven't been allowed to see him for over a week. It's been wearing me down."

She turned her face away from his chest. "I don't want to get your clothes wet. How was work today?" Kellie dabbed at her tears with her handkerchief.

"It was nice to get out early, since it's so cold out. I'm looking forward to church tonight. I can escort you, can't I?"

Kellie sat back up and looked him over. "Of course you can, and I'll be the envy of all the girls there. I know I shouldn't stoke your vanity, but we're going to turn heads." She stood up to begin carving the turkey as Justin rejoined them in his church clothes.

"There's no one else I'd rather go with than you, but I'm sorry that your fiancé can't take you," Jack said compassionately. "Anyway, I don't know what good it does to turn heads when none of the mothers here will ever let their daughters near me."

"Come now! You're just seventeen, and the war won't last forever. Their feelings will change when it's over, and God will bring you a woman in His own time," Kellie said, shaking her head at the notions Jack came up with.

"You were seventeen when you got married. Gosh, I hope I'm not old like Justin." Jack looked like he would rather die than not marry until he was twenty-four, and Kellie giggled at the drama in his face.

"It was different with me, and it's a long time until you're as old as Justin. Speaking of which, Justin, are we going to swing by the house for Rebecca before we go to church?"

"Yes, ma'am."

"You should use some of my hair oil. It's no wonder you've never married," Jack told him, looking at his older brother disapprovingly, but Justin just rolled his eyes at him.

"Just this spring, we were having to remind you to button all your buttons, but now that you're employed, all of a sudden there's hair oil in this house," Justin said in amusement.

Kellie took her seat, and Justin grasped her hand, squeezing it tight as he bowed his head. He blessed the food and prayed for Kellie and for Luke as his body fought the infection and fever raged.

Having her brothers there, praying for her and doing their best to comfort her as they ate Christmas Eve dinner together, was good medicine for Kellie. For Jack's sake, she did her best to put her grief aside yet again and be fully present in the Christmas Eve service, allowing herself to be reminded of God's good gifts and choosing to find joy. Luke wasn't beside her like she wanted him to be, but Jack was, and that was such an answer to her years of prayers that she couldn't ask for anything more.

-31-

January 19, 1865

Elisan finished stacking the last of the empty crates in the wagon after a nippy morning of distributing vegetables with Pick. She was shocked and pleased to see him still wearing his new mittens that somehow had escaped getting confiscated, but after weeks of sneaking him oranges, he still was obviously ill. He'd barely spoken all morning, and she could tell that the months of misery were wearing on him.

"Come here," she said softly, and Pick followed her to the back side of the wagon, glancing around for the camp police. Reaching down, she gently took his hand and pulled the mitten off, revealing his cracked, bloody skin, before producing a small bottle of salve from her pocket. Elisan tugged her own mittens off and held Pick's hand in hers as she rubbed the salve wordlessly on his hand and his eyes didn't leave her face. After finishing one hand, she carefully replaced his mitten and did the same thing for his other hand. She lingered, clasping his hand in hers when she finished, the first time she had ever voluntarily touched him, and the way Pick's pulse raced had nothing to do with the camp police.

"How are you?" she finally asked without letting it go.

Pick watched her closely as he hoarsely replied, "I'm just fine when you're here."

"But I'm usually not here, am I."

"No. Not nearly enough."

"I'm sorry this has been going on so long. Your sickness and . . . being here." Elisan slowly raised her eyes to meet his, and the way he was looking at her took her breath away.

"Nobody would be surviving if it weren't for what you do for us every week, Elisan. They don't have any desire to keep us alive."

"But prisoner exchanges have resumed this month, right? There's hope now."

Pick lifted his finger and traced her cheek and jaw with a slow, shaky hand.

"We'll see. There is hope now. How is Luke?"

"He's finally improving," Elisan said, forgetting to breathe, wondering if Pick could hear her heart beat as he turned his hand and ran his knuckles gently over her cheek.

"Really?"

Elisan nodded. "I think he's finally beat the fever. I got to see him for the first time on Monday, and Kellie has started coming back over again."

She stood motionless, her eyes locked with Pick's, allowing him to touch her as neither spoke for the space of several breaths.

"I had a letter from my father," Pick said, licking his lips and swallowing. He was quiet for a moment, dropping his hand and shoving it in his pocket.

"He wrote to tell me that we've lost almost everything. I've suspected for a while, but he finally admitted it. Beyond that, about half of the Negroes left when the Yankee army came through."

Elisan's heart broke for him and her countenance fell despite herself, but she said nothing, allowing him to continue.

"I'm sorry for his sake," Pick finally added. "He's a good man, and it's going to be difficult for my parents to adjust to a different life."

"But you?"

Although Pick didn't answer right away, his eyes never left hers. "The strange thing is that I'm not really sure what I think. It's painful to watch an empire fall, and to know that the beauty of my childhood is gone." He spoke slowly and carefully. "I know you're happy about the slaves, Elisan, and you should be, but you've never watched your homeland crumble, and I hope you never have to. This world isn't my home anymore and my life is in Christ now, but I'm not going to pretend that surrendering everything that I used to find my identity in isn't gut-wrenching."

"I'm so sorry, Pick," Elisan said, her eyebrows knit together in sorrow.

"It's just a matter of time until we lose this war, and we're all sitting up here helplessly, needlessly dying." Pick waved his hand in the air. "But it's different for me now, and I don't think I can explain it."

He paused, then quoted from the Psalms: "'My flesh and my heart faileth, but God is the strength of my heart, and my portion forever.' I can't say it any better than that. In Jesus, I have peace; peace that the United States will be intact, peace that the slaves will be free, peace that I have learned to live on nothing, peace that God's perfect will will be done. It hurts like the dickens right now, but at the same time, I'm at peace in a way that I wouldn't have been in the past. I think I partially have you to thank for that."

"Me? I think it's God, not me," Elisan said, but Pick shook his head.

"But He used you to help me learn to see things in a new light."

Just then, they heard voices around the corner of the chapel, and Elisan gave him his mitten.

"I'm going to go write letters now, but know that I've been praying for you every day," she said softly, holding his gaze for another moment. "And I'm truly sorry about your parents."

"Thank you."

Elisan left Pick limping towards the chapel, and she headed next door, her mind swirling with everything that just happened: the way Pick looked at her and opened up to her, the way his fingers felt on her skin, the way she was getting attached to him, all terrified her.

February 14, 1865

Justin called on Rebecca after dinner on Valentine's Day, handing her a large bouquet of pink roses when she came into the parlor where he was waiting.

"Oh, Justin!" she exclaimed, burying her face in the bouquet to hide her smile. She knew that he'd brought the only flower that he knew the meaning to, and she found his effort endearing. He looked dashing, and although she'd always liked how he dressed, she was fond of him showing up at her house in the suits and cravats that he wore to work these days.

"I know your birthday isn't until tomorrow, but I didn't think I'd get you to myself then, so I had to see you today," he explained. "I wanted to give you your birthday gift."

"I'm glad. It seems I've hardly seen you lately since you've been working so much."

Justin gently took the vase from Rebecca's hands and set it on the tea table so that her hands would be free, and handed her a small box that he produced from his pocket. Rebecca pressed her lips together expectantly and her eyes grew large as she opened the box to find a diamond ring inside. It was the same size as Kellie's, but with a single stone on a gold band, and it sparkled as the light from the fireplace hit it.

"It's beautiful," Rebecca breathed.

Justin plucked the ring from the box and slid it on to her finger. "I tried not to get one that was too big, since you insisted that I can't shower you with money. But I did want you to have something pretty."

"It's lovely. Thank you." Rebecca held her hand out at arm's length and ran her thumb over the stone. "I love it."

Justin slid his hands around her waist, stepping closer to her. "I want you to know, Rebecca, that my face lights up when you walk in the room. I want you to know that I love you and I will never get over the fact that you waited three years for me so that I can call you mine for the next hundred. And I want you to know that you take my breath away and I love having you by my side, and the best decision that I ever made was letting you in again."

Rebecca hung her arms around his neck, unable to wipe the joy from her face. "I love you too."

Justin leaned forward, closed his eyes, and kissed her slowly. He stopped without opening his eyes, pressing his forehead against hers. "You make me feel alive, too," he whispered, then pulled back to kiss her forehead and let her go.

As they settled onto the settee together, Justin asked if she was planning to go to the orphanage the next day as usual, and Rebecca nodded.

"Are you going to continue teaching there after we're married?"

Rebecca looked Justin over. "I don't know; I suppose that's up to you. I didn't think that I would keep my other students, but you know I'd be happy to keep going to the orphanage."

"I'd actually like to cook dinner on Tuesdays so that you're free to continue there. And as time goes on, I'm hoping that we can get even more involved there together."

The corners of Rebecca's mouth turned up affectionately at him. "How so? Do you mean we could find a time when we can both go?"

"Yes, for starters, and possibly more down the road. Such as . . . adoption."

Justin watched Rebecca closely, his lip between his teeth, but her face revealed no shade of hesitation or concern.

"I think it's definitely something that we should consider," she said calmly, and Justin's eyes crinkled as he relaxed.

"I adore you," he whispered.

Rebecca looked at her ring and adjusted it on her finger with her thumb. "I started going there because of you, you know."

"No, I didn't know."

"Growing up with you made me more aware and compassionate towards orphans and their caregivers. I'm grateful to the Wests for the care they gave you, and I've always wanted to do that for someone else."

"You've been grateful to the Wests," Justin repeated, thinking how she had never even met them. "Because you loved me."

"Yes. By falling in love with the orphan boy, I've come to love orphans. And on the same vein, I don't think that God gave you this job because He wanted you and me to have a big house and the nicest clothes," Rebecca added.

As Justin looked at her, he failed to understand why he hadn't already married her.

"We've been blessed to share with others, and it's no mistake that God has given us the same heart and brought us together like this. I thank God for you, Rebecca Dinsmore, and for the wisdom He's given you. I need you in my life, and God knew that."

"I'm thankful for you, too, and for the way you always put everyone else ahead of yourself and love more deeply than anyone I've ever met. I can only hope that I'll learn from your humility and generosity by living with you."

Rebecca sat thoughtfully for a moment before turning back to the original question. "I'm looking forward to having you come and meet my little students, though. I'd love to invite them to our wedding."

Justin's face brightened. "Let's absolutely do that. There will be room for them, won't there?"

"We can make room," Rebecca said. "I'll tell them tomorrow then."

Justin stood up and prepared to take his leave. "I hope your birthday is very happy, my love. You make the world a better place," he said, and kissed her goodnight.

The bitter cold wind cut through Elisan's cloak and she shivered to keep warm as her father drove through the gates of Camp Douglas that week. As soon as Reverend Dinsmore stopped the wagon, she jumped down and set to work, hoping that the activity would help in the frigid cold.

She didn't see Pick, but some of the other men helped unload the crates, and she had almost finished passing out the vegetables when her father came out of the chapel.

"I'll write the letters today," he said as he approached her, wrapping his scarf around his neck. "Pick is in the chapel and he wanted to talk to you."

"Oh! Okay then," Elisan said with surprise. Finishing the last crate, she left him for the chapel. Pick stood up and came near when she entered, holding his hat in his hands. A couple of men she didn't know were on the front row talking quietly together, but they didn't pay any attention to Elisan and left a few minutes later.

"Hi," Pick said with a warm smile, reaching to take her hand. "Come here. I have something to tell you."

Befuddled, Elisan followed him to a bench near the back of the room and took a seat next to him. "What is it?"

Pick leaned toward her and grinned largely. "I'm being exchanged. I'm going home."

"What? Oh!" Elisan exclaimed, and she couldn't figure out if she was happy about it or not.

"What do you think about that?" Pick asked, searching her face.

"I'm thrilled for you. This place is awful, and I'm thankful you even survived it. It must be something to be free again. And you must be so anxious to see your parents."

"But what about you?"

Elisan cracked a smile. "Are you trying to get me to admit that I'll miss you?"

"Something like that."

"Of course I'll miss you. I look forward to Wednesdays every week."

"I do too. Well," Pick said, glancing down at his hands and then up into her eyes. "I'd like you to come with me."

"Come with you?" Elisan gasped. "I said I would come sometime, but now? Like this? It . . . it wouldn't be appropriate."

"It would be if you married me."

He spoke quietly but without hesitation, and she knew he was serious. Elisan's mind swirled and she didn't know what to think or say. She had never actually considered marrying him before, and she wasn't sure what to do. She sat blinking, looking at him for a few moments in shock.

"But you can't know me very well. What if I'm a terrible dancer, or chew with my mouth open?"

"That's not important, Elisan. I know the important things about you."

He seemed confident, as if he didn't realize how her stomach was churning. "I know that you have a big heart because you give up time every week to serve the enemy in deplorable conditions. I know you're loyal and brave because you put yourself in great danger to help your friend find his family. I know you work hard. I know you stand up for yourself and for people who are below you in life. I know you make me laugh. I know you love God. I know you're a good cook. And," he finished, "I know that you're in love with me."

Elisan choked, but didn't even attempt to correct him. Pick waited for a minute, then relaxed and smiled again when she had no retort for him.

"I love you, Elisan. I don't want to leave without you by my side," he said softly, and Elisan's eyes filled with tears.

"I love you, too," she admitted. "This is such a shock though. I never thought of marrying you and leaving before."

"I know it's very fast. I got a second chance with you when you showed up here and then came back, and we built something here, serving side by side every week." Pick reached down and picked up her hand. "I need that. I need you, serving next to me, challenging me, making me laugh and think. And you need someone who understands you the way that I do and who will give you space to follow your conscience and fulfill your purpose. But if I leave now, we might not get another chance."

"I know," Elisan said as tears ran down her face. "All of it. But I don't think I can do it, Pick. I love you, but I also love my family, my father, my church and friends, my home, my book club, I love Chicago and these horrible winters. I would be leaving everything, Pick, everything for you. Nobody in Carolina will want to be friends with me. All that I'll ever have there is you. And here . . . I have everything else. I'm happy here, and I never dreamed of leaving. What would I do there? What are you going to do there?" Elisan shook her head in confusion.

"I don't know," he whispered, and shifted in his seat. "I'm not sure what I'm going to find down there. The best I can say is that I need to go do what I can to help my father pick up the pieces and give support to him and all of our Negroes as everyone figures out their new lives. And honestly, I was hoping to have you there to help me with that."

"Oh, Pick," Elisan breathed as she wiped at her tears.

"Elisan," Pick said gently, deliberately. "You've never let fear stop you before. You're not that type of person."

"Nobody has ever asked me to give up everything before, and so suddenly. It's too much even for me."

Elisan leaned her head on his shoulder, sniffling at the thought of the end of her closest friendship, broken-hearted that he was leaving and that she didn't have the courage to go.

"This doesn't have to be the end for us, does it? Can't we write? Please don't ask me to say goodbye."

Pick swallowed and slowly lifted his hand to stroke her back.

"Of course not. I'm not ready to say goodbye either. I'm not offering you an ultimatum. It's an invitation, and the invitation will still stand even after I leave. Don't cry. We will write." He pulled her close and whispered, "I'll miss you so much."

"I'm so sorry, Pick," she cried, holding tightly to him for the first and last time. She'd known that as time passed, food quantities had become a problem in the camp as the prisoners' rations were reduced, but it was still distressing to feel how bony his body was as he hugged her. She had to let him go; he would be free, and could go home to regain his health and strength. As difficult as it was going to be to watch him go, he needed to, and her comfort was in the fact that she knew he would be okay now.

Elisan was ashen but composed when her father came to get her later, and as he helped her into the wagon, she quietly told him, "I turned him down. I told you there could never be anything between us."

The reverend nodded understandingly, and nothing more was said of the matter.

-32-

Elisan was quiet on the way home, all that week around the house, and the next Wednesday when they drove back to camp. It was going to be different and empty without Pick there, and she wasn't sure how she was going to handle it.

She felt hollow as the wagon rolled through the gates and up the road to the square. They rounded the corner to the chapel, Reverend Dinsmore pulled on the reins, and the wagon stopped next to a singular lanky figure with straw colored hair, sparkling brown eyes, and a jaunty gray kepi on his head.

"Pick," Elisan whispered. She climbed down, stunned, to stand in front of him as he removed his hat and held it in both hands. "What are you doing here?"

"I told them to exchange someone else," Pick said, and Elisan gaped at him.

"Why?"

"I can't leave you yet, Elisan. Maybe you can let me go, but I can't let you go."

Elisan swallowed around the lump in her throat. "What are you doing, Pick?" she exclaimed as tears formed in her eyes. "This place is like hell, and you've been sick for months. You can't mean that you stayed here for me. Please don't tell me you did that."

"I couldn't say goodbye, Elisan. We needed more time."

"This place is going to kill you," Elisan cried. "You're lucky you're still alive now with all the disease, you should have gotten out while you could! I didn't know you were going to be suicidal and decide to stay!"

Pick said nothing, but he stood in front of her as she sobbed. "Papa, I . . . can I please . . . I can't."

"We'll handle this," her father said gently, and nodded his head toward the chapel. She ran into the building, to safety and solitude, and Reverend Dinsmore summoned Robertson and Clark to help with the wagon.

"What should I do?" Pick asked, standing uncertainly between the chapel and the wagon.

"Help us unload, then you can go talk to her," the reverend said, reaching for a crate. "Give her a couple of minutes."

Pick nodded and as he turned to join in the work, he felt a hand on his back.

"I'm glad to see you, son," Reverend Dinsmore said in a low voice, then lifted his crate with a smile and carried it to the line.

When the wagon was unloaded, Reverend Dinsmore and the two others began distributing the vegetables and Pick headed into the chapel. He found Elisan on a bench with her face buried in her hands. He quietly came over and sat beside her to wait for her to be ready to talk to him.

"I can't bear the thought of you putting yourself in danger unnecessarily like this," she finally said from beneath her hands. "I told you the truth last week." Elisan slowly sat up and turned her tear-filled face to him. "I love you, Pick. And if something happens to you here . . . it would be my fault."

"It would not be. I stayed because I made a decision out of fear, when I accused you of doing the same thing last week. I feared losing you more than I feared what will become of me in this place," Pick told her honestly. "And they exchanged Whitley in my place. He has a wife and children, and now he'll be going home to them. I should have given up my spot anyway, even if I wasn't in love with you."

Elisan took a wavy breath as tears rolled down her face. "What if time isn't enough?" she whispered. "And you stayed for nothing? What about your mother? What about smallpox, and cholera? How could you have chosen to stay in prison . . . for me?"

"That's just it, Elisan. It was my choice, my risk. You don't need to bear the weight of it," Pick said calmly.

"Then you don't know how being in love works," Elisan cried, and Pick couldn't help but laugh. He quickly composed himself, gently took her by the shoulders with both of his hands, and ducked his face to look her in the eyes.

"Elisan. I didn't stay to put pressure on you or make you feel guilty. The risk I'm taking does not put an obligation on you, okay? I wanted more time with you, and that's all this is. More Wednesdays passing out vegetables with you, teasing you, and watching your smile light up the camp. Don't go thinking that you're God and control whether I live or die."

Elisan laughed through her tears and wiped at her face with her fingers.

"But how did you know that I'd come back?"

Pick smiled fondly at her. "You don't come here just for me, Elisan. I knew you'd be back."

"I really am happy to see you." She sniffled, knowing he was right. "I'm just in shock. That you love me that much, and that I actually fell in love with a Confederate. You are the last person on earth I ever imagined I would fall in love with. You've changed me, there's no doubt about that."

"You've changed me, too," Pick said with a crooked grin. "Whatever else happens, I'll bear the marks of your influence on my character for the rest of my life." He watched her, content in his decision to stay that gave him even this one more moment with her, then stood up.

"There's something you said last week that's been bothering me all week, though. I must know if you're really a terrible dancer or not," he said, offering her his hand.

"In the chapel, Pick?" Elisan hesitated, looking at his hand disapprovingly.

"King David danced before the Lord, and we can too." Pick beckoned to her with his fingers. "I have a lot in common with David."

"You do not." Elisan rolled her eyes at him. "I'll just tell you then; I'm not a terrible dancer, and I'm not that good, either. Somewhere in the middle."

Pick sighed loudly, his hand still extended. "Miss Dinsmore. May I have the pleasure of this dance?"

"Only if no one comes in and sees us," Elisan said, taking his hand and standing up.

Pick moved the pulpit to the side of the front of the chapel, saying, "Since we don't have music, we have to sing it. How about *Dixie*?"

Elisan laughed outright. "I am absolutely not going to dance to *Dixie* with you."

"Fine then." Pick shrugged. "*The Bonnie Blue Flag*?"

"Oh no, let's do something slower. And neutral. How about *Danny Boy*?"

Pick nodded and offered her his hand again. "*Danny Boy,* then. You have to sing it though, I can't sing."

"This really is ridiculous." Elisan sighed as Pick pulled her close.

She softly began to sing, and as they danced through the first verse and the chorus, she realized that singing actually helped her to stay on count and she made it through without mishap. As she expected, Pick was a phenomenal dancer, and she was sure that his parents had spared no expense on whomever it was that had taught him.

Before she could start the second verse, Pick said her name, so she stopped singing and quietly hummed the tune so that she could listen to him talk.

"Elisan, you said that all you would ever have in Carolina would be me, but that isn't true," he breathed. "If you married me, you would be leaving everything you know here, and that is true, but you would have more than just me. You would also have my parents, who I don't doubt would love you; the opportunity to show love to three hundred former slaves, who I think would benefit from your presence; you have God with you always, wherever you go, and His love that will never fail you; and you'll always have your tenacity and confidence, the strong character that God blessed you with, to help you through any situation. You may be right that North Carolina might not be willing to accept you for a long time, but I'm not all that you'd have there." He looked at Elisan with hesitation. "I'm not intending to sway your decision, but I wanted to give you another perspective."

"You're sweet, Pick," Elisan murmured. "I promise that I'll put it to serious consideration. I'm sorry . . . that I'm not ready and you needed me to be."

"No, you were right. It was too sudden. I panicked when I thought I'd be leaving you forever, and I knew I had to ask."

He stopped dancing, and Elisan quickly moved apart from him, terrified of someone entering the room and seeing them.

"I should probably get back outside," she said, heading back to her seat to gather her cloak and mittens. "Have I met your expectations, kind sir?"

"More than enough," Pick said with a sly grin that stopped Elisan in her tracks.

She stepped back towards him, pulling her mittens on. "You will not start flirting with me, Mr. Thomas," she warned him in a low voice. "I'm not going to be distracted by you, nor will I be the talk of the camp."

"You're already the talk of the camp," Pick said cheerily. "I'm not particularly sorry for distracting you, either, but I promise I'll respect your wishes when we're outside working."

"Thank you," Elisan said. She paused briefly, then headed out into the sunshine alone before he could delay her further, and Pick stayed behind to move the pulpit back. She could hear him whistling *Danny Boy* behind her as the door closed, and even the sharp February wind didn't chill her this time.

Winter lingered relentlessly on, blowing in a brutal start to March as the death toll rose at Camp Douglas. It felt like a fitting mirror of the war, never ending and deadly. Pick and his friends bravely kept putting one foot in front of another, holding Bible studies despite their own weaknesses and watching their toil bear fruit as the gatherings multiplied in number.

Not a few miles away, Luke continued to fight for his life through ups and downs, but by March, he was definitely building up his strength and was, by all appearances, finally out of the woods. His loved ones breathed a collective sigh of relief, and Kellie continued to come most mornings, keeping him company when he was awake and staying busy with fancywork when he was resting. It was still far too cold for March one Tuesday when Kellie arrived at the Dinsmores', walking into the room where Luke sat in bed propped straight up on pillows.

"Good morning," Luke said cheerfully when she entered.

"Good morning. You're looking well today." Kellie set a couple of books on the nightstand and adjusted the fichu crossing her bodice.

"I'm feeling well, just waiting for my old bones to catch up with me so I can get up and start learning to walk again."

"Soon."

Standing next to the bed, Kellie leaned over and kissed him on the lips before straightening up and taking her seat.

"Wow," Luke said, staring at her in shock. "When I pictured my first kiss, I never pictured it like this."

Kellie's eyes flew to his face and her mouth hung open in dismay. "Oh, Luke, I'm so sorry. I didn't even think. I didn't mean to take that from you," she said, aghast.

"No, don't be sorry." Luke quickly reached out to place his hand on hers before she could continue. "It was better than I ever would have imagined. Thank you."

Kellie could tell that he meant it, so she relaxed.

"I only meant that I never pictured being an invalid when it happened. But that was special, and I'm glad it was you." He caressed her hand, rubbing his thumb over the ring she wore. "I'm sorry you've had to wait so long for it. But I guess you see that I could use some practice."

"Nonsense." Kellie leaned towards him and ran her fingers through the hair that was finally growing over the scar on his head, admiring how much better he looked with it than with a bandage covering it. "It's not terribly appropriate to kiss you in here, anyway."

Luke's eyes watched her wistfully, but he nodded acceptance. "Well then, I'll have to get better if there's nothing else to it."

"That would be an excellent plan. When do you think you'll be strong enough to begin working on walking?"

"I think I'm about ready now. I'm feeling stronger every day."

The next time Kellie visited Luke two days later, Rebecca proudly showed Kellie into the drawing room, where Luke was sitting in a wheelchair with a book on his lap. Rebecca beamed at the surprise on Kellie's face before leaving them alone.

"It's so good to see you in here!" Kellie exclaimed, coming over to him. "Is it wearing you out to be up?"

"Not yet; I'm doing pretty well so far. But I really do think that a drawing room is a much more appropriate place to kiss my fiancée," Luke suggested hopefully, and Kellie laughed.

"It certainly is," she said, leaning over and kissing him slowly. "If you need more motivation, we can get married as soon as you can walk again."

Luke wordlessly lifted his hand to the back of her neck and kissed her again. When he let go, she stood next to his seat and wrapped her arms around his shoulders.

"I love you so much."

"I love you, too," Luke said, watching Kellie get settled in the armchair across from him. "Rebecca's been working on her things. She told me this morning that she had started piecing together the bodice of her wedding dress, and I think she's anxious to start making plans. How does the first Saturday of June sound to you?"

"It sounds perfect. Let's get the four of us together after dinner on Friday and get some things figured out," Kellie said, pulling out her lacework and making her hands busy.

Luke reached his hand out and fingered the material she had made already. "I really like this one. What's it for?"

"Probably my dress." Kellie held it up so they could both see it better. "I think I'll take it off and reuse it for something else after the wedding, though. Rebecca wants a white dress, so I figured I'd have one too, but I can always change it afterwards. Did you see Justin last night when he came to call on Rebecca?"

"Briefly. He poked his head in to say hello and he told me that he's been making it home in time for dinner every night again."

Kellie nodded. "I still don't see a whole lot of him, but he told me that he'd promised Rebecca an abundance of conversation during their engagement. I'm just glad to see him thriving again and getting enough rest at night."

"He's looking much better, and Rebecca is happier these days too. I've been spoiled to have all this time with you." Luke took her hand in his and squeezed it. "I think my biggest challenge will be buying a house. I have the money, but I thought I'd have more time to look around, and now it looks like I might not be able to even begin until right before the wedding."

"God will provide," Kellie calmly reminded him. "I'll let you know if I see anything around, and you just work on walking again."

Luke did start putting a great deal of effort into walking, but found, like everything else about his recovery had been, that progress was slow and painful. Kellie couldn't be of much help since she was half his size, but Titan and Rebecca worked with him tirelessly every afternoon when Titan was home from school.

Kellie found him one Friday morning on the settee in the drawing room, discouragement written all over his face.

"Good morning, handsome," she said with a smile, leaning down to greet him with a kiss, but he didn't smile back. "I take it that practice has been difficult?"

Luke sighed and looked at his hands dejectedly. "I'm twenty-five years old, Kellie. I'm supposed to be in the prime of my life right now, and I'm supposed to be marrying the love of my life, but I can barely take two steps, and I'm losing my mind sitting around for months on end."

Kellie took his hand in hers and placed it on her lap. "You're alive, Luke, and that's a tremendously good gift right now. We feared for your life for months, feared that if you woke up that you would be a different person, or not remember who we were. But here you are, sitting, eating, talking, even kissing me. After what your body has been through, you shouldn't even be here today, but you are."

Luke swallowed and dropped his eyes contritely as Kellie continued. "If you're going to tell yourself what you're supposed to be right now, well honestly, you should be dead." She dipped her face to look into his eyes, and squeezed his hand compassionately. "You will walk again. It will come."

"I'm sorry. You're right, and I shouldn't complain to you," Luke said, realizing how much his accident had put Kellie and his whole family through as well. It didn't feel good to be corrected, but Luke was grateful to have a fiancée who wasn't afraid to correct him when he was wrong. He lifted her hand to his lips and kissed it softly. "Thank you for keeping me in line."

"I'm sorry it's been so slow going, but you'll be able to get back to work soon. Do you think you'll get your old job back at the station?" Kellie asked in an attempt to keep him thinking forward.

"I don't know," Luke replied without concern. "Since I'm a trained telegrapher now, even if I'm not able to return to Great Central, I should pretty easily be able to get a job at one of the other stations. At the least, I'm sure I could just work the counter again until something opens up, but I don't think it would be hard to find a job in this city."

"Well then, that's another good gift. And you're making progress, even though it's not as quick as you'd like. For one thing, you don't have to be spoon-fed anymore, as fun as that was."

Luke chuckled wryly. "I'm glad that was fun for you, at least. You've been awfully patient and gracious with me all these months."

"I love you, and I haven't done anything that you wouldn't have done for anyone else. Now, are you going to read today or am I?"

"I'll start, and you can pick up when I get tired," Luke suggested, picking up the biography in his lap and cracking it open.

April 5, 1865

The first Wednesday in April, Elisan was anxious to get to camp and see her friends. The whole city had been buzzing with the news that the end was imminent—Richmond had indeed fallen, and it was reported that General Grant was currently pursuing what was left of General Lee's battered Confederate army. If General Lee surrendered, which everyone seemed to think would happen anytime now, the war would be over, and no one could say for sure what that would mean to the remaining prisoners at Camp Douglas. Would they remain imprisoned, or be immediately boarded on a train without a chance to say goodbye, or . . . ?

Each Wednesday, Elisan wondered if it would be her last time with them, and today more than ever with the news of Richmond's fall. Uncertainty hung thick in the air: fragile hope that they would be free soon coupled with paralyzing fear of what a Confederate loss would mean to them, all dependent on what the terms of the surrender would be. If, that was, a surrender indeed took place.

There were no more quiet moments alone with Pick, since everyone crowded near her father and herself from the moment they arrived until they drove away, but he was close, assisting with the work like any other Wednesday. As he helped her down from the wagon, she noticed that he was looking better now that winter was past, and she was encouraged to see his eyes clearer and his gait steadier.

With twenty other men around vying for last moments with them, the wagon was unloaded in record time, but then distribution was slow with everyone wanting to stop and chat with her on their way through the vegetable line. She could feel Pick's nearness even though they barely managed a word to each other throughout the course of the morning, but from time to time, her eyes would meet his twinkly brown ones, making her grin like a fool every single time. She didn't want to be dramatic, but she also didn't want to miss her last chance to say goodbye to him either, and found it difficult to be patient.

When he gave her his hand to help her into the wagon at the end of the morning, he spoke in a low voice so the others couldn't hear.

"I won't leave without saying goodbye."

"You won't?" Elisan said hopefully, losing herself momentarily in his eyes, and Pick shook his head.

"You'll come next week though, if you can, right? If nothing's changed?"

"Of course, silly." Elisan grinned from her perch. "I'll come as long as they'll let me through the gate. And after that, I'll dress like a Confederate soldier and sneak in."

Pick laughed and backed away from the wagon as Reverend Dinsmore picked up the reins. "I know you well enough to know that you would actually do that," he said. "Anyway, I'll see you again. Take care."

He waved his hand and stepped back to join the others as Elisan rode away, reassured and hopeful.

April 9, 1865

Justin was seated at the kitchen table that Sunday evening, folding up a letter he'd just finished writing to Robert, when he heard a loud shout in the street.

"What was that?" he asked, standing up and walking to the kitchen window. There came another shout and then clattering as the noise in the street grew louder, and within a minute, the reason became apparent.

"The war is over." Justin turned from the window to his siblings who had come up behind him, his voice calm and full of wonder.

"General Lee surrendered!" a shout came from the street as people poured out of their houses.

Jack grabbed his brother and sister in a bear hug. "The war is over!" he cried, repeating Justin's announcement jubilantly. He pulled back and still holding Kellie's hand, swung her around and began dancing around the table.

"Let's go," Justin called, heading to the door and tugging his boots on.

Soon they were running down the stairs to join the excitement outside, where their neighbors were shouting, dancing, and shooting off blanks into the air. They made their way down the street together, greeting everyone they passed and shaking hands with neighbors and strangers alike. Without stopping to make a conscious decision, they automatically walked in the direction of the Dinsmores', arriving at the same time as Deacon Hennessey and his wife.

The family was gathered in the drawing room, where Luke was seated, but he carefully stood when the guests entered and everyone hugged each other, laughing and crying with joy. Kellie stood by Luke with her arm around his waist as Reverend Dinsmore called attention to the group.

"Let us pause and thank God for this wonderful news and for the preservation of the Union," he said, and they all bowed their heads and joined in the time of prayer.

The city-wide celebration continued late into the night and the next day, so Justin kept the warehouse closed on Monday like many other businesses around town.

Elisan could hardly think of anything except for her friends at Camp Douglas. Her father confirmed her fears on Tuesday that he'd heard from Reverend Tuttle that the camp was closed to visitors as the parole process began. The fact was that only General Lee had surrendered, and in North Carolina, General Johnson had not yet done so, but oaths of allegiance were being offered to the prisoners in exchange for their freedom. Elisan could only wait and hope, trusting Pick's promise that he would not leave without seeing her again.

To her great joy, on Friday morning she had a letter from him, the first time she'd seen her own name in his scrawling script. *We celebrated all night when we heard the news of the war ending,* he wrote. *Not much has changed around here this week, but everyone's spirits are high, and I think we'll get out of here soon. See you before too much longer, lady.*

On Saturday morning, Elisan dawdled over her toilette, unsuccessfully attempting a new hairstyle twice before giving up and pinning her hair up the usual way. When she finally stepped into the dining room for breakfast, the sun was high and Luke and Rebecca were still at the table together, although they had long since finished eating.

"What's wrong?" Elisan asked, seeing their grim faces.

Before Luke could reply, Reverend Dinsmore returned from taking a breakfast tray to his wife, entering behind Elisan and placing his hand on her shoulder.

"President Lincoln was shot," Luke said somberly, and Elisan gasped, her hand flying to her mouth.

"What? Why? Who would do something like that?"

"We don't have the details yet, since it just happened last night. I imagine it was Confederate sympathizers."

"And he's dead?"

"We don't know that, either. It sounded like he was still alive last night."

Elisan fell into a chair at the table, sure that she couldn't eat anything now. "I can't believe it. We were supposed to be united now, friends again, and he's such a good man. How could they do this?"

"Every group has its extremists," her father said, taking a seat beside her. "The Confederates that I know all respected him, whether or not they agreed with his politics."

Elisan shook her head. "It doesn't make any sense. Jefferson Davis is on the run with his cabinet, and President Lincoln is the one that gets shot? And right after everything was looking up again for our country?"

No one responded, because there was nothing else to be said, but by lunchtime, the news had arrived that Abraham Lincoln was dead. Bells tolled across the city, and flags everywhere were lowered as the joy that had enveloped the atmosphere all week dissipated into deep grief.

As the month passed, Pick wrote to Elisan twice a week to let her know that he was still in the city, still waiting for parole, and she knew that it meant that he was therefore still weak and starving. She always wrote him back and collected his letters in a little carved wooden box in her trunk, looking at them often, but handling them made her feel sad, as if she had already lost him.

Luke began to be able to take three steps unassisted, then four, and by the end of the month, he could walk across a whole room if he was careful. Still, he felt that it would be too strenuous to join his family when they all went out to see President Lincoln's funeral procession when it arrived in Chicago on the first of May.

Justin closed the warehouse again the following day so that none of his employees would have to miss the event, and all three of the Youngs went with the Dinsmores and 125,000 other residents of Chicago to the funeral. They waited in line for hours in the rain to pass the grand funeral arch that the city had erected, underneath which the beloved president lay in state.

"I'll never forget the times we came to hear him speak," Rebecca said to Elisan as she hung on Justin's arm on the walk home. "He was a truly inspiring man."

"I know. I still don't understand how anyone could hate him," Elisan said, stepping gingerly around a mud puddle. "I can't believe how many people were there today, either. I've never seen crowds that big in my life."

"I think Chicago loved Mr. Lincoln as much as he loved his country," Justin said. "We have a lot to be grateful for that he was the one leading our nation for the past four years. I can't imagine what would have happened if it was anyone else."

"You're right," Rebecca said. "I've been worried about what will happen now without him, but I need to be thankful that we had him when we did. I'm not sure if anyone else would have had the nerve to free the slaves in the middle of the war, or could have handled all the negativity that he had to deal with. I thank God for Mr. Lincoln."

"God bless Mr. Lincoln," Elisan echoed sadly.

-33-

May 8, 1865

Reverend Dinsmore looked up from his desk at the church the following Monday morning to see Pick Thomas entering his study, gaunt, ragged, and dirty, despite his attempts to make himself presentable. The reverend came to his feet, and rather than extending his hand, pulled Pick into a warm hug.

"Praise be to God, you're finally free," the reverend said, patting him firmly on the back for a minute and letting go.

"Yes, sir," Pick agreed as they took their seats.

"I want to thank you," Pick began right away. "I truly thank you, sir. I don't know if you'll ever know how much your weekly visits meant to me, or how deeply I appreciate your presence and teaching over the past year. I will never forget you, and I believe that I'm a different person because of all that I've learned from you. I can't—" Pick swiped his hand across his damp eyes, and he found himself too choked up to continue.

"Ah, son, God is good. You've been like a son to me, and we will never forget you, either," Reverend Dinsmore said, giving Pick a moment to recover his composure.

When Pick could speak again, he continued. "They gave me my papers and a voucher for my travel home, so I intend to leave as soon as possible." He took a deep breath, and looked at the reverend steadily. "Sir, I really would like to have another chance to ask Elisan to come with me. I . . . I have to go home, you see, but I can't imagine my life without her in it. It doesn't seem worth living without her."

Reverend Dinsmore gestured with his hand. "You can ask her if you like, but do you think she'll reconsider?"

"I hope so." Pick paused and cocked his head. "Do you?"

The reverend couldn't hide his smile. "Elisan always surprises me. I didn't think that she would turn you down the first time, to be honest, so I really couldn't say. But you do not have my permission to ask her looking like that. I would require you to get some proper clothes first."

"Well, you see," Pick said nervously, biting his lower lip. "I quite agree with you, but I'm in a difficult position, which perhaps you should know about anyway, before you agree so quickly. I don't know if Elisan told you, but I don't have anything waiting for me when I get home, except for my parents and the house. The life that I had before the war has been obliterated, and to the best of my knowledge, I have nothing to offer her. I'll be working with my father, but I'm not entirely sure yet what that will be looking like."

The reverend did not know this, but he immediately saw the implications of Pick's admission. "So you're unable to afford clothes," he surmised.

Pick scratched his chin. "I'm unable to afford to get Elisan to Raleigh, either."

"And you would like to discuss the matter of her dowry," Reverend Dinsmore concluded.

Pick squinted his eyes unbelievingly at the discovery that Elisan would even have one to discuss. "Actually, I thought perhaps you could help me find work to do this week," he corrected.

The reverend pulled out a paper and a pencil and continued talking as he scratched numbers out on the paper. "I would be happy to put you to work myself, since there are projects here at the church that need to be done, but let me go over these numbers with you. Elisan has this sum available to her upon her marriage," he said, waving his pencil at Pick. "So if she doesn't agree to it, it stays with me. Subtract the cost of her ticket . . . "

Pick waited while he did the math out loud. "Meals along the way, and the cost of a small family wedding, and twenty dollars for her to prepare whatever she needs to take with her. You'll need room and board for the next week, a haircut and shave, and at least one decent set of clothes and boots."

He finished his sums and examined the paper, reviewing it to ensure that he hadn't forgotten anything. "It looks like that would do it," he said, showing Pick the numbers. "I can give you an advance for what you'll need today, and if she turns you down, it will be my gift to you." He looked up, and saw that Pick's eyes had filled with tears again.

"I wish I didn't have to accept your kindness, but I'm a desperate man," Pick confessed, and the reverend's eyes dropped with compassion.

"Son, if anyone loves my daughter as righteously and honestly as you do, I don't have a problem with them being desperate, and I know your work ethic." Standing up, took a small gold box off of the bookshelf, opened it, and counted out some money. "If she agrees to marry you, are you willing to wait a week for her to get her affairs in order? We could do the wedding on Sunday, and you could be on the Monday train."

Pick nodded readily. "Yes, I would be willing to wait one more week for her."

"Well, then. Head on up to 16th Street now, and you'll find a boardinghouse next to the bank, run by Mrs. O'Reilly. The barber is just two blocks further, on the west side of the street, and the clothing store is actually three blocks this way when you go out from the church. Once you get yourself taken care of and take a room for the week, you're welcome to call on Elisan at any time up until nine o'clock. She's usually home on Tuesday mornings, if you run out of time tonight."

Reverend Dinsmore reached out to hand Pick the money, then dug into his pocket. "Please get yourself a good lunch, too," he added, dropping another quarter into Pick's hand.

Pick put the money in his pocket and shook the reverend's hand firmly.

"Thank you, sir. Thank you from the bottom of my heart," he said with conviction, and took his leave.

When Pick knocked on the Dinsmores' door that evening, dinner had recently ended and the family was just retiring to the drawing room.

"You can get the door, Elisan," the reverend said as he settled into his favorite chair, and Elisan headed to the foyer.

She gasped as the door swung open, and could not imagine a happier surprise than what was waiting for her on the other side.

"Pick!"

Pick's bright brown eyes and crooked smile were the same, but almost everything else looked different from when she had seen him last at the prison. He'd had a bath and a haircut, his new clothes hung loose on his skeleton frame, and it was the first time she'd seen him cleanshaven.

"You're free! I'm so happy to see you! Please come in."

"Thank you, Miss Elisan," Pick drawled, stuffing his hands in his pockets. "Actually, can I talk to just you first before I come meet everyone?"

"Yes, sure. You must be starving. I'll be right back."

Elisan left him at the door and hurried into the house. As she passed the drawing room, she called out, "Papa, it's Pick! He's free!" She retrieved a roll from the kitchen and nearly ran back through the house, failing to notice Reverend Dinsmore's lack of surprise.

"Could someone make him a plate of dinner? We'll be in shortly."

"Slow down, Elisan," Mrs. Dinsmore said tiredly. "No need to run."

Elisan took her shawl from the hook by the door and met Pick outside. She handed him the roll and pulled her shawl around her shoulders. It was almost dusk, but there were still a few minutes of daylight remaining of the spring day.

He took a bite of the roll and looked over at her as they descended the stairs together.

"You look so pretty. I've never seen you in pink before."

Elisan glanced down at her ruffled pink chiffon dress. "I wear my work dresses to the prison. This one's kind of new; I finished it about a month ago. We were shopping today, so I dressed up."

"You made that?" Pick looked surprised as he took another bite.

"Of course, we make all our dresses." Elisan paused, realizing that Pick was probably used to having someone else make his family's clothes. "Well, Rebecca's better at hems so she usually does those, and I do hooks better so we help each other."

She chatted on, happy to just be with him. Other than looking malnourished, he was even better looking than she had ever seen him, and she couldn't get over the excitement that he was indeed alive and free. Pick, however, didn't relax. She sensed his sadness and looked up at him.

"You're really leaving now?"

Pick nodded soberly and finished chewing his bite. "My family needs me. I have to go this time." He took a deep breath and wiped his hands on his pants.

Elisan held her breath and waited as he looked past her into the night, and as time stood still, she began to wonder if his pensive silence was a prelude to goodbye. What was he thinking? Was tonight her last moment with him? Her heart began to beat fast, and her hands went clammy.

"Pick," she whispered, almost in tears.

He swallowed hard and fervently whispered back. "Elisan, how can I even dare to ask you again to leave all of this to come with me? Can I be selfish enough, crazy enough, to hope against hope that you would?"

His eyes moved to her face, but he didn't pause for an answer. "Five years ago, I would have asked the woman I loved to come down to be mistress of Ashton Hall, to luxury and comfort, but you wouldn't have accepted that anyway. Now all I can offer you is to come down and work with me, because you're the only person on earth I want by my side, and the only one who I think really would. You're everything that I want and need in a partner, and I want to be everything you want and need your husband to be. Will you come? Will you marry me?"

Elisan made the mistake of glancing toward the house and discovering faces pressed in the window, and she realized that her family was watching them. She blinked and ignoring them, turned her eyes back to Pick as she strongly, sincerely, replied. "Yes, I'll come."

Pick's eyes widened, as if he hadn't expected her to actually accept, and he looked like he was going to cry. "You will?"

"Yes, I will."

Pick pulled her to his chest and pressed his eyes closed as he hugged her tightly, kissing her hair.

"Pick . . . they're all watching."

"I know." Pick pulled back just enough to look down and see her face. "Let's give them something to watch then," he said impishly, and pressing his hand low on her back, he tipped her backwards and kissed her soundly.

Inside the house, Rebecca stood at the window with her brothers, her insides swirling in confusion.

"Papa. Why is the Confederate kissing Elisan?"

"Oh, she must have accepted his proposal then," the reverend replied with a smile, and his children stared at him as though he had spoken in a foreign language.

"She's marrying him? But we don't even know him," Luke said, bewildered. "She said his name is Pick?"

Reverend Dinsmore held up his hand to stop the questions, surprised to discover that Elisan had never told her siblings about Pick. "You can talk to her about it when she comes in. I'll let her tell you what she wants to."

Rebecca turned and peered back out the window as knots turned in the pit of her stomach, watching her sister being caressed by a man she had never seen in her life. The scene was so uncomfortable that she soon left and took her seat, picking up her lace with shaking hands.

Elisan stood in Pick's arms with her hands grasping his shoulders. "How much time do we have until we leave?"

"I can give you a week. They gave me a voucher so I can use it on my ticket anytime, but I've already delayed getting home too long. Your pa said we could get married on Sunday and leave on the Monday train. Is that enough time for you to get everything together?"

"I'll take as much time as you give me, but we can do a small wedding at the house with the family and Jack's family. What are you going to do until then?"

"I'm staying at the boardinghouse up on 16th, and your pa said he has projects around the church that I can do. If you need help with anything, I'll be around, though. I was thinking about seeing if Jack would stand up with me in the wedding. Do you think he will?"

Elisan's face suddenly fell, and her eyes widened. "Oh Pick, I'm supposed to stand up with Rebecca, and now I'll be leaving before her wedding. I hope she understands. But I think Jack would be happy to do it. He'll be standing up with Justin in a few weeks."

"I'll ask him tomorrow then," Pick said, pulling Elisan close against his chest. "Are you ready to go in? I think your family is getting impatient."

"After you kiss me one more time," Elisan said with a sigh, and Pick was delighted to comply, kissing her sweet and long.

When Elisan and Pick joined her family in the drawing room, a plate of dinner was waiting for Pick, and Rebecca had cups of tea for the others so that Pick wouldn't feel awkward being the only one eating. Elisan preceded Pick into the room, stopping inside and clasping her hand on his arm as her family sat stone-faced, watching her.

"Pick, this is my family," she announced, gesturing to her parents and then introducing her siblings. "Everyone, this is Pick Thomas, of Raleigh, North Carolina. I met him when he was in Jack's company in Virginia, and we've been working together every Wednesday for the past year and a half. I've just agreed to marry him, and we're planning to have a small wedding before leaving for Carolina on Monday."

The Dinsmore family didn't move or speak, and Elisan realized with horror that Rebecca was fighting tears. After a difficult silence, Reverend Dinsmore came to his feet and extended his hand to Pick.

"I'm pleased to see you again and welcome you into our home. Let me be the first to congratulate you, Sergeant Thomas."

"Thank you sir, though I'm not a sergeant anymore," Pick said. "Just a normal citizen of the USA once again. I'm grateful to meet you all," he added, nodding towards the others.

"Come, have some dinner," Elisan said, ushering him towards the empty settee and handing him his plate of food. She sat down beside him and swallowed hard, not wanting to look at Luke or Rebecca especially, annoyed by their rudeness.

"What do you do, Mr. Thomas?" Luke finally asked, refusing to refer to Pick by his Christian name.

"Um, well, until today, I worked for the United States Engineer Corps, constructing buildings and maintaining the property at Camp Douglas," Pick said, and his answer was so humorous that Elisan cracked a smile despite the tension. "I'm not sure yet what I'll be doing when I return to Raleigh, but I'll be working to help my father rebuild what we can of his businesses."

"What are his businesses in?"

Pick inhaled, holding his fork and unable to take a bite. "Tobacco and real estate, primarily. He owned several plantations outside of the city and multiple companies in the financial district in Raleigh."

"I see," Luke said. "So you'll be figuring out how to turn a profit without the free labor you've been used to."

"Luke!" Elisan exclaimed, disturbed by his blatant disrespect.

"Elisan, you're bringing us a man you're planning to marry that we have never even met, and you've given us very little time to get to know him before you run off together," Luke said, his manner tearing Elisan's heart to pieces. "I'm trying to learn as much as I can about him."

"You could at least be more courteous towards him, since he's going to be your brother," she protested. "I'm in love with Pick, and I would like for you to be happy for me and more respectful to him."

"What courtesy did you show us by preparing us for this? By letting us know that you were seeing someone at the camp, or that he was going to come tonight, or that you were planning to leave for North Carolina? I would like to be happy for you too, Elisan, but all I see is you making an impulsive decision and marrying someone with whom you have nothing in common."

Pick took the opportunity to quietly begin eating his dinner, while beside him, Elisan became livid.

Before she could reply, Rebecca cut in with tears in her eyes. "Luke's right, Elisan; we had no warning. How could you be falling in love with someone all this time and not say anything to me? I thought we told each other everything, and this—this is huge. And I don't understand how you could leave before our wedding."

Rebecca started to cry, so Elisan started to cry as well. "I'm really sorry about your wedding, Rebecca, and you too, Luke. I wanted to be there too, but Pick hasn't been home in three years and I can't be selfish and make him delay further. He's been in a prison camp, and his parents need to see him alive and well as soon as possible. And I'm not being impulsive, Luke, you can ask Papa, he's been there all along, and he liked Pick long before I did. I actually have a lot in common with Pick, which I found out the more that I spent time with him and got below the surface of our different life experiences," Elisan said, wiping at her face.

"Different life experiences?" Luke's voice rose. "He's a slave owner, Elisan, and you *hate* slavery. That's not a surface issue; that's something you've been passionate about your entire life. It's like I don't even know you anymore."

"Was a slave owner," Pick quietly corrected, but no one paid attention.

"No, you don't," Elisan cried, coming to her feet. "You have made no effort to know me since you started seeing Kellie, so you can't blame me and therefore have no right to judge me."

"I do, though," Rebecca said. "I don't understand this at all. I sleep with you every single night, and maybe twice you mentioned your friend Pick at the camp, but you never said anything to make me think there was something between you two. Now all of a sudden, you're marrying him and are offended that we're surprised."

"I turned down Pick's first proposal in February because I didn't want to leave my family that much, and he has stayed in prison for three extra months so that I could have more time with you, and now you're making me regret that I didn't leave with him then," Elisan sobbed from the center of the room. "Why can't you trust me?"

"First proposal? He asked you to marry him three months ago and you never said a word to your family about it?" Luke stared at her. "And how could you presume that I'm the one at fault when I couldn't even get out of bed all those months?"

"Papa knew! I didn't think I was going to leave though, so I didn't think it mattered, and I didn't think you all would understand. Clearly, I was right about that. I didn't think you would understand that I fell in love with a Confederate, but he's one of the most caring and honest people that I know, and he loves me for who I am. He loves God, and he has shown far greater character since we entered this room than you have."

Elisan's shoulders shook with sobs; Pick found himself unable to continue eating while the woman he loved was in such distress and he felt that he should leave, but couldn't find a good way to make an exit. Elisan turned to her father, who was sitting quietly sipping his tea and watching the proceedings with her mother and Titan.

"Papa," she pleaded, "Can you tell them I'm right to marry him? Can you tell them he's a good man?"

Reverend Dinsmore placed his mug down on the table next to him. "I will gladly vouch for Pick's character, Elisan, but you're the only one who can say if you're right to marry him. Although you have my blessing, it's your decision to make, and the consequences of it are yours as well. If you haven't been honest with your siblings and are breaking your word to be present at their wedding, I can understand why they would be upset."

He looked past his weeping daughter to Luke and Rebecca as Pick lightly tugged on Elisan's arm and convinced her to sit back down.

"I gave Pick my permission to ask Elisan for her hand in February, because over the past year and a half, I've watched him serve the men in his camp in humility, dedicating himself to the study of the Word of God and becoming a leader after God's own heart. I personally have not met anyone else who is as qualified to take Elisan in marriage as Pick, but of course," he finished softly, looking at Elisan, "we're going to miss you dearly, and wish you didn't have to live so far away."

Still too angry to apologize to anyone, Elisan buried her face in her hands and cried as her family fell silent. After a moment, Luke got up and quietly limped from the room.

She felt Pick's hand on her shoulder. "I should probably go," he whispered.

Elisan heaved a sigh and straightened up, wiping her eyes. "I'll walk you out," she said, and they stood together. Pick shook the reverend's hand again and bowed to Mrs. Dinsmore before Elisan escorted him out in the silence.

"I'm sorry," Elisan whispered to him on the front step. "I'm so sorry."

Pick held her face in his hands, gently wiping away her tears with his thumbs. "I wasn't expecting that, from the way you described them to me."

"They've never been like that before," Elisan said, sniffling. "I've never seen Luke or Rebecca so angry at me." She slid her arms around him and hugged him tightly, leaning her head on his shoulder.

"I'm sorry, Elisan. Let them sleep on it, and maybe they'll be calmer when they get used to the idea. Are you going to try to smooth things over with them?"

Elisan nodded. "With Rebecca, at least. I'll see you in the morning?"

"Sure. I love you."

Pick leaned down and kissed her gently, then placing his hat on his head, turned and walked away into the night.

When Elisan reentered the house, she went straight upstairs to her bedroom and found that Rebecca was already there, sitting on the bed and still crying. She reached her hands out to Elisan, who came and took hold of them, standing before her.

"I'm so sorry, Ellie," Rebecca cried, looking up into her eyes. "I know we hurt you, and I can't bear it. We're in shock right now, but I can't fight with you anymore."

"I'm sorry I didn't tell you." Elisan plopped down on the bed next to her. "It never made sense, Rebecca. I couldn't make sense of it or figure out how to talk about it, because I really used to hate him but eventually we became friends, and by the time he proposed to me in February, I realized I'd fallen in love with him. He was going to be exchanged, but when I turned him down, he stayed for me, just to have more time with me." Elisan pulled out her handkerchief and wiped her falling tears.

"But how could you not say anything to me then? You got a marriage proposal I never even knew about! That had to have been life changing for you."

"It wrecked me," Elisan admitted. "Especially when I came back the next week and discovered he was still there. I don't know, Rebecca, but I was wrong not to tell you, and I'm sorry. And Luke doesn't understand that I do still hate slavery, and Pick knows that, but I learned that I can respect him anyway. I'm as surprised that I fell in love with him as you are, but I really love him so much. I wouldn't leave you for just anybody, I promise."

She leaned over and hugged Rebecca. "I hate that I'm missing your wedding, truly, but he already stayed this long for me, and his family needs him."

Rebecca's shoulders slumped and she laid her head on Elisan's shoulder. "It feels a little bit like you're upstaging us. We've been in love for years and planning this wedding together, and all of a sudden you swoop in with a mystery fiancé and are going to get married two weeks before our wedding. There's nothing to be done about it, but we're struggling with it."

She sighed and Elisan stroked her hair compassionately. "I'm going to miss you so much, Ellie. I never imagined life, or my wedding, without you. It's going to be dreadful."

"It will not; you'll have Justin now, and a new life and your own home, and soon, babies to distract you. However much you'll miss me, I'll miss you more. You've been my rock for my whole life, and I'm scared for what the world will think of me when I'm on my own, without you to protect them from me."

Rebecca sat up and turned to look Elisan in the eye. "Elisan, the world needs you. You can't shirk back and hide yourself because you're afraid of what they'll think of you. You go down to Raleigh and shine your brightest, whether or not they appreciate it, because God made you with the passion and courage and strength that I've always wished I had. They don't need to be protected from you, or have half of you, they need you to bring all of yourself and shine God's love in the way only you can. Goodness, Ellie, you said that Pick loves you for who you are, so don't hold back or waste your effort trying to fit into a mold. Promise me."

Elisan nodded through her tears. "I promise."

"On the days that are hard and I miss you especially, I have to know that you're down there living out the gifts and talents God gave you, and that will make me feel better," Rebecca said, squeezing Elisan's hand. "Now dry your tears, because we have to plan your wedding. I'll write to Christina tomorrow and see if she'll stand up with me, since she'll be there at my wedding anyway."

Rebecca stood up and began untying her undersleeves. "You can wear my wedding dress, if you'd like to."

"Really?" Elisan sniffled. "You don't have to do that. You've worked so hard on it, and it's special."

"It will be even more special if I'm wearing the dress you wore," Rebecca said, pulling off her sleeves and unhooking her bodice. "Since you won't be there, it will make you feel close."

"If you're sure."

"I am. What all do you need? Mostly underthings?"

Elisan nodded slowly. "I'm not going to worry about new dresses or bonnets at this time. I don't think it would be appropriate to show up in the south all decked out right now, and I think the money Papa would have spent on my trousseau will be used for my train ticket. But I should have new underthings."

"Okay. We'll go to the ladies' boutique after breakfast for lace, and get started. I'm sorry we don't have time to make the lace ourselves."

"I don't know how you have time to put towards my trousseau at all," Elisan protested. "Your wedding is in three weeks, and you have your own things to work on."

"I have plenty, and I can always make more after the wedding if I need to, but you only have a week and haven't started on anything," Rebecca reminded her.

She sat down at the vanity to brush her hair, and looked at Elisan in the mirror, sitting on the bed behind her. "Now tell me all about Pick and how all this happened."

Happy to oblige, Elisan pulled her knees up to her chest, although she carefully selected how much of their first meeting in Virginia to tell her sister and left dancing in the chapel out of her story altogether.

"He made it sound like he was rather wealthy tonight," Rebecca said, but Elisan shook her head.

"Not anymore. He used to be, but he told me a few months ago that they lost it all when Confederate money crashed. Isn't that terribly ironic?" Elisan's eyes sparkled. "Justin was always the poor orphan boy, and look at him now, you're marrying into money. On the other hand, Pick used to be richer than I can even imagine, and now he has nothing."

"I always thought you'd marry someone who was rich, and I only ever cared about marrying Justin. It is ironic," Rebecca said with a laugh.

The two sisters chatted about their lovers and weddings until late into the night, finally falling asleep curled up on the bed together.

Rebecca made it to the Youngs with the news first, arriving early the next morning before Justin had left for work.

"Do you know Pick Thomas?" she asked Jack, taking a seat at the table and accepting the cup of coffee that Justin handed her.

"Yes, we were friends in the war, and I visited him a few times at the camp," Jack replied from across the table.

"Well, he showed up at the house last night, made an offer to Elisan, and she accepted. She's going to marry him on Sunday before they leave for North Carolina together."

"Are you serious?" Justin asked, thunderstruck.

"Quite."

Jack blinked, wide-eyed. "I knew they were friends, but I didn't know there was anything more between them."

"None of us did, but apparently he had proposed in February and she turned him down. We're all shocked, to say the least. Luke and I have had a difficult time with the news, and I think he's still pretty angry," she added, directing the last point toward Kellie.

"I can imagine," Kellie said. "He's so protective of you two."

"Still." Justin raised his eyebrows. "I didn't know Luke was capable of being angry."

"You should have seen him last night. He's furious," Rebecca said. She looked back at Jack. "What can you tell us about Pick?"

Jack shifted in his seat, feeling that it was best that he didn't say too much. "Well, he got saved before Gettysburg. He's changed a lot now from when we fought together, and he leads Bible studies every week in the camp. He's from a prominent family in Raleigh, and his sister died during the war."

"We didn't get much of a feel for him last night, since we were all rather . . . touchy . . . about the news," Rebecca admitted. "I hope we can get to know him a little more this week. I'm going to miss her horribly."

Justin stood up and set his plate by the dishpan, then leaned against the counter. "So she's leaving before our wedding, then."

"Yes, sadly. I was actually wondering, Kellie, if you have time this week. We're heading to the store shortly and then need to spend the week working on some new things for her, and can use all the hands we can get."

"Oh, I'd be happy to help. I don't have that much more that I was working on myself; I'm pretty ready for the wedding. I was just doing some doilies, but that was mostly to pass the time."

Justin grinned at Rebecca. "You had better have your doilies ready before the wedding, Rebecca, or we might have to postpone."

"My doilies have been ready for years," Rebecca said with a laugh. "I hope they haven't grown musty waiting in my trunk all this time."

"Well, that's good news. The wedding can continue, and I promise we'll get them aired out in just a few weeks," Justin said, coming up behind her and resting his hands on her shoulders.

"I should get going now, since I have to meet her at the store in a bit," Rebecca said, and drank the last of her coffee before she and the others stood up.

"I'll be over to the house in a little while," Kellie said, and everyone headed their separate ways.

-34-

The week passed quickly with all the sewing that Elisan had to accomplish, but they managed to get together the pieces that she needed the most and freshened up some of her dresses before carefully packing her trunk on Saturday. It was hard for her to know what to take, but since it sounded like she would be living with her in-laws, she figured that she didn't have to worry about bringing many things for the house.

Pick kept out of the way next door, whitewashing walls and repairing loose pews for the reverend, but he had dinner every night at the manse and spent the evenings in the drawing room, doing his best to give Elisan's family time to warm up to him.

Luke remained icy towards him, however, and even escaped to spend Wednesday evening with Kellie to spare himself another painful episode of watching his baby sister swooning over the man. He didn't approve of Pick and didn't think that he ever would, but there was still time for Elisan to change her mind, and he held out hope that she would do so before Sunday.

On Friday morning, Elisan donned Rebecca's altered wedding dress, and she and Pick sat for their wedding portrait, and that night, Justin brought a lemon meringue pie with three inches of meringue to dinner.

Elisan and Pick got one last quiet moment together before their wedding on the front step before Pick left for the boardinghouse on Saturday night.

"Are you scared?" he asked her tenderly, noting how tired she looked.

Elisan leaned against the door frame and squinted. "I am, a little bit, about leaving and not knowing anything about what my new life will be like."

She smiled reassuringly at him and the brown eyes that she was so much in love with. "I'm not scared about marrying you, though. I'm over the moon happy to be spending my life with you."

"I'm over the moon happy, too," Pick said, his face shining. "Is there anything I can do to help? Anything I can say that would ease your fears?"

"Mmm, I don't know. I suppose I'll face them head on soon enough, but it helps knowing you'll be with me."

"I absolutely will be with you and watching out for you," Pick said, and kissed her. He stopped for the space of several breaths, just holding her and feeling her become calm in his arms.

"When was it when you first realized it? That you had fallen in love with me?"

"Oh, that's easy," Elisan said. "It was during the four hour conversation we had. I was so touched by the fact that you cared enough about our friendship to have that conversation with me, I sat there the whole time, thinking, 'This can't be happening.' I actually was rather mad at you at the time for getting me to fall in love with you."

Pick chuckled. "Are you still mad at me?"

"Only a little bit," Elisan said, laughing. "I think I'm still more surprised by it than anyone. When was it for you?"

"For me, it was the first time you hit me with a carrot. I thought, 'I'm going to marry this girl.'"

Elisan giggled, trying to remember when it was that had happened. "I've hit you with a lot of carrots. That was pretty early on though, wasn't it?"

"Pretty early. Well, you need to get some rest before tomorrow so I should head out. I'll meet you at church in the morning?"

Elisan thought, then shook her head. "No, come get me here at nine and we'll walk over together. I think word has gotten out about us, and the church will be in a tizzy."

"Okay. I'll see you in the morning," Pick said, and leaning forward, kissed her on the lips.

Reverend Dinsmore performed the ceremony to unite Elisan and Pick in marriage on Sunday evening in the Dinsmores' drawing room with just the family and Youngs in attendance. Rebecca stood beside her sister, bravely fighting back tears throughout the ceremony. Elisan had no tears herself; she was glowing, beautiful, and she and Pick were both clearly ecstatic. She wanted dancing more than anything at her wedding, so they moved the chairs back in the drawing room and Rebecca and her mother took turns playing the piano and they all danced. Luke would have preferred to sit it out, but Kellie wanted to dance with him and he wouldn't turn her down, managing two slow dances before he had to rest.

Everyone else danced with each other until they were tired and Elisan finally went with Rebecca to change out of the wedding dress and into the pink chiffon gown that she had worn the night Pick proposed. She had altered it into an evening dress, changing out the sleeves and remaking the bodice, and looked stunning when she rejoined her family for dinner.

They closed out the evening with a candlelit turkey dinner in the dining room, where for the first time, Elisan felt her emotions catch up with her. It was her last meal with her family, and dreading the moment when she would have to say goodbye to them, she picked at her food and sat watching them chatter and laugh together.

Eventually the time came, and Reverend Dinsmore was ready to drive the newlyweds to the hotel across the street from the train station, where they would be leaving at first light. Pick was patient as Elisan made her goodbyes painfully long and drawn out, hugging everyone twice, thanking them, telling them how much she loved them and how she would write soon. She hugged Luke, and he hugged her back, but it was strained, and everyone could feel it.

"You know you can't let her leave like that," Kellie said softly, turning aside to a mellowed Luke as he stood watching the carriage drive away.

"I know."

He didn't move for a long time, standing lost in thought on the front step as storm clouds formed in the spring night sky and the air hung thick around him.

Justin decided to go ahead and walk home and try to beat the rain, rather than waiting for the carriage to return, but he stopped next to Luke on his way out the door as Kellie and Jack walked on ahead.

"Are you going to be okay?"

Luke took a deep breath. "I'm going to miss her," he admitted. "I hope she's made a good choice. I don't like it, and I'm scared for her."

"Boy, I know that feeling," Justin breathed, and Luke looked sideways at him.

"Yeah, I guess you do. I keep telling myself it's Ellie though, and somehow she's always managed to land right side up. Well, good night. It looks like you'd better hustle if you want to make it home dry."

He turned toward the door, and Justin slapped his hat on his head and hurried to catch up with his siblings.

It just started to rain when Pick and Elisan made it into their room at the hotel and removed their jackets, shaking the wet drops off of them. Pick waited until the footmen had deposited Elisan's trunk and left them alone before he turned to her.

"Would you like me to leave and give you a few minutes?"

"Oh, no," Elisan replied. "You can stay. I can't get out of this dress by myself anyway; the hooks are in the back."

"Ah, well that is just the type of thing I can help with." Pick grinned, setting his jacket across the back of the chair and coming over to her.

She began pulling pins and combs out of her hair while Pick stood behind her, carefully undoing her hooks, one by one.

"This isn't your first time, is it?" she asked quietly as her hair tumbled down around her shoulders.

"No, it isn't." Pick paused for a moment as he brushed her hair over her shoulder, out of the way of his hooks. "It's the first time since God made me a new man, and the first time with the woman who has my heart and soul, though. I can talk to you more about it sometime, if you'd like."

He leaned down to press his nose lightly against her silky cheek. "Nothing else ever felt like this," he whispered. "Ever."

He ran his palms down her arms and clasped her hands in his as she leaned her head back against his chest and closed her eyes. The safety she felt in his arms relaxed her. *As long as I have these arms around me, I could make a home anywhere,* she thought.

Straightening up, Pick set to work again on the hooks. "I was right about you from the beginning, Mrs. Thomas. How many rebel babies do you want, anyway?"

Elisan instantly swung around, exclaiming, "Oh, you!" and Pick caught her in his arms. He tried to kiss her but was laughing too hard.

"This is going to be fun, living with you," he chortled, his eyes twinkling.

He gently ran his fingers under the waist of her bodice to find the hooks that attached it to the skirt. "I believe your exact words were . . . " Pick released the hooks and pulled her dress bodice off, leaving her in her skirt and four layers of crisp white underthings. "' . . . You have no more access to me, Mr. Thomas.'"

He circled his arms around her corseted waist and leaned forward. "I think I was a lot more right than you were."

"I assure you, none of this was in my plan, but it seems like it was always in yours," Elisan teased, and Pick didn't argue back.

"I was thinking at least six children. As long as it's safe for you, I think a nice big houseful would be fun."

Elisan wrapped her arms around him and looked up into his eyes, tossing her long honey brown hair behind her shoulders.

"Does that have anything to do with the fact that you're the only one in your family?"

"I'm sure it probably does," Pick replied, tucking loose strands behind her ear as Elisan cocked her head.

"I think at least six sounds like a good plan, as long as you admit they'll be half Yankee too."

"I hope they all turn out like you," Pick said devotedly, but Elisan looked horrified.

"Oh goodness, no thank you. I was a terrible child."

Pick tried not to grin and failed as he leaned his forehead on hers, holding her close and breathing her air.

"You have no idea how happy you've made me today. I still can't believe that I get to keep you for always."

"I still can't believe you stayed in prison for me." Elisan reached her hands up to run her fingers through his hair and enjoyed how it felt. "I love you."

Her lips met his and she melted into the kiss.

May 15, 1865

It was still dark and drizzly when the newlyweds approached the ticket counter at the station early the next morning, and Elisan noticed a tall brown-haired figure in a long raincoat standing near the door with his hat in his hands.

"Luke!" she exclaimed, dropping Pick's arm when she recognized her brother.

"I'll be right back," Pick said in a low voice and headed to the counter, leaving Elisan with Luke.

"I'm sorry, Elisan," Luke said without hesitation, stepping towards her. "I was harsh, and I was wrong, and I don't want you to leave with this between us."

He took a deep breath, and she could see the familiar sincerity in his eyes. "I saw yesterday how much he really loves you, and you really love him, and that's all I ever wanted for you."

Elisan nodded, swallowing back tears. "Thank you," she whispered. "It means the world to me, and I forgive you. I'm sorry for accusing you of not caring, and for not telling you earlier."

Luke hesitated. "Will you keep in touch with me and Kellie?"

"Yes, please! I'm going to miss you so much; you have no idea."

Elisan started to cry and stepped forward to hug him. Luke held her and stroked her back.

"We're going to miss you, Ellie," he said softly. "I wish you all the happiness in the world."

"You too, Luke. I've been lucky to have a big brother like you."

Pick started back towards them with the tickets, so Luke released Elisan and turned to his new brother-in-law.

"Take good care of her, Pick. She's a special lady," he said, and Pick looped his arm around Elisan and smiled lovingly at her. "Have a safe trip."

"Bye, Luke. I love you," Elisan said through her tears, and she watched him turn and walk away.

"I'm glad he came," Pick said as he escorted her toward the train. "I hated for you to be leaving with unresolved conflict with your family. I have a lot of respect for him."

"Me too." Elisan lifted her skirts and climbed aboard. They made their way down the aisle and settled into their seat.

"His opinion has always been really important to me. Not enough to keep me from marrying you, but I'm thankful that I don't have his displeasure hanging over my head anymore. Are your parents really going to handle it better than my family did?"

Pick inhaled and clasped Elisan's hand in his lap. "I think so, but I haven't told them yet that I was planning to propose."

"So I'm just going to show up with you, the first time they've seen you in three years?"

"Kind of," Pick admitted with a lopsided grin. "I've told them about you, but they don't know that you're coming. I'm fairly certain that they'll be happy about it, though."

"Oh goodness," Elisan said with a sigh, looking out the window as the train lurched forward.

"Elisan." She turned back to her husband when he said her name softly, and saw his brown eyes watching her closely. "You trust me."

It wasn't a question, and it wasn't spoken lightly. The words carried with them the weight of months spent carefully, tenderly, cultivating that trust, and the respect, listening, vulnerability, and understanding that had eventually earned it for him.

"I trust you, Pick."

Elisan thought of their first night together and how sensitive he had been of protecting her trust even then, and there on the train she felt the safety that she had felt in his arms. He had never promised her an easy life in the south, but he had promised her himself. Gazing into his eyes, her thoughts continued on, and she smiled up at him.

"I trust you, but I'm on this train because I trust God more. Everything isn't about you, Pick."

For the first half of the train's journey, Pick and Elisan were pink-cheeked and obviously in love as they chatted the hours away. As the train neared Corinth, Mississippi, where they turned east, however, the terrain changed. The effects of the war were clearly visible as they traveled through Mississippi, Tennessee, and then North Carolina. Food was scarce and expensive at the stops, and they repeatedly passed shelled out buildings, burned homes, returning war veterans in rags and missing limbs, and sometimes delays as repairs were made on the track or the train was rerouted.

The impact all of this had on Pick was obvious, and there was sadness in his eyes that even Elisan couldn't take away as he looked out the window surveying mile after mile of destruction to his homeland. Elisan didn't know what to say, as the scenes were heartbreaking, yet she knew that it was all at the cost of saving the union and freeing the slaves. She remembered Pick's command a year ago to respect the people of the south, so she stayed quiet, although experiencing her husband's grief broke her heart.

It was late into the evening when they arrived in Raleigh later that week and disembarked into the Carolina humidity. Pick arranged for the delivery of Elisan's trunk at the station, then turned and extended his arm.

"Are you ready for this?" he asked, looking down into her eyes.

"I don't know that I am. Are we walking?"

"Yes, it's close," Pick said, starting off in the direction of his home.

They were in the center of the city, and walked just a few blocks to the east before Pick turned in at the gate of a huge stone mansion.

"This is it?" Elisan asked, realizing that Pick was right about it being a short walk, and turned her head up to take in the massive building.

"Ashton Hall," Pick said with a happy sigh. "I can't believe I'm home after all this time. Three years."

"You're free, and you're home," Elisan said watching him, trying to imagine how it must feel to be him in that moment. She thought about the last time he had been there, for his sister's funeral. "Are you okay?"

Pick took a deep breath and nodded. "Come on." He squeezed her hand and headed up the stone steps to knock on the enormous glass-paned door.

Elisan stepped backwards into his shadow as the door opened and Andrew Thomas stood in the light of the hall.

"Margaret!" he called, and reaching out his arms, pulled Pick into a firm embrace. Pick's father had Pick's twinkling brown eyes, thick gray hair, and a nice set of whiskers that curled out to the edge of his face. He was dressed in a burgundy smoking jacket and striped gray pants, and to Elisan, he looked tired and drawn.

In a moment, Pick's mother appeared alongside her husband. She was as beautiful and youthful as Pick had described, with blond hair swept in perfect rolls over her ears into a chignon at the nape of her neck. Elisan immediately felt dirty from the trip and plain in her navy plaid dress and traveling bonnet as she surveyed her mother-in-law's dinner dress draping off of her shoulders, made of chocolate brown silk with pink and white paisleys, cinched by a belt of the same brown color at her slim waist.

"Pick!" the lady cried, and Pick hugged her tightly as Elisan realized this elegant woman was the one that had been the first to love her husband, and she pictured her hugging Pick as a little boy.

Pick was quick to pull back and reach his hand behind him, and Elisan took it as he brought her forward.

"Mother, Father, I've brought us a very special gift. My wife, Elisan."

"Your wife," Margaret breathed, holding her pretty white hands out to Elisan. "Oh, you darling thing. You must be exhausted. Please, come in."

She escorted Elisan into the house, and Elisan found herself in a huge marble hall with a grand gilded staircase in the middle, leading to the second story. Pick took Elisan's bonnet and jacket and placed them on the table along with his own hat, and followed his wife and parents toward the drawing room.

"We've heard of you of course, dear," Margaret was saying to Elisan, "but we didn't know to prepare for you. Please, come sit and tell us everything, and we'll get some dinner for you."

From the start, Elisan found Margaret's British accent enchanting and her manner endearing, and she hoped that she was as sweet as she seemed. They passed an older black man in the hall, and Margaret stopped him to ask for him to bring food for Pick and Elisan.

"It sure is good to have you home, Mr. Pick," the man said, and Pick reached to shake his hand.

"It's good to be home, Zechariah. I'm glad to see you. How is Nanny?"

"She's just fine but boy, will she be happy to see you. As soon as I get back to see her tonight, I'll let her know you're here, and she'll be bounding over to see you first thing."

Pick introduced Elisan to his nanny's husband, then the man turned to do as he was asked. Pick lightly touched his mother's arm.

"We really should clean up first, Mother."

"Yes, of course, I'm sorry. There's no water in your room yet, but we can get some. We've changed the sheets to be ready for you whenever you arrived, but nothing else is ready. Unless you'd prefer a larger room now; you can have your choice."

"Oh no, my room will do just fine," Pick said. He and his father left to get the water and firewood, leaving Margaret to lead Elisan up the stairs to Pick's old room.

Elisan stared upon arrival at a bedroom that was at least twice as large as her and Rebecca's room and had a sparsely furnished sitting room adjacent to it. In the center of the room was a four poster bed with a cotton coverlet the color of the sky, but except for the wash basin and a small nightstand, the room was empty and the floor was bare.

Margaret watched Elisan as she stood taking in the room, took a good look at her new bright-eyed daughter-in-law.

"So you're the lady who was finally able to win Pick's heart," she said lightly. "Pick mentioned you often in his letters, and told how he looked forward to seeing you and your father every week. I could tell he thinks highly of you, and I'm glad to get to know you myself. Of course, we had no idea that he intended to marry you, but we'll get over the surprise of it, won't we?"

"I'm glad to know you too." Elisan paused awkwardly. "What would you prefer I call you?"

"Oh! Well, Pick calls me Mother, but if it's too soon for that, you can call me Margaret," she said, and Elisan relaxed.

"I'd be happy to call you Mother, if only it's not too soon for *you*. I know it must be a shock for me to show up like this." Elisan sounded apologetic, anxious to start off on the right foot with Pick's mother. "My family was surprised by the whole thing too, except for my father. He liked Pick from the beginning, but none of the others had met him until a week and a half ago."

"There are many things that we're adjusting to around here these days, dear, and I'm sure it will be for you more than anyone. I'm a transplant too, you know, and the culture is so different here," Margaret said sympathetically. "We'll do our best to make you feel at home."

Pick and his father entered the room in time to hear the last sentence, and Pick winked at Elisan on his way to stack his armful of wood on the hearth. Once Andrew had filled the pitcher with water, he set the pail on the floor beside the wash basin.

"Take your time, and we'll have food for you in the dining room whenever you're hungry," he said, and left with Margaret, shutting the door behind them.

Immediately, Pick came over to Elisan and put his hands on her waist.

"Well?"

"Well, she's delightful, and the first ten minutes have been lovely," Elisan said, smiling up at him.

"I knew she'd love you," Pick whispered, leaning down to nuzzle his wife.

"She doesn't know me yet!"

"Well, when she does, she'll love you even more, I promise."

He kissed her, then pulled back and went to wash his hands in the basin, and Elisan unhooked her cuffs.

"When will my trunk arrive?"

"It should be on its way. Do you need it now?" Pick asked, splashing water on his face.

"No, I'll just change my collar and sleeves now, and I have extras here in my satchel." Elisan peeked in the mirror, disturbed to discover that she had met her in-laws for the first time with frizzy stray hairs and gray skin from the trip, and quickly set to work freshening up.

"Um, Elisan, I never told my parents that I was offered the exchange in February," Pick suddenly said from across the room. "I think it would be best if we not mention it yet. They don't know you really, and they might feel slighted to hear that I chose you over them at that time."

Elisan decided that it would be wise to follow Pick's lead when it came to how to communicate with his parents. "I won't bring it up then."

A few moments later, Pick added, "It's so different being home already. I've never seen my father haul water before, my mother's had that dress since before the war, and my Egyptian rug is gone. You won't notice what's different, but it's definitely not the atmosphere I'm used to here. But then, I showed up forty pounds lighter and with a wife, so things are strange all around."

"I think your parents are handling the surprise very well," Elisan said, looking around the room. "And I can't wait to hear all your memories of this place and how it used to be."

"It used to have Evangeline, so all the memories are of her." Pick's voice dropped. "It will never feel the same without her."

Elisan stopped and her eyes met his. "I suppose it wouldn't."

She finished buttoning her cuff, and smoothed her skirt as best she could. "Are you ready? I'm hungry."

"I am. Let's go," Pick said, offering her his arm. "Mrs. Thomas, may I escort you to your first dinner at Ashton Hall?"

Elisan grinned up at him and put her hand on his arm. "Why thank you, sir," she said, adding as they left the room, "I never in my life thought I'd be a southern belle, but here we are."

As they rejoined Andrew and Margaret in the dining room, Elisan felt the exhaustion of the trip catch up with her, but not wanting to be the cause of the evening ending early, determined to power through at any cost. She wanted to get to know Pick's parents as quickly as possible, and didn't want to waste this early opportunity in any way.

They seemed equally desirous to talk, but they let Pick and Elisan eat first, making small talk until they were full, and then moved together into the drawing room. On their way across the hall, Zechariah stopped them to inform them that Elisan's trunk had arrived, and she was glad to know that she could make herself more presentable the next morning.

Margaret immediately seated herself next to Pick on the settee, so Elisan sat on a lady's chair nearby and Andrew settled into his armchair and lit a pipe. Elisan took in the carved scrollwork on the mahogany furniture, recognizing that

Margaret Thomas shared her love of renaissance revival furniture and had used it throughout her home.

"Oh!" she exclaimed as her eyes fell on an oil painting mounted over the fireplace, a portrait of two children.

Elisan stood back up and moved to have a closer look of what was obviously a depiction of Pick and his sister. Pick looked to be about eleven or twelve, and stood with his hand on the shoulder of Evangeline, who was seated next to him, her light blonde hair in ringlets around her shoulders. She had her mother's delicate features, her hands folded daintily on her lap and ankles crossed neatly together, and her brown eyes were not unlike Pick's. Elisan took great pleasure in seeing her husband in his past life for the first time, as something other than the malnourished twenty-three-year-old that she knew.

"It's beautiful," Elisan breathed, standing for some time admiring the portrait. Pick and his parents watched her, enjoying her obvious appreciation of it.

"There's another one upstairs of us when we're older, before I went to college, and we have some daguerreotypes we'll have to show you as well," Pick said.

"I'll look forward to seeing them," Elisan said, taking her seat again.

Margaret held Pick's hand in her lap, clasping it tightly with both of hers.

"I'm so glad to have you alive and well, after everything you've been through," she said, looking him over. "Are you here to stay?"

"We definitely are." Pick leaned over and kissed her hair. "Let us know what you need us to do, because we're here to help however we can. What's been going on around here these days?" Pick looked up at his father expectantly with his question, and Andrew let out a puff of smoke.

"We have a lot of wheels spinning right now and we're looking to see which ones get some traction. We can talk more business later, but the short of it is that everything that we had in the stock market and the plantations that the Yankees burned are gone. Everything that we have left in gold and real estate, we're using to get the Negroes on their feet. We still have the Millbrook and St. Matthew's plantations, and the crops are in there, and we've already given loans to a few returned veterans that will bring a bit of income after the harvest. Here at the house, we really only have Zechariah left. Nanny's been taking care of all of her grandchildren while their oldest daughter cooks for us and some of the other houses in the neighborhood, and their sons work at St. Matthew's. We hope if we give them income, it will allow them to stay in the area."

"I'm pleased that you are, Father," Pick said, obviously relieved. "Are the rest of the field hands working for hire now?"

Andrew shook his head and shifted in his seat, and Elisan listened attentively.

"The field hands could really be divided into three groups. There are those who want to stay on and work for hire, mostly older ones. There are those who want to work in return for eventually being able to own the land they are working on themselves and have their own farms. I would say that these are largely fathers with young families. And then there are those who are working here for now, but are looking for an opportunity to start something on their own, when we can get together the resources to help them. Our greatest need for all of them, especially the last group, is education, since they won't get very far if they can't read or figure the numbers. We've been talking about how we can start evening classes, but there are too many that want to learn, and we don't have the resources to do it ourselves right now."

"Elisan and I are here and are anxious to be a part of that," Pick replied to Elisan's delight. She tried to keep her demeanor dignified despite her excitement. "We would love for you to take us around this week and give us a fuller picture of the current situation and discuss how our time will be best used."

Andrew smiled appreciatively at his son and recognized that it was enough business talk for their first night. "There is plenty of time to get into it all in further detail. For now, though, we want to hear about you two, and allow you as much rest as you need to recover fully."

"Yes, we do," Margaret chimed in. "Do tell us about your wedding and how this all came to be."

Pick looked at Elisan, and even the sight of her sitting in his drawing room in Raleigh made his heart skip a beat to know that she was actually there, and that she wasn't leaving.

"Well, you know my side of the story already," he began, but Margaret shook her head.

"You never directly said that you were in love, and you *never* said she was this pretty."

Pick winked at Elisan and couldn't contain his big grin. "But you know that we first met in Virginia, and that last January we met again when she showed up at the camp with her father, and that when she started coming to volunteer every week, it gave us all something to look forward to. And you know that we worked together nearly every week since, and that she's the staunchest abolitionist I'd ever talked to."

"Yes, I did know those things," Margaret said. "Now we need the rest of the story."

"It's Elisan's turn now," Pick said.

Elisan wished she could glare at him, wondering how in the world she could convey the wild first ten months of their friendship to her husband's parents.

"It took me a long time to warm up to Pick specifically, because I thought he was too different from me," she finally said. "But he was always so cheerful, no matter how bad things were, and never complained, even when he was sick. In time, I came to see that under the lightness, he has a good heart and that he cares more about doing the right thing than what I or anyone else thinks. For example, when we disagreed, he took the time to find out why I thought the way that I did, and that went a long way in helping me learn to trust him."

"At the same time, I had a lot of respect for the way that Elisan stands up for what she believes is right and how she uses what she has to benefit others," Pick put in. "I think it's safe to say that by Christmas, we both knew that we were in love but we didn't know that the other one felt the same way."

"No, I knew you loved me," Elisan corrected, and turned to Margaret. "He thinks that I can't read him like a book. At any rate, it was a couple of months after Christmas that he finally admitted it to me. So then the next three months I had to decide what to do about it, but it really wasn't until after the war ended that I knew that I couldn't let him go."

Pick nodded. "It was a big decision. It was easy for me to choose her, but for her, she wasn't just choosing me, she was choosing to leave everything else. When I got out, I went straight to her father, and he was fully supportive of me proposing to Elisan, so I did that very night. I would have written you about it sooner, but it seemed foolish to think that anything would come of it until she accepted me, and then I stopped thinking that I was crazy for the first time."

"I wasn't sure if he was going to ask me, or if he was just coming to say goodbye," Elisan said. "Thankfully, he asked me, and by that point, I would have followed him to China if he'd asked me to. I got my things in order, and we were married in my home with my family the Sunday after Pick was released. First thing the next morning, we started for here. We did get our wedding portrait taken, and my sister will send us a copy of it when it's printed, so you can have it."

"It's such a lovely story." Margaret smiled approvingly, squeezing Pick's hand.

"Margaret had the same difficult decision to make, so we know the weight of it," Andrew said. "I'm still not sure how she decided that I was worth more to her than all of England, but humans will do some incredible things in the name of love."

"There haven't been any celebrations around here since the war ended, but people might be happy to have some gaiety if you'd like to have a party to announce your marriage." Margaret's eyes brightened, but Pick pursed his lips warily.

"Under any other circumstances, Mother, but I don't think that it would be the best idea right now. I can't imagine that the people here are going to take kindly to my coming home from the war with a Yankee wife."

"Not likely," Andrew agreed.

"I'm just so happy to have you home, my whole being wants to celebrate, and I want to show off my new daughter," Margaret admitted, looking at Elisan sadly. "Despite our joy at having you, perhaps the timing isn't the best for a party."

Elisan clasped her hand over her mouth, catching a yawn too late, and Pick glanced at her.

"I'm afraid it's been a terribly long trip for us," Pick said as Elisan apologized. "I really should get her to bed, but we'll be here in the morning, and we'll be all yours."

"Yes, dear, you must always take care of your wife first," Margaret said, standing up. "I'm sorry we've kept you up so late. Do you have everything you need in your room?"

"Yes, ma'am." Pick crossed the room to light a lantern and returned to offer Elisan his hand. They bid his parents goodnight, and left the room together, fingers locked together like newlyweds.

"He's grown up so much," Margaret said, sighing proudly when they'd gone. "It's lovely to see him matured and married, and I think he's chosen well."

Andrew smiled in agreement. "Did you see the way he looks at her? He can hardly contain his happiness."

"I love it. He looks dreadful, however, and I shall talk to Carrie tomorrow about getting the fattiest foods she can find to put some weight on his bones. It's abominable what they did to him up there."

"He's here, though," Andrew said softly. "Many people's sons aren't returning."

"Yes. I couldn't be happier to have him home." Margaret exhaled contentedly, watching the fire lick the logs in the fireplace. Her son was here, alive, and happily married, and her mother's heart was full.

-35-

May 19, 1865

The Friday after Elisan left, dinner at the Dinsmores' felt painfully quiet, even with the Youngs there, and it made everyone cognizant of how much more their lives would be changing with the upcoming wedding. Thankfully, there was plenty to talk about, and everyone made effort to fill the noticeable void at the table.

"I went around to the railroad stations today, looking for a job," Luke announced as dinner wound down, smiling across the table at Kellie. "I can't be on my feet all day yet, but I'm strong enough to sit and work, and walk when needed, so I think I'm ready."

"If you're sure. You know you don't need to feel like you have to be employed before the wedding," Kellie said, her eyebrows furrowing.

"No, but there isn't a need to delay it either, if I'm doing well enough now. Wells Station needed a telegrapher, so I did a demonstration for them and they gave me the job. It's an early shift that starts at five in the morning."

"Congratulations," Justin said. "That's a nice station. Not as big as Great Central, but quite a bit closer."

Luke's eyes twinkled as he looked around the table. "It's quite a bit closer to the cottage we're going to look at tomorrow too."

"What cottage?" Kellie exclaimed, hearing about it for the first time.

"Well, when I swung by Great Central, my former superintendent, Mr. Edwards, told me about some cottages that were recently built on the near west side, and said that we should check them out. So if you're free, why don't we go over there in the morning?"

"The near west side? Can we afford that?" Kellie asked in astonishment, but Luke grinned at her.

"Previously, no, but it sounds like the neighborhood has been shifting lately, and several middle class families have been moving into these cottages. It would also only be a mile or two from the station, but I could take the Kinzie Street streetcar until I'm strong enough to walk it."

"I'm certainly free tomorrow to go with you, and that sounds perfect," Kellie said, delighted at the prospect, as well as the joy on Luke's face.

Reverend Dinsmore cleared his throat, and she turned her attention to him as he looked in Jack's direction.

"With the wedding two weeks away, and living quarters being determined, I wanted to extend an invitation to you, Jack, to come stay here until you leave for college in August and fill some of the empty space we'll have in this home."

Jack's eyes immediately widened, but then he looked slyly at Rebecca.

"I'd consider it, sir, but I know that Rebecca was looking forward to having me around at the apartment, and I'd hate to take that joy from her."

Rebecca snickered without even trying to hide it, and Justin shot back, "You mean to say, you were looking forward to Rebecca's cooking. You've never yet not followed your stomach when an important decision was to be made."

"I hardly think that Rebecca is anxious to expose herself to your moral instruction," Kellie said, and glanced at Rebecca. "Since Jack has been reading the Bible more, he's been quick to let Justin and me know when we aren't measuring up, and always has the chapter and verse with the needed correction ready."

Everyone laughed, but Jack only shrugged. "I'm doing it for you, Rebecca, and you too, Luke. I'm making sure that when you marry in two weeks, you're getting the best possible versions of Justin and Kellie, and you should be thanking me. They've come a long way in the past three years." Jack winked at Rebecca. "I know you always loved Justin, but you really are getting one that is far better prepared for marriage now than the one you would have gotten three years ago."

"Oh, you can hardly take credit for that, Jack!" Kellie retorted. "That was almost all my efforts, and you're quite welcome, Rebecca."

"And let us hope," Justin interjected, holding up his hands, "That the husband that Rebecca has three years from now is a better Justin than the one she's getting next month. May we all," he said, looking at Jack, "continue in growth throughout our lives."

The mirth around the table was good medicine for Rebecca, and she was still laughing when she replied, "I do appreciate it, Jack, and especially your kind offer to stay and keep Justin and me company during our honeymoon, but I won't be selfish. I know you'd have so much more space and privacy here, and perhaps I can cook for you once or twice. The piano is here too, so you'll have more time to practice, since you've been doing so abysmally in your lessons lately."

"I am sure that you could hardly expect more from me when I'm spending my days laboring under the iron hand of Justin Young, and by the time evening comes and I can practice, my energy is depleted," Jack said defensively before turning back to the reverend.

"Despite the great pleasure that teasing Rebecca affords me, I am grateful for your invitation, and I would be happy to stay here this summer. Thank you kindly."

Reverend Dinsmore smiled at him. "We will look forward to having you. Will you all continue to gather for Friday night dinners here? It would be a shame if next week were our last one of these."

"Would it be too much for you, Mother?" Luke asked, but Rebecca quickly cut in.

"I can come on Fridays and help cook, if we could only continue this tradition."

"Then it would be just fine," Mrs. Dinsmore replied, and it was settled.

Rebecca looked around the table. "I might as well let the rest of you know, that I've told Papa and Justin that I will be retiring as the church organist before the wedding as well," she said, and Luke blinked at her.

"Really, why? I know you love to play."

"I do, but I can still come over and play during the week whenever I want. I've been the organist for ten years now, and I'm looking forward to sitting in the pew next to my husband. Besides, there is no lack of applicants who are anxious for the position, so I know Papa won't have a problem replacing me."

"I'm afraid I have organist trials scheduled all next week, if any of you want to take pity on me and come listen to help me make my decision," Reverend Dinsmore said, shaking his head.

"Won't Mr. Kirk be the one making the decision?" Luke asked, referring to the song director.

"He will be quite opinionated on the matter, but the deacons and elders have the final vote. They were none too happy that I stuck Rebecca in there as a substitute when Mrs. Keene fell ill years ago, and basically gave her the job without consulting with them first. Nonetheless, I shall be subjected to all manner of cacophonies in the process of determining which musician is worthy of my vote."

"They may have fussed about it to you, dear, but those same deacons were also terribly proud of her, and used to boast about town about the twelve-year-old organist at our church," Mrs. Dinsmore reminded him. "It would never do nowadays, but when Chicago was just an up-and-coming frontier town, we used to get away with quite a bit more. These days, everything must be done the proper way, and there's no harm in that."

"I remember how surprised and impressed I was the first time that I came and saw Rebecca up there," Justin said, his smile affectionate and nostalgic. "It was one of my first clues that things were different here from Kentucky. Goodness, I can't believe that was ten years ago now, and I was even younger then than Titan is now."

"I think it's about time to make you officially part of the family," Reverend Dinsmore said, pushing back his chair and standing up, "And about time to retire to the drawing room. Shall we sing tonight, Rebecca?"

"I can play, Papa, but I won't be able to sing a note. Without Elisan here to harmonize with me, I'm afraid I'd be a puddle of tears."

"Then we'll enjoy your playing." The reverend offered his wife his arm and led the way out of the room and everyone pushed back their chairs and followed: first Luke and Kellie, then Justin with Rebecca, and Jack and Titan brought up the rear together.

June 3, 1865

"I'm here," Kellie called, knocking on Rebecca's bedroom door early the morning of the wedding. She opened the door when Rebecca replied, and peered inside.

"Have you started yet?"

"Just now," Christina answered as Kellie entered and dropped her carpetbag on the bed. Rebecca was seated at the vanity in her dressing gown, her straight brown hair falling down her back, and Christina was behind her, pins in hand.

"How are you this morning?" Rebecca asked her.

"I'm well," Kellie said and then quietly added, "Just thinking about Jed today. He should have been here."

Before Rebecca could reply, Kellie seated herself on the rug next to Annette, who'd been given buttons on a string to play with while her mother was occupied with her sisterly duties.

"Good morning, sweetheart," Kellie said, reaching out to touch her little blonde head. "Remember me from yesterday? I'm going to be your new auntie. Where's George?"

"He's with William and Titan," Christina replied. "He would tear this room up since I wouldn't be able to keep a good eye on him, but hopefully they'll help him get all of his energy out before the ceremony."

The eldest Dinsmore sister looked like her father, Kellie thought, while Luke favored their mother more. Her hair was a shade lighter than Rebecca's, but she had the same hazel eyes and since Titan's latest growth spurt, she was now the shortest of the siblings and had morphed into a more matronly shape in recent years.

"Are those our flowers?" Kellie asked, noticing jars full of flowers covering Rebecca's bedside table.

"We picked them this morning," Rebecca said. "Do you want to start making bouquets? You could pick out whatever you like for yours; we don't necessarily have to have them match exactly."

Kellie picked up Annette and took her over to look at the flowers together. There were pale pink peonies, various shades of pink and white roses, hydrangeas, azaleas, baby's breath, and an assortment of greenery. "It smells heavenly, and they're beautiful. What are you wrapping yours with?"

Without moving her neck, Rebecca picked up a necklace from her vanity. "I have my grandmother's pearls and some ribbon I bought. You?"

Kellie stood looking the flowers over and plucked a peony bud that she handed to Annette. "I'll just use some ribbon since I don't have anything special."

She glanced up at her dress bodice that hung on the wardrobe next to Rebecca's, and setting Annette back on the floor, began to make her flower selections, holding them up to the dress every now and then as she worked.

"Do you think you're going to cry in the ceremony?"

"Oh, there's no doubt," Rebecca said with a laugh, and Kellie smiled at her. "And you know that Justin is going to sob like a baby, so once he starts, I don't have a chance of making it through dry-eyed. Are you going to?"

"Well, Luke won't, even if the whole rest of the church was crying. I didn't think I would, but I probably would have cried in Justin's wedding, so I'm not sure."

Rebecca's hand flew to her forehead in dismay. "Oh, that's a good point; I didn't even think of the fact that it's going to be Luke's wedding, too! Goodness, I may even start crying before the ceremony then."

Christina chuckled as she busily worked over Rebecca. "Did Elisan cry at her wedding?" she asked, taking the hairpins out of her mouth.

"No, she was euphoric the whole time," Rebecca said. "She was so happy and beautiful, and I know she wished you could have been there."

"I was sorry to miss it, and to not be able to say goodbye before she left. It's been so long since I saw her, but she was beautiful in her wedding portrait. She needs to put some weight on her poor husband, though." Christina picked up Rebecca's mother of pearl hair combs and carefully inserted them into place, then continued pinning around them.

"I know she's anxious to. What are you wearing today, Christina?" Kellie asked, looking around the room.

"My dress is still in my room, but it's mint green silk. Rebecca's favorite color," she said affectionately, and Rebecca's eyes widened.

"You made a new dress for my wedding?"

"I needed a new tea dress anyway," Christina said with a wave of her hand. "Nothing's fit since I had Annette."

Kellie came over to the sisters holding her bouquet. "How do you like this? I think I've finished."

"Oh, I like that a lot," Rebecca said. "I think I do want mine to match yours after all. I like the peonies especially."

"Me too. How do you like this?" Christina asked, patting Rebecca's hair one more time and stepping back.

"Gorgeous." Kellie admired Christina's work. "You're going to do mine too, right?"

"If you'll let me. I was hoping to have the chance to work with your pretty curls, and I'm finished with Rebecca."

By the time Christina had Kellie's hair set perfectly, it was nearly time for the wedding to start. Kellie and Rebecca carefully donned their new petticoats and began hooking their dresses into place, so Christina left to quickly dress herself and deliver Annette to her husband. Dozens of carriages were already arriving next door at the church, and the three women were the only ones left in the manse when they descended the stairs to the foyer.

Rebecca looked at Kellie, and Kellie looked at Rebecca, both beautiful in their wedding splendor.

"I'm so happy that you're marrying my brother," Rebecca exclaimed, and Kellie hugged her.

"I'm so happy that you're marrying MY brother. Thank you for being willing to have a double wedding. It's so much more fun."

"Are you ready?" Christina opened the door and peeked outside. "I think we're a little late."

She pulled the veils over the brides' faces, and together they walked across the courtyard to the church door, where the strains of the organ could be heard from the outside. Stepping inside, Christina made eye contact with her father in the front of the full church, and he began the ceremony.

Luke and Justin came out and stood together at the front of the sanctuary, and Jack walked up the aisle alone, carrying the Young family Bible that Kellie had taken from home as a child, and placed it on the altar. Christina entered next, standing across from Jack.

The organ belted out and bells tolled as Kellie stepped up the aisle, followed by Rebecca.

The ceremony progressed without mishap as Reverend Dinsmore led the recitation of vows. True to Rebecca's prediction, neither she nor Justin were able to keep their composure as they promised to love and honor each other until death, but Luke and Kellie remained serene and enraptured in one another's gaze as they did the same a few moments later.

And so they were married; for Justin and Rebecca, it was a long awaited union that was the fruition of more than five years of patient, quiet love, the realization of a dream that had of necessity been buried for a time but had bloomed into reality sweetly and beautifully in the right time.

For Luke and Kellie, it was the surprise of a new day, like digging through the ash of a heart destroyed in a raging fire and finding love growing there, a vine reaching out of the rubble and desperately grasping hold, spreading and flourishing until it was unable to be rooted up.

They ate, drank, danced, and celebrated with their families and loved ones for much of the remainder of the day. When the last trampled flower was gathered up and the crumbs all swept away, Justin and Rebecca settled in together at the little apartment above the bakery, and Luke and Kellie made their home in a cottage a few miles away.

The newlyweds' new lives together had a blissful start that summer. Justin and Luke continued to thrive in their respective careers, and the thrill of coming home after a day of work to their own adored wives never got old. They all gathered on Friday nights at the manse as promised for dinner, music, games, and robust conversation, everyone bringing along any letters they had received from Elisan that week to share with the others.

She wrote captivating letters with every detail of her strange new life, honest about the ups and downs but always speaking rapturously of her new husband and his parents. She'd begun teaching former slaves to read and write, and although it was more difficult than she'd expected, having never done such a thing before, she found it deeply meaningful and loved her work despite its challenges.

Titan started college in the fall at Rush Medical College at the same time that Jack headed to Northwestern, and although they both stayed in the city, their studies kept them too busy to spend much time with their family during the semester.

For the newlyweds, their wedding day was one step, a decisive step, in their journey of love, and they continued to move forward along the path, cultivating their love with faith, humor, patience, and fortitude after their wedding as they had done before it.

-36-

February 20, 1866

Kellie heard the front door open and close, telling her that Luke was home from work, as she stirred dinner's soup one more time and began to tidy up the kitchen. He would need a few minutes until he would be ready to eat, so she let the pot continue to simmer after she straightened up and came out into the front room to greet him.

She had started across the room towards him when she glanced over and suddenly stopped short. Propped up on the table was a framed painting that she had never seen before, a still life of hibiscus flowers in bright pinks and whites. Luke stood quietly checking something on his ledger, but his eyes moved up to watch her.

"Where did this come from?" Kellie asked slowly, an odd look on her face.

"It was just delivered. There wasn't a note."

Kellie walked over to the table and stood looking at the painting as if in a trance, staring at the bright blossoms and taking in the details. The simplicity of the bouquet felt slightly unusual; in the center was one beautiful pink hibiscus in full bloom, surrounded by three white ones in a clear vase of water, and stuck in the side of the bouquet was a small pink bud, not fully open. Kellie wasn't entirely sure yet what it meant, but something about it seemed deeply meaningful. Searching for a signature on the painting, she didn't find one. She felt herself beginning to unravel and she swallowed hard as her body trembled and tears came to her eyes.

Luke's expression became alarmed. "Are you okay? Do you need your smelling salts?"

"Did you know that hibiscus is my favorite flower?"

Luke thought for a second and shook his head. "No, I thought hydrangeas were your favorite."

"Mm-mm. I like hydrangeas, but I grow them because I can't grow these here. I don't get enough sun in our yard, and I've never seen these in Chicago. My mother called them rosemallows and grew them outside her bedroom window, and they always make me think of her."

Kellie stared at the flowers and took a shaky breath, tears falling.

"You don't have any idea where this came from?"

"Do you?" Luke countered without answering the question.

"I only ever told two people that these are my favorite, and they're both dead."

From across the room, Luke watched her closely as she continued.

"Nathan and . . . "

Kellie instinctively looked up at the doorway, whispering, "Jed," as from the hall stepped a six foot tall man with curly black hair and smoky gray eyes.

Kellie's whole body shook as she blinked, not believing her eyes as Jed stood uncertainly across the room, letting the reality of his presence sink in before moving towards her.

"Jed," Kellie repeated when he stopped in front of her, looking through tears up at the brother she had thought she would never see again. She reached out slowly and touched him, and knew that he was real.

Jed enveloped her in his arms and held her as huge sobs shook her entire being. She pressed her forehead against his chest and wept, unable to regain her composure.

It wasn't the greeting that Jed had expected, but it was sobering for him to realize the pain that he had put her through for the past two and a half years. He let her cry for a few minutes, but the tears continued when she tried to stop, so he finally began to rub her back to help her calm down as Luke watched mutely.

"Kellie . . . Kellie. I'm so sorry. Shhh . . . Kellie, I'm sorry," he whispered, until eventually she was quieted.

Jed pulled her away from himself and held her by the shoulders, leaning down to look into her puffy, wet eyes. "I'm so sorry, Kellie."

Kellie's tears never stopped, but she was calm enough to speak. "Where have you been?" she cried.

Jed let his breath out. "Running. I've been running. But I'm . . . not. Anymore."

"Why? Why didn't you write? Why didn't you come home?"

"I—" Jed looked up at Luke helplessly, but Luke didn't move. "A lot of reasons. I couldn't at first, and then . . . I don't know. I thought you were probably doing better without me," he admitted. "Do you . . . want to talk about it all right now? Like this?"

Kellie remembered herself, and wiped at her eyes. "No, I'm sorry, we can have dinner first." She looked at Luke with a request in her eyes, and he moved to put dinner on the table. She turned back to Jed and dropped her head.

"I'm sorry, Jed."

She stood quietly with him for a moment, then slowly reached her arms around him and hugged him. "I love you so much."

"I love you too. I missed you every day."

"I just wish you would have let me know you were alive." Dropping her hands, she turned to the painting. "Did you do this?"

"Yeah," Jed said, taking a deep breath. "I did."

"It's beautiful. I love that you even included Katie," Kellie said, referring to the small bud in the side of the vase. "When did you start painting?"

"After the war ended. It was all part of the journey for me."

"Will you tell me about it? About . . . what brought you home?"

"Of course."

Luke opened the door and Kellie led Jed into the dining room, where they took their seats around the table. After Luke blessed the food, Kellie stood up to ladle the soup into the bowls, picking Jed's bowl up first.

"Does anyone else know you're back?"

"No, I just arrived at the station today, and Luke brought me here because I wanted to see you first. He said that Justin and Rebecca are at the apartment and Jack's in college, but that's all I know so far." Jed paused. "I was thinking about going over to see Justin after supper." He took a sip of soup and swallowed before asking, "Do you think he'll want to see me?"

Kellie gave him a reproachful look. "Justin loves you a lot more than you ever knew, and he's forgiven you. Have you forgiven him?"

"He never did anything that I needed to forgive," Jed said softly.

They ate quietly for a couple of minutes, then Kellie set her spoon down. "Jed, have you found God?"

Jed straightened up and bobbed his head. "He was there all along. I just needed to have my eyes opened to see Him."

Kellie pressed her hand to her lips as tears dripped down her face, never really having dried up from before. "There were so many dark nights, when I thought that you were gone without Him. I stopped hoping; I stopped believing that this could happen. I stopped praying for you even, because I thought you were dead."

Jed reached his hand across the table, and she lifted hers to touch it. "Kellie, I'm sorry for what I've put you through, and I wish I could've let you know. I wouldn't be alive today if it weren't for your prayers, and I wouldn't be here if it wasn't for your love."

He picked his spoon back up and continued eating before he remembered they hadn't settled the matter of calling on Justin. "I want to talk to you, but I can do that tomorrow while Justin's at work, and I shouldn't put off seeing him further . . . if it's okay to go tonight."

Kellie nodded, drying her eyes again. "It's actually been a rough week for them, and you probably won't see Rebecca, but it might help Justin to see you."

Jed cocked his head. "Is she . . . " He tried to remember the proper word. "Is she in confinement?"

"No." Kellie shook her head sadly. "She was, but it . . . didn't make it."

"Oh. I'm sorry to hear that." Jed took another bite, glancing from the silent Luke to Kellie. "What about you?"

Kellie's face turned into a half smile, amused to see pieces of the Jed she'd known before, blunt, clueless, and so lovable.

"It's probably not going to happen for us, Jed."

They continued eating in silence until Jed was the one to break it yet again. "This is great, Kellie. Your cooking has really improved."

She smiled, touched that he noticed. "I've learned some things from Rebecca. I'm glad you like it. How about your cooking; has it improved as well?"

"A little," Jed said wryly. "You were right that it's a good skill to have, but I should have done a better job of trying to learn when you were teaching me."

When dinner was over, Kellie excused herself to the bedroom to fetch her cloak and bonnet, and Luke followed her there.

"Are you doing okay?" he asked, alone with her again.

"Yes." Kellie looked up into his eyes and took a deep breath. "I'm deeply happy right now, more than anything. But there are a lot of other emotions too, that I wouldn't have expected, and I'll need to sort them out."

She wrapped her heavy gray wool cloak around her shoulders and clasped it, and Luke pulled her into a hug.

"It will probably help when you're able to sit down and talk to him. I think Justin's going to need some time with him tonight too, since he'll be as shocked as you were."

"You're right, we can give them some space if he needs it," Kellie said. "I'm still in shock myself, to be honest."

"If you're ready, I'll go hook up the buggy."

Luke kissed her and let her go, and Kellie picked up her bonnet and muff.

"I'm ready." She led the way out of the room, rejoining Jed in the front room as Luke headed outside.

She found him standing in front of the painting again, and clasped his hand in hers.

"You're looking really well, Kellie," Jed said, smiling down at her. "I'm glad to see you with Luke, and you seem happy together."

"We are happy. You were the missing piece, and now you're here, although I still haven't believed it to be true."

Jed offered her his arm, and they slowly made their way outside into the cold darkness.

Justin was taking dinner to Rebecca in the bedroom when he heard Kellie's knock, so it took him a couple of minutes to finish before he could get to the door. He was glad to see Luke and Kellie though, and opened the door further to let them in. Kellie hugged him as they entered the apartment, but Luke stood with his hand on the open door.

"How are you both doing?" Kellie asked as she unpinned her bonnet.

"We're alright. Rebecca's still resting, and you know we're sad. But she's young and strong, and we're grateful that she's okay."

"Sometimes, God gives us a miracle long after we stop believing, and sometimes, He raises the dead," Kellie said, biting back a smile and looking over his shoulder at the doorway. "That's what I learned today."

Justin turned around to look questioningly at Luke as Jed stepped from behind the door.

"Oh, dear God," Justin breathed. "Jed?"

His eyes filled with tears like Kellie's had, but he quickly stepped towards Jed and embraced him firmly.

"Are you really alive? How is this possible? Come in, come in." Justin gestured for them to take seats around the warm fireplace, but Luke touched his arm.

"Can I see Rebecca?"

"Yes, you can go on in. She's up and awake," Justin said.

Luke left as Justin sat, turning expectantly towards his brother.

"It's really me. I'm sorry . . . Kellie told me about the baby. But congratulations on your wedding," Jed said, settling into one of the old familiar armchairs.

"Thank you. What have you been up to? We had a letter that you were wounded or probably dead. I guess that was October two years ago now?" Justin leaned forward. "What brings you back?"

"Ah, well." Jed stopped and cocked his head. "Which question do I answer first?"

Before Justin could answer, Jed continued. "I suppose, um, that I came back because I woke up to a lot of things, and because I needed to tell you that I'm sorry. I know that I hurt you, and that I left badly. Really badly. But I understand a lot more now about things, about how you weren't a failure and about why I did a lot of the things I did. And . . . I'm sorry."

Justin dropped his hands heavily onto his knees. "Oh, man, I forgave you a long time ago. I'm sorry that I didn't take more time with you when I had it, Jed. I've regretted it every day. And I mishandled a lot of things back then."

"Well, I've come to appreciate everything that you did for me." Jed's face twitched. "I've had a lot of time to think about it, and about a year ago I started reading the Bible you gave me, so I guess it was in the fall, I started praying and gave my life to God. So He's walked me through a lot of things." Jed scratched his forehead. "And here I am."

A huge grin took over Justin's face, and he shook his head unbelievingly. "Praise God," he exclaimed, blinking back tears. "Praise God for his faithfulness to our family." He took a deep breath and wiped at his cheeks. "Where have you been all this time?"

"West Virginia at first, then Pennsylvania. So yes, I was wounded in the raid in West Virginia, and it was . . . quite a long and difficult recovery." Jed held up his right hand. "I actually can't use this hand anymore. My shoulder was shattered and originally I couldn't move my arm at all, but now I can lift it but it isn't good for anything."

"I didn't even notice tonight," Kellie admitted. "Did you eat with your left hand?"

Jed nodded. "I've been working on it, so I've gotten to the point where I can manage okay. But, um . . . well, it's a long story. But once I had nearly recovered, I ended up near Philadelphia and that's where I've been for about a year. I've been driving, doing deliveries, since there's not much else I can do one handed, but I worked for some Christian brothers. So I spent that time building up my strength, thinking, reading, praying, saving up money so that I could come home."

He looked around the room. "Lots has happened around here since I left. I can't believe you all let Jack go to college. So I guess he's found new things to do on Friday nights?"

"Yes, Jack got saved soon after we found out that you were probably killed," Justin said with a smile. "He completely turned a corner after that, and then started working with me at the docks."

Justin and Kellie took turns briefly catching Jed up on everything that had happened since he left, including Luke's accident, Justin's promotion, their wedding, and Elisan's departure.

"If I write to Jack in the morning, I think he'd come home on Saturday," Kellie said. "He hasn't been home since Christmas, so I think I could lure him down here if you want to surprise him."

Jed's face lit up. "I would love that."

Kellie nodded and glanced from Justin to Jed. "We didn't want to stay late, Justin. Are you staying at my house, Jed?"

"Sure, if you'll have me."

"I was hoping you would." Kellie stood up, and her brothers joined her.

"Are you in Chicago to stay, then?" Justin asked, reaching out to shake Jed's hand.

"For the time being. I have some opportunities I'm considering, but even if I don't end up living in the city for good, I'm planning to be around from now on. As far as the family is concerned, I'm here to stay."

Kellie grinned as Justin hugged him again, slapping him on the back. "This is the best news we could have gotten all year. We're happy to have you home."

"Thanks, man. It means a lot."

Kellie was tired when they got home that night, but long after she climbed into bed, her mind hadn't stopped swirling and she still lay awake an hour later. She finally sat up and lit a candle, and reaching for her journal, began to put words on the paper in an attempt to figure out what was going on inside her heart.

At first, the words were scattered: *Thrilled beyond belief. Complete and utter shock. He looks good. Who has he become? He's a stranger again. We used to be so close, but now I barely know him anymore. Why can't I believe this really happened? Why did I stop praying?*

After a few minutes, however, she began to dig out what was hiding under the surface. *Don't think for a moment that my heart isn't overflowing with happiness, but why does it hurt? When we've all forgiven him for hurting us years ago, his very appearance on my doorstep cuts a new gash, the pain of discovering that he could have written to me a year and a half ago, and he chose not to. He could have spared us a year and a half of heartache, and he chose not to. It was easier to believe that he was dead than to believe that he would do that to us.*

And now again, I must choose to forgive him, but this time, my heart wonders, now that he's back in our lives will he only continue to hurt us again and again? When did I become such a cynic that I can't even receive my long dead brother back to life with anything other than sheer joy? Jesus . . . have mercy on me; I am ashamed of these thoughts.

But tomorrow, I will let him speak for himself, and I will extend him honest forgiveness, regardless of his story. Thank You for forgiving him Yourself . . . I will follow You.

In the morning, Kellie had second cups of coffee for herself and Jed after breakfast as they settled in across from each other on the sofas in her front room.

Jed took a sip of his coffee and looked out the window, through Kellie's lace curtains to gray skies tempting snow, and bleak, barren trees.

"You're angry," he said softly, and Kellie's heart caught in her throat to be found out.

"I'm mostly happy," she defended herself, then sighed and dropped her eyes. "A little bit. I've been praying about it, though, and I'll work through it. You've already apologized and there's nothing else you can do, so please don't let it get to you." She paused. "Where do you want to start?"

Jed accepted her statement and moved on. "I think . . . I'll start with West Virginia. I'm not sure that I know how to start from before that."

"It's okay. Just do what you can," Kellie said, and Jed took a deep breath before diving in.

"So . . . when I got hit, I was in enemy territory, and my unit had to leave me there. And I was bleeding quite a bit, but I was alone and I couldn't get captured, not as one of Mosby's men. I managed to drag myself away from the scene so that I wouldn't be found, but I kept passing out. Well, I guess you don't need all the details. But by the next day, I got myself to a shelter and I was there for a few days before I was found, and by then, Mosby was long gone, and I'd torn off and buried anything that would possibly identify me as a Ranger. At that point though, I was barely hanging on. Starving, bleeding to death, and you know the pain was unbearable, but I thought it was just a matter of time before I'd be gone, and I'd rather accepted it."

Jed licked his lips and then chewed on them for a minute. "It was this pastor that found me, and he took me home, and him and his wife Alice hid me and took care of me for months. Months. I can't even tell you what all happened during that time, but I was really ill and Alice took care of me. Eventually, I started getting my strength and started being conscious more, and then I realized what was happening in the house around me. And I started to realize that he was beating Alice."

Jed stopped then, covered his mouth with his hand, and his eyes glistened with tears. He swallowed, lowering his hand to his chin. "To this day, it shakes me up when I think about it. It was the worst feeling I've had in my life, and I do mean that. As soon as I was well enough, and I mean, the very moment that I thought I could walk, I took Alice and we left."

He sat motionless, breathing heavily, while Kellie sat quietly across from him. She remembered the conversations she'd had with Jed over the kitchen table years before, and tried to reconcile those memories with the man she was seeing before her. As close as they had been, she had never seen this side of him; but then she remembered the deserter that Jed had refused to shoot, and she was cognizant of the fact that as glaring as the differences seemed to be, this Jed had been there all along, cloaked in the shadows behind the one she'd known.

"I just took her and ran," Jed continued shakily. "And I don't know that she would have come if I hadn't made her. But I took her straight back to her family outside of Philadelphia. I just took her home, Kellie. You know, I didn't have any other intentions. And I thought I'd leave her there and I'd leave, but she wouldn't have even gone in to her family, she was so ashamed to come home. So I took her in there, and you know what, they just embraced her. Her brothers were there, and her parents, and they did exactly what they should have done. They wrapped her up and loved her and told her that she never had to go back to that man again. Her brothers were pretty livid at her husband, though, because I told them what he did. She wouldn't, but I told them.

"They wanted to repay me and be friends, but it's not as though they could let the neighbors know, 'Oh, this is Jed, he's a Confederate who ran off with our sister,' you see, but they got me an attic room in town and gave me a job driving for them, and I've done my best to try to be less noticeable by the way I talk, so I made myself fit in there while I saved up money to come home."

Kellie sat drinking her coffee, enraptured by his story, as Jed thought through how to say what he needed to.

"So Alice . . . when I had her and we were traveling, a lot of things became clear for me. I looked at what happened to her, and how she acted, and all of a sudden I understood some things that had happened to me. For the first time . . . I felt that there was someone who understood me."

Jed paused. "When I came here, it was the first time I'd let myself be around women, and I came and allowed these really incredible women into my life. I was here with you, and Rebecca, and Elisan, and you are all strong, confident women. So Alice was the first woman I knew closely who wasn't like that, and I saw myself in her. She was broken and scared, and I was there at a really tender time in her life. You . . . you had opened up things in me that I'd never thought about or talked about before, and then Alice came along and I discovered . . . well, there was a whole new level I'd never touched before.

"When we got to Philadelphia, we didn't really talk anymore, only occasionally, and we'd see each other at church, but I started spending a lot of time thinking through things, and I started reading the Bible. I started painting then, because I needed to strengthen my left hand, so I painted to practice it, and it helped me think."

Jed looked down at his coffee mug. "I thought about you a lot. Every day. And I cried more than I've ever cried in my life, but I really thought that you were happy without me and that I needed to let y'all live your lives. But I couldn't stop thinking about Alice's family either and how they just took her right in, and they didn't tell her she'd done anything wrong or turn her away. Her brothers woulda probably killed that man if he'd come then, and that's for sure what I woulda been like if it was you, and I began to figure out what family meant, and what love meant, what God meant, what my life meant. So it was the fall when I started praying and God started working in my heart, and by Christmas I'd decided to come home, but I just had to finish saving enough money . . . since I don't gamble anymore, you know."

Jed looked like he had finished his story, but he still sat looking at his coffee, and Kellie remembered how he needed quiet, so she waited. When minutes had passed and he looked up at her again, his eyes were full of tears. Kellie had never seen him cry before, and her tender heart broke at the sight.

"I fell in love with her, Kellie. I really didn't mean to, and I wish I hadn't. But I never knew how powerful it is to be understood by someone before her. And right now, it's tearing me up and it feels like my world has ended, because I had to walk away from her."

"Oh, Jed," Kellie breathed. "Did you ever tell her?"

Jed shook his head. "No, she doesn't know, and that's the way it should be. She's safe now, and she's with her family, and I have to leave her there."

He chewed on his lip and furrowed his eyebrows as tears slipped from his eyes. "It was the right thing to do, but I wish it didn't hurt so much."

Kellie stood up, set down her coffee, and moved to sit next to Jed, wrapping him in a hug as he struggled for control.

"I know how it feels to lose someone I love dearly," she murmured. "I know how it feels to walk around every day feeling like I've been punched in the gut from the pain. But I don't know how it feels to be brave enough to walk away myself. You did the right thing, Jed, even by rescuing her, and I'm proud of you."

"Does it ever stop? Does it ever get better?" Jed cried, running his hand up and down her back.

"In time, yes, but it changes you. It gets to where it doesn't sting as much, but you're never the same afterwards, and that's okay." She held Jed until he was calm again, and he picked up his cold mug of coffee.

"Thanks, Kellie. I haven't been able to talk to anyone but God about it, but you've always been safe for me. It's good to be home."

"I'm glad you still think that, after all this time. Thank you for telling me, Jed. It sounds like God has taken you on quite the journey and used it to bring you to Himself."

"He's been patient with me." Jed inhaled and fell silent.

"Now, tell me about these opportunities you have now," Kellie said brightly, patting his knee. "What are you considering?"

"Well, I'm going to be honest, I think I'm done with city life," Jed replied, watching her. "It doesn't agree with me, and I can't sit still. My soul needs space, but I only have one good hand, so that complicates things. I was thinking about getting a job riding on a ranch in Wisconsin or on a barge on the Mississippi. Somewhere close enough that I can still come home at Christmas, or in the summertime. I have a couple names to reach out to whenever I'm ready."

"That sounds good, Jed. I think those are good ideas for you, and I hope something works out. In the meantime, you can stay here as long as you like."

Jed leaned over and kissed her hair. "You're wonderful to offer. Did you write to Jack yet?"

"No, I should do that now." Kellie stood up. "I can't wait to have us all together again."

Jed looked out the window again, at Chicago's endless winter. "We should go ice skating again. Do you still have the skates?"

"Yes, we do," Kellie said with a laugh. "We haven't used them since you left, though. Remember how it was harder than it looked?"

"I remember how that was the happiest day we ever had together, and I've wished a thousand times that I could go back to that day."

"It was a beautiful day," Kellie said softly. She paused, then turned to her desk and pulled out a sheet of paper to send for Jack.

"What time are you expecting Jack today?" Luke asked Kellie on Saturday morning, buttoning his shirt as they dressed together.

"He should be here by lunchtime. Justin's going to come over in a little while so that he's here when Jack arrives."

Luke tucked his shirt into his pants and buttoned his suspenders in place. "I'm going to go spend the day with Rebecca, so Justin can stay here as long as he needs to."

"Are you sure?" Kellie glanced over at her husband. "Don't feel like we don't want you here."

"No, it's fine. You all are going to need time, and Rebecca would appreciate my company. You can tell me about it all later."

"I'm sorry you have to miss seeing Jack's face. I can hardly wait."

Luke smiled, picturing that moment in his mind. "It's going to be special, sweetheart."

He walked over and hugged her tight, in celebration of the long-dead dreams that were alive again and coming true, and he thought of all the hurt and sorrow that she had endured that now was birthing a joy, complete and beautiful.

"We thank God," he whispered tenderly. "He has brought dancing from our mourning, joy from our sorrow, and He has brought the dead to life."

Kellie closed her eyes and leaned her head against his chest, the chest that she had breathlessly watched barely rise and fall on a hospital bed and was now strong and healthy.

"God was good in the valleys, and He is good to us now in our season of refreshment. And He will always be good around the bends in our journey, wherever He takes us."

Luke bent down and kissed her lips softly. "I love you. I'm thankful that this is the stretch of the journey that He's allowed us to walk together."

Kellie exhaled, resting in his arms, and she couldn't agree more.

Jed and Justin were in the kitchen later that morning with Kellie, helping her slice bread and cheese for lunch and chatting together when Jack came through the door without knocking.

Everyone looked up at the same time when he entered sooner than expected, and Kellie turned around, exclaiming, "Oh, you're here!"

"Jed?" Jack stopped in the middle of the room when the realization of his brother's presence hit him. He blinked and shook his head, as if trying to wake himself up, but there was no denying that he was awake and Jed was actually there.

"Surprise!" Jed stood up and stretched his arms out. "Gosh, Jack, you're almost as tall as I am now."

Jack grabbed Jed into a fierce hug, laughing out loud as Justin and Kellie watched teary-eyed.

"I can't believe you're alive! Welcome home! Wow, my goodness, I never thought I'd see you again. How long has Kellie been hiding you?"

"Just since Tuesday," Jed said, pulling back to have a look at his brother. "It's good to see you, but I wish I could've come up to see you at college with your robes on. Maybe I still will."

"I still don't care for having to wear a necktie every day," Jack said. "You weren't helping Kellie make lunch, were you? She should know better than to let you touch the food."

"You're not wrong." Jed lifted his right hand. "I can barely use this hand for anything anymore, so I can't even slice bread for her properly."

"Oh man, that's rough. Was that when we got the letter that you were hit?"

"Yeah. I almost died, but I've spent the last year after my recovery making my way back to God and working through a lot. But I finally came to the place where I knew that I had to come back to you all."

Jack beamed at Jed, grabbing him by the arm. "I can't tell you how much we missed you. We really struggled with losing you. Wow. I can't believe this."

He perched on a stool while Justin and Kellie finished up making lunch, and Jed leaned against the table telling him his story, including for the first time in Justin's presence the part about taking Alice to Philadelphia. He didn't share the intimate details he had told Kellie, but she couldn't help but notice how different he was now from when he'd lived with them, by even being willing to open himself up to them at all.

They moved to the dining room for lunch, talking around the table long after they'd finished eating, unraveling together more about the mysteries of their pasts and how their year together had impacted each of them.

"Every day, all I saw was how I didn't fit in here, and I felt like an imposter. I'd convinced myself that you all would manage better without me," Jed said slowly, tilting his chair back the way he always had. "I saw what Jack was into, and I knew that I couldn't be the example that he needed and I was getting in the way of the impact that Justin could have on him. Because I knew that I would never be good enough, and I would never deserve to be one of you."

"I didn't think I would ever be good enough, either," Jack said. "I explained to Justin and Kellie before that I wanted this to be home so much, but I was terrified of it, because I thought that I would be rejected when I was known. It was wanting something so badly but not being willing to step into the light to receive it."

Jed's eyebrows arched and he nodded slowly. "That's it, for sure. Scared of home, because home is where you're known. That's exactly why when I saw myself getting close with you all, I ran, because I couldn't face it, being known. But when God came into my heart and changed me, I . . . finally felt free to come back. And accept that I belong here, with you."

"I honestly don't understand." Kellie wiped at tears in her eyes and lowered her hands to rest on the table. "I don't think either Justin or I rejected you or meant to make either of you feel that you didn't belong here just because you weren't a Christian. We tried to love you the best we could, and we know we didn't do it perfectly, but I don't think we ever offered you conditional love. How did both of you came to the conclusion that until you were a Christian, you couldn't consider this family to be your home? We loved you anyway."

Jed shook his head, and Jack reached out to cover her hands with his own. "It's not at all what you did, Kellie, and honestly it wasn't even about you and Justin at all. Neither of us had ever known a home or a family before, and we had a fairy tale dream of wanting it, but when it came down to it, neither of us could stand the feeling of unworthiness when we came into the light of being known."

"It was the exposure," Jed said with a nod, and Justin looked at him wryly.

"Goodness, even I struggled with that. I don't think any of us were capable of living up to the expectations that we thought came with having a family."

Jack continued. "I realized that this wasn't the home that I was searching for, really, and that it was God that I needed to come home to. My soul wasn't longing for people who have the same black curly hair as me, it was longing for my true, heavenly home. When I finally accepted that, when I finally stood before Jesus with all of my sin and shame, and like Jed said, took on His righteousness, then I came home. And when I came home to Him, coming home to you was just an aftereffect."

"God was merciful," Justin said softly. "He's pursued each of us, gently calling us to Himself, and He led us home. And now, because of His great grace, we've all found home."

Jed looked around the table at his family, unable to wipe the smile from his face.

"Thanks be to God, we've all found home."

I would love for you to visit me online at https://www.heatherwoodauthor.com

(Sign up for my newsletter to get the short story Until Hope Holds True here!)

If you enjoyed *Until We All Find Home*, please leave a review on Amazon and Goodreads! Indie authors rely on reviews to get our work noticed.

Also by Heather Wood

Until We All Run Free

Jed and Jack Young may be brothers by birth, but as orphans, their separate upbringings produced polarizing results. Now that the Civil War is over, the brothers look forward to settling into the next chapter of their lives as they learn to walk in their new faith. Each brother's ideal happily-ever-after is the other's worst nightmare—and when that nightmare becomes their own reality, their relationship with each other is threatened. Mary Pierce has a picture-perfect life with three beautiful daughters and a husband who adores her. When tragedy alters the course of her life, Mary has to lean on God in deeper ways as she learns to navigate a confusing and painful new path. Face to face with their greatest fears, Jed, Jack, and Mary must anchor themselves in the unchanging character of God, holding fast the belief that what God is doing in them is greater than their pain. As they each overcome sin, learn everyday obedience, and find peace in surrender, they discover there are no dark corners in their lives that God's grace won't illuminate and His power can't resurrect.

Until The Light Breaks Through

Jack Young's past comes back to haunt him in the third installment of Heather Wood's Christian family saga as the Great Chicago Fire threatens to destroy everything he loves most.

Newly graduated from seminary and on the cusp of taking a pastorate in Kentucky, Jack discovers devastating consequences of the licentious life he put behind him six years ago. To move forward, he must go back. But each encounter with his old life brings lasting reverberations for his future and further chips away at the peace he's pursued so desperately all these years. The revival of an old friendship sparks feelings he's worked hard to keep dormant and challenges his determination to reject anything that could come between him and the Lord again. When the city of Chicago burns to ashes, it leaves his family tragically altered—and Jack more unsure of his place in God's plan than ever.

Until We All Share Joy

Titan Dinsmore loves his family, but as the youngest of five, he craves his older siblings' respect—and a little distance. A chance meeting at the train station with a forlorn young lady turns into a growing attraction between them. But Titan quickly learns there is a difference between wanting to be treated as an adult and truly stepping up to lead. How can he help tenderhearted Nora see beyond her father's abandonment and rest in the love of her Heavenly Father? And will his secret plan to restore her family for the ideal Christmas together win Nora's undying admiration or only lead to greater heartache?

This warm, standalone Christmas novella highlights a lesser-known member of the beloved Dinsmore family in the *Finding Home* series.
With all the charm of a Victorian Christmas and yet the realities of navigating difficult relationships in a Christlike manner, this book is one to be savored throughout the holiday season and beyond.

Made in the USA
Middletown, DE
14 April 2024

53016055R00187